I0823353

PRAISE FOR ELIZABETH LOWHAM

CASTERS AND CROWNS

"An exquisite tale of love surpassing curses and the magic of embracing all facets of yourself. *Casters and Crowns* is a lush romantasy that enchanted me from start to finish."

—KATHRYN PURDIE, #1 *New York Times* bestselling author of *Bone Crier's Moon* and *The Forest Grimm*

SONNETS AND SERPENTS

"With fascinating world building, a slow-burn, enemies-to-lovers romance, and plenty of twists, *Sonnets and Serpents* will ensnare you, holding you captive until the final breathless moments."

—SARA B. LARSON, best-selling author of *Defy and A Promised Vengeance*

"An absolute delight! With shapeshifting scholars, poetic princesses, and a city full of mystery, Elizabeth has created a story that leaves you not only swooning, but absolutely enchanted."

—ALLISON ANDERSON, author of The Cartographer's War series

"*Sonnets and Serpents* had me gasping, laughing, and wistfully sighing from the first page to the last. With an immersive world full of lovable characters, magic, and plenty of swoon, Lowham's latest work is the perfect enemies-to-lovers romance! This book will hold a permanent spot in my heart and on my shelf."

—ASHLEY BUSTAMANTE, author of the Color Theory trilogy

BEAUTY REBORN

"Suspense-building flashbacks. Soul-searching, cautionary realism. Beauty herself is an intriguing, well-crafted original. . . . Readers who appreciate narrative risk-taking are well served."

—*KIRKUS REVIEWS*

"Lowham adeptly wrangles classic elements of 'Beauty and the Beast' to craft a sensitive and slow-burning retelling. . . . The creator's narrative stands out in its portrayal of themes surrounding trauma and recovery alongside familiar musings on perceived differences between humans and monsters."

—*PUBLISHERS WEEKLY*

SONNETS AND SERPENTS

OTHER BOOKS BY

ELIZABETH LOWHAM

Beauty Reborn

Astra Remade

Casters and Crowns

SONNETS AND SERPENTS

ELIZABETH LOWHAM

SHADOW MOUNTAIN PUBLISHING

Map illustration by Elizabeth Lowham

Visit us at shadowmountain.com

Library of Congress Cataloging-in-Publication Data

Names: Lowham, Elizabeth, author.
Title: Sonnets and serpents / Elizabeth Lowham.
Description: Salt Lake City : Shadow Mountain Publishing, 2025. | Audience term: Teenagers | Audience: Ages 13–19. | Audience: Grades 10–12. | Summary: "A shape-shifting serpent and a romantic princess, bound by magic, must work together to uncover legendary secrets, confront danger, and discover an unexpected love"—Provided by publisher.
Identifiers: LCCN 2025010224 (print) | LCCN 2025010225 (ebook) | ISBN 9781639934355 (hardback) | ISBN 9781649334718 (ebook)
Subjects: CYAC: Shapeshifting—Fiction. | Magic—Fiction. | Princesses—Fiction. | Fantasy. | Romance stories. | BISAC: YOUNG ADULT FICTION / Fantasy / Romance | YOUNG ADULT FICTION / Fantasy / General | LCGFT: Fantasy fiction. | Romance fiction. | Novels.
Classification: LCC PZ7.1.L77 So 2025 (print) | LCC PZ7.1.L77 (ebook) | DDC [Fic]—dc23
LC record available at https://lccn.loc.gov/2025010224
LC ebook record available at https://lccn.loc.gov/2025010225

Printed in Canada
PubLitho

10 9 8 7 6 5 4 3 2 1

To Brady.

A hundred dedications could never cover it, but this specific book wouldn't exist without your level-headed support, your love for me and our kids, and the many times you reminded me I actually like writing.

I love you as you are.

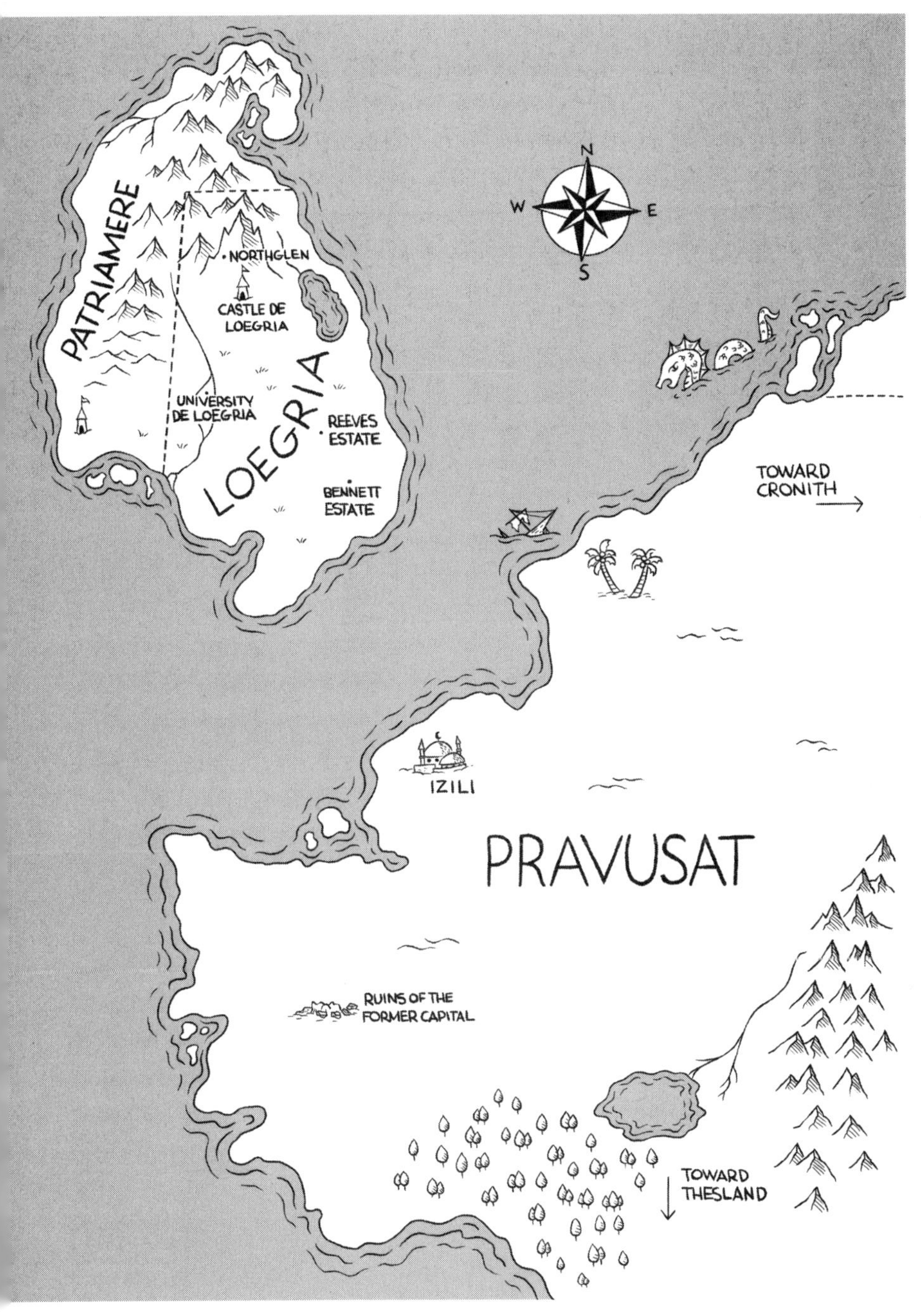

N
W
E
S
PATRIAMERE
NORTHGLEN
CASTLE DE LOEGRIA
LOEGRIA
UNIVERSITY DE LOEGRIA
REEVES ESTATE
BENNETT ESTATE
TOWARD CRONITH
IZILI
PRAVUSAT
RUINS OF THE FORMER CAPITAL
TOWARD THESLAND

PROLOGUE

Princess Eliza's first words to Lord Henry Wycliff were practiced. Not that she'd anticipated meeting *him* at the ball for her seventeenth birthday, but all her life, she'd anticipated meeting *someone.* She'd read romantic adventures and poetic promises at every opportunity, waiting seventeen impatient years to come of courting age and finally lock eyes with true love.

When Henry approached from across the ballroom, bowed, and met her brown eyes with his stunning hazel ones, Eliza said, "Fate is surely kind, arranging for us to meet tonight."

The specific greeting was essential. After all, if he *was* her true love, then she would spend all her days reciting the story of their first meeting, and such a thing deserved an opening more profound than, "Enjoying the ball?" or "Pleasure to meet you."

It was also a test, because Eliza had tried her romantic opening on other young men, and so far, she'd been met with blank stares, confused blinks, or stammers of small talk.

Henry grinned. He tossed his head, shifting his brown hair off his shoulders, and he shrugged, the casualness charming amid the formality of court. He held himself as straight-backed as a hero, yet he wore his shirt untucked.

"Is it fate?" he asked with clear teasing. "I thought it was a party invitation."

Trying to hold back her smile, Eliza adopted mock horror. “You dare diminish fate?”

“Not if it led me to you.”

All her words fled, and her cheeks flushed with a pleasant warmth. The ballroom seemed to widen around her, like her heart filling her chest. She bit her lip.

Finally, she said, “I like your confidence.”

In response, he ducked his head. “I’m only confident on tournament grounds, Highness. This is just hopeful.”

“What exactly are you hoping for?”

“A dance?” He offered his arm.

When Eliza took it, her heart began the dance before she did, and she prayed this was the beginning of much more than a turn around the ballroom.

Her hopes were quickly realized. Henry brought her flowers and whispered promises of courtship to come. When he competed in a tournament at the castle, he wore a token of her favor, and he even snuck into the castle early to see her. He left her with a tingling kiss on her cheek and a swoon in her step.

Eliza had found the dream she’d longed for. She’d found it in a knight with swirling hazel eyes and a smile that melted her soul. She’d found it in Henry Wycliff.

Until her father banished him.

CHAPTER

 1 

Water crashed over the gunwale and swept across the deck, swirling anything not tied down. Eliza caught a mouthful of the salty spray just as she emerged from belowdecks.

"Keep that hatch closed!" one of the sailors bellowed at her.

Sputtering, she swiped the water from her eyes and scrambled onto the deck, securing the hatch behind her. The blackened sky snarled with thunder, and clouds crackled lightning threats. Wind howled against the sails, making the entire ship a symphony of creaking fabric, wood, and ropes.

With the approaching storm, Eliza and the handful of other passengers on the merchant galley had been ordered belowdecks, which she'd been happy to obey—until she realized how terrifying it was to be locked in a little room, tossed madly about in the gloomy darkness. She'd emptied her stomach into a bucket, then decided facing the storm head-on had to be better than this.

Now she wasn't sure.

Tipping with the ship's motion, she stumbled up the stairs to the quarterdeck, where she wrapped both arms around the railing and clung like a thistle to wool. Nearby, the helmsman strained at the wheel and shouted an order lost in thunder. Eliza had meant to help, but that seemed foolish now, surrounded as she was by full-grown men battling a storm. She had no strength to haul on a rope or reef a sail, no ability to direct in the dark. Everyone around her knew what they were doing while she was simply a bystander, far out of her depth.

Her stomach knotted, wondering if the same was true of her search for Henry.

Purple lightning split the world from sky to horizon, and a moment later, deafening thunder rattled her bones. Eliza whimpered, pressing her cheek to the railing and wishing she were back home, bundled beneath quilts, enjoying the pleasant crackle of flames in her hearth.

Another wave swirled around her ankles, trying to drag her away. She curled stubbornly into her position, and with a burst of defiance, she looked up at the storm. Rainwater dripped from her chin.

There was no going home. She would only go forward.

It seemed to take an eternity for the storm to blow itself out. By the time the sky lightened to a grumbling gray and the rain retreated, Eliza felt like all her strength had been washed away. She sank to the deck like a limp, tattered sail, every bit of her aching as she released her grip on the railing.

The helmsman cast her a glance. "Hoy! Still with us, girl? Should've stayed below."

"I thought it would be better to see what was happening," Eliza said weakly.

"You're lucky this was just a baby storm—barely any legs at all."

At her horrified expression, he laughed. Though he must have been exhausted from holding the ship steady against a storm, he never lifted a finger from the helm while the rest of the crew reset the ship.

It was a ten-day voyage from Loegria to Pravusat, and they'd already traveled most of the distance. Eliza prayed the next two days would not bring further storms.

Suddenly remembering, she gave a little cry of despair and fished a damp, sad book from her pocket. The cover's red fabric was threadbare at every corner, and the ridges of the spine had grown mushy, no longer sharply defined as they'd been when her sister, Aria, had gifted the book to her for her fourteenth birthday. Three years of constant reading wore out even the sturdiest books. But reading was one thing; she'd never subjected the book to salt water before.

With great care, she peeled the pages, relieved to find them dry except for the wrinkling edges. The words of familiar sonnets swirled before her eyes, comforting her heart in the wake of the storm.

And on the page of her favorite sonnet, a dried flower remained nestled and safe, tucked against the binding. A white snowdrop blossom.

Henry's voice echoed in her mind, his nervous smile fixed in her memory. *I just picked these along the path. Next time, I'll get you real flowers.*

No, she'd told him. *They're perfect. Just like you.*

In two days, she would see him again. That thought was like the sunbeams breaking through the clouds.

A strange hush fell over the ship, lifting Eliza's attention from her book. Though the sailors continued their work, they did so stiffly, and even the helmsman stood rigid, his jaw clenched. She followed his gaze to a crew member who seemed out of place with the rest.

Then she tensed as well.

The man moved like a ghost—silent and without touching another sailor—but the true eeriness came from the brand on his neck, an elongated S that warned what he was capable of.

Anywhere water had gathered on the deck, he made it vanish with a mere touch and a dim flash of light.

A Fluid Caster.

He disappeared belowdecks, and Eliza found the helmsman looking at her.

"You ever seen a Caster at work?" he asked grimly. "Most haven't."

Eliza shook her head. She closed her sonnet book with the instinct to protect it, and she resisted pulling it to her chest, since her shirt was still drenched from the storm.

"Handy to have a Fluid Caster out on the ocean, I'll say that, and Ed's never given us any trouble." The helmsman's expression grew dark, and his gaze fixed on the horizon. "But with all that Morton business, feels like we'd be better off if no one had ever heard of magic."

Eliza's mouth had grown dry, and though she struggled to keep a neutral expression, she couldn't help but wince.

"That Morton business" that most people danced around was a curse laid on Eliza's family by the Fluid Caster Clarissa Morton. It had started with Eliza's older sister, Aria. For months, Aria had been unable to sleep at night, her strength sapping away. Then the same effect had passed to Eliza.

The exhaustion from the curse was bad enough, but her father's response was worse. His need for control and his refusal to look weak drove him to turn the curse into a challenge. Whatever man of court was able to break it would be given the privilege of marrying Crown Princess Aria.

And then, presenting it as a *prize* for winning a royal tournament, he'd forced Henry to be the first challenger.

The shock still vibrated in Eliza's chest. Her father had *known* she wanted to court Henry, but he didn't care. He addressed her feelings in one clipped, dismissive answer:

"Eliza's romantic whims are such that she'll find a new boy within the week."

Gripping the sonnet book, her hands trembled. The gray clouds still pressed too heavy and low for comfort, as if threatening to unleash another storm at any moment. She longed to see the sun.

"Do you know where you're going, girl?" the helmsman asked.

Eliza tensed. The sailor's tone wasn't threatening, but her senses prickled with danger all the same. He sounded too . . . interested. She'd given a false name while booking passage, and the last thing she wanted was anyone looking too closely at "Jenny," who was the same age and height as a certain runaway princess.

She should have stayed belowdecks.

The helmsman didn't wait for her answer. "If you're that pale after seeing one Fluid Caster, you'll have a hard time in Pravusat. Whole country's infested with magic. No laws, no restrictions."

Magic. That was still his focus. Eliza held back a sigh of relief.

"I'll be careful." With stiff movements, she forced herself to her feet, swaying on the deck.

"Careful don't mean much against shapeshifters," he muttered darkly.

Eliza gripped the railing. Unsure what else to say, she began the descent down to the main deck, her joints aching.

She couldn't allow herself to think of what dangers waited in Pravusat; they didn't matter. When Henry had failed the king's challenge, her father had banished him, leaving Eliza with a choice.

She could stay at home, where everything was falling apart, or she could seize her one chance at happiness and love.

Eliza's romantic whims.

Her father's words burrowed inside her like a parasite, eating away at her confidence. In his eyes, she was nothing but a collection of frivolous impulses. Like a flitting butterfly blown by light breezes, unable to settle on a flower.

She'd sworn to prove him wrong. She'd sworn to prove her devotion to Henry. If she could choose to live in exile with him, an entire ocean away from home, without the aid or resources offered to a princess, it would mean she wasn't all whims. It would prove she had substance, that she could be trusted, that she *meant* something.

Whatever dangers Pravusat held, she would brave them all for Henry's sake.

The entire ship buzzed with the call from the crow's nest: "Land ahoy!"

Avoiding the rushing sailors, Eliza pressed herself to the gunwale along with several other curious passengers, watching the sandy stretch in the distance grow closer and clearer. Pravusat was almost ten times the size of Loegria, or so her geography tutor had told her, but unlike her homeland, it was more desert flatland than green countryside and mountains. A nervous excitement built in Eliza's chest, and even when the other passengers retreated to gather their belongings or prepare to dock, she remained at the railing, watching the harbor grow to encompass them.

She'd brought only one bag from home, filled with as much silver as she dared carry, a spare change of clothes, a nightgown, and a hairbrush. Plus the sonnet book in her pocket. Most of what she loved at home—like her sister—couldn't fit in a bag, so she'd been forced to leave it. Now her entire world rested on a strap on her shoulder and a hope in her heart.

Henry, I'm here.

The ship anchored, and the crew lowered a gangplank, wasting no time in unloading the boxes of woolen fabric that served as the merchant ship's livelihood. Eliza seized the first opening to rush down onto the docks, laughing as her steps wavered drunkenly after the voyage. She chose to think of it as a dance she couldn't help participating in.

Ahead of her, the port city of Izili stretched in a gently rising landscape, full of strange colors and architecture she never saw at home. Around her, the docks echoed with the chatter of sailors and the creak of masts and rigging swaying in the ocean's cradle. Eliza grabbed the first dockworker she could find and asked for news of *The Unbroken Duke*, the ship Henry had sailed on.

Which was when she remembered one big problem: She was in Pravusat, and she did not speak Pravish.

As a princess, she'd received instruction in foreign government and languages, but she'd daydreamed through many of the lessons and snuck poetry books into the rest. She'd always assumed Aria was the only one who *actually* needed to know such things. Eliza was never going to wear a crown or meet with ambassadors. She was certainly never going to visit a country all the way across the sea.

No matter—she could ask for help.

She returned to the Loegrian crew of her own ship, searching until she found a crew member who claimed confidence in Pravish. He took her to the dockmaster and translated her request.

The dockmaster was a compact man with greedy little eyes, striding around with a logbook and a jingling purse. He recorded their ship's arrival and took his docking fee before even gracing Eliza's search with an acknowledgment. Then he demanded an inquiry fee for any information on docking.

"You can barter it down," the Loegrian sailor told her. "Pravish people are all about arguing."

Eliza didn't have the patience for that. She shoved a few silver coins at the dockmaster, and his eyes lit up with glee. He consulted his log, quickly speaking a few words.

The Loegrian sailor's face turned grim.

"What is it?" Eliza lifted on tiptoe, peering at a book she couldn't read. "Has it been delayed?"

She didn't know much about sailing, but she'd heard the palace tailor complain about the ocean's unpredictability when a shipment of silk for the queen had been delayed an entire week. Henry should have arrived several days ago, but if he'd been delayed, she would take a room at the closest inn and wait.

The dockmaster spoke in broken Loegrian, closing his logbook with a sense of finality. "Sad, very sad. Ship sink."

Sink.

The harbor sounds grew louder around her as she became aware of the ocean's insistent pulse, washing in and out, slapping against the hulls of ships and the posts of the winding docks. White gulls cried out from above.

Slowly, Eliza rocked back on her heels. She looked at her translator, waiting to hear what she was clearly misunderstanding.

The sailor shook his head. "There was a shipwreck. I'm sorry. Whoever you're looking for is gone."

CHAPTER

2

ONE WEEK LATER

The worst day of Silas Bennett's life was the day his father tried to kill him.

Second-worst was the day Silas agreed to track down a reckless princess. When taking the assignment, he learned exactly three things about the girl he was supposed to find.

One: Her name was Eliza de Loegria. The "de Loegria" was not a true surname but simply a mark of her royal lineage. She was, quite literally, "Eliza of Loegria," as if every other Loegrian citizen were not "of Loegria." A prime example of royal arrogance.

Two: She was a princess. Not heir to the throne—that title belonged to her older sister, Aria. Considering Silas hadn't known of Eliza's existence until Aria requested his assistance, he could say that being second-born in a royal household held as many perks as being second-born in any other. The privilege of the second-born was to always be a second thought, which Silas knew from his father's treatment of his own younger sister.

His father had tried to marry Maggie off to an abusive drunkard, which was the only reason Silas had made a deal with a royal. Crown Princess Aria stopped the marriage, protecting his little sister, and in return, Silas agreed to protect hers.

He knew only one additional thing about Princess Eliza, and it was the worst of the list.

Three: She was a fool, of the variety commonly known as "a hopeless romantic." She'd run away from home—and in her sister's direct words—chasing a *boy*.

It would be one thing if Eliza had just gone to a neighboring town, but no. She'd crossed the ocean to Pravusat, a country where she presumably didn't speak the language, didn't know the dangers, and definitely didn't belong.

Silas sighed. The Izili outer market bustled around him, a sprawling collection of blankets, canopies, wagons, and crates, where merchants hawked everything from fruit to furniture, bartering in brightly violent tones that charged the air with passion.

Unlike Eliza, Silas knew the markets and streets of Pravusat well. Izili—the capital city—had been his temporary home for the two years he'd studied at its university.

After crossing the ocean between Loegria and Pravusat, then bribing two dockworkers and almost losing a finger to a cranky old lady, Silas had tracked Eliza to this market, the biggest in Izili. Now he just had to find her among the packed, colorful crowd.

A horn-nosed snake slithered beside him, its dusty yellow pattern blending with the sand, and Silas could feel its pulsing anxiety—hundreds of people packed into a single market with all their baggage and noise and trampling.

"We're looking for the girl out of place," Silas said quietly. His magic didn't need words, and the snake certainly didn't speak either Pravish or Loegrian, but he found it easier to direct commands with spoken language than through focus alone.

The horn-nosed snake darted off, disappearing into the cluttered merchant stalls pressed against the city wall. That left Silas to search the crowded main thoroughfare.

Unlike the markets of Loegria, where everyone arranged things in neat, orderly rows and used permanent wooden stands to display their goods, the markets of Pravusat were like a big family picnic, where everyone threw down a rug in any available space. Untethered chaos in the form of a winding maze that changed daily. But there was always familiarity, if one knew where to look, and although merchants changed specific location, they favored the same general areas of the market.

So he wasn't surprised when Baris called out a loud greeting in Pravish, waving a hand missing the last two fingers. "Silas the student! Come to buy a papaya!"

Before Silas could dodge it, Baris shoved a basket of fruit into his legs, bruising his shins. Silas stepped back with a hiss, which only made the large, dark-haired man laugh.

"Soft as a snake!" The Pravish idiom was a compliment meaning someone led such a blessed life, they were allowed to have a soft underbelly, though Baris used it for more literal reasons.

Ducking out of the walkway, Silas crouched on the merchant's rug. "I'm looking for someone. Another Loegrian, like me."

Like me was the wrong description. They may have been from the same country, but Eliza belonged to the ruling family, who created laws to persecute magic users—registration and branding for Casters and death for Animal Affiliates.

Silas was one of those Animal Affiliates.

So, no, he and the princess were nothing alike. And while Silas had no desire of his own to help her, he would swallow the poison for his sister's sake.

Baris scooted closer on his rug. "I heard you'd gone back to your country. Izili University is no longer good for you?"

"I finished my studies, so I went home for a while."

Specifically, he'd gone home for a single week where everything had gone horribly wrong. He'd been disinherited, banished, and even forced to strike a deal with royalty. It had been a mistake, going back to Loegria.

At least it was a mistake he'd never make again.

"Obviously," said Baris, "your country does not appreciate snakes as we do, since you are back to us so soon."

He had no idea. Loegria enforced a bloodthirsty prejudice against *shapeshifters*—the derogatory term for Animal Affiliates—which included ridiculous myths about infants being eaten by demons who then assumed their forms and lay in wait to devour others.

Silas was very, very careful to keep his magic a secret back home. But here in Pravusat, there were no laws against Affiliates. He could have transformed into a viper right in front of Baris, and the man would have only put him to work guarding the papaya baskets.

Baris cocked his head. "Will you take more classes now?"

"Studying costs money."

"Pay for them with papayas! After you buy them from me, of course."

"Oh, I have something else in mind for the university." Silas smirked. "I'm going to have *them* pay *me*."

Baris gave a full-throated laugh. He turned his attention for a moment, threatening a woman who'd been about to leave without buying. They haggled until she carried away a dozen papayas, and Baris admired a new bronze ring much too small for his hands; perhaps he intended it for his wife. In Loegria, Silas had never seen anyone trade for goods or jewelry; the market operated solely on the exchange of money. In Pravusat, *everything* was money.

"Do you think the university *would* take papayas?" he asked.

The question earned another laugh before Baris assured him the university was "uptight like your country." Hard silver only.

It didn't matter. In the morning, Silas would speak to Iyal Afshin, the dean, and offer his services as a professor. With a position at the university, he could settle permanently in Pravusat. Build a life. Forget all about the one he'd left behind in Loegria.

First, he had to find the lovesick princess and convince her to go home to her sister.

"You are, what, sixteen?" Baris demanded.

"We've had this discussion before. I'm nineteen."

"Sixteen and a half, then. The university will not allow sixteen and a half to teach. Come work for me! Gather papayas, twist-twist and done. Even sixteen and a half can manage."

"I've done orchard work before, and it's miserable." Silas's best friend, Guillaume Reeves, owned a lemon orchard. Since meeting Gill, Silas had worked four harvests at the Reeves estate, because even though he *hated* it, the torture of sweat on his back was preferable to the torture of enduring his father's expectations at home.

"I'm an academic," he told Baris, "not a hired hand."

"Bah, then you are of no use to me. Be gone with you and your hands until you can buy papayas! If I see your Loegrian friend, I will send them to the university."

Baris waved him off, and Silas stood, ducking to avoid the canopy over the stall. But he'd only gone a few paces deeper into the market when a quick succession of impressions flashed through his mind.

Girl smell. Shadow men. Loud. Fear.

Silas cursed.

The horn-nosed snake had found Eliza, all right, and she was being arrested by the kuveti.

When Eliza first heard the shouts, she didn't realize they were directed toward her. Everyone in the market was shouting; it seemed like how all Pravish people communicated.

She'd been in Pravusat exactly one week and had hated every minute of it. It was loud and aggressive and *blazingly hot.*

When she'd left home, the castle grounds had suffered frost each night, and the thick clouds promised oncoming snows, with all the delights of her favorite season. Pravusat did not believe in winter. It believed only in sand and chaos.

When two men grabbed her by the arms, Eliza glared up at them, demanding to be unhanded, but she quickly realized these were no random marketgoers. The two men wore dark uniforms with veils, only the slits of their eyes visible. One of them spoke in Pravish. Eliza caught a few of the most common words—*you, quiet, come*—but the context was clear.

She was being *arrested.*

"There's been a mistake," she protested, trying and failing to yank free. Her mind spun. She couldn't have broken any laws. She'd only been going from person to person in the market, trying to find someone who spoke Loegrian, someone who might have seen Henry.

For the past week, that had been her quest, though all she'd earned for it was a lot of cursing and dismissals. She'd returned twice to interrogate the dockmaster, and he answered her only by shaking his head, but she refused to believe there were no survivors of the *Duke*'s shipwreck.

She refused to believe the last time Henry had smiled at her had been the *last.*

The ship she'd arrived on had already departed, so she'd hired a room at an inn near the harbor, and she'd spent every day embroiled in her search. She was exhausted, her strength as frayed as her clothing, her soul as hungry as her stomach, but there was nowhere to go except forward. She would not accept any other path.

"Let me go!" she snarled again as the uniformed men began to drag her forward. "I'm a—"

She clamped her jaw shut before she could say *princess.* She'd kept her identity a secret thus far, because she knew a princess far from home without a single guard would be an easy target. She also knew her father was searching for her, probably cursing her name and swearing to drag her back home before she did something to embarrass him and the crown of Loegria.

"I've done nothing wrong," she amended. "You can't arrest me for *nothing*!"

The guards ignored both her protests and her struggles, steering her toward the city, its scattered rooftops visible above the battered Izili wall. That wall would have been a disgrace in Loegria. Gaping holes riddled the soft yellow sandstone that no one had bothered to repair. It couldn't keep out a thieving child much less stop any kind of assault on the city. Her father would have burst a vein to see it; he kept the infrastructure and defenses of Loegria immaculate, even though their country hadn't seen war in centuries.

"Help me!" Eliza shouted, turning her focus on the people of the market instead of the guards. In response, they only bartered more fiercely, customers and merchants alike avoiding her gaze in such a pointed way that she *knew* they saw her need.

They simply didn't care.

She fought more fiercely, kicking at the guards' shins, driving her weight to one side and then the other. They were clearly accustomed to struggling prisoners because they never broke stride.

Then a *whoop* echoed above the market noise, and a pair of papayas came sailing through the air, each one smacking her guards in the face.

Eliza blessed whatever kind stranger was throwing fruit.

Laughter bounded through the stalls, and her guards began their own furious shouting. Eliza seized the opening, twisting free of the guards, then took off running. She was short and slim, so she squirmed through cracks between stalls, ducking beneath low canopies.

Glancing back, she saw someone chasing her, but the man was both younger and taller than the guards, and he was alone.

Had he thrown the papayas?

If so, he might be chasing her to demand payment. Pravish people didn't believe in generosity; she'd learned that while trying to get a chart of the course Henry's ship had taken. It had cost her five silver dubs just to *get* the chart, and then another three for the dockmaster to mark it with the route and the location of the shipwreck.

Safest not to get caught again. By anyone.

But just as Eliza made that determination, she tripped. Not over a merchant rug or crate.

Over a *snake*.

Eliza shrieked, scrambling away from the dusty yellow serpent, which watched her with a lifted head and hungry eyes. Thankfully, it darted off as the man approached.

She was so shaken, she allowed the stranger to grab her hand and haul her to her feet, and when he directed her toward a hole in the city wall, she followed. It was the opposite direction the snake had gone.

Eliza clambered through the broken barrier, her silk clothing snagging on thorns of stone. She banged her head on the rock, leaving a pounding ache in her skull and snarls in her carefully braided hair. Rubbing her head, she glared back at the wall.

And then she realized she was alone in a shadowed alleyway with a stranger.

CHAPTER

3

Who are you?" Eliza demanded. "And why were you chasing me?"

Her foot still crawled with the memory of *snake*, and she absently rubbed her ankle against the back of her opposite calf.

"Who you?" she demanded again, this time in Pravish, since he hadn't responded to her Loegrian. She spoke Pravish haltingly, so perhaps he still wouldn't understand, but she'd been practicing for a week.

He heaved a long-suffering sigh. When he responded, it was in the smooth silk of Pravish. She caught *name*, followed by *Silas*.

Up close, Silas was younger than her first impression of him, perhaps even her own age, but he was also more intimidating. For one, he was unreasonably tall with a broad chest to match. He could have thrown her over his shoulder like a sack of potatoes without even noticing the weight. His cold, dark eyes said it wouldn't bother him to heave people around like potatoes.

He was light-skinned for a Pravish person, more honey-brown than brown, but even Loegria had a variety of skin tones, with people from the southern half darker than those from the north. Eliza had the great misfortune of pale skin that turned splotchy red and freckled in the sun—courtesy of her mother, who hailed from Patriamere, a country of fair skin and fair hair. At least she wasn't blonde; she'd not seen *anyone* blonde in Pravusat, and though her brown hair was noticeably light, it wasn't quite out of place.

Silas had hair the color of spilled ink, combed back on one side and dripping over his forehead on the other in long, straight strands that reached his eyebrow. Her attention must have made him self-conscious, because he raked his fingers through that section, forcing it back, though a few strands rebelled, falling loose once more.

He was probably a thug. He looked like a thug.

Eliza itched to reach for the dagger tucked through her belt, but she didn't really know how to use it, and she would have only one chance for a surprise if things turned ugly.

"Go away," she said. She'd certainly learned that Pravish phrase after hearing it directed at her so often in the last week.

"No," Silas replied.

Rats. There had been little hope that would work, but still.

In contrast to his dark hair, eyes, and expression, Silas wore a loose shirt of bright blue fabric, reaching partway down his thighs, belted with a sash of orange that also crossed one shoulder. Eliza had seen the Pravish style scattered everywhere in combinations of pink and green, purple and yellow, red and orange. Loegrian fashion was never so flamboyant in its colors, and Eliza found herself wishing she could trade her muted silks for a flowy rainbow.

It wasn't only the Pravish fashion that was remarkably different. Chatter echoed from the city streets nearby, where people strode along by themselves or in groups, all in a seemingly great hurry to get somewhere. Since arriving, she'd seen no carriages or even solo horseback riders in the streets. She had seen a few carts carrying people, but they were pulled by other *people*, not horses, and the roads were all pitted and in need of repair, just like the wall. She wondered how Pravusat's king spent his money if not in caring for his cities and people.

"Why you follow?" she demanded in Pravish, trying to make the question understandable even though she couldn't conjugate it.

Silas drawled something too quick to deconstruct. She thought she heard the word *money*.

As she'd expected—he wanted payment for saving her.

"No money," she snapped. "Go home!"

Wait, she thought. *That isn't right.* Pravish added extra words she wouldn't need in Loegrian. Go *to* home. How did she say that again? *Gik ne seyahat.*

Or was it *seravat*?

"Go home," she repeated forcefully. *Seravat* sounded better. It was definitely the right word.

Silas snorted.

Eliza blushed. She turned to leave, and the thug didn't stop her, yet she found she couldn't go more than a few steps. She turned back, face flaming.

"You be . . . ashamed." *Is that "ashamed" or "gentle"? Utanmas.* "Steal money, ashamed. Follow girl, ashamed." She ended with an emphatic *hmph!* Then she turned again to leave.

"You're too old for that," he said.

It took her a moment to process that he'd spoken Loegrian. Her jaw dropped, and she whirled around.

Silas leaned against the alley wall and shrugged. "In Pravish, the *genc* root—either *gencal* for boys or *genca* for girls—references children, ten years old at most. *Genca,* you said—so you're claiming to be a seven-year-old girl? As far as disguises go, Your Highness, shaving ten years off your age won't fool anyone. In addition, I'm not sure it's possible to 'steal money gently.'"

She gaped. The humidity made her mind feel as sticky as her clothing, and her thoughts scrambled to grasp what was happening. Her face burned more fiercely than before.

Finally, she asked, "What's the word for 'ashamed'?"

"*Utamas,*" he supplied, his smirk clearly expecting her to use it regarding herself.

"You should be *utamas,*" she snapped. "For being a thug *and* for pretending to be Pravish."

"I pretended nothing."

He had the audacity to say that while wearing Pravish fashion and speaking the language as smoothly as anyone she'd heard in Izili.

"You called me 'Your Highness,' so clearly you know who I am. Well, if you're hoping to turn me in for a reward, you can forget it. King or not, my father's not the rewarding type."

Silas's eyebrows rose, though his expression betrayed nothing else.

"Your sister sent me," he finally said.

Eliza's insides shrank. When she'd run away, she'd been too cowardly to give her sister one final hug. She'd simply left a note in the night.

Would Aria tell her to abandon her search and come home?

She knew what her father would say—that running away was the worst of her whims. That she'd accomplished nothing.

"I'm fine," she whispered. "Tell Aria not to worry."

Aria had enough to worry about as it was. Ever since the Caster rebellion started, she and their father had grown more and more at odds, a struggle between current ruler and future ruler that Eliza had no part in.

Or maybe that was the excuse she told herself to ease the guilt of running away. Of abandoning her sister.

Only days earlier, Eliza had felt the curse lift. She no longer carried a deep chill in her bones, no longer spent restless nights awake or felt the constant exhaustion in her limbs. Having the curse broken should have thrilled her.

Instead, it terrified her.

She didn't know if her sister was responsible or if some man of court had finally passed the king's challenge. If it was the latter, Eliza couldn't even hope for a handsome gentleman her sister might be happy to marry—because Aria was already involved in a secret romance, one their father would never approve. She loved a Caster.

But there was something worse about the curse breaking, a truth Eliza could hardly bring herself to acknowledge.

The truth that something had *changed* about her since being cursed.

The truth that, long before the curse had broken, it had broken something *inside* her.

The truth that it was broken still.

She'd convinced herself that everything would return to normal once the curse was removed. But although the sleepless nights had vanished, she remained altered. Wounded. It was like someone had removed an arrow from her shoulder, but they'd only pulled the shaft and left the arrowhead buried.

Her one remaining hope was finding Henry. She couldn't explain why, but she *knew* that if she could find him, she would be fixed. She would fall into his hazel eyes again, and everything would be like it once was.

With more conviction than before, Eliza squared her shoulders, and she looked up into Silas's dark eyes. "You can tell Aria I'm staying, and you can go home. *Seravat*."

"*Seyahat*," he corrected.

Rats. She'd had it right the first time.

"I am home," he added. "You're the one out of place." He held her gaze with a pointed look, and based on attire alone, his words held weight. But they didn't change anything.

"I have to find someone," Eliza insisted.

"Henry Wycliff."

Hearing Henry's name from someone else sharpened the ache, like removing the cover from a basket of feelings she'd tried to keep pressed down and unseen. Henry's face rose in her memory, smiling and warm, his head cocked and his brown hair brushing his shoulders as he offered her a white snowdrop.

"I happen to know—" Silas began.

She gasped, struck by the sudden realization of what was *happening*. Her soggy, tired mind had finally caught up. She was speaking Loegrian with someone who also spoke Pravish.

"*You* can help me find Henry!" she burst out, grabbing his arm.

He stepped back, clearly unnerved by the contact, slithering out of her grasp. "I—"

"You speak Pravish! I've been searching . . ." Fumbling, Eliza pulled the folded map from her pocket, where she kept it beside her book of sonnets. "I have a map of the ship's route, and I've been searching for the survivors, but even if I can phrase a question, I can't understand answers. You can fix that!"

Silas stared at her. Something about his dark gaze made her skin crawl until she leaned back.

"Survivors?" he repeated.

She realized what she was shrinking from. *Pity.*

"There was a shipwreck," she said with forced calm. "He's missing. But if you translate for me, we can—"

"He's gone, Highness." Silas's voice was surprisingly gentle for a thug.

Eliza clenched her trembling jaw. "You don't know that, and I won't accept it. That isn't our ending."

"You can't just *not accept* truth."

"It isn't truth. It's what some choose to believe, but I don't."

"Ignoring truth out of personal discomfort is the act of the foolish."

"Then I'm foolish!" she snapped. "*Aptal.*"

Silas smirked. "You're a man now? *Apta* is the feminine form."

"The point is," she said sharply, "foolish or not, I'm not going anywhere until I find Henry."

The princess was worse than Silas had feared. Brash, stubborn, and delusional. It was a shame about Henry—Silas was fairly certain he'd crossed paths with him at the Reeves estate, since Lord Reeves had always been close to Lord Wycliff—but it was life. War, illness, shipwrecks. The unavoidable swallowed even the best of people.

He tried to keep his voice consoling. "Highness, wouldn't you rather grieve at home? With your family?"

Part of him wondered if anyone at home grieved *his* absence. Not his father, certainly. When the king had announced his challenge—break the crown princess's curse and win her hand in marriage—Lord Bennett had volunteered Silas without even consulting him, and he'd made it clear the king's wrath for failure would be nothing compared to his own.

If you can't win this contest, he'd said, *you'll never hold my title. If you can't win this, you're not my son.*

Silas's father believed in motivation by threat, but Silas had grown tired of threats.

So here he was. Exiled and disinherited.

Trying to reason with the daughter of the very man who'd exiled him.

At the mention of grief, Eliza's eyes hardened. She drew herself up in regal posture. "You *will* help me find Henry. That's an order from your princess."

More motivation by threat. For a moment, Silas was tempted to leave her to her well-deserved fate.

Instead, he drawled, "Or what?"

"What do you mean?"

"Or what?" He gestured at the alley, empty except for themselves. "If I disobey your royal order, you'll what—call the guards? Lock me in prison? *Banish* me?"

He let the last example hang in the air until her cheeks colored. Then he said, "I suggest you shelve the arrogance, Highness. Power isn't inherent, no matter what any monarchy claims. It's enforced. You can't force me into anything. Not here."

When she ducked her head, picking at her shirt, he gave a satisfied nod.

"Come on," he said. "I'll take you to the harbor and help you arrange for a ship. That's all the translation I can offer."

CHAPTER

The princess walked behind Silas with her head down. It was unnerving, like having an extra shadow that might attack him at any moment.

Everyone they passed on the street darted a curious glance her way. Some of the men's gazes were appreciative, lingering. Loegrian clothing was formfitting, so her silk shirt and woolen trousers meant the princess's curves could be clearly seen, but it was more than that. She was *different.*

Between the human trafficking and wanton violence, it was unwise to stand out in Pravusat. Even the king kept the ornamentations of his palace to a minimum.

When Silas had first started university, Izili had not been the capital of Pravusat. Barely two months into Silas's studies, the nephew of the former king had wrested the crown for himself, his revolution setting fire to the then-capital. Once he'd burned his uncle's city to the ground, the Nephew King built a palace in Izili, declaring the city the seat of his everlasting power.

Everlasting? Not likely. But he'd held power for two years now—long enough that people sometimes referred to him by name, King Orzan, rather than simply the Nephew King. If he survived another two years, his reign would surpass that of his dead uncle's, but the odds were not in his favor. Silas had witnessed one attempted rebellion against the Nephew King already.

Pravusat was the land of revolution.

When the air was still, the Izili streets carried the dank smell of too many people and too little sky, but every so often, a fresh ocean breeze cleansed that scent with salt. Nature's own little revolutions. As they approached the harbor, those breezes grew more frequent.

Eliza came to a halt on the street. She gestured to a voyager's inn, the upper windows shuttered and the main floor windows thrown open to tantalize passersby with the wafting scent of roasted fish, sumac, and ale.

"This is where I'm staying," she said. "I need to get my things."

Of *course* she'd chosen a voyager's inn. They were established for travelers arriving by ship and double the price of most other lodgings. By staying at one, she was practically waving a banner declaring herself a foreigner. No wonder the kuveti had been able to find her.

Silas clenched his jaw. He didn't like that she'd nearly been arrested. The kuveti were the peacekeeping force in Pravusat, which ought to have been beneficial for a war-torn country. Unfortunately, their version of peacekeeping was less altruistic and more "peace as defined by the highest bidder."

He had a terrible feeling about anyone bidding on Eliza. Either they wanted to ransom a princess, or they wanted to capture a seventeen-year-old foreigner no one would miss.

I just want to know she's safe—that had been Aria's exact request when they'd made their deal. But she'd also said, *I want you to ensure my father's soldiers don't drag her back. She deserves to make her own choices.*

The crown princess didn't know the contradiction of her own request. There was only one safe haven in Izili, and that was the university. Since Eliza wasn't here to enroll, her quickest path to safety was across the ocean, back to Loegria. For all that Silas hated the place, it was at least a safe country for those *without* magic.

"Aren't you coming?" Eliza asked impatiently.

Had she brought a royal wardrobe she couldn't carry by herself?

Silas rolled his eyes, but he followed her into the bustling inn. Rather than making for the stairs to the upper floor, she marched straight to the innkeeper, who was distributing drinks from behind the bar.

She turned back to Silas. "Ask him what the Sarazan is," she ordered.

Silas narrowed his eyes, glancing between the girl and the innkeeper.

The dark-skinned innkeeper lifted a mug in his direction, asking if they wanted ale or fish.

"No, thank you," said Silas in Pravish.

Eliza folded her arms. "When I asked him about shipwrecks, he kept repeating the word *Sarazan*. I know it has something to do with Henry, so I need you to tell me what it is."

Sarazan tabernacles were houses of refuge and healing, scattered throughout the desert. There was one on the other side of the cliffs, directly on the beach, that took in shipwrecked sailors if they washed up outside of the Izili harbor.

"Did you really think you could trick me into this?" Silas asked coldly.

"You're here already! Just ask him."

He turned and strode from the inn. Eliza darted after him, blocking his path forward on the street. Despite her small size—she was a full head shorter than he was—she was as quick as a scurrying mouse.

"Wait! You can't just leave!"

"I offered to get you home," he shot back. "Nothing more." It was already more gracious than he wanted to be.

Eliza glared at him. "Of course it's fine for *you* to be here but not me. I'm a fragile princess. I shouldn't do things myself. I should cower at home and order guards around instead."

"You ordered *me*."

"I'm sorry I ordered!" She seized his arm again; he'd never met anyone so touchy. "My sister paid you to get me home, didn't she?

Please. Just do this *one thing* for me, and you can consider your service finished. I'll write and tell Aria it's all my doing!"

"I'm an academic, not a servant." He shifted his arm, sliding it free of her grasp.

Eliza frowned. "Why did Aria choose *you*?" she finally asked.

He bristled at the implication—that *he* was somehow the one falling short in this encounter.

"An alliance of necessity, *apta*," he said.

Her linguistic failings had provided the perfect moniker for her. *Foolish girl.* That translation wasn't totally satisfactory; in Loegrian, the etymology of *fool* had to do with being useless, or, more literally, a bellows emptied of air. The Pravish counterpart of *apta* and *aptal* had a spontaneous connotation. A person charging forward without thought.

Silas couldn't afford to be that way. He had a plan, and he would be living off papayas until he could accomplish it—assuming Baris hadn't already resold his basket because he'd taken too long to collect it. Silas had paid for a full basket in exchange for Baris throwing fruit at the kuveti.

"You *have* to help me," Eliza insisted, the desperation clear in her voice.

Ironically, he was trying to do just that. He sighed.

"Oh, I see." Her desperation transformed to derision. "You were happy to take the first command and the money that came with it because it didn't require any real work on your part. Just a quick, 'Go home, princess.' A messenger bird could do the same and be half as annoying about it."

Silas clenched his teeth, a surge of irritation bringing out a faint pattern of snake scales across his arms, thankfully hidden beneath his sleeves. He drew in a deep breath, eyes focused on the overhead clouds until the itch on his skin retreated. In Loegria, a surprise transformation would have condemned him as a shapeshifter and cost him his life, but in Pravusat, anyone passing on the street would have given him a respectful bow and a whispered, "*Iyanal.*" *Snake-blessed.* There was no better home for a Snake Affiliate than Pravusat, where they revered snakes as symbols of good fortune and rebirth.

Respect for being an Animal Affiliate. The concept felt like an impossibility, even though he'd transformed repeatedly in Izili. Yet, when his magic rose within, his instinct was still to resist. To fear the repercussions.

The girl before him was responsible for that. Her family had created the laws of Loegria that inspired the fear that divided him inside and had driven him from home. He'd already saved her from the kuveti, which was more than she deserved.

More than she would ever do for someone like him.

"I've reconsidered," he said, waiting for her response.

Just as her expression lifted and brightened, he added—

"Your sister's exact request was to know that you were safe and to let you make your own choices. Now that you've mentioned letters and messenger birds, I realize I've been trying too hard. I'll write Her Royal Highness a letter, informing her of your safety and your continued ability to make all your own reckless decisions, unhindered by me. Goodbye, Highness. *Bikmayak kalamak.*"

It wasn't often he got to use one of his favorite Pravish idioms—*My sword breaks here*. It meant the severing of a relationship. Quite literally, it meant he expected to die before seeing her again, and thanks to his tone, the implied connotation was that dying was *preferable* to seeing her again. It was a shame all that clever meaning fell on ignorant ears.

He skirted around her, heading back toward the market.

"Don't you *dare* leave!" she called from behind him.

Watch me, he thought.

If she wanted attention, so be it.

Silas closed his eyes, embracing the warmth of magic that he'd rejected a moment before. When he opened his eyes, he sent out a pulse in the air, a ripple visible only to him. Then, to direct his magic, he whispered, "*Buraya ne ka.*" *Come to me.*

A moment later, he was rewarded with a faint hiss.

Just as Eliza was about to grab him, she pulled up short, turning. "What was that? Did you hear . . ."

Her eyes drifted down as two gray adders slithered across the rough paving stones toward her. She shrieked, then leapt onto the steps of the closest building, as if reptiles couldn't climb.

"Relax," said Silas cheerfully, his stride never wavering. "Snakes are a religious symbol here, and seeing two at once means a great fortune is headed your way. Congratulations on that—it seems you can continue to afford your expensive lodgings."

As he kept walking, the snakes quickly divided him from the princess.

"Silas!" she shouted. "Silas, help!"

The shrill panic in her voice almost turned him back. He hesitated, then shook it off and kept his eyes forward. Adders were venomous, but these wouldn't attack her while under his instruction. It was only a message.

A message that she wasn't the royalty here. *He* was.

Eliza stared at Silas's retreating back with slack-jawed horror quickly turning to fury.

He was the one who'd chased her down in the market. She'd spent days searching for anyone who could possibly help, days beating her head against the wall of an unknown language, and then he'd arrived like a Loegrian-speaking beacon of hope.

Only to laugh at her plight.

He mocked her powerlessness, told her to go running home. After all, she wasn't a *person*, just a princess. What problems could she possibly have?

Eliza had encountered such an attitude before. Some of the servants at the castle liked to gossip about the royal family with pitying smiles—*How quaint that* royalty, *with all its wealth and finery, thinks it knows anything about real trials.*

As if Eliza didn't know what it was like to hear her parents fight. As if she'd never been lost or lonely or forgotten.

As if she'd never been afraid.

The two snakes rested in tightly curled shapes at the bottom of the steps, flicking predatory tails, tasting the air with forked tongues, waiting for the moment to come uncoiled as a lightning strike.

Eliza tried to restrain her trembling, tried to hold as firm as the building behind her, but it was no use.

Her focus slid, calling to mind an old memory. A horse ride with her mother. A happy picnic—or what should have been a happy picnic. Instead, a viper. Eliza remembered her mother's arms around her, remembered her own frantic scream.

And more than anything, she remembered her beloved white pony, Daisy, struggling to rise from the grass. Too slow. The viper's fangs pierced the horse's neck, pumping deadly poison.

The queen dragged Eliza onto her own mount, racing back to the castle, while Eliza screamed and sobbed for Daisy. The guards were dispatched, but they only brought word that it was too late. Daisy was gone.

Eliza knew what it was like to be afraid. She knew the sharp bite of loss.

She struggled to breathe. Slowly, she reached behind her, feeling for the door to the building. Her hand found the doorknob, but it was locked, and no matter how she rattled it or pounded her hand against the door, no one answered. People continued passing on the street, but no one moved to help her. They only gave deferential nods to the *snakes.*

This country—and everyone in it—was *poison.*

If she tried to leap over the vipers, they would strike. All she could do was stand at their mercy. The snakes held frightfully still, eyes fixed on her, measuring her life with each little tongue flick.

She didn't know how long she stood. Long enough for her knees to ache, for her vision to begin creeping black at the edges, presumably from a lack of air as she failed to control her strangled breathing.

Until, finally, the snakes slithered away, disappearing into the shadows.

Eliza sagged against the door, gasping in air, striking the angry tears from her cheeks. She glared out at the people on the street, but, of course, no one cared.

Truthfully, as much as she hated them for not helping, it was nothing compared to the fury she felt toward the boy who'd joked about *good fortune* and walked away. Silas had ignored her pleas for help, leaving her alone with her search and the snakes.

With one shaking hand, Eliza gripped the small dagger tucked into her belt, and she glared down the street where he'd disappeared.

Realms help him if they ever met again.

CHAPTER

Eliza woke in the night to furious shouting. She kicked against the thin cotton blanket tangled around her legs. Her silk nightgown stuck to her skin, and once more, she longed for the cold winter back home.

Orange light flickered outside her window. Was there a fire?

She threw open the shutters, squinting down into the street.

There was no uncontained fire, only a collection of torches, held aloft in angry hands. Eliza recognized the stocky innkeeper, shirtless and shouting in Pravish. He stood in the circle of torchbearers.

At their center was a lone, short-haired man, perhaps in his thirties, grinning wildly at those surrounding him. His hands twitched at his sides, and Eliza gasped as she realized his fingers had been replaced by scaled talons, the type a large eagle might have.

The innkeeper took a threatening step forward, bellowing a clear accusation.

The man laughed.

Eliza finally saw past the man's animal features to the bloodied corpse at his feet, and her stomach flipped. She clamped a hand to her mouth.

One of the women in the circle screamed something, charging forward along with the man beside her.

In a puff of golden mist, the shapeshifter disappeared, replaced by an enormous eagle, his wingspan at least as wide as Eliza was tall. His piercing shriek cracked the night air, and he swooped at his attackers, raking his talons through the woman's arm and the man's cheek, leaving them bleeding.

The world tilted in Eliza's view. She stepped back from the window, struggling to breathe as her throat closed. From outside came the sound of more shouting and another scream. Torchlight flickered, shadows crawling across her wall.

She had never seen a real shapeshifter before. She'd heard the legends, the horrifying stories of children consumed in their cribs, replaced by a monster adopting human skin. When she was young, she'd laughed at those stories, the way she laughed when performers came to the palace and pretended to be the legendary Einar, brandishing a sword against a three-headed chimera. *Stories* never frightened Eliza.

Until her father told her sternly that shapeshifters were not a story. His mother had executed one when she'd been queen, and sometime during Eliza's life, there would be another loose in the kingdom, and no one would see it coming until it was too late. Until it was already a monstrous killer on a rampage.

Then Eliza no longer found the legends funny.

I need to help, she thought. She fumbled for her sheathed dagger, which rested against her pile of clothes, but once she held it in her hands, she froze.

What could she do against a demon?

Slowly, she inched back to the window and peeked out. Stripes of blood painted the street, glistening in the orange light. Four people lay collapsed, but four others had captured the shapeshifter and wrestled him to the ground. He was a man again, spitting at his captors, howling and bucking as if possessed. Inhuman.

Eliza clutched her small dagger to her chest.

A group of veiled men arrived, identical to those who'd tried to arrest Eliza in the marketplace. *Kuveti*, she heard them called. She shrank against the edge of her window, unable to close the shutters lest that draw attention. In glimpses, she watched the kuveti knock the shapeshifter unconscious, bind him, and drag him away.

What kind of nightmarish place had she come to?

She sank to the floor, back against the wall, both hands around the only weapon she possessed. The helmsman's warnings made sense now, his concern that she didn't appreciate the dangers of magic in Pravusat.

Silas's voice taunted her from memory. *You're the one out of place.*

If she'd let him arrange a voyage for her, she could have left behind the shouting and the miserable humidity and the fresh memory of blood spilled in the street. She could have left behind the fear that those veiled men would catch her again and drag her all the way to prison.

The way they'd dragged off a shapeshifter.

Did they throw their prisoners in cages with shapeshifters to fight for entertainment? She'd read of gruesome practices like that in fables, and in this country, anything seemed possible.

She was beginning to doubt everything, spiraling like a ship caught in a whirlpool. Abandoning the dagger, she stumbled across the room and snatched up her book of sonnets. The light from the window was faint since the torchbearers had dispersed, but she knew this poetry better than her own name, and the bindings remembered all her favorite pages.

So even in a dim blur, she could see the words, crisp and clean. She could see the individual petals of a dried white flower, pointing her to the first two lines of her favorite sonnet.

Love, my crown, most precious gems within its settings gold;
Patience abiding, unceasing hope, and mine endurance bold.

"Unceasing hope," she whispered. "Endurance. Bold."

She would not lose herself to fear or to a lawless country or to whims. She would finish what she'd started, even if everyone else deemed it impossible. She would hope. She would endure.

That was the essence of love.

She'd already searched the docks and markets. She could not go to the royal palace without revealing her identity and making herself a pawn in political games. There was one other noteworthy part of Izili.

On the northern side of the city, the land rose sharply into its highest point atop a set of cliffs. Eliza had noticed a collection of buildings set back from the cliffs but still raised above the city. White with blue accents, towering and yet somehow welcoming. Obviously important.

Henry surely would have noticed them as well. Perhaps he was recovering there. Perhaps it was safer than the run-down streets of the city proper.

Tomorrow, she would search there.

After spending a night in the dorms, the first person Silas sought out on campus was not the dean; it was his favorite professor.

The university had a quieter atmosphere than the city, likely because its arrangement gave the impression of a shelter from the world. All the buildings faced inward, as if they held council the same way the people within them did, and the ground had been cultivated by Stone Casters to grow towering trees, shading the paths. It was a haven—part of Izili in name but separate in every practicality.

In the city proper, faded yellow stone mingled with dark-grain wood to create striking two- and three-story buildings. Every so often, a splash of orange, red, or pink added another contrast to the wild color scheme, though the paint was always splotchy in application, as if the building's owner only had a few hours for the task but simply *had* to have something set their home apart. The entire city was like an art student on a deadline, throwing haphazard colors on the canvas and telling themselves that, really, *any* construction counted as art.

If Izili was the splattered canvas of a student, the university was its composed professor, dressed in a sharp alabaster suit, looking down at the work with a concerned frown.

The university's main building—the Yamakaz—was domed and arched, tiered in four massive levels. It carried no harsh angles at all, everything rounded and softened beneath the touch of magic. Lines of blue lapis accented the white alabaster on each dome, and statues or stone murals marked each curving wall and arch, depicting the mythology of Pravusat, the history of the university's founding, and significant discoveries made by the university's greatest minds. If a Stone Casting student showed particular excellence, they were allowed to contribute to the Yamakaz's decoration when they graduated. Silas was wildly jealous—his magic, for all its benefits, didn't lend itself to art.

He stepped through the Yamakaz's arched doors and breathed deeply the scents of ink and incense. He'd told Eliza that Pravusat was home, but that wasn't entirely accurate.

This was home.

Students milled in every open space, books open before them on tables or the floor. They studied in groups or talked with assignments pushed aside, forgotten. They hurried up and down the spiral staircases, coming to and from lectures on the second floor.

Directly ahead, the main floor held the library, a collection of endless shelves Silas could lose himself in for days. But the library wasn't what he'd come for.

He climbed to the third floor where the staff offices were located and followed a curving hallway down a series of doors interspersed with narrow windows. One door gave him pause—not the one he'd come in search of, but one with a string of braided *yaslari* flowers draping its handle. Purple, the color of mourning. A small boat of incense burned at the foot of the office. Silas frowned. The plaque on the door read *Iyal Havva.*

Pravish mourning traditions were private and rarely included graveside or memorial offerings. Something truly awful must have happened to the professor. Silas had only been gone a month—a week in Loegria plus the twenty days of sailing to get there and back—yet there'd been a tragedy in his absence. That seemed ominous.

He continued until he came to the door marked *Iyal Kerem*. Out of habit, he tried to walk right in, but the door had been locked.

"Who is it?" called a gruff voice from inside.

"Just a passing adder." Silas lowered his hand, rubbing his palm self-consciously on his tunic.

A moment of silence, and then a rush of footsteps to the door before Kerem threw it open. The top half of his black hair was pulled back in a ponytail to keep it out of his face, and he wore thin-rimmed spectacles over his dark eyes. Seeing Silas, he gave a rare smile.

"Silas! Oh, good. I know I wished you well and all that, but I hoped you'd return. You belong here."

Silas offered a smile of his own, and when Kerem gestured, he stepped into the office. A dry, musty smell rose from the research shelves where Kerem kept snakeskin, fangs, and preserved bones, familiar and more comforting than it should have been.

While attending university, Silas had been Kerem's research assistant in everything but name, and together with a Fluid Casting professor, they'd studied the properties and applications of snake venom. Kerem was well-known in Pravusat for developing a way of treating snake bites with antivenom. Revered though they might be, that didn't stop venomous snakes from being deadly when crossed.

"Since when did you start locking your door?" Silas asked. He felt like he'd never left, yet at the same time, he'd been away too long.

"Oh." Kerem waved a hand. "Precautions, I suppose."

"I saw Iyal Havva's door down the hall, with the *yaslari*."

"Nothing like that," Kerem said quickly. "It's protection for my students, not me. I've had more dangerous materials on hand lately."

"More dangerous than vipers and venoms?"

"The most dangerous vipers and venoms, then, let's say. You'll love this." From a shelf, he snatched a vial containing fine white powder, like limestone dust. "Hold that, but don't open it."

With care, Silas turned the vial in his hands, examining the powder. "You didn't," he said, fighting a grin.

Kerem reclaimed the vial, lifting his spectacles to peer at it up close. "Powdered venom. Can you believe it? Mazhar was ready to give up when we finally got it."

Silas's shoulders drooped. "I'm gone a single month, and you make the breakthrough without me."

Working with Kerem had been an unexpected bright spot in Silas's university career. The research was thrilling and challenging, but the largest comfort lay in working alongside someone who truly understood Silas's situation. Kerem wasn't just a fellow Snake Affiliate, but in his youth, he'd been captured by Cronese slavers who traded Affiliates like exotic pets to wealthy buyers. He knew what it was like to be targeted for magic, what it was like to almost die for it.

Kerem lowered his spectacles with a smirk. "Innovation is an ever-progressing river, you know that. But in this case, Mazhar did all the work; only a Fluid Caster could have dried the venom. Now that you're back, let's make the next innovation a feat of Affiliate magic, shall we?"

"I'd like that." Silas swallowed. "I'm trying to make my stay permanent, but I need to speak to Afshin. When I left, I told Iyl Myrna to donate my things, but she said you claimed them."

Kerem pointed to a closet on one side of the room. "I knew you'd be back, Silas. You belong here."

It was the second time he'd said it, and it felt truer than ever, especially once Silas opened a chest to find his clothes and books tucked neatly inside. His old life in storage, just waiting for him to resume it.

This time, he wouldn't look back.

CHAPTER

6

Dressed in a proper suit—which, in Pravish fashion, was not a tailcoat but rather a heavy brocade jacket that extended almost to his knees—Silas made his way, at last, to the dean's office.

Afshin resided on the fourth floor of the Yamakaz, directly beneath the center of the grandest dome. Like the building itself, his office had no corners or hard edges, only curved ceiling and walls, like open arms ready to embrace. The dean stood at a far shelf, murmuring as he rearranged books, as if looking for one that had been misplaced.

Iyal Afshin was a dark-haired man quickly graying, with more wrinkles than it seemed reasonable for his middle-aged face to hold, although anyone who knew him could attest they came from an excess of smiles rather than years.

Silas rapped the back of his knuckles against the open door, and the dean looked up, melting into his signature smile of prominent teeth.

"Our standout Loegrian pupil!" he said. He spoke Loegrian, since he preferred to speak to students in their native tongues. "Silas Bennett, back on Pravish shores."

Afshin welcomed Silas in, striding over to meet him on the rug. He gave a forceful handshake and a shallow bow, which Silas returned.

"Iyal," Silas greeted. It was the same respectful title given to every male professor, and the dean insisted he was no more important than anyone else at the university.

"I must say, Silas, I was hoping you'd go home and make some changes to that little country of yours. Maybe bring it out of the dark ages."

Silas snorted. "You'd need a herd of elephants for that, and I'm just one snake."

Afshin waved Silas over to a sitting corner with wide, flat cushions. Although he used his desk for working, it wasn't where he preferred to hold council. Silas crossed his legs beneath him as he sat.

"Speaking of Loegria." Afshin's eyes gleamed with curiosity. "I've just today gained significant news."

Though Silas's insides knotted with anticipation, he kept his tone light. "Knowing history, it can't be anything good."

"It seems you have a new monarch on the throne. Queen Aria de Loegria, first of her name."

Silas blinked. That *could* be good news. He hoped.

"I'm told the transition was something of an upset," Afshin went on. "How do you think your court will take it?"

Silas's father would be livid, that was for certain. Lord Bennett practically worshipped the king.

He shifted on his cushion. "Honestly, Iyal, Loegria hasn't had a real change in centuries. When I spoke to Aria twelve days ago, she claimed she would reverse the laws against magic users, and I imagine it will cause an uproar if she follows through. More likely, she'll buckle under pressure from tradition and the upper class."

His throat tightened as he thought of his best friend, who had fallen in love with the crown princess during all the recent turmoil. Gill Reeves was a smart man, but he was a tenderhearted one, and a magic user in a hostile country.

You could go back and help, said a voice inside. Aria had promised him a pardon, and if she was queen, she could make good on that.

If she'd been sincere to begin with. The only reason Silas had asked her to protect his sister was because of the way he'd seen her defend Gill before the court, but he still wasn't convinced Aria's motives were selfless. After all, Gill was the strongest Fluid Caster in Loegria, and for a princess facing conflict with Casters, there was an obvious reason for her to keep him on her side.

The more he thought about it, the more certain he became that his friend was facing betrayal down the road. He felt ill.

The shadows beside Afshin's bookshelf took on the shape of Silas's father, looming with a raised sword. He closed his eyes briefly, pushing down the memory.

Afshin clapped his hands together. "This is a wonderful change. I can feel it. Perhaps your country will advance after all. I'd love to welcome more Loegrian students to our campus."

Silas nodded but pushed eagerly to a new topic. "I hope you're willing to do more than that. I'm requesting a position as a professor of warlockry."

The dean frowned, causing Silas to tense. He hadn't allowed himself to consider the odds of winning in this gamble.

"I can't offer that," said Afshin.

"I was top of every class," Silas protested. "In two years, I did double the studies of any other student, and that was after my delayed start, coming from a country *in the dark ages*."

Afshin raised his hands, offering peace. "No one's criticizing your work as a student. Surely, no one *could*. Your research on both Casters and Affiliates has been exemplary. I know Iyal Kerem has been staggered by your contributions to his projects. You're a credit to the field of warlockry."

Silas heard the caveat coming, and his anxiety manifested in a faint scale pattern across his arms.

"But you're still years behind any other professor on my staff."

Slowly, Silas breathed in, then out, calming himself. Afshin waited; he was accustomed to dealing with Affiliates and the accompanying volatile emotions.

Once Silas could speak evenly, he said, "Age shouldn't hobble education. I know I'm only nineteen, but—"

"This is not about your age of living; this is about your age in the field. In two years, you've done twice as much as any student, that's true, but my professors have ten, fifteen, *more* years of research and discourse beneath them. They have revolutionized this and other countries. Iyl Yvette raised the Great Eastern Wall. Iyal Nikolai restarted a stopped heart. And Iyal Kerem . . ."

He didn't need to finish that comparison. What could Silas offer the university that Kerem didn't already supply?

Silas clenched his jaw, holding back the fangs threatening to manifest.

"Continue your studies," Afshin said gently. "Another two years, a sponsorship from another professor to be included in their research, and you will stand shoulder to shoulder with the finest Izili has to offer. Don't mistake me—I *want* you on my staff. I'm thrilled at the prospect. But we have rigid standards here, and it serves no one to lower them."

Silas would love another two years of study, another *ten* years of study, but as he'd told Baris, studying cost money. If the university wouldn't hire him, Silas would have to take a job wherever he could. Harvesting papayas. Working the docks. He would lose everything he'd ever worked for, and he'd spend his days missing a home that had never loved him. It couldn't end like that.

For a moment, he remembered Princess Eliza and her words: *That isn't our ending.*

Perhaps he was *aptal* after all. Perhaps they were both looking truth in the face and denying it. He scowled at the idea.

"What about my final thesis?" Silas tried. "No one had drawn the correlation between activation age for Casters and subsequent Casting strength."

"Dvorik and others had established that Casting potential increased in younger subjects."

"Yes, but I made the connection to *activation* age."

"You expounded on groundwork already laid, but you did not break new ground."

"So if I break new ground, I'll have my position?"

Afshin turned away too late to hide a smile, and Silas felt a flash of triumph. With effort, he remained silent, allowing the dean to consider. And because it couldn't hurt, he also sent a silent prayer to the heavenly realms. After leaving behind his sister, his best friend, his native country and kin, all he had left was the university. He couldn't lose this too.

Slowly, Afshin said, "What is your proposition?"

Silas cast his eyes desperately around the office, trying to spark any idea for *groundbreaking* research in a single moment.

Gill came to mind. His best friend was the strongest Caster alive, activated at birth, and Silas had been itching to write about that ever since he'd realized it. But he'd kept Gill out of his thesis for a reason. As an orphan responsible for two younger brothers, living in the worst country for magic users, the last thing Gill needed was a group of curious researchers breaking down his door to put his Fluid Casting through a battery of tests.

No, Silas couldn't betray Gill. Not for the sake of his own future. Not even to advance the field of warlockry as a whole.

There was something else . . .

An unproven hypothesis about nature's balance and how, if magic users existed, then they must be countered by anti-magic users. Magic stealers.

"Proof of magic stealing," Silas said.

Afshin shook his head. "That has been exhausted in study, by Casters and Affiliates both. Magic cannot be stolen by any—"

"Mine almost was."

The dean fell silent, leaning forward with intrigue.

It had been what finally sent Silas home. One month ago, he'd almost lost his magic, upending everything he knew. He hadn't told anyone, not even Kerem. The moment had felt so surreal, it was hard to believe it had even happened.

But if it could open a future for him, he would face it.

"Someone tried to steal mine," Silas restated with force.

Afshin smiled, wide with raised eyebrows, a man who couldn't resist betting on a horse race if only to see what a certain majestic creature was capable of.

"Put me up in a university dorm for three months," Silas said. "Threadbare budget for living."

But the dean shook his head again. "I haven't the funds for that. The warlockry department is over budget as is, and I've had to refuse most of the latest research proposals."

No, no, no. He couldn't be *this* close and lose it.

"Kerem will pay me," Silas said desperately. "I'm practically his research assistant anyway, and he wants me here."

"If he's willing, then it seems we've found an agreement."

Silas stuck his hand out, quick as a viper strike, and Afshin laughed as he shook it. His grip was firm, and with his other hand, he pointed at Silas's heart.

"I expect great things," he said.

Without hesitation, Silas answered, "I'll be back with proof on your desk. So tell the school of warlockry to prepare for Iyal Silas."

There was a snake in the library.

Eliza stood, petrified, looking at a wide planter nestled between bookshelves, home to a stretching tree. Wrapped around its branches sat a brown python, nearly invisible despite its enormous size, ten feet long at least.

She'd climbed the hill to the mysterious white-and-blue buildings only to discover it was a school, filled with students rushing around with books and papers and even musical instruments. They all seemed to be her age or not much older. A university?

They had a university back home, on the western side of Loegria. Eliza had never visited it, but she knew they taught students from Patriamere as well as Loegria. Sometimes her mother gave music lectures there in either language.

Excitement bubbled to life within her. Even if Henry *wasn't* here, she could at least find a translator. If any place was likely to have people who spoke other languages, it was a university.

She charged into the largest building and gasped in awe at its massive domed ceilings and sprawling library. Surely they'd lost students in the stacks and had to send out entire search parties. She climbed a ladder and stretched her neck but still couldn't count the number of shelves.

Focus, she told herself.

But when she tried to approach the front desk, she found the python.

No one else was bothered by its presence. One girl walked by and gave a polite nod to both Eliza *and* the snake.

They're a religious symbol here, Silas's voice taunted her.

Eliza would never understand this country. But they did have a lovely library, minus allowing a snake to inhabit it.

Slowly, Eliza inched to the side until she reached a bookshelf and could disappear around it. With the python out of sight, she pressed her hands to her chest and breathed. At least until she heard a familiar voice.

"Morning, Tulip. You'll never believe the conversation I've just had with the dean."

It was so cheerful, she almost didn't recognize it at first. But when she peeked around the bookshelf, she saw a familiar tall figure, dressed in a brocade jacket with stunning embroidery. Silas could have been headed for a social event in Pravusat's royal court instead of holding court with a snake.

He smiled at the python stretching its head out of the branches, and he bopped it on the nose with one finger. Fearless as a madman. "Oh, did you? We've both had exciting mornings, I see. That'll teach the rats to stay out of the history stacks."

Eliza shivered. He was lucky they weren't in Loegria. Talking to an animal, even jokingly, would have cast suspicion on him for being a shapeshifter.

At least now she understood why he *fit* here. He was a student at their university. Aria must have chosen him for that reason without understanding that his personality was as rotten as month-old fish.

After leaving her to *die*, he was skipping around a library, cheery and remorseless.

She clenched her teeth, closing her eyes and fighting the impulse to throw her dagger at his back. Or at least a book at his head.

Ever since her curse, she had to be so very careful about controlling herself. Most days, she felt fine, but sometimes a storm brewed inside, growling with thunder that made it hard to hear logic. Navigating that storm led her to impulsive actions.

Lashing out at others. Running away from home.

She had to stay busy, had to stay focused. That was how she maintained control.

I have to find Henry.

Hopefully the python would swallow Silas, and she would never have to see him again.

Staying carefully out of sight, she crept to the library's front desk and asked for someone who spoke Loegrian. The librarian's eyes widened, and she gestured for Eliza to wait. A few minutes later, she returned with a handsome young man in tow. His shoulder-length brown hair reminded Eliza of Henry, and her heart cracked at the edges.

Haltingly, but in blessed Loegrian, the man asked, "You new student?"

"No, I—I'm looking for someone. There was a shipwreck, and I—" Eliza forced herself to take a deep breath and keep things simple. Speaking clearly, she said, "I need a translator."

The man's smile froze, and he didn't speak right away, as if trying to pick her words apart in his mind. She knew the feeling.

At last, he said, "We have . . . translation people. None talk Loegrian." Leaning forward slightly, he gave an apologetic shrug. "Not a popular country."

Well, she wasn't fond of Pravusat either. Far too many snakes.

Desperately, she asked if he would translate for her, and he shook his head. His lack of fluency was clear enough, so she wasn't surprised, only disappointed.

This had been her best lead, and it was a dead end.

CHAPTER

 7 

A heavy pressure built inside Eliza, like a storm on the ocean's horizon. She tried frantically to think of her next step, the next thing to do, while ignoring the billowing clouds.

After the two librarians consulted in Pravish, the young man addressed her again. "For translation, maybe you can buy one Caster in the market."

She blinked. Her mind took a moment to sort through the words and meaning before she asked breathlessly, "Buy magic, you mean? Can a Cast *translate* for me?"

He gave an enthusiastic nod. "The market can buy stone and water and animal. Every magic."

Even in Loegria, Casts could be purchased from certain Casters, as long as they were registered and branded. After her experience with curses, Eliza never would have steered herself toward magic, but now it was the only path before her, and with the storm rising at her back, she plunged forward rather than face it.

If this was her one way to find Henry, so be it.

Eliza ran from the library, barely remembering to throw a Pravish *thank you* over her shoulder.

By the time she reached the market outside the broken wall, she was sweating. She doubled over, gasping for breath, then pushed on. A hundred conversations swirled around her from people jostling her in all directions. After a particularly violent shove, she almost ran into a hot plate sizzling over a contained fire, and the merchant's only response was a wide smile as he offered her whatever dripping meat he'd just pulled from the cooktop.

Her stomach rumbled, and she bit her lip, but paying for the inn had eaten up almost all her money, and what little silver remained was now dedicated to whatever magic could lead her to Henry. It was the only hope she had left, and she had not crossed an entire ocean only to fail now.

Scanning the market, she saw a few stone statues on a striped rug. A Stone Caster, perhaps? Eliza forced her way through the crowd until she knelt on the woman's blanket.

"*Nirhaba*!" the woman cried out, smiling widely. She wore a bright-pink scarf wrapped to cover her hair, vibrant against her rich brown skin, and her green shirt was embroidered with matching pink flowers. Leaning forward, she said, "*Seykeli atin al*!"

Eliza pulled her shoulders back, strengthening her spine, and she tried to speak in a voice loud enough to be heard over the chaos of the market.

"*Nirhaba*," she repeated. The greeting was easy. After that, the woman had said to buy . . . something. She didn't know any Pravish words for magic or Casting, and she hadn't thought to ask the male librarian to teach her. Eliza fought back a groan. "*Seykeli* . . . Cast?"

The woman lifted a stone statue carved in the shape of a woman. She chattered away in Pravish, gesturing between the statue's face and Eliza's own.

"Very pretty," she kept repeating. "Very pretty."

"Yes," Eliza agreed. "Very pretty."

"You buy!"

"No, I . . ." Eliza flopped her hands uselessly, trying to think of how to communicate her need. She stitched words together like the most horrendous of scrap blankets. "I need . . . thing . . . Speak Pravish?"

The woman laughed, amused. She waved her hand. "*Arakl sana Pravish konusturamaz.*"

Well, at least Eliza heard the word *Pravish*. And she was fairly certain *sana* was "cannot." *Konustura* was a verb for speaking—and, embarrassingly, the *-maz* ending meant Eliza had conjugated her own attempt incorrectly. Pravish conjugations would be the death of her.

But if she understood correctly, that meant *arakl* was something like "Casting."

"*Arakl*!" Eliza said.

With an approving nod, the woman reached behind her to a pile of rocks. They were the same porous yellow as the Izili wall, and she easily pulled one from the top, suggesting it was lightweight.

Eliza's heart pounded. She'd never commissioned anything from a Caster of any kind, but she'd always admired the creations of Stone Casters. There was even a bit of their work in Castle de Loegria, in the observatory tower, which stretched higher than any other part of the castle, with thin stone rafters that appeared delicate and yet remained stable through the roughest storms.

It was one thing to commission a statue or a feat of architecture. Another to ask for a Cast that affected herself. Eliza rubbed her hands on her thighs, her palms damp. She remembered cold nights spent in the cage of a curse.

After knowing the terrible touch of magic, she was asking for it again? Perhaps she would come out even worse. Perhaps after magic infected a person deeply enough, they lost themselves.

Or maybe magic canceled itself out? Maybe if she requested a blessing, it would wash away the remaining effects of the curse? That seemed too convenient to hope for.

There was so much she didn't know. Eliza swallowed heavily. "Wait," she whispered in Pravish. "I . . . wait."

She fumbled her red book from her pocket. The words slid like ice in her grasp, and she found nothing to tell her the right way to go.

Suddenly, the woman reached out and patted Eliza's hand.

Eliza jumped, dropping her book to the striped rug beneath her.

With a sympathetic, motherly smile, the Caster asked, "It is boy?"

Despite herself, Eliza smiled back, releasing the tension from her shoulders. She laughed, retrieving her book and sliding it back into her pocket. "Yes, there is . . . boy. I . . . I *need* boy. Need to speak Pravish." She licked her lips, then added nervously, "Understand?"

Or maybe that was "memorize." *Analamak. Enelemek?*

"I help," said the woman, giving another reassuring pat.

Eliza sagged in relief, shoving her coin purse forward, not caring how much it cost. She couldn't bear to hit another delay, couldn't bear to lose hope again. This *had* to work. It *had* to lead her to Henry.

The Stone Caster tucked away the rest of Eliza's silver and then lifted the rock again, rolling it between her palms. She closed her eyes, humming a low, drawn-out note that rumbled pleasantly in Eliza's bones, somehow piercing the din of the marketplace—quieting it, even. For a moment, a blanket of peace settled over Eliza.

The yellow stone glowed faintly before rounding and elongating as if it were soft, pliable clay rather than solid rock. With a quick twist, the woman wrenched the stone apart, splitting it in two. The glow sharpened, flaring through her fingers like rays of sunlight through broken clouds, dotting Eliza's vision with spots.

Suddenly, the woman held out two golden bands, flattened and curved. Eliza had seen similar bracelets worn by other Pravish people.

Gesturing to the first and then to Eliza, the Stone Caster said, "You wear." She pointed at the second and then away, toward the city wall. "Boy wear."

Eliza's tentative smile vanished as her jaw dropped. "*Boy*? Oh, no, I—he isn't—" She struggled to switch back to Pravish. "Only me. Cast me."

But the woman shook her head. Enunciating, she said, "Boy speak Pravish?"

Eliza swallowed. This had gone so terribly wrong.

But she thought of Silas instead of Henry. Thought of his smug dismissal and carefree demeanor in the library.

She did know a boy who spoke Pravish.

So she said, "Yes."

The woman gestured with the bracelet. "Boy wear." She lifted the other bracelet. "You wear. You speak Pravish."

Apparently, the Cast could not summon language ability from thin air. She had to borrow it from someone who already possessed it.

So? It was not too much to ask Silas to wear a *bracelet*. In fact, this was the perfect compromise. He wouldn't have to lift a finger to help Eliza himself.

You can't force me into anything, his voice taunted from memory.

Watch me, she thought.

Before she could second-guess herself, she closed the first bracelet over her wrist, holding her breath. But she felt nothing. The woman pressed the second bracelet into her hands with a wink, and Eliza understood that message well enough. They would only work together.

This was her path to Henry. She just had to believe in it.

"Thank you," she said to the Stone Caster. And then, since she didn't know a stronger gratitude phrase than the standard *tezekurler*, she said a nonsensical *tezekurler kol*. "Thank you very."

Beaming, the woman inclined her head and said something too quick and wordy to fully catch. Something about *your boy*.

With heated cheeks, Eliza bowed in return, tightened her grip on the other bracelet, and fled.

CHAPTER

8

The day Silas had almost lost his magic, it had been raining all morning—a light drizzle that annoyed and dampened but kept no one at home—and when the overhead gray broke at last, he'd been on the outskirts of campus, basking in the rays of sunlight. There was a path out to the cliffs that he sometimes liked to walk, though he hadn't made it that far yet. With a few other students on the path around him, he thought nothing of a jostle when someone passed.

Until the girl caught his hand. His eyes widened as she went up on her toes, and that moment hung frozen, her face and his, a breath apart, her blue eyes approaching like a sudden wave to capsize an unsuspecting ship.

Then she kissed him.

He should have been appalled to kiss a stranger, but Silas enjoyed the unexpected, and there was nothing more unexpected than being suddenly kissed by a girl he'd never met. Curiosity flared in his mind. Why him? Why this way? Most likely, she was a Fluid Casting student on a dare. Because of the increased heart rate during a kiss, maybe she was experimenting with his blood.

She'd be expelled for unsanctioned experiments on other students, but he was having difficulty focusing on the lecture she deserved.

It was only his second kiss; the first had been an innocent peck at boarding school, followed by a lot of giggling from the girl and a lot of confusion from Silas about why people chose to do this repeatedly. Now he had a better idea. He could have written an essay about what this girl's lips were doing to his senses.

Until he realized what they were doing to his magic.

Silas shoved back. The sense of magic within him flickered like a candle threatened by wind. He breathed slowly, trying to guard the flame.

Even though she'd been the one to attack, the girl with ocean-blue eyes stared at him with wild panic in her expression, like he'd drawn a weapon on her. A scale pattern appeared along her cheekbones—gray lined with black, just the way Silas's skin looked when he was in danger of transforming. He was certain the scales hadn't been there before the kiss. In her hands, she clutched a small box, obscured by her fingers, peeking through in slits of bone-white angles and thick black decorative lines.

Then she bolted away, almost knocking over one of the other students. The few bearing witness gawked at the drama, some laughing, some rolling their eyes.

Silas should have grabbed the retreating girl, but he was struggling to breathe, paralyzed by the feeling that any sudden movement would extinguish the most vital part of him. She'd drawn his magic out like a thread, and he had to somehow wind it around his core again without letting it snap.

Scales flickered on his skin, fleeting as ghosts. Even with fierce concentration, he couldn't transform, and he began to tremble. Though he stood in a ray of sunlight, he couldn't feel the warmth, and he finally stumbled forward—not following the girl, just reaching desperately for something to ground him.

"*Come*," he rasped. He couldn't see a ripple in the air, couldn't be sure he'd sent a command at all.

His knees gave out, and the other students finally took note.

One of them ran for a physician. Silas clenched his fists, pulled his knees up, and tucked his head down, like he could hold everything inside by sheer force of will.

A faint hiss met his ears before Tulip slithered up beside him. The python almost never left the Yamakaz, but he was grateful she'd answered. When he extended his hand, she curled once around his wrist, and magic surged through every bone. Warmth returned to the world. He let out a gasp, no longer candle-frail, and his gaze finally searched campus, dreading the view of a girl who was, thankfully, long gone.

Magic stealing. It had been hypothesized for decades but never proven. Iyal Kerem had a volume of extensive research on the subject, documentation of a hundred experiments conducted by Affiliates and Casters alike, all ending in failure.

Yet Silas couldn't deny the truth screaming to him from every bone, the fear vibrating his chest with every heartbeat.

He was an academic, not a coward. He chased new information, new experiences. He lived far from home in a culture not his own. While witnessing a failed revolution against the Nephew King, he'd stood in a doorway as the street before him was torn between Stone Casters in a living earthquake. While others ran, he'd waited out the conflict, and, the next day, he'd turned in an essay about it to Iyl Yvette.

But this girl was different. She'd been a threat with no warning. The sheer casualness of the encounter made it more callous, more frightening than any impassioned revolution. She'd not torn apart the cobble of streets; she'd reached between his ribs and torn the fabric of his soul. With a single touch, she'd almost unraveled him entirely.

His academic instincts told him he should track down the ocean-eyed girl, chase the discovery that could change the world.

Instead, he did the unthinkable.

He ran.

He boarded the first ship back to Loegria, only to have his home country reject him in the one moment he actually needed it. He should have known. Whether it was his father's sword or the king's banishment, all his home had to offer was betrayal.

Now he had nowhere to run.

His terror hadn't vanished—even the memory of the near loss of his magic held sharp edges. But if proving magic stealers existed stood between him and his future, then he would fight a revolution of his own, and, fangs bared, he would show the world what he was capable of.

One should be very careful about cornering a snake.

Silas worked out an agreement with Kerem for a paid position as his assistant. It was a meager salary—Kerem couldn't spare much—but it was enough for Silas to secure the university's cheapest dorm, and as long as he was living on campus, he could use the dining hall for evening meals. The rest of the time, he would make do. All that mattered was that he'd seized his opportunity.

Now to succeed in it.

For the next three months, he would spend his effort in three ways: One, assisting Kerem. Two, tracking down the ocean-eyed girl. Three, attempting his own experiments to steal magic. He didn't have any insights greater than those who'd already conducted failed experiments except knowing for certain it was possible. Sometimes, knowledge like that was all it took to open new angles of creativity on research.

Although he was tempted to ask for Kerem's insights, Silas refrained. If he was going to prove himself worthy of a professorship, he had to do this project alone. All his study, all his ambition, would serve or fail him now.

He grabbed a few books from the library and settled into his new dorm. The room he'd rented left a lot to be desired, but that was the point. Most people wouldn't pay for it, so he'd negotiated the cost down to almost nothing. Iyl Myrna, the housing matron, had been generous while bartering, especially after he'd given her one of Baris's papayas.

The room itself was cozy, furnished with a sturdy bed, a wide dresser, a floor desk, and a washbasin. The biggest trouble was that, while most of the university enjoyed water piped directly to their rooms courtesy of Fluid Casters, this particular dorm did not.

That was because it stood next to the Stone Caster training yard, which suffered frequent earthquakes that would have broken the pipes.

As Silas sat cross-legged on a flat cushion beside his desk, turning his pen in his hand and feeling the heavy flow of ink inside slide from one end of the barrel to the other, the ground beneath him rumbled, signaling the start of Stone Caster training. He leaned one elbow on his desk, which was low to the ground and sturdy enough to anchor him through the tremors, and while the room rattled around him, he kept reading *Tales of Nightmare Beast*.

His other books were all research on magic stealing, but this one was a mythology from Cronith, one of the countries bordering Pravusat. When he'd seen it on the shelf, it had tickled the back of his mind, and Silas knew better than to ignore his instincts.

If he only knew what they were trying to tell him.

A particularly large quake made his books hop, and he dropped his wrist atop the stack to hold it steady.

He couldn't write notes during the tremors. Although his pen was an immense improvement on the quill and ink of his childhood—Fluid Casters had fashioned it to release ink at just the right rate—it still couldn't save him from an unsteady environment, and he'd rather not have jagged lines all over his journal. So he merely absorbed the words of the text, letting his mind chew through them like a heavy piece of meat at a banquet, savoring the spices and trying to identify them.

Ever hunger, the text read. *Never sated. Monster dwelling. Blood and ash.*

The translation was choppy at best and gibberish at worst. Silas should have grabbed the book in its original Cronese rather than Pravish. Cronese was the weakest of his three known languages, but he'd specifically learned it because the Cronese syllabary script didn't lend itself to translation.

All at once, he knew why he'd been drawn to this text, what his mind had been trying to tell him.

"Blind as a burrowing snake," he muttered, closing the book. He grabbed his bag, stumbling as another tremor shook the dorm building.

The black symbols on the magic stealer's box—even obscured, he'd recognized something about them. They reminded him of written Cronese.

At a brisk pace, he crossed campus back to the Yamakaz. He returned the translation of Mollier's text and asked for the original, only to learn it had been signed out by another student.

"Other works in Cronese?" he asked.

He followed the librarian's directions, seeking a shelf of historical texts about Cronith.

Until he turned a corner and came face-to-face with the reckless princess.

"*Disi dokmek*," he cursed. *Swallowed tooth*. It was the best expression of bad luck—the idea that, while biting lunch, a snake could lose and swallow its own fang. It certainly *felt* like Silas had something sharp lodged in his throat.

Eliza had been sitting at a table, as if waiting for something, but she leapt to her feet when she saw him. What was she doing at the university?

Her brown eyes fixed on his and began smoldering like embers, and Silas found he didn't care for reasons. He didn't have time for this.

The princess surged forward, clearly intent on intercepting him, but he ducked into a passage between shelves, certain he could lose her between the historical accounts of the Century War and the research by Fluid Casters in the medical field.

He'd forgotten how fast the mouse could scurry.

Just as he rounded a corner, he glanced back only to realize she was nearly upon him. At the same moment, his magic tingled with awareness—*snake below.* Tulip was down from her tree, stalking the library for her next rat, and he'd almost stumbled right into her. She lifted her head, hissing her displeasure, even though he'd halted at the last second.

With premature triumph, Silas smirked, knowing the snake would drive Eliza back.

Instead, it did the opposite.

She launched herself directly into his arms.

With a grunt and no other choice, Silas caught her, keeping them both from falling onto an innocent python. The trembling princess pressed her face to his chest, eyes squeezed closed. He appreciated the irony that she found him a safer option than a snake. That was the trouble with ignorance; it motivated hypocritical decisions.

He cleared his throat, trying to extract himself from her grip, which was more constricting than any python's. She whimpered, and he rolled his eyes.

"Tulip won't hurt you," he said. "First, because she's a lazy thing, and she has plenty of easier prey available. Second, because even small as you are, you're not *that* small. Third, because you have a problematic shape for swallowing, particularly in the shoulders. Need I go on?"

Slowly, Eliza loosened her grip, straightening but not releasing him. Despite himself, Silas softened. In the past, only Maggie had ever trusted him to be her defender, and no matter how irritating the princess was, she'd stirred fond memories.

So he spoke more gently when he said, "Just because I have no fear of snakes doesn't mean I can't see the reasoning in it. You know, my sister—"

With the speed of a striking cobra, Eliza pulled her arms free, revealing something clutched in her right hand. Something she clamped around Silas's wrist.

His magic roared in his ears. *Intruder*, it screamed. *Threat!* A pulse of magic not his own wrapped him with invisible cords, binding him in a cage. With a snarl, he ripped free of Eliza, clawing at the unwanted shackle. But the magic had already fastened, and the bracelet fit him perfectly, a band sealing his wrist without seam, without hinge or release.

Distantly, he heard the princess's smug voice. "Since you wouldn't help me willingly, I'll be borrowing your language proficiency to find Henry. You won't have to lift a finger, so—"

Silas looked up, and her voice died in her throat, her eyes widening. He could guess what she saw in his.

Red eyes, pupils narrowed to slits. His viper eyes.

Beside him, Tulip reared, lifting her head almost to his waist, her gaze also trained on the princess.

Eliza's face drained of color. Her lips trembled.

Silas felt the press of fangs in his mouth, the desire to lash out at being cornered, to strike with venom. It was a good thing the princess didn't run. If he didn't strike her, Tulip would. Silas wasn't her brood, but the python was poised to defend just the same. Eliza wouldn't die if Tulip struck, but she'd be in for a few miserable days and a pair of nasty scars.

No more than she deserved.

Silas tried to keep his boiling emotions under control, tried to exhibit restraint, but there was little of that left to him. Not after being chained like an animal.

His hold slipped, and he transformed in a puff of gray mist.

draining the warmth from his father's eyes. It was an inward decision, made in a bare moment without entertaining other options.

Lord Bennett chose to believe all his country's superstitions about shapeshifters.

He drew his sword.

And when he slashed it toward Silas's throat, Silas couldn't say what his father's vision looked like in terms of warmth and colors, but whatever he saw, it wasn't his son.

The university library filtered through Silas's waking nightmare, prompted by Tulip's approach. The python slithered against his leg, pausing to lift her head and flick her tongue, as if telling him to snap out of it. Silas reached out an unsteady hand, brushing Tulip's patterned brown scales, and within him, his magic slowly settled.

He pressed his other hand to the long, thin scar below his jaw.

The only reason he was still alive was because Gill had stepped in. His best friend had used magic to stop Silas's bleeding and to make Lord Bennett forget seeing the transformation. But even without the memory, nothing between Silas and his father had ever been the same.

Since that day, he'd never been his father's son.

"He—he's a sh—he's a *shapeshifter*!" Eliza cried, barely choking out words past her obvious terror. She pointed at Silas in condemnation.

Silas glared up at a spoiled princess.

The three librarians looked helplessly between the two of them. Seeing no real emergency, the others retreated, leaving only the one who spoke broken Loegrian—although he did not address Eliza. He addressed Silas in Pravish.

"Mr. Bennett, is this girl harassing you? Did she harm you?"

Despite everything, Silas almost managed a smile, the librarian's concern helping him regain his composure.

"I'm fine," he said in Pravish.

He *belonged* to campus and was such a frequent visitor at the library, most of the workers knew him by name. Eliza was the stranger.

"He's an animal!" Eliza gasped out again, her skin deathly pale.

"Please calm," the librarian said in accented Loegrian.

"Affiliate," Silas corrected, finally standing. He narrowed his eyes on the princess. "*Animal Affiliate.* Not animal. Not shapeshifter. But I don't suppose there's any purpose in educating you on proper terms when you're the most selfish, unmannered creature I've ever encountered. Now tell me what you've done to me."

Eliza tried to run, but she hit some kind of unseen barrier. An invisible cord yanked her back a step at the same time it pulled on Silas's arm. In horror, she stared down at her own bracelet, identical to Silas's. Apparently she'd purchased some kind of Cast in an attempt to control him, tangling with magic she didn't understand.

Silas regarded her coldly. "You were so eager to seek me out, Highness. To gloat. To attack. Now you realize being royalty doesn't make you the biggest threat in the room." He tilted his head, and with his emotions still churning, a faint scale pattern rippled across his skin, evident in the way his cheeks itched. "What's the matter? Are you afraid I'll bite?"

Through the worst misunderstanding imaginable, Eliza had bound herself to a living deception, to a creature who wasn't even human. Just a snake in human clothing.

She grabbed the librarian's arm. "Help me, please!"

But the librarian only gave her a disapproving frown. Then he said something about campus rules and Animal Affiliates while Silas just watched with cold eyes. Cold, dark eyes. Eliza remembered how they'd turned solid red with just a slit for a pupil. She'd thought he was selfish and uncaring, but it was so much worse.

He was a monster.

Eliza's limbs shook, and she tried to lock her knees, tried to put on a brave face when she didn't feel it because she knew the adage about fear and animals. The python finally slithered away, but that gave no comfort, because the remaining snake was far, far worse.

Silas reassured the librarian, the two of them exchanging quick, casual words in Pravish, and with a final glance, the other man moved off.

Leaving Eliza at the mercy of a demon.

She thought of torches in the dark, of a man transforming into an eagle and tearing through innocent people with deadly talons. She thought of his gleeful, unhinged grin.

"Will you kill me?" The question squeaked from her without permission, and her voice broke. She gripped a bookshelf to remain standing.

If anything, Silas looked even angrier. For an instant, his eyes flashed red again, like a window catching a glaze from the setting sun.

"No, Your Highness," he said. "I'm an academic, not a rampant murderer."

Did he really believe that? Maybe he was a skillful liar, or maybe the creature side of him wasn't even in his control. Maybe it overtook his consciousness like a nightmare, wreaking havoc he didn't remember come morning. Was that how shapeshifters managed to stay hidden so well? Hiding even from themselves?

Eliza knew something about losing control, and she could feel herself on the precipice of that now, hanging above a steep drop she wouldn't know how to survive—because worse than any reckless action or angry outburst was the feeling of drowning. The feeling she'd kept at bay thus far by focusing on her search for Henry.

The storm inside rumbled with growing thunder.

Don't fall, she begged silently.

She wished she'd never met magic of any kind, shapeshifter or Caster. She wished she'd never been cursed. She wished she could be back in that ballroom on her seventeenth birthday, cradled in Henry's arms.

Though it betrayed her desperation, she pried at the bracelet with everything she had, cutting bloodless lines into her fingers, breaking a nail. But the band around her wrist did not budge.

All she'd managed to accomplish was binding herself to a shapeshifter, offering herself up as prey to be consumed at any time. Henry was still lost. She'd chased her whims and wound up here. Useless. Foolish.

She'd failed.

Thinking the words was like a blow to her spine, cracking what remained of her foundation. Her knees hit the polished library floor.

Curling against a shelf, she buried her face in her arms in a poor attempt to hide, and her shoulders shook as she tried and failed to suppress everything spilling from inside. The shapeshifter might kill her now, not because she was easy prey but just to silence her. She didn't care. There was nothing left to care about.

Yet no attack came. There was only the storm inside. She'd tried to pretend the thunder was just rolling in, but she was already a shipwreck. She'd been clinging to broken scraps of hull to stay afloat, and all she could feel now was a grasping current, dragging her down.

Then Silas heaved a sigh.

With a disgruntled *whump*, he sat beside her.

Eliza jerked her head up, looking at him through bleary eyes as he flicked a handkerchief onto her face. She swatted it free, irritation slowing her tears.

If he'd given her a handkerchief the day before, she would have thought him half a gentleman. Now she wondered if it was some kind of trick. He didn't say anything, so after a moment's hesitation, she wiped her face. The tears still trickled, her breath coming in hiccups.

Silas pulled a book from the shelf behind them and started reading.

Eliza stared at the strangeness, and eventually, the pressing force on her chest eased, allowing her to breathe without a catch in her throat. She didn't know how long it had been, only that Silas had turned more than a few pages.

"Come on," he finally said. "Stand up. We'll get someone to reverse the Cast."

After returning the book to its shelf, he climbed to his feet, clearly waiting for her to follow.

Eliza swallowed. "You can—can do that?"

"I know a revered Stone Caster. She's a professor here. Helped build the Great Eastern Wall."

Eliza pressed her hands to her cheeks, which were dry now but raw from the tears. No doubt her nose was red and her eyes much worse, but she'd never been much of a pristine princess. Her father had scolded her for that many times, but her mother had told Eliza to be her own person, no matter her station.

She'd gotten herself into this, and if there was a way out, she would take it. One step at a time. That tiny sense of control gave her enough strength to stand, even if her knees still wobbled.

Silas watched her with dark, unreadable eyes. Then he nodded toward the library exit. He kept his hands in his pockets as they walked, like he was as afraid to touch her as she was to touch him.

Like they were both monsters to each other.

The princess's breakdown had been a blessing; it had given Silas a chance to gather his own emotions, to view things with a level head once more. Clearly, neither he nor Eliza wanted this arrangement, so the easiest thing to do was fix it. He knew just the person for that.

Iyl Yvette had her office door open, and Silas knocked as he crossed the threshold. He expected a warm greeting, maybe even a hug, but instead he received the fiercest of scowls, enough to stop him in his tracks.

"Silas Bennett!" she snapped, rising from behind her desk. "You dare show your fanged face in this office?"

Silas blinked. "What did I ever do to you, Yvette?"

Yvette was barely taller than Eliza, and her demeanor was suited to being a Stone Caster—between her stoic expression and stocky frame, she often gave the impression of being a statue herself. While many Pravish women wore scarves as head wraps, Yvette wrapped hers around her throat. No matter what else she wore, that scarf was always the same, inherited from her mother, red as wine and striking against her beaded black hair.

"That's *Iyl* to you. I expect sufficient groveling before you earn back your first-name privileges." She stomped over and jabbed him in the chest, making him hiss.

"Grovel for *what*?" Silas demanded.

"You left without saying goodbye."

He shifted his weight to the other leg, and not just because it drew him one step back from the threat. "You knew I'd finished my studies."

"Yes, and every time I saw you in the library, you said, 'Any day now,' 'Just a few loose ends,' and what did I say to you, Silas, *aptal*?"

He rubbed his chest; she'd poked quite hard. One of the books on her shelf had a skull carved on the front leather, its gaze offering an empty-eyed condemnation.

"*What* did I *say*?"

Begrudgingly, Silas admitted, "You said, 'Don't leave without—'"

"*Don't leave without saying goodbye*. Oh, so you do have human ears in that snake skull!"

"I saw your husband in the market," he said, as if that made it better.

From her expression, it did not. "You spoke to *Baris* but not to me?" She loosed a string of colorful curses. Yvette was the source of

Silas's most delightful Pravish expressions. "What did I waste all my time on you for? Ungrateful student!"

She threw her hands in the air, and, beside him, Eliza flinched as if the professor had threatened a strike.

Yvette turned, finally noticing Silas wasn't alone. "Who's this one? Your wife? Is that why you're gone and back so soon—your father arranged a marriage?"

"I'm not his *wife*!" Eliza squeaked out, face reddening like a tomato.

It was Silas's turn to blink. Yvette knew Loegrian, but she hadn't spoken any in this conversation, so Eliza shouldn't have been able to understand anything.

Addressing the princess, he asked, "Since when did you learn Pravish?"

"She's speaking Loegrian," Yvette said.

"Yes, I—" Silas huffed. He raised his wrist, shoving the golden band into Yvette's view. "It's this cursed thing. This is why we're here."

Yvette's ranting demeanor vanished, replaced by the intrigued professor hooked on a mystery. She took Silas's wrist and turned it this way and that, rubbing her thumb across the flattened stone. Where her touch passed, a faint golden glow trailed, quickly fading.

"Oh," she murmured. "*Oh.*" Anything left of the statue softened, and she looked up at Silas with concern, reaching out to grip his shoulder. "Are you all right?"

He frowned but nodded. "I just want it gone. Can you read the Cast?"

"As clearly as any book. You won't like what it says."

Before he could ask, Yvette moved to stand in front of Eliza and crossed her arms like a chastising parent.

Eliza shifted from one foot to the other, head bowed before the stony professor.

In Loegrian, Yvette said, "Eyes forward, girl, and give me your name."

To her credit, Eliza followed the instruction without bluster. Then she grew nervous and stumbled into the rest of the story—Henry Wycliff and the shipwreck.

Yvette studied the girl's bracelet just as she had Silas's before she prompted, "Dear Eliza, what have you done?"

Eliza looked at the floor, whispering, "I just wanted . . . I needed to speak Pravish."

"And the Caster you hired to help—you told her you needed a leash for this boy who slithers out of everything?"

"Excuse me?" Silas spat.

Eliza's face turned red once more, and she sputtered.

Yvette lifted the girl's arm calmly, gesturing at her bracelet. "This Cast binds you together. I'd estimate you can't go more than twenty feet apart without one bracelet pulling the other. This is a wrist-to-jaw Cast, a common bone pairing, so the magic is rooted in the jawbone and worn against this prominent carpal on the wrist. It's surprisingly strong. You found a good Caster, or one who was particularly enthusiastic about your request."

Silas seethed more with every word. "What exactly did you request?" he demanded of the princess.

Eliza shrank. "I—I just said I needed to speak Pravish! Then she started talking about a boy, and I didn't realize—"

"And you made this request *in Pravish*? Which you *don't speak*?" Silas groaned, imagining the vast multitude of malapropisms she might have performed in that single request. "How did you refer to me? *Erkal*?" He gave the most common, age-neutral male identifier, already knowing it would be wrong.

Eliza huffed. "Well, I thought we were speaking of Henry. Besides, she's the one who mentioned it first, so I only mimicked her phrasing. *Erkek*."

Yvette busted out laughing. Silas gave her a flat stare.

"*Erkek* is a drippingly affectionate term for males," he said. "Either you're hopelessly in love with me, or I'm your darling little son you never want to leave home."

Yvette gave a conspiratorial grin, releasing Eliza's arm. "I don't think your Stone Caster interpreted it as the second."

"If you'd just helped me!" Eliza exploded. "None of this—"

"Don't you dare blame me! Entitled royal—meddling with magic you don't understand. Did you even consider if we're bound for life?"

"We're not!"

"You were so certain of the terms before you purchased? You didn't even know the right words to use!"

He pried at the bracelet again, but it did not release. He let out a string of curses revolving around people who never deserved to see a snake in their lives.

"Well, I . . . We can't be." Eliza swallowed. "That's not the way it should work."

"You seem to have this belief that you can warp reality to suit your own wants. I have news for you, *apta*—truth is objective. And reality does not care what you want it to be."

"Don't call me that," she growled.

"I'll call you whatever I please, considering what you called me—and where we stand as a result."

"Enough," said Yvette, cutting her hand through the air as if she could sever the conversation. Her expression still held enough enjoyment to make Silas's skin bristle with gray scales.

"Jawbone," she said, gesturing to her own. "Symbolic of language, among other things. My best guess is that you found this Stone Caster in the market, you told her something about a darling boy and Pravish, and she took that to mean you'd fallen in love with some Pravish boy but couldn't tell him because of a language barrier. As long as you're both wearing the bands, you'll understand any language the other can speak, and it should assist with learning it as well."

"Why limit how far we can go?" Silas asked, glaring at the princess. "Did you throw that detail in too?"

"I didn't say anything about distance!" Eliza protested.

"A side effect only," said Yvette. "A language Cast like this needs stability, which can be offered through proximity. Since she assumed you wanted an intimate conversation anyway, why not have it in the same room? Not a problem."

Silas could have given a few choice thoughts about problems and the princess causing them.

"How do we break it?" he asked. Unless it was a curse, the Cast would come with an inherent unraveling feature.

"Ah . . ." Yvette pressed her lips together, separating them with a small *pop*. "Well, presumably, after your romantic intentions could be made clear and understood, this Stone Caster had faith you'd be a love story for the ages."

Silas tasted something sour. "How do we break it, Yvette?"

"You kiss, Silas. And don't look at me like that—I didn't Cast it."

CHAPTER 10

"*Kiss*?" cried Eliza.

Silas would rather be skinned in snake form. He'd rather be milked for venom. He'd rather be shipped back home to the mercy of his father.

Perhaps not that one. But the list of *rathers* was still nearly infinite.

Especially when Yvette said, "Nothing quick, either. You'd have to mean it."

Silas turned away from the princess, banishing her from even the corner of his eye because if he looked at her, he'd suffer another rage transformation. Instead, he breathed steadily and counted Yvette's books by multiples of three.

For a moment, he wished he'd never agreed to Aria's deal, but he couldn't make that resentment last. He'd been the one to request her help first, and she'd saved Maggie from a miserable future. He'd pay any price to save his sister. Even this one.

"Can you break it?" Eliza asked before Silas could, and he angled to see her clutching Yvette's hands, pleading. "You're a Stone Caster!"

Yvette squeezed the princess's hands and dropped them, stepping back. "Breaking a Cast I didn't lay comes at high cost. But more than that, I'm not sure it's for the best in this case."

Silas stiffened. "What do you mean 'not for the best'?"

Yvette caught him by the arm, pulling him to the other side of the room for a hushed conversation.

"I'll tell you what I mean," she said quietly, speaking Loegrian. Her sharp eyes pinned him like a research subject. "I remember two years ago when Iyal Afshin brought a new student to my office, fresh off a boat from Loegria, full of fragile hope."

Silas shifted uncomfortably. "What do I have to do with—"

"Afshin told me your father did all the talking for you, enrolled you in university and demanded you be taught a *respectable* field. Economics. Your father said by the time you returned in two years, you'd have a true appreciation for your own country and be ready to inherit your title."

"I remember well enough," Silas muttered.

"Then you'll remember why Afshin brought you to me instead of to the head of economics."

"Because you spoke Loegrian."

She snorted. "Because the only question you asked during your university tour was, 'Is it true Pravusat has no laws against magic?' Because you still wore a bandage on your throat from a fresh wound that was nearly fatal, and you flinched whenever your father lifted his arm near you. We're not fools, Silas, and our primary objective on this campus is to help every student, in whatever way is best for them." With clear meaning, she tipped her head toward the princess.

"She's not a student," said Silas, with more petulance than he cared to admit.

Yvette raised a smooth eyebrow, and she held her pose, firm as a statue, until Silas fidgeted.

"*You* are," she said. "You were, at least. And if there's one lesson I never managed to pierce through that snake's skull, it's that life is about *more* than lessons. It's about saying goodbye to friends when you leave the country. It's about looking at a lost girl, far from home, wounded and in need of help, and thinking of how, just two years ago, you cast the same shadow."

"You can't condemn me to *this*"—Silas lifted the bracelet—"out of a grudge that I didn't say goodbye. That's petty."

Yvette looked far too smug. "I am not above pettiness. This is good for you, Silas. I feel it with every bone. And what a horror I condemn you to—take your head out of the books, out of the political bitterness, and spend some time with a beautiful young woman. Other young men would *beg* for this opportunity."

Silas hissed. She took him by the shoulder in a firm grip and turned him to face Eliza.

"Well, Your Highness, you are fortunate," she said. "There is no better guide to Pravusat than a snake. Give it a week, and I'm sure my reliable student will find Henry. Once that's done, come back, and I'll see what I can do about breaking the Cast. That is, unless you fall madly in love and break it yourselves with a passionate kiss."

She grinned as if such a thing was the most desirable outcome. As if it was even *possible*.

Eliza stared, her jaw slack, her brow furrowed. Silas waited for her protest; maybe if she broke down in tears again, she'd soften Yvette's stubbornness.

But in the end, the princess didn't cry. She shuffled closer to Yvette and whispered, "How can you . . . trust him?" But not quietly enough for Silas not to hear.

He clenched his teeth. He looked down at the bracelet and considered taking a hammer to it. A broken wrist might be worth the subsequent freedom. Unfortunately, it was his writing hand.

Yvette said, "You seem like the kind of girl who understands a leap of faith. Take one now, Eliza. He won't hurt you. He knows too much of hurt himself."

Silas resisted the urge to fidget. Instead, he resolved to never ask Yvette for help again. He would find a way out of this situation on his own.

And it would *not* involve kissing a reckless princess.

Eliza missed Yvette as soon as they left. She'd been gruff, but like a concerned aunt, and more than that, she'd been compassionate. After hearing Eliza's story, she hadn't insisted Henry was gone. She'd even said Silas could find him, and she'd seemed to really believe it.

Perhaps Eliza's mistake with the Cast was not as world-shattering as she'd feared. If she couldn't quite believe that yet, she could at least *hope* it.

As she and Silas emerged into the sunlight on campus, Eliza steeled herself for what needed to be said.

"I'm sorry. I didn't mean for . . . *this* to happen, so I'm sorry about that. But I'm not sorry to have your help, not if it means finding Henry."

Silas hardly glanced at her.

Eliza tensed, trying not to think about how she'd seen snake scales on his skin while he'd argued with Yvette. The professor's words echoed in her mind—*He won't hurt you*—and she willed herself to believe it. Perhaps Silas was a . . . mild shapeshifter. One who abandoned people to his fellow snakes but did not swallow them himself. In stories, some demons were tricksters rather than devourers.

This is not a story. The memory of her father's voice cut through her imagination, making her flinch. *Shapeshifters are real, Eliza, and they are monstrous.*

The setting sun cast an orange glaze across the alabaster university buildings, reminding her of torchlight. Of a man-turned-eagle spilling innocent blood in the street.

With purpose, Silas set off across campus, and Eliza kept pace behind him in a spot he couldn't reach without turning. She determined not to speak, not to provoke him or offer him any reason to become savage when he'd been civil thus far.

Yet a moment later, she asked, "Where are we going?"

Clamping her jaw shut, she tried and failed to glare at herself without a mirror.

"I'm hungry," was all he said.

Truthfully, so was she. The hunger pangs had only grown worse since her trip to the market, but Eliza had spent all her money. She couldn't depend on Silas for a meal; he would say something about entitled royalty. She'd taken to paying for dinner every other day at the inn and stashing bread in her pockets for the days between. There were two rolls waiting back in her room, but if she couldn't go more than twenty feet from Silas, what hope did she have of returning to the inn or gathering her things?

Her cheeks heated with a sudden realization. If she couldn't go more than twenty feet from Silas, she would have to stay near him all night. Did shapeshifters grow more dangerous at night? Was that what had happened with the eagle?

While she worried, Silas led her to the university's dining hall, and upon entering the arched room filled with long tables, Eliza felt a sharp sting of loss. For a moment, she could pretend she was back home, and her father was throwing a feast for the members of court. By instinct, her eyes moved to the front of the room where the royal table would have been, and she could almost picture her parents and Aria already seated, waiting for her.

But no one was waiting for her.

She'd lagged behind Silas, and, suddenly, her arm yanked forward, pulling the rest of her along with it. He halted, glancing back at her with a scowl, causing her ears to burn.

When they reached the food table, it wasn't as Eliza expected. In the formal feasts back home, everyone sat in their place to be served their meal. In less formal settings, one edge of the room held anywhere from one to three refreshment tables, laden with food, and guests were free to select whatever offerings they desired.

At the university, the food table was guarded by a set of workers in aprons, who divided food onto plates in identical manner and handed them out. Silas accepted his without pause, but when a worker handed one to Eliza, she tried to hand it back.

"Oh, I'm not—" She swallowed, lost in Loegrian. "I'm not a student."

Silas caught the back of her shirt collar, tugging her away from the confused worker. She heard him offer Pravish thanks on her behalf, which only increased the heat in her face. She could have offered her own gratitude, at least.

"I was trying to be honest," she whispered, following him toward one of the tables.

"A noble thought," he said, and she couldn't tell if he was mocking or not, "but I belong to the university, and as long as we're linked, so do you. I suppose you're my research assistant now." Before Eliza could sort out how she felt about that, he added, "A useless, resource-draining assistant."

She scowled, then almost tripped on an uneven stone in the floor, so she refocused on following Silas to a group of empty seats at the table closest to the west windows. She didn't think it a coincidence that he sat somewhere with a view of the ocean, as if reminding her she should be sailing back home across it.

Her stomach growled loudly at the rising aromas before her. The majority of her plate held some kind of pastry, oblong like a boat and filled with a dark mixture of mashed beans and vegetables. Besides that, she had a collection of olives and a pile of what seemed to be wheat. Not milled, but simply dumped on her plate. When she poked the yellowish-brown substance with her spoon, she found it too soft and fluffy to be raw wheat, though it was still a collection of grains.

"Rice," said Silas. She glanced up to find him halfway through his own grain. "Loegria and Patriamere share an island without any rice fields. On this continent, rice is the most common agricultural resource."

Eliza's lips curved into a faint smile. "Agriculture. Economics. Magic. Is there anything you didn't study?"

"Sailing. Otherwise, I'd sail you back to Loegria myself."

She regretted her smile. It was wasted on him.

"You're the most disagreeable person I've ever met," she said, "and that's a fact."

She jammed a spoonful of rice into her mouth, then instantly forgot about her dining companion. The rice was the strangest thing she'd ever eaten, a bizarre texture on her tongue as the individual grains came apart. It was lightly flavored. A bit sticky. People lived off this?

Silas stared at her, a shadow in his dark eyes. She braced herself for a lecture about not appreciating rice, but what he said was, "I can't be the most disagreeable person you've ever met. You don't even consider me a person."

Goose bumps pebbled Eliza's skin, a chill from within. In the staring contest with a shapeshifter, she looked away first.

They finished their meal in silence.

Dusk fell as they exited the dining hall, and Eliza followed Silas toward the dormitories. He passed all the largest buildings until he reached one at the edge of campus. Eliza wasn't surprised that he chose to live as far as possible from everyone else.

The building had a squat, sturdy look to it, with thick foundations and pillars, as if constructed to withstand storms. Unlike the other buildings, it was only a single story, and inside, the dim hallway divided into four doors. Either the other rooms were unoccupied, or the occupants were all engaged in silent meditation.

Silas turned a key in the first door on the right, then pushed it open to reveal the room he was staying in. It would have been meager accommodations for a single person. For two . . .

Well, for starters, there was only one bed.

Silas sat on it, eyeing Eliza as if waiting for her protest that she was a *princess*, she was a *lady*, she needed *privileges*.

She did not give him the satisfaction. Instead, she hovered in the doorway, eyeing the door across the hall and the one just down the way, trying to judge which was closest. Surely the room that shared a wall made the most sense.

She strode down the hallway to the door.

"What are you doing?" Silas called after her.

Locked. She should have anticipated that. So much for her grand idea. With a sigh, she released the knob and returned to Silas's room. "How do I get a key for the next room over?"

Silas raised an eyebrow. He'd lit a lantern in her absence, and it glowed on the floor beside his bed. "Simple. Petition a professor to put you up on a research budget for three months, then produce groundbreaking research that revolutionizes your entire field of study and proves you impressive enough to stand next to career professionals with decades of experience."

Frowning, Eliza cocked her head, but he said nothing more. He unlaced his boots and kicked them into a corner, then spread the materials from his bag—a few books, a thin journal, a collection of writing supplies—across the low desk that rested practically on the floor. It had no chair, only a wide, flat cushion.

"Why is your desk on the ground?" Eliza asked. She'd seen normal tables and chairs in the university library.

"So it doesn't topple when the Stone Casters are in the yard."

He certainly enjoyed being cryptic.

Taking the cushion, Eliza dragged it over to the wall opposite the bed, as far from Silas as she could get. She sat with her back pressed to the smooth wall and closed her eyes.

After visiting Yvette, she'd felt renewed, but now the heaviness was settling in again. She'd had mood swings in the past, fits of temper or excitement that came normally from growing up, or so her mother said. But her volatile emotions in the wake of the curse were different. These swung from highs to lows without warning and with unfair strength.

Truthfully, Eliza felt exhausted from fighting the storm inside. In trying to escape it, she made her most impulsive decisions—crossing an ocean, buying a language Cast, trapping Silas. It was like her only choices were either drowning or climbing to the crow's nest, but every time she reached that peak height, she inevitably leapt from it without even meaning to. Then she was just drowning again.

Would this be the cycle for the rest of her life?

Something flopped down on top of her, startling her into a yelp. She opened her eyes to find a cotton blanket across her legs and a pillow beside her. Silas had stripped the bed, leaving only the mattress for himself.

He didn't say anything, just settled on his side with his back to the wall.

"Your surname is Bennett?" she asked. Yvette had said his full name when she'd chastised him, and it had remained on Eliza's mind. *Silas Bennett.*

Silas grunted. "What of it?"

There was a Bennett family in the Loegrian court. Lord Bennett was a viscount from the southern end of the kingdom, and while Eliza couldn't remember ever meeting him directly, she'd kept track of the eligible men of court, and someone had told her Lord Bennett had an unmarried male heir. Unfortunately, that was all they could say; they'd never met the son. It seemed no one had. When she'd tried to investigate, she'd found the mysterious Heir Bennett had no friends at court. He was a ghost.

Was it only that he'd been abroad in Pravusat?

She opened her mouth, then closed it.

Why was she trying to find commonalities with a shapeshifter? Besides, Silas carried too much animosity against ruling classes to be a member of the nobility himself.

Silas extinguished the lantern on the floor, ending the chance for conversation and plunging the room into darkness.

In the corner of her vision, a pair of red viper eyes lurked.

Stop that, she ordered herself.

She pulled the blanket around her shoulders like a hug, snuggling into the only embrace available. When she shifted, her book of sonnets pressed painfully into her hip, and she worked it free of her pocket, curling it into her chest along with one corner of the blanket. Her clothes were not meant for relaxation or sleeping; they were too fitted. But even if she'd had her nightgown, she would not have worn it. She hadn't even taken her shoes off.

Straining her ears, she could make out Silas's breathing, already steady and rhythmic. Maybe he was exhausted from the day.

Maybe he was faking sleep in order to lull her into a sense of security.

With trembling hands, Eliza drew the dagger from her belt, still in its sheath. She held it with the book of sonnets. As her eyes adjusted to the dark, she could make out every shape in the room, shadows wreathed in darker shadows.

The lump on the bed.

No matter how much she trembled next to the memory of those red eyes, she wasn't about to stab a person in their sleep.

Silas's voice rang an accusation in her mind. *You don't even consider me a person.*

The minutes passed in agony as her mind chased itself in circles. All she could do was listen to Silas's breathing and wait for dawn, ready to defend herself if he broke the farce.

CHAPTER

11

At some point during her vigil, Eliza had fallen asleep. When she woke, the first rays of dawn streamed through the dorm's only window, and she scowled at the light before realizing that wasn't what had woken her.

The ground was shaking.

Eliza gasped, pressing herself against the wall, heart hammering—or perhaps it was merely the earth shaking every part of her.

"Silas," she rasped. "*Silas*!"

He was sprawled out on the bed, head pillowed on his arm, fingers dangling over the side of the mattress. And he was, apparently, immune to earthquakes.

Another rumble creaked the floorboards and jittered Eliza's heart. She threw her pillow at the sleeping snake, and he finally lifted his head, squinting at her, his black hair tousled and hanging in his eyes.

"There's an earthquake!" she cried out. "What do we do? Should we leave? Should we—"

He waved a dismissive hand, tucking the pillow under his head and settling again, even as the bed rocked along with the rest of the room. Perhaps shapeshifters could not be killed by earthquakes, but Eliza was only human, and she could not help imagining the ceiling coming down, reducing her to one more piece of rubble beneath it.

The dresser had scooted a few inches away from the wall. If it had been tall instead of wide, it would have toppled on her already.

Another tremor rocked the room, and she tipped, barely catching herself on her hands before her face met the floor. In a split second, she made a decision born of self-preservation. She crawled over to the edge of the bed and heaved herself onto it.

Unfortunately, she moved just as another tremor hit, so the ground bucked, and she lost her balance.

Falling directly onto Silas, her elbow jabbing his stomach.

"Ow!" He sat up, glaring at her. For a moment, a line of gray scales rippled across the edge of his cheekbones, and she held her breath, but they vanished, and then he was a grumpy human again. "What is the matter with you?"

It felt too pathetic to say, *I'm scared.* Instead, she returned his glare.

"You wouldn't communicate, so I was forced to take matters into my own hands. Now, use your words, Silas Bennett, and tell me what's happening!"

He rolled his eyes, as if she were more bothersome to him than the room-shaking tremors. Then he grumbled, "It's Stone Caster training. They tear up the ground and put it back together. Give it an hour."

"An *hour*?"

Eliza struggled to sit up, extracting her limbs from where they'd tangled with his. Meanwhile, he sighed and scooted to press his back against the wall, leaving her a paltry space.

"I'm sure it feels worse on the floor," he admitted, which was more than she'd expected.

He wasn't wrong. The mattress absorbed some vibration, and the presence of another person—even an enemy—brought a sense of security as well. When the next tremor hit, Eliza abandoned her attempts to sit up straight and instead curled tightly into the abandoned bed space, still warm from his body heat. By necessity, she was lying over his arm, and her knees bumped into his. She darted a glance up to see if her proximity annoyed him.

But that wasn't what she saw.

Up close, he was more handsome than she'd realized. Perhaps that was because he was still groggy with sleep, blinking his dark lashes lethargically. His ink-black hair fell in strands across his eyes, and his jawline carried a shadow of growing stubble against his honeyed skin, which accentuated his lips. Eliza had never known *disheveled* to look so attractive on anyone.

"Don't get any ideas," she mumbled, cheeks flushing. "This doesn't mean anything."

He yawned. "You're the type to assign meaning to things, *apta*, not me."

When he lowered his head again, it knocked softly into hers on the shared pillow. She pulled hers back to the far edge.

The tremors still shook the bed, and no matter how stiffly Eliza held herself, they seemed determined to roll her directly into Silas. Her arms bumped his chest, though she held them tightly against her own. Her heart pounded with each rumble of the earth, but now it also pounded at the thought of the boy beside her, because she was close enough to smell the soap he must have bathed with—almond and spice—and to feel his warm breath coursing down her cheek.

Did he have to breathe so forcefully?

She peeked up at him through her lashes only to realize he had fallen asleep again. His eyes were closed, and that breathing rhythm was too deep, too even.

She stared, aghast, at the traitor. Earthquakes were one thing, but did he not even care he was sharing a bed with a girl? If he thought himself a regular person, this was surely evidence to the contrary.

She realized the hypocrisy of that thought, since *she* was the one who'd climbed into his bed uninvited, but it lingered with her all the same because she couldn't believe he was not affected by her *at all* while she was hyperaware of his breath and his scent and his every tiny shift against the mattress and the way his lips looked impossibly soft for a monster.

Twice, she tried to leave the bed, but as long as the quakes continued, she could not convince herself. At least she didn't have to attempt conversation in this awkward spot—although, perhaps that would have been better. Perhaps it would have distracted her, stopped her from letting her gaze sneak back repeatedly to his face, relaxed in sleep.

At last, the tremors ceased, and Eliza's stress drained from her like a releasing flood. Her eyelids drooped. Her head rested heavy against the pillow, her entire body aware of how little sleep she'd managed during the night.

Yet that indignant part of her was still indignant.

"Silas?" she whispered, barely a breath.

He gave no response. No care. Sleeping as if she didn't exist.

Eliza forced herself from the bed, sliding carefully to the floor, finding it cold and hard after the softness of the mattress. What was wrong with her? She could have stayed. If Silas didn't care, she should at least take advantage of that apathy to prevent her own discomfort.

Then she thought of waking next to him, coming alert to find him staring at her with those dark eyes—or, worse, the red version—and she shivered.

After surveying the room, she pulled her cushion back to the desk, sitting with her legs tucked beneath her. For a while, she read her sonnets, finding comfort in the familiar pages. Then her mind returned to the task of finding Henry, and she remembered something Yvette had said about the Cast helping her learn Pravish.

If she could learn it on her own, she wouldn't need Silas.

Eliza searched the desk, baffled when she could find plenty of parchment but neither quill nor inkpot. Silas *wrote*, didn't he? A peek into his journal showed her pages of handwritten notes. So where was his—

Her attention caught on a reed-like object, rolled against a book.

It had a wooden shaft and a pointed, metal nib, like a miniature spear. It was much heavier than a quill, and it felt awkward in her hand. Too thick. But when she tried it against a sheet of parchment, ink flowed from the tip like magic.

It *was* magic, no doubt. This country was full of it, like the bracelet on her wrist.

Her father had been certain that magic left unchecked would overtake everything else—like the tremors from earlier, bringing down a building.

Except the building was still standing.

Focus! Eliza snapped her eyes back to the desk. She grabbed a sheet of parchment and began writing in Pravish, ignoring the awkwardness of the not-quill. She wrote the words she'd learned not to mix—*seravat* and *seyahat*, *utamas* and *utanmas*. She wrote the new words she'd learned. *Arakl* for Cast or Casting. *Erkek* for never-to-be-said-about-any-boy-ever.

And when she filled the first sheet of parchment, she reached for another.

CHAPTER

12

Silas woke aching and tense. The first thing his eyes did was locate the reckless princess, who, sure enough, had not popped out of existence to make his life easier. She was writing something at his desk.

"It's a bit early for poetic composition," he grumbled, sitting up in bed. He covered a yawn and swept one hand through his disheveled bangs, shoving them out of his eyes.

"Early?" Eliza scoffed without turning. "You've slept through a dozen earthquakes and half the morning. Are you certain you're a snake and not a hibernating bear?"

He was surprised to hear a joke about his magic. Did that mean she was beginning to reevaluate her prejudices, or was she simply mocking?

Unfortunately, he found her impossible to read.

"*Gunadin*," he said, testing something.

She frowned at him over her shoulder.

He waited.

"Good morning?" she finally said.

"Does the Cast make everything sound like Loegrian, or does it give you meanings while still letting you hear the language?"

"I can tell you're speaking Pravish."

Interesting. As irritating as the situation was, at least he was still learning new things. Warlockry was a difficult thing to study when so much of it changed in specific application.

"*Gunadin*," Eliza repeated hesitantly.

Despite himself, he smirked. "You're using a Loegrian 'uh' sound, but in Pravish, the *u* is a diphthong. Your vowel needs to glide at the end."

"What does that mean?"

Scooting to the edge of the bed, he leaned forward with his elbows braced against his knees. "It means move your lips. Watch mine."

Slowly, he repeated the first syllable a few times, then the word as a whole. Eliza dutifully watched his lips, but she must have grown disheartened with the pronunciation because an embarrassed red stained her cheeks.

"Just try," he said. "From a linguistic standpoint, Loegrian and Pravish are actually—"

With a clear scowl, she cut him off. "You do realize I'm a woman, don't you?"

Silas blinked. "I hadn't questioned it until now."

"Well, you sleep quite easily with a woman in your bed. Is that a common occurrence for you?"

He stared at her flatly. "If you're referring to earlier this morning, Your Highness, I'll remind you that you're the one who climbed in. Is that a common occurrence for you?"

Her blush spread to her collar.

"*No*!" She buried her face in her hands. "Forget it. Forget I said anything."

He snorted. While she remained in hiding, he stood and used the top of his dresser as a work surface to cut open two papayas for breakfast. Eliza finally peeked, no doubt enticed by the scent of fresh fruit. Without a word, Silas set a bowl of papaya pieces on the desk before resettling on his bed. Since he had only one bowl, he scooped his fruit directly from the peel.

As he ate, he stole a glance at the princess. It *had* been startling to share a bed with her, especially without warning, and though he'd forced a calm demeanor, he'd been certain she would hear the pounding of his heart.

Retreating into sleep had seemed the safest way to deal with a reckless *apta*.

After finishing his breakfast, Silas wiped his hands and mouth on a handkerchief and set the peel aside. He drew in a deep breath.

"Since your boundaries are clearly lax," he said, "we should just kiss."

Eliza choked on her papaya. She turned away, hacking and coughing. Silas found his inner response to be mostly the same, but that didn't change the straightest path forward.

For clarity, he added, "Yvette said the Cast will break with a kiss."

It took another few moments for the princess to get control of herself, and her eyes were still watering when she glared at him with near-physical force. "Absolutely *not*. How could you even—we can't just kiss!"

"Why not?" he challenged with a glare of his own.

It wasn't very academic of him to ask a question he already knew the answer to. In her eyes, he wasn't a person. Just a monster. Funny how that hadn't deterred her when she was fearing for her life in an earthquake.

"Because I don't love you, that's why not!"

Silas opened his mouth and then closed it. His mind had to catch up with the answer.

"That's all?" he finally managed.

She stood, apparently trying to emphasize her argument with height. But even sitting on the edge of his bed, Silas was nearly as tall as she was.

"That's *all*?" Eliza repeated. She planted her hands on her hips. "Does love mean so little to you?"

It would be more accurate to say love meant nothing to him. People declared love for selfish reasons or with the intention to manipulate. For example, his father's love had been brandished like a flag to other nobles whenever Silas performed admirably in what his father expected of him—his academic excellence at Fairfax, his performance of estate duties, even his table manners. But that love had been withheld whenever Silas's feet slipped from that path.

"I've been kissed twice," Silas said. "Neither one related to love. And to answer your question more specifically, love is an excuse people give to justify their actions."

Eliza sputtered. Slowly, her hands dropped from her waist, and she stared at him as if he'd made a funeral announcement.

"You're wrong," she finally whispered. "You're so very *wrong*. Love is all that gives life meaning."

Before he could dispute that, she whipped around, snatching a small book from his desk. It wasn't one of his; judging by its worn cover and rippled page edges, it had seen more use than any of his books, and that was saying something. She flipped to a page near the beginning and shoved the book under his nose, forcing him to lean back before it clipped him in the face. He took it on instinct.

"*There*," she said, as if she'd offered the grandest proof in the world.

He restrained the smile tugging at his lips, and he let his eyes scan the page. A Loegrian sonnet. Curious, he glanced at the book's first page for the author.

"Fernsby is better known for his nonfiction than for his sonnets," he said. "Have you read his *Treatise on Instability*?"

Eliza's furrowed brow said she hadn't.

"He claims every structure in life is fragile and inevitably collapses. Even love." Silas closed the book and handed it back. "It's a depressing read. Understandable why you skipped it. Now, back to *our* situation—this is our way out, and a kiss doesn't mean anything."

After glancing between him and her worn-out book, she tucked it into her pocket like a cherished treasure.

"Yes it does," she insisted. "*You* may have gone around kissing girls you don't love—"

"They both kissed me," he drawled.

"—but *I've* never kissed anyone. Because a kiss is *meant* to be a declaration of love."

He opened his mouth, but before any new argument could leave his tongue, she cut in again.

"Besides, Yvette said I had to mean it, and I couldn't mean it with anyone but Henry."

Magic *did* intertwine fiercely with intention. Silas grimaced.

"There's an easy solution." Eliza gave what was clearly meant to be a charming smile. "You help me find Henry, and then Yvette breaks our Cast. Done."

"Right. I'll just set aside my life and obligations in favor of yours for however long it takes. That's fair."

"It will only take a day!"

She seemed to really mean that. A headache stirred in the back of his skull.

"A schedule," he ground out. "We'll make a schedule."

He knelt at the desk, reaching for his pen. Eliza scurried off the cushion, the mouse fleeing a snake, and he did his best to ignore the sting of that. With quick strokes, he sketched two schedule options in his journal, turning the page for her to see.

"Either we each take part of a day to pursue our goals, or we alternate days—the exception being if I'm needed in Kerem's office."

She clenched her fists against her knees. Clearly, her royal entitlement urged her to say her search deserved first priority.

"Finding Henry will only—" she started.

"No matter which one we choose," he said, "I have to work for Kerem today. I've already committed. Unlike you, if I neglect my work, I lose my livelihood."

"I suppose you really can't be a lord, then." When he frowned, her gaze slid away. "There's a Lord Bennett at court. I thought you might be his heir."

"No, he wouldn't claim me as such." Silas kept the words droll, but they left a bitter taste in his mouth.

She gathered in a breath, clearly planning a scheme, and Silas clenched his jaw.

"You can finish your work," she said, "and then we can search tonight."

"Tonight," he repeated flatly. "In the dark. In Pravusat."

"I'm not going to sleep anyway," she muttered. Raising her voice, she added, "We can take a lantern—"

"Light isn't the problem, *apta*. It's the exponential rise of violence at night. Most of the slave trafficking doesn't happen at high noon."

She reared back. "There's . . . there's *slavery* here?"

"It's actually a Cronese trade invading on Pravish territory. Regardless, no, we're not going out in the city at night."

"Well, if you intend to sleep the full morning, there's hardly any day to split!"

"Alternating days it is." Silas snapped his journal closed.

He was concerned with how Eliza would react once they found proof Lord Henry had gone down with the shipwreck, which was still the most logical conclusion.

Or maybe the bigger concern was that she would never accept proof of any kind, that she would rather continue a hopeless search indefinitely than face a dismal reality.

Either way, a problem for tomorrow.

"I need to change," he said, gesturing for her to turn away.

She gave a disappointed glance at her own clothing. Silas rolled his eyes. She could have bought better clothes in the market, but, instead, she'd performed wild negotiations for magic. A mixed sense of priorities was entirely her own fault.

"I'll wait outside," the princess said, ducking from the room.

He pulled on fresh clothes, then packed his bag. When he met her in the hallway, he found her fighting a war with her hair, an agitated general offering commands her troops clearly did not follow.

"Stay *down*," she ordered, trying to flatten a line of wispy hair with her palm while holding sections of a braid between the fingers of her opposite hand.

Silas raised an eyebrow. "You don't experience much humidity at the castle, do you?"

Maggie had always complained about the humidity in southern Loegria and what it did to her hair, especially when Silas's hair remained indifferent to it. She'd cried jealously whenever readying for a big event.

Eliza surrendered the battle with a huff. She finished her braid, pinned it in place, and threw her hands up with clear dismissal.

"Cover it with a scarf," he suggested. "That's what most Pravish women do."

"I can't afford a scarf," she muttered.

"Not my problem."

With a glare, she jerked her chin at the door. "Let's go. Henry's life may hang in the balance, but I wouldn't want you to lose your very important *livelihood*."

CHAPTER 13

Eliza determined to stay silent for the day. She had no reason to make small talk with a shapeshifter. Yet they hadn't even reached their destination before she found herself saying, "I've never seen a building like this."

She and Silas had climbed several flights of stairs in the Yamakaz, and she looked up from the landing at a dome, sunlight sparkling through the windows. The inside curve of the ceiling displayed colored murals with physical depth—sculpting and painting hand in hand.

Silas flicked his gaze toward the dome but kept walking, following a curved line of doors. "That's because it was built by Stone Casters."

Of course it was.

He went on, unprompted, like a tutor in lecture mode. "Most of the advancements in Pravusat are courtesy of its freedom for magic. The few scholars who bother dedicating any interest toward Loegria theorize that the island is a full age behind the rest of the world, trapped in a state without enlightenment. Unless we see a major revolution, the schism will only grow."

"I experienced the attempted Caster revolution," Eliza returned hotly. "All it did was hurt."

It hurt still. The cursed sliver in her soul that never quite faded from her awareness, the quiet fear that, at any moment, she'd realize she wasn't acting as she should. Wasn't acting as *herself.*

"Change always hurts, Highness. It's growing pains."

He waved her to a halt in front of a door, then pulled a set of metal picks from his belt and crouched to begin working them in the lock.

Eliza gasped. "Your livelihood is *thievery*?"

He gave a quiet laugh, never lifting his eyes. "I have a key. But being able to enter a door without one is a good skill, and, deprived of practice, good skills fade."

With a twist of the knob, the door swung inward, and he smirked up at her.

It was charming, in a roguish way, but she would have died before telling him as much. She stepped past him into the opened room.

Only to immediately retreat, pressing one hand to her nose.

"Ugh." She made a dry retch, eyes watering. "Are you sure this is an office? It's not an uncleaned washroom?"

Even Silas wrinkled his nose. "That's snake musk. Hold on."

He entered the room, head cocked as if listening to something. After a moment, he lowered himself to his stomach in front of a set of shelves, extending his hand into the shadows beneath.

Eliza tensed, expecting him to be bitten by an unseen viper. She should have remembered who he was.

What he was.

He withdrew his hand, and a thin white snake had threaded itself through his fingers and around his wrist. It flicked its tongue rapidly, head swinging back and forth, looking for something to bite.

Eliza inched backward.

"You're safe," Silas cooed, not to her but to the snake, as if the creature were something innocent and cuddly. He turned his hand, evaluating the reptile, not seeming to care how close its swinging head came to his eyes. "An albino—and a young one. No wonder he's helping you. Get into some trouble?" After a moment's pause, he nodded. "Well, you're lucky you weren't eaten."

He was *talking* to a *snake*.

She remembered witnessing him in the library, talking to the python. She'd ignored the sign of a shapeshifter, attributing it instead to Pravusat's love of snakes.

How dearly she'd paid for that mistake.

Eliza backed up until she reached the end of her invisible tether, which, unfortunately, tugged on the bracelet. Silas's arm rose in her direction, the snake along with it, and both of them fixed their cold eyes on her.

"Relax, *apta*. If Tulip can't swallow you, this one definitely can't."

"It could poison me," Eliza rasped.

"Most snakes *aren't* venomous." Silas raised his eyebrows. "Even Tulip."

"It has fangs!"

"You have teeth as well, Highness, and somehow, I think you're more inclined to bite me than she is. Should I be concerned about *your* venom?"

As if *Eliza* were the danger here.

All the same, heat rose in her neck, and she folded her arms across her chest, ignoring his smug expression. He took the snake to a back corner of the office, forcing Eliza to follow him, pulled by her bracelet. Then he cleaned whatever had caused the assaultive odor, opened a window, and lit a stick of incense on the room's desk.

Under the calming fragrance of sandalwood, and with both snakes on the other side of the room, Eliza finally had a chance to survey the office. The two windows let in a good amount of natural light, and the desk held an oil lamp for evenings. There were more shelves than she'd seen in Yvette's office but with fewer books and more creepy bottles of substances she wasn't sure she wanted to evaluate closely.

When Silas moved, she kept him in the corner of her eye while pretending to study some kind of hooked stick hanging between shelves. He picked up a sheet of parchment from the desk, lips pursed as he read, and when he turned it briefly to look at the empty back, she could see the front looked like a written list.

Curiosity tickled her throat. She cleared it.

"Settle in, *apta*," he said without looking up. "These'll take me a while."

"What am I supposed to do?" she asked.

"Not bother me," he shot back. "Otherwise, it'll take longer."

Easier said than done. Eliza had never been a skilled manager of boredom, and it was more dangerous now than ever.

If she didn't keep moving, she might drown.

"Maybe I could help," she offered begrudgingly.

He squinted at her. "You want to handle snake bones?"

When she blanched, he snorted. Setting the list down, he came over to a nearby shelf.

"Here." He plucked a book, extending it. "Pravish dictionary. I saw you writing words this morning."

With a sigh, she took the dictionary and seated herself on a cushion in the corner opposite from the white snake, who'd settled into a little area of branches and rocks clearly meant for vacationing such creatures.

Silas gathered materials from the shelves, and she shivered, picturing bones and everything else. With effort, she forced herself to focus on the pages before her.

Only to realize she couldn't read them.

"Useless Cast." Eliza glared down at her bracelet. "If it makes me understand Pravish, why can't I read it?"

"People can understand a spoken language and still be illiterate," Silas said offhandedly. He spread his chosen materials across the desk and took a seat. "Sound it out. Pravish uses the same alphabet Loegrian does, minus a few letters, like *x*."

Tipping a bottle, he emptied a collection of what looked like small rib bones into his hand, carefully counting out a dozen at a time, which he then bound with thread, as if preparing a bundle of kindling for a fire.

His side glance made Eliza's cheeks burn, and she looked down at the dictionary's first page.

"*Abajur*," she said slowly, feeling silly. It meant nothing to her.

"Softer *j* sound," said Silas. "*Abajur*."

As soon as he said it, she understood. *Lantern.*

She glared down at her bracelet once more. For all the things magic could do, it certainly didn't like to be straightforward in them.

"*Abakar*," she tried next.

"The tip of your tongue should flick your palate on the *r*."

Eliza glared at him. "Are you going to do this with every word?"

"Depends." His side glance was now decidedly taunting. "Are you going to get every word wrong?"

"Ha!" She smacked her finger into the page. "This one's the same as Loegrian. *Abide*."

He winced as if she'd caused him physical pain. "Same letters. Different pronunciation and meaning. *Abide.* Ah-bee-day."

As soon as he said it, she understood. *Memorial.*

"Of *course*," she said, rolling her eyes. "So *obvious*." She huffed. "They should have different letters so it's not confusing."

He mimicked her sarcastic tone. "Of *course*. How thoughtless of Pravish not to consider the Loegrian princess's confusion when developing its language."

Despite herself, she laughed, noticing the way Silas flashed a quick smile when she did.

"Give me your magic writing thing," she said, extending her hand.

He pursed his lips. Then, after a moment, he rifled through his bag, extracting the writing instrument. He brought it over but pulled back as she reached for it. "Be careful. If it breaks, it'll ruin books and clothing alike."

"I know the dangers of an inkpot," she said, stretching for it again.

He held it just out of reach. "It's a *palem*."

Eliza frowned, because for the first time, the word didn't come with an understanding of what it meant.

Silas grinned, as if she'd given the exact reaction he'd hoped for. "I was curious about that one. There's no Loegrian equivalent, since we haven't embraced this advancement. I wondered if the Cast communicated in ideas and images, like an Affiliate bond, or in words, like a translator. Seems it truly is a translation Cast."

"Are you actually *enjoying* the magic that's stuck us together?"

"What I enjoy is any opportunity to learn something new." He handed her the instrument at last. "I call it a pen. 'Quill' has no verb form, so we sometimes say we 'pen' a letter. 'Pen' derives from the archaic 'penna,' or feather. It seems only right it gets to be a noun again."

Eliza stared at him in a way that seemed to drain his enjoyment. As the smile left his face and he slid his hands into his pockets, she felt a pang of guilt, which was foolish. Why should she care about killing a shapeshifter's mood?

Unless he killed her in return.

"Say it again. The Pravish."

He'd turned away, but he glanced back. "*Palem.*"

And she understood: *pen.*

There *was* a little wonder in that.

"I hear it now," she said. "So I guess we both learned something new."

He didn't say anything in response, just tilted his head like he was evaluating her in a new way. A few strands of hair fell into his eyes, giving him that roguish look again. Eliza shifted.

Before she could tell him to go back to his snake bones, a figure appeared in the doorway. The newcomer was a well-dressed man in his late thirties, and by the confidence with which he entered, this was clearly his office.

"Good, you're here," he said, sparing Silas a quick glance before setting his bag on the desk and unpacking a few books. "Any trouble with the Artifacts? Some of my snakeskin might be too aged to hold the magic."

Eliza clutched the dictionary to her chest, unsure if she should rise or not. The professor hadn't noticed her yet.

"I haven't finished the bones." Silas rubbed the back of his neck, clearly embarrassed.

He'd told her not to distract him. Of course, he'd also told her to read a dictionary out loud and then insisted on correcting every word.

The professor waved him off as if it didn't matter. He left his bag and moved to the snake den in the corner, bending slightly to evaluate the white snake. The serpent lifted its head and flicked its tongue once.

"Ether's calmed down, I see." Wrapping one finger around the snake's tail, the man lifted his wire spectacles to peer closely at the scales. "She's a ribbon snake—can you believe that? Can't even see her stripes. I've never found a true albino before."

"She told me about some trouble with a hawk," Silas said.

"Yes, excellent luck on this one. By rights, she should have been dead before I found her." The professor suddenly looked over, locking eyes with Eliza as if he'd been tracking her gaze the entire time. "Would your friend like to hold her? Ether might abide it with two Affiliates here."

At the professor's sudden attention and offer, Eliza blushed, jaw flapping uselessly.

"She's terrified of snakes," Silas deadpanned.

He was right, and yet, hearing it from him set her teeth on edge. Silas Bennett didn't get to speak for her. With clenched fists, she climbed to her feet, nearly tripping as the cushion slid beneath her. Out of habit, she dipped a curtsy, remembering too late that she wasn't in Loegria anymore, and Pravish people only bowed.

"I'm Eliza," she said.

The professor looked at Silas with a raised eyebrow, but when

Silas responded, it was directed at Eliza. “He only speaks Pravish, so now’s your chance to practice.”

With feigned confidence, she repeated her introduction in Pravish.

“Kerem Aytac,” the man said in return, bowing slightly. He adjusted his round spectacles. “A fear of snakes raises questions about your choice of company.”

If it hadn’t already been obvious that he knew about Silas’s condition, it was now. How could he be so calm? Yvette had been the same way, lecturing a shapeshifter like he was just another student, even *threatening* him. As if she wasn’t at all scared about what kind of dark magic she might receive in return.

“There are, after all, three snakes in this office.” Kerem pointed at Silas, Ether, and himself.

Even though the Cast provided a translation of every word, Eliza’s comprehension lagged. By the time she understood, the professor had already moved back to his desk.

She gaped at Silas. “He’s a . . . you’re both . . .”

His return expression was hard, nothing like the relaxed enjoyment he’d shown while inventing new words.

“Get used to it, Highness. Out here, we’re allowed to exist.”

He joined Kerem at the desk, and Eliza found herself with no better option than to return to her cushion. Since she still had Silas’s pen, she attempted to write the new words she’d learned on the parchment tucked in her sonnet book, but her hands were trembling.

She set the pen aside and read. Her mind tried to bring up issues of shapeshifters—or even her morning conversation with Silas, when he’d claimed the author of her sonnets had called love “unstable”—but she forced all concerns aside, burying them beneath familiar, comforting words.

Even if the author himself denounced what he’d written, Eliza never would. She felt the truth of it every time she read her favorite sonnet.

Love, my crown, most precious gems within its settings gold;
Patience abiding, unceasing hope, and mine endurance bold.
Love, my armor, gleaming steel, the guard above mine heart;
To pointed axe and hardened falchion, ne'er will it part.
Love, my sword, a sharper blade will ne'erwhere be found;
Which severs lies, defends the truth, and holds me honor bound.
Love, my cup, and to it raised;
Drink deeply now and all my days.
For with thy love, a king I'll be;
And with my love, all's well with me.

Somewhere in the city, Henry was struggling just as she was, surrounded by magic and unfamiliar customs.

She could only hope he'd encountered fewer snakes.

CHAPTER 14

I'm not offering my best work today," Silas said quietly. "I'm sorry."

The distraction felt doubly ungrateful, since Kerem's generosity was the only reason Silas had been able to stay on campus at all. The only reason he had a chance at a professorship.

The princess had returned to her cushion in the corner, and he resisted the urge to glance over his shoulder at her. Even without looking, he could feel her there, a prickling awareness like what he felt for snakes, except this didn't come from magic, only from annoyance. How did she manage to distract him so easily?

By contrast, Kerem worked with relaxed shoulders and his signature calm, reading through a stack of student essays and marking notes as he went. Rather than filling his office with comfortable chairs, he kept only a few stools at his desk, and he never sat for long. Motion prompted ideas, he taught.

Silas sat on his own stool, wishing it was a chair with a back because that would have been one barrier, however slight, between him and Eliza.

"You're agitated," Kerem said. "No Affiliate can do their best work with emotions churning." He glanced up, gesturing with his pen at Silas's bracelet. "That's new. Something to do with this?"

Embarrassment heated Silas's ears. "Stone Cast. It was an . . . ambush."

"Looking for a way to break it?"

He found he'd rather discuss anything else. "What happened to Iyal Havva? The *yaslari* was still on his office door today, and I've never seen a shrine like that in Pravusat."

Kerem's lips pressed to a grim line. He underlined a paragraph in the current essay, jotting *unsupported* beneath it. After adding another line of direction, the professor finally said, "An experiment gone wrong, most likely. He was on a research leave from teaching, and his body was found, missing bones. About a week after you left."

Silas frowned. "I've heard of Stone Casters breaking their bones"—Yvette had broken her arm while overexerting herself on the Great Eastern Wall—"but never them *vanishing*. Still, I would have expected him to survive, however painfully."

Kerem held his gaze for a moment, then clarified, "Missing *all* his bones."

Suddenly the shrine made sense. Silas swallowed, his own research into magic stealing seeming tame by comparison.

What kind of experiment had the professor been attempting?

"No one knows what could cause such a thing," Kerem said. "It's never been seen before."

Setting the essays aside, he rose from his desk and opened a chest on a shelf, removing a roll of tanned snakeskin. Tension lined his shoulders now, and Silas regretted raising the subject. The closeness of relationships might have varied, but the warlockry professors were a tight-knit group, and it must have been disturbing for Kerem to lose a friend in such a gruesome manner.

Silas rededicated himself, and they worked in silence, crafting Artifacts. But by the time he moved from snake bones to snakeskin, his head started pounding, magic slipping from his grasp. It felt pathetic not to be able to finish a batch of Artifacts he'd done a dozen times before. Was the bracelet interfering with his own magic? Or was having the princess around really that much of an agitation?

"Silas," she whispered, as if summoned by his thoughts.

He almost slipped off his stool, banging his knee on the desk. Then he turned on Eliza with a glare.

"I'm not happy either," she told him curtly, planting her hands on her hips. "I feel like a child saying this, but I'm in need of a washroom, and somehow, I doubt there's one within twenty feet."

Annoyance though it was, he could hardly blame her for being human.

She peered over his shoulder at the desk, then shuddered. "What do you do with . . . all this?"

"Artifacts," he said flatly.

She frowned. "I thought Casters made those."

"Casters have their type, and we have ours."

For Casters, creating an Artifact meant anchoring a Cast to a related object to increase the magic's strength. They served no one but the Caster. For Affiliates, creating an Artifact meant imbuing an object with magical properties relating to their animal link. They could be used by anyone, although they could only be created from a piece of the Affiliate's animal link, like snakeskin.

"As for what we *do* with them," he added, "we sell them at market to fund research. I infused these python bones with a snakelike flexibility and strength. Orchardists near the coast drive the bones into their trees during hurricane season."

Baris would be eager to trade Silas's work for his best papayas.

"These"—Silas gestured to the squares of snakeskin sewn to leather backings—"are sun protection. By drawing heat to themselves, they keep people cool and prevent sun sickness."

"You protect people?" Eliza stared at him as if she couldn't comprehend the idea.

Silas scowled. "I misspoke. These are both deadly weapons. Used for ending any student who misses a deadline." He stood, grabbing his bag with too much force. "There are washrooms on the main floor."

Kerem didn't ask for details, only handed him another list, this one a collection of reference books he wanted from the library.

Eliza tried her best to be patient, truly. She repeated to herself a silent mantra of *patience abiding, patience abiding.* Sometimes she recited the entire sonnet.

Still, the hours were no longer filled with minutes. Each minute had become an hour itself.

After the washroom, Silas collected a stack of books from the library, and on their way back to Kerem's office, Eliza realized her first impression of his physical build had been wrong. She'd thought he might haul people around like sacks of potatoes; now she realized his broad shoulders and tall frame were only ever put to use hauling around books. Had she carried the tower he currently hefted, she wouldn't have been able to see over it, and she would have been puffing after a flight of stairs. Silas shifted his hold on the books once, but his breathing wasn't labored. If anything, he seemed more energized returning up the stairs with a pile of books than he had been coming down empty-handed.

It wasn't only being a snake that made him strange. It was everything about him.

While Silas delivered the books to his professor's desk, Eliza eyed the cushion in the corner. It sat like the open maw of a monster, beckoning her to be swallowed. If she was idle any longer, she would lose her mind.

"How can I help?" she asked in Pravish—or at least tried to. It might have been something more like *how helpful I am.*

But if she'd gotten it wrong, Silas would have corrected her. Instead, he squinted, as if trying to detect a snare beneath a pile of harmless leaves.

"There's nothing for you to do," he said.

But Kerem shrugged. "I won't turn down an extra pair of hands."

Smugly, Eliza gave him a shallow bow of thanks, and Silas muttered something under his breath.

Just no snake bones, she thought. She didn't know how to say that in Pravish, so the best she could do was offer it as a silent prayer.

The professor put away the bones and other disgusting materials, which was a relief. Then, rolling back his sleeves, he asked, "Have you ever milked a snake?"

Eliza didn't like the sound of that at all. The look on Silas's face said he clearly expected her to run, and the thought of being a coward in his eyes irked her. She wasn't a coward. *Apta*, maybe, but she would rather be known for foolish actions than for retreat.

She licked her lips, managing to string a few words. "Snakes . . . have . . . milk?"

Kerem flicked his hand. "No, no, snakelets fend for themselves from birth. 'Milking' is a term used for venom extraction."

She cast a side glance toward the enclosure holding Ether, where the white snake moved restlessly along the rocks. Silas had sworn the creature didn't possess venom.

Following her gaze, Kerem shook his head. "Not her. I need a venom collection from Silas."

Eliza froze. Meanwhile, Kerem stepped past her to the shelves, gathering supplies. Silas remained by the desk, avoiding her gaze, focused on combing his unruly hair back. After she stared long enough, though, his dark eyes finally met hers, narrowing in distaste. Or possibly challenge.

"You get milked?" she blurted in Loegrian.

She was certain he blushed. Though his darker skin concealed it better than hers, he looked rosy along the ears, and the way his posture stiffened certainly spoke to embarrassment. She bit her lip, finding the response cute even if the subject was the strangest she'd ever broached.

"You can leave," he said, more threat than invitation.

Eliza should have. She should have hidden right outside the door, out of reach of any snake fangs, especially the venomous set belonging to the shapeshifter in front of her. But, honestly, with his blushing ears, he didn't seem as much of a threat.

Besides that, his voice from earlier haunted her. *She's terrified of snakes.*

This country seemed determined to continue throwing them at her, perhaps because it thought she would abandon her purpose and flee. Perhaps because it thought she was just blown by *whims.*

Let it watch, then. Eliza could conquer terror and anything else.

Mimicking Kerem, she unbuttoned her silk cuffs and rolled back her shirt sleeves. She planted her hands on her hips and said, "I'm not afraid of you."

The brave image was ruined by Kerem startling her from behind as he said, "Hold this vial."

The container's opening had been covered by a thinly woven sheet of linen tied securely at the neck. Eliza breathed calmly to keep her fingers steady around the glass.

"To prevent spills," said Kerem, indicating the linen, "and avoid venom on skin."

Eliza frowned. Surely it wouldn't hurt him if he was also a snake. She struggled to put that to words. "Snake can't . . . pain you. Right?"

He raised his eyebrows, and the round, wire frames of his spectacles exaggerated the disbelief.

"Is this snakeskin?" he asked, opening and closing one hand, displaying his long brown fingers. "Blood will bleed, and tissue will rot, even with magic beneath. Magic is a powerful weapon, not a shield against all ills. Ready, Silas?"

In answer, Silas gave a surly grunt. His eyes darted to Eliza, then away. She tensed, expecting them to be red viper eyes, but they were his usual deep brown. She was almost surprised when he vanished in a puff of vapor.

The gray snake with a string of black diamonds down its back looked like an ordinary—if deadly—animal, and Eliza's throat filled with questions that she held clenched behind her teeth. Was he still aware as a snake? Could he communicate? Could he control himself?

Reaching down, Kerem lifted the viper like it was nothing more than a fallen scarf. The reptile twisted around his arm.

He stared at her expectantly.

"If you're too fearful," he said, "set the vial on the desk and step away."

She looked down and found her hand shaking. Images of Daisy rose in her mind, joined by the echo of the pony's terrified scream mingling with Eliza's own. She forced the memories back down.

She was not afraid. She would *not* be afraid.

She was more than a whim.

Swallowing, she braced the vial with both hands, one palm beneath it, her fingers around it.

Kerem watched until he seemed satisfied. Silas's snake eyes were watching her, too, but a mere glance at their crimson coloring made sweat break out across her skin. She focused on her hands, on the glass warm in her grip.

Holding tense, she waited for the viper to lunge for the vial. Instead, Kerem took hold of the snake's head, holding it with the same firm grip she'd seen her father's hound trainers use on unruly puppies. He pulled his arm away, and Silas's deadly snake body fell limp, dangling from Kerem's hand like a lifeless body from the gallows. Kerem could have crushed his head.

Was it that easy to kill a snake?

Was it that easy to kill a shapeshifter?

Kerem pressed the snake's mouth to the linen covering on the vial, and Eliza watched a colorless liquid drip from twin fangs that looked too thin and fragile for their murderous capabilities.

Until, finally, Kerem said, "There we are. Set the vial on my desk. Carefully."

While Eliza had her back turned, Silas transformed into a human once more. She found herself staring at him. She hadn't expected the whole experience to be so . . . vulnerable. It almost felt as if she'd witnessed something she shouldn't have. Something private. He wouldn't meet her eyes.

Kerem examined the vial, replacing the linen covering with something more permanent, then spoke to Silas about toxins and experiments and something about Fluid Casters. Silas nodded and gave curt answers, the muscles of his neck visibly tense. He looked at his professor but still wouldn't glance at Eliza.

For the first time, she realized he had a scar along his neck, pale against his skin. It was long and thin, perfectly straight, paralleling his jaw. Like he'd been caught by a blade.

"Did someone do that to you?" she asked before she could reconsider. Nervously, she touched her own throat. "The scar on your neck."

At Kerem's raised eyebrow, she realized she'd spoken right over the professor, and her cheeks heated, but it wasn't as if she could take the question back. The silence stretched awkwardly.

Without looking at her, Silas finally said, "Well, I didn't fall out of a tree onto the sword, if that's what you mean."

He spoke Pravish, as if to spite her. Or to distance himself.

Someone had tried to *kill* him. They'd nearly succeeded.

Taking the vial from Kerem, Silas transferred it to a locked chest beneath one of the shelves. Though his body obscured the view, Eliza assumed there were similar vials within. A box of poison. Did the professor sell it to assassins? Her skin crawled at the thought.

Kerem leaned against his desk, and even though it was a nonthreatening action, Eliza took a step back. His sharp eyes said he didn't miss the movement.

"I'm given to understand," he said, "that a sword to the throat is the most common greeting for Affiliates in Loegria. Weren't you aware?"

Eliza's jaw worked wordlessly as a shiver rattled her spine. However laid-back he presented himself, however non-red his eyes were, she had to remember that Kerem was a snake as well.

He waved a hand as if to ease her.

"Your shock must be at a father trying to kill his own son, choosing law over family in any country. It's a shock to me as well. Certainly not the decision I would make. After all, the loss of Silas Bennett would rob this world of its finest young mind."

He motioned Silas back over, and the two of them resumed work. Eliza stepped into the hallway, needing the fresh air. She stood just outside the door, at the end of her leash. Out of sight.

For a moment, she'd been lulled by false vulnerability. She'd doubted. The law in Loegria was to kill a shapeshifter upon discovery, no exceptions. If even Silas's *father* thought that was the best course of action, what kind of monster was really hiding within the snakeskin?

Eliza had almost been lured in by a shapeshifter. *Two*. Of course they trusted each other.

She rubbed her arms, shivering, and didn't return to the office.

Once Silas finished his work, she followed him to the dining hall, where they ate in silence. That night, she sat wrapped in a blanket on her cushion, both hands on her dagger, watching him in the dark and pinching herself to remain awake.

In the morning, they would find Henry, and she would be free of this nightmare.

CHAPTER 15

Normally, Silas did his most diligent studying in the quiet of night by the warm light of a lantern. With the princess sharing his cramped dorm room, there was no chance of that. She scattered his thoughts, jittered his nerves.

They were both up at dawn. He wasn't sure she'd slept at all, and he couldn't convince himself to fall back asleep with her watching.

The day before, she'd boldly declared, *I'm not afraid of you*, and he'd thought maybe she was finally willing to see him in a realistic way. But she'd sat all night with a dagger in her hands. Come morning, she'd stashed it beneath her blanket, but not quickly enough he didn't see.

So as he dragged himself from bed and dressed, he had to fight the fangs trying to manifest in his mouth.

"Today, we find Henry," Eliza announced in the hallway, as if he could have forgotten.

Stiffly, he said, "You came after my language skills with such vigor, Highness. Where would you like me to put them to use?"

Only to discover that her grand plan amounted to *asking everyone if they'd seen Henry*.

When she first marched down the hill into Izili proper and knocked on a door, he thought it was a place of significance, that she had reason to believe the person inside had information on Henry. Perhaps they were a ship's captain or other dockworker.

But it was a beleaguered housewife who answered, her hair bound up in messy loops, a young boy's hand clenched tightly in hers to keep him from escaping into the street.

"Ask if she knows Henry," Eliza prompted, bouncing on her toes.

Silas would have preferred turning invisible. Or at least turning into a snake and slinking away. But Eliza gestured urgently to the woman, who was growing more exasperated with each passing second.

"Have you seen a Loegrian boy?" he finally ground out.

"About this tall"—Eliza held her hand above her own head but below Silas's—"with shoulder-length brown hair, sort of tan skin, tanner than mine, anyway, um, dreamy eyes, and, what else—"

Silas's eyes were far from dreamy at her prattling. He was certain they were red.

He drew in a sharp breath and released it. "Brown hair. And he'd look as out of place as she does."

The woman glanced between the two of them before shaking her head, and Silas apologized for the interruption.

"Do the eyes again!" shouted her son, pointing up at him.

Observant little thing.

"Do you one better," said Silas with a grin.

He transformed into a snake and slid across the boy's bare feet, which sent the child into giggling shrieks. The woman cracked a smile and might have said something had her child not run back into the house, shouting about magic. The door swung closed as she darted after him.

Silas slithered down the steps, forcing the princess to tiptoe behind. Half of him was tempted to remain transformed all day. With a bit of focus, he could still speak as an animal—one of many benefits of being an Affiliate rather than a true adder.

But, in the end, he turned human again, adjusting his clothes, which somehow always wound up skewed after a transformation.

"He really . . . liked that," Eliza said in wonder. "He wasn't afraid. Neither was the mother."

"Incredible, isn't it," Silas said coldly, "how some people don't need to sleep with daggers just because they're around someone different?"

She had the grace to blush, and her gaze sank beneath his.

"I just didn't want to get hurt," she finally said.

"Ironic, coming from the one holding the blade."

"It's not as if I used it!"

"Am I meant to *thank you* for not stabbing me in my sleep?"

"No." She jabbed a finger toward him, looking up with sudden fire. "No, *you* don't get to act like this is unfair. You have fangs and venom, which is no different from a dagger. I haven't stabbed you, and you haven't bitten me, so let's keep it that way. Help me find Henry, and we can *both* get away from the sharp threats—deal?"

For a moment, she almost seemed Pravish, impassioned and unapologetic.

And maybe she wasn't entirely wrong.

At the very least, she was a step above the last person who'd pulled a blade on him and actually used it.

Slowly, he slid his hands in his pockets, and he nodded at the house they'd left behind. "Tell me your plan isn't going door-to-door all day interrogating random citizens. Tell me you're smarter than that."

Pink colored her cheeks, but she planted her hands on her hips. "Oh, how silly of me—I ought to have directed us to the single group of people most likely to have seen a lost Loegrian. Remind me, do they live by the palace? Or perhaps by the hole in the Izili wall?"

Though he tried to restrain it, the corner of his lips twitched. *Apta* or not, he couldn't help but appreciate the way she responded to challenge. Honest and direct and full of fire.

"They might run a few inns," he drawled. "Maybe an alehouse—*birahan*. The usual places travelers congregate."

She opened her mouth again, then snapped it shut, clearly hating that he was right. In the end, she mumbled something about finding a *birahan*, and Silas's good humor faded as he resigned himself to a long morning. It turned out to be exactly that as they searched out public gathering space after public gathering space, interrogating innkeepers and bartenders alike about a wandering Loegrian no one had seen. No one, except, Silas was still convinced, the fish circling the sea floor.

To that end, he steered their search closer and closer to the docks.

"What are we doing here?" Eliza asked suspiciously, glaring at the moored ships. "I already got information about the shipwreck."

"I'm being thorough," said Silas.

He found the dockmaster, who confirmed the shipwreck, though the man's greedy eyes kept darting toward Eliza in a way Silas didn't trust.

"Was the captain recovered?" Silas asked. "Have any of the crew come back to join another ship?"

"No one, no one." The man didn't look at him, only at Eliza. "All gone. Very sad."

He was heartbroken, obviously. Silas resisted the urge to roll his eyes.

The princess, however, looked heartbroken for real. She'd wrapped her arms around her middle, like she needed help holding everything inside. For as often as the dockmaster was trying to catch her eye, she was avoiding looking at anything, just staring into the depths of a wall.

"We'll be going then," Silas said, though his original plan had been to obtain this exact information and confront the princess with it. It was hard to think about confronting her when she'd become smaller than usual, ready to fold up and disappear entirely.

The dockmaster suddenly burst into Loegrian. "Your Princess! Family so sad. I help you home. Big help, I—big help to you! I can."

Eliza's arms dropped, as did her jaw. She stared in horror, not at the dockmaster, but at Silas.

"I never told him," she said.

"Princess—" The dockmaster tried to grab her, even as she shrank back.

Silas stepped in the way, baring fangs. The man had enough sense to halt. Reaching back blindly, Silas caught Eliza's arm, steering them both from the dock house. He didn't stop moving until they were a few streets away without pursuit.

"At least we solved one mystery," he drawled at last. "Your arrest by the kuveti. They must be looking for a princess."

Eliza pulled away, pacing. "My father must have sent guards after me. Or a . . . an offer of reward. Why couldn't he—just *once*, why couldn't he—"

Her voice muffled as she pressed her hands to her face.

"It would have been before your sister took the throne." Silas knew firsthand that Aria wanted Eliza to come home by choice, not by force.

Eliza came to an abrupt halt, lowering her fingers to rest against her chin. "Before my sister . . . what?"

"She's queen now. I was told by the dean."

"I missed the coronation," Eliza whispered as if dazed.

For the first time, Silas felt a sliver of pity for the princess. She'd done this to herself, of course, but he knew what it was like to be far from home, to receive news late, if at all, to miss things he could never make up.

He'd missed Maggie's seventeenth birthday, when she came of courting age. Rather than having Silas there to intercept undesirable suitors, she'd been left entirely to their father's agenda, which was how she'd almost wound up in a disastrous marriage.

Now he'd miss every future milestone too.

In a moment of decision, Silas said, "We're going to the Sarazan tabernacle."

“The what?” Eliza frowned.

“When we first met, you wanted me to get a translation from the innkeeper about Sarazan. I’ll show you what he was talking about.”

She could have yelled at him for not explaining that the first time. He expected her to.

Instead, a hesitant smile budded on her face. Her eyes sparkled in the sunlight, a light brown speckled with copper that Silas hadn’t noticed before.

They were pretty.

“Thank you,” she whispered.

He cleared his throat, looking away. “Don’t thank me yet. Prepare for a hike.”

CHAPTER 16

Silas had not exaggerated the hike.

At first, they climbed the winding paths that led to the top of Izili's cliffs and the university, but when the paths diverged, Silas took the route directly along the cliff edge.

At the peak, Eliza paused, marveling at the beauty of the ocean from this height. The horizon stretched into eternity, a never-ending expanse of sparkling water. She stood on a divider. To her left, the cliff overlooked civilization, bustling city streets and brightly painted buildings. To her right, the edge fell away into an empty, sandy landscape, a long stretch of tan and beige bordering the ocean, marked only by a worn footpath.

"I come out here sometimes to read," Silas said. An ocean breeze ruffled his hair, tossing it all to the left in an adorably lopsided way.

Eliza couldn't help but laugh. "To *read*? Not to . . . I don't know, look at the ocean?"

"I look at the ocean between pages. Unless the book is particularly enthralling."

All her life, people had told Eliza she read too much. She should have introduced them to Silas.

As soon as she had the thought, her chest tightened.

Introducing him to anyone in Loegria would mean his death.

The world tilted, like her body thought it was back on the ship to Pravusat, swaying without solid ground.

"Highness?" Silas frowned.

"It's high," she managed, though that wasn't the problem at all. She didn't want to think about the real problem.

Silas led the way down the other side of the cliffs, and she followed in silence. Beneath the withering afternoon sun, her clothing quickly grew sweat-soaked and constricting, the silk of her shirt trying to escape the heat by becoming one with her skin.

Her cheeks tingled, little pricks in her skin warning against the sun's burn. At home, the palace physician could have given her cooling balms, but here, she would have to live with the blistered skin. She attempted to shade her face as she walked, but the path continued, and her arms grew weary.

Eliza flapped her shirt against her chest. The puffs of air against her throat were almost more torture than relief.

Then, finally, she saw it. Or at least, *something*.

It wasn't a building so much as a tent. A very *large* tent, rectangular and blocky, with thick posts holding its shape. It was both larger and closer than she'd realized because it was the same dusty beige of the landscape, camouflaged against the sand.

As they drew closer, she saw a limestone statue near the entrance, an enormous serpent with fangs bared. Because of course it was.

And Silas, of course, paused to admire it.

"They probably worship it, don't they?" Eliza said, and her bitterness really had nothing to do with snakes at all.

Actually, it did. But just with one.

"Sarazan?" Silas smirked. "Well, he's what they named all the tabernacles after, so I suppose that's answer enough. He's a mythological sea serpent, but there are conflicting legends. Some say he's the transformed state of the god of the ocean. Others claim that he's only a guardian, protecting the gate to the spirit world."

"Do you believe in him?" It would be just like him to call love a myth while believing in a big magic snake.

But Silas shook his head. "Once, I thought I sensed something out there in the ocean, something big. Perhaps there's a sea snake grown so large, it's inspired legends. Or perhaps people are seeing the shadows of driftwood in the dark and spinning tales."

He stepped through the tent flap, and Eliza followed.

The interior had a *breeze*. It startled Eliza so greatly that she stood in the entrance, feeling blessedly cool air swirl against her face and clothing, until she almost shivered beneath the silk. Her eyes adjusted to the shaded surroundings, and she realized the tent had been divided into multiple sections by sheets of gauzy material, offering a measure of privacy but also openness. Shadows moved behind the barriers, and the light smell of incense tickled her nose until she sneezed.

One of the curtains parted, and a girl perhaps a few years older than Eliza approached, dressed in flowing robes with her hair tied beneath a green scarf. She smiled and greeted them in a soft, friendly voice, introducing herself as a "sister of Sarazan."

Silas wasted no time.

"There was a shipwreck two weeks ago," he said. "Loegrian crew and passengers. Did you care for any survivors?"

Eliza took a step back. This was the answer she'd been searching for, and now that it was directly in front of her, she couldn't bear to hear it in case it was the end of everything. She needed a moment to prepare. Needed—

"Yes," said the sister.

Like a shooting star, Eliza's heart shot from her chest, right into the sky, almost tugging her along with it. She grabbed Silas's arm, shaking it. "Ask about Henry!"

"I'm getting there, *apta*." But his voice was hardly chastising. Quickly, he outlined Henry's description.

The answer was *another yes*.

He *was* here. Definitively. The sister described his unconscious state and the long gash on his arm, slow to heal. Eliza barely heard the details because her ears were full of the sound of his name, repeating in her mind like a chant, like a prayer. *Henry, Henry, Henry.*

She was floating. She was flying. If she closed her eyes, surely she would fly right to him.

Silas was frowning. He couldn't even enjoy good news.

Then he asked, "Were there any others?"

Guilt sliced through Eliza for not considering anyone but Henry.

The sister nodded. "One other, but she was a Pravish girl, and she bore no serious wounds. She brought the boy for treatment, and when he woke, they left together."

Silas looked at Eliza sharply, as if he expected her to be able to explain that, but all she could do was stare.

Finally, he said, "So she found him washed up on the beach?"

The sister shook her head. "No, she was on the ship. I could not speak to the boy, of course, but he showed no panic around her, the way he did around most of our staff. She seemed trustworthy to him. Familiar, at the very least."

Silas looked at Eliza again, and this time, she bristled. "What?"

He shrugged, but the movement was far from casual.

Eliza huffed. "I'm here with *you*. Why shouldn't Henry have depended on this girl for help?"

Then she thought about the bracelet on her wrist and everything she'd hopelessly tangled herself in, and she prayed Henry's situation wasn't as complicated as that.

"Do you remember anything about this girl?" Silas asked the Sarazan healer.

The sister gave a brief description—taller than Eliza, dark hair, blue eyes.

"She protected a small white box," the woman added. "Strange black markings."

Silas stiffened at that, his jaw tightening. Clearly it meant something to him. All at once, he was out of questions, thanking the tabernacle worker for her time and taking his leave.

Eliza scrambled after him. "What was that?"

Silas shook his head.

She grabbed his arm, pulling him to a stop on the sand. "Don't you *dare* keep this from me! You know something!"

He grimaced. "I've met that girl before—the one with the box."

"That's wonderful! So you know where to find Henry!" This day just kept climbing.

Until he shook his head. "It was a chance meeting. She's . . . dangerous."

"Like you?" Eliza said heatedly.

He narrowed his eyes. "More so. And if she's interested in Henry Wycliff, it's not for any charitable reason. Henry may not be who you think he is."

Every good thing, he had to sour. Eliza turned away, shaking her head. "You don't know him. And the important thing is that Henry's *alive*. We'll go back to Izili, and . . ."

Her voice trailed as she realized the angle of the quickly lowering sun, saw her shadow thrown out long beside her. By the time they made it back up the cliffs, it would be dusk.

That's fine, she thought, setting her jaw. They'd pick the search up again.

"Tomorrow—" she started.

"Is my day to work," Silas said.

Eliza ground her teeth, but she refused to let him dampen her spirit. Henry was alive. The entire world felt alive again.

She began a determined march back to the university, and Silas fell into step beside her, looking at her strangely.

"Is Lord Henry a Caster?" he asked.

"What?" Eliza frowned. "No, he's a knight."

"The two are not mutually exclusive. Does he come from a Caster bloodline?"

"I . . ." She faltered, stumbling over a rough piece of brush. "No, he's just—he's just Henry."

Silas squinted, his lips thin, and Eliza suddenly felt like she'd exposed a secret.

"How well do you know this boy?" he demanded.

She glared at him. "I know Henry."

"How *long* have you known him? How much time have you spent together?"

"Long enough and time enough."

"You've met his family?"

"I've met his . . . father." Heat grew along Eliza's neck, and she blamed it on the lowering sun, even though its fierceness had gentled into sunset.

Silas was relentless. "How many months did you court before he was banished?"

"We never had a chance to officially court, but he'd declared his intentions. At least to me." Had the tournament not gone so horribly wrong, Henry would have asked her father's permission at the celebratory feast. Instead, everyone had spent the feast congratulating him on his chance to marry *Aria*.

Eliza swallowed the bitter memory.

Silas gave a short, incredulous laugh. "You didn't even *court* him. What, did you see the chivalrous knight compete in one tournament and 'fall madly in love'?"

She flared as red as the setting sun, and he turned away with a groan.

"*Sarazan kurta beni*," he muttered. *Sarazan save me*. Of course he would appeal to a mythical snake.

"I don't need your approval," Eliza huffed. "And I plan to spend all the time in the world with Henry, as soon as I have him back."

"This is why I can't take declarations of love seriously. What exactly are you in love with? How good he looks while galloping on a horse? Yes, I see—*the ultimate meaning of life*."

Eliza came to an abrupt halt, spraying sand. Fiercely, she glared at the boy beside her, who matched her dangerous expression with his own.

He was trying to embarrass her, make her feel ashamed about

loving Henry, but he couldn't. She may have been blown by whims in other things, but not in this. She loved Henry, and she was right to love Henry.

"I met Henry at the ball for my seventeenth birthday," she said softly, "and we shared the final dance of the evening. He was kind, and he made me laugh. After that, he invented an excuse to see me again as soon as possible. He brought flowers. When he competed in the next castle tournament, it meant everything to him, but he still snuck away to see me beforehand. When I say I love Henry, it's because I love his thoughtfulness and his easy humor and his genuine interest in me. I love the way he makes me feel and the way I feel like I could do anything to help him."

Her tone grew challenging. "And, as a matter of fact, he *does* look good while galloping on a horse."

For once, Silas made no retort. He slid his hands in his pockets, and his gaze dropped from hers first. Satisfied, Eliza continued walking.

Wherever Henry was now, whoever he was with, she was going to find him. If she had to endure the presence of a cynical shapeshifter a few more days to accomplish that, then she would.

CHAPTER 17

After enduring a second day of Silas's work and projects, they searched again.

Only to discover *nothing.*

Have faith, Eliza ordered herself. *Hope. Endurance.* Every motivating word and sonnet she could think of.

But no inn claimed any Loegrian guests, not even one who had stayed for a night and moved on. No alehouse could remember a foreigner of his description coming in to seek a meal. It seemed no one in Izili had seen Henry.

It seemed he'd walked off the face of the world.

She hated being out in the city, because it wasn't just Henry in need. There were beggars in the street she couldn't feed and thieving children dragged off by the kuveti to some unknown, terrible fate. Everyone turned a blind eye, just as they had when Eliza had been cornered by snakes. Aria's heart would have shattered to see such a lack of compassion, and Eliza could at least take comfort knowing Loegria's queen would never allow such things.

Eliza wrote her sister a letter, but it only made her feel worse. Because instead of saying, *I'm with Henry*, she could only say, *I'm determined to find him.*

And her determination felt less adequate each day.

She never got to claim her own belongings from the inn. Silas informed her that abandoned possessions in Pravish inns were bartered away. Because everything was rotten in this rotten country.

He suggested she buy new clothes in the market, but Eliza had neither money nor time for that.

With each search, she pushed their pace faster and faster and made more outlandish demands of who to interrogate. She ignored Silas's protests. If he so much as breathed the words *slow down*, she glared daggers at him.

And she still slept with her real dagger, although she did sleep. The exhaustion was too severe not to.

On Silas's days, if Kerem didn't need his help, he spent most of his time in the library, doing research of his own. In the first week, he'd already filled half a journal with notes—though, based on his frustration, they weren't very successful notes.

"What are you hoping to find?" Eliza finally asked.

"Hoping to prove," he corrected, then said, "The unprovable."

She almost made a quip about how he'd called *her* quest impossible, but it died in her throat. Because she still hadn't found Henry.

She was starting to fear—truly fear—that she never would.

The storm inside was growing, and Eliza was fighting desperately to hold her ship together. Silas suggested that Henry might have gone to another city in Pravusat or left the country entirely, and Eliza's frustration snapped at him to mind his own business.

"You don't care about Henry anyway," she snarled.

He didn't argue, just returned to his never-ending stacks of books.

She found she couldn't watch another minute of him seated calmly at a table, taking notes with all the leisure in the world while her legs physically *ached* to start the next search. So she dove into the shelves, searching for a book of her own. It was foolish; she couldn't hope for a book titled *Exact Directions on Solving Your Problems*. Had it existed, it would have already been checked out, with a waiting list made up of everyone else in the world.

Her body halted as if an invisible hand had grabbed her wrist. She glared down at her bracelet.

"Forgot, didn't you?" Silas called out from the table, sounding entirely too smug. He was certainly a snake, because only a creature with an eye in the side of his head could have been watching her while keeping his nose in his book.

"No," she said stubbornly. "I found what I was looking for."

She snatched a book off the shelf and brought it to his table. She examined the blue linen cover before carefully opening the pages. The illustrations were breathtaking, but, of course, she couldn't read a word.

This had been a stupid idea. Just like all her others.

With a curious gleam in his eyes, Silas shifted in his chair, peering over the table at her chosen book. Then he laughed.

"What's funny?" Eliza asked crossly.

"You're not missing anything."

"You've read every book in the library, have you?"

"Nearly."

Half of her wanted to throw the book at his head. The other half went ahead and recklessly said, "Well, I don't need an interpretation. I can tell this story just from the pictures."

"Oh, do tell."

She couldn't discern if he was mocking or challenging. Either way, she snapped the book open to the first illustration and threw herself into the story with dedication.

"In a far distant land"—all her favorite stories began "In a far distant land"—"a group of pixies danced beneath the moon."

"Well, you have the beginning correct," Silas said, writing as he spoke.

"Don't interrupt me. I'm reading." Eliza turned to the next illustration. "A pair of humans stumbled into the pixies' revelry. 'Terribly sorry!' they said. The pixies, of course, forgave the honest mistake and invited the beautiful couple to dance along with them."

Silas scoffed, but Eliza ignored him, flipping to the next vivid painting.

"The revelry was so great that they danced all night and fell asleep by morning. The woman woke alone, and she panicked, unable to find her beloved. She begged every pixie for help, asking if they'd seen him."

Eliza swallowed heavily, regretting the direction her mind had taken the story, although there wasn't much else she could have said for the illustration of the lonely, crying woman. She almost closed the book.

But if she stopped now, the lovers would remain separated, so she continued. "Together, they all scoured the forest."

After glancing at the next illustration, she swept past it, but Silas's voice halted her.

"You skipped one."

Since she'd been caught, she forced herself to incorporate the strange donkey on the page. "Then the woman met . . . an enchanted donkey? He said he knew where to find her beloved. She was so overwhelmed by gratitude, she cried, thanking the kind donkey."

Smiling, Eliza turned to the next illustration. "She ran with haste to the meadow he'd told her about, where she found her beloved, wandering in a daze. The lovers were reunited once more, never to be parted again."

Just as a story should end, she thought. Her fingers trembled slightly at the edge of the page.

Then Silas said, "There's one more." He didn't even glance up as he spoke, too busy reading lines in his own book and making notes.

"How do you know this?" she grumbled.

Eliza turned to the final illustration, and stared.

"Um . . . the donkey watched from afar," she finally said. "He was overwhelmed with joyful tears for the couple's reunion and pleased he was able to help it happen."

She closed the book decisively, and before she could think better of it, she said, "See? Even an enchanted donkey wants to help other people reunite with their loves. And he's more helpful in the search than you've been."

Silas chuckled, but it was a dark, low sound, hardly amused. He made a final, decisive note, the scratch of his pen sharp. Then he reached out and flipped her book over, beginning again at the first illustration.

"In a far distant land," he said, "a group of pixies danced beneath the moon. It was the advent of the lunar year, the most precious and sacred holiday in their tradition, and every pixie in the forest came to celebrate together, from the oldest whose wings no longer fluttered to the newest-born, barely the size of sunflower seeds nestled in their mothers' arms."

Eliza meant to cut him off, but she couldn't—not when his words flowed like a river, sweeping her along despite her resistance.

He turned to the next painting, his voice unfolding the story with it.

"Yet before the moon even crested, a pair of intruders disrupted the celebration. The human couple had been married just that evening, and they demanded the pixies bless their new union. Though the humans were rude and arrogant, they were met with gracious hosts, and in the spirit of the sacred occasion, the pixies welcomed the invaders to their celebration, with only one stipulation.

"'You may dance with us beneath the advent moon, and we will bestow upon you a blessing of fortune. But you must not drink any of our wine.'

"The couple scoffed about how anyone could drink from such tiny acorn-shell cups, and they gave their word to abide this rule. However, the man found himself drawn to the wine. The heady and floral scent permeated the air, intoxicating even in fragrance. While his new wife wasn't looking, he drank a single acorn-cup of it, rationalizing that such a small amount could not hurt anyone."

Eliza fixed her eyes on the fair-haired man in the illustration, scowling and wishing she could shout at him through the ink.

Silas turned to the next illustration. "The bride woke alone in the forest, and no matter how she searched, she could not find her husband. She blamed the pixies for hiding him and demanded they return him at once, but the pixies only shook their heads. In silence, they mourned tragedy on a sacred day.

"The woman ran through the forest, shouting her husband's name, until, at last, she collapsed beside a hideous donkey. To her shock, the donkey spoke to her in her husband's voice. He wept his regret and sorrow, confessing, 'I drank the wine after I was warned. I brought this tragedy on myself. But the pixies have told me that a kiss from my beloved will free me once more. I am deeply sorry for my mistake, and I will never break another vow. Only give me the chance to prove it.'

"But the wife fled, screaming at the hideous creature to be gone. She would neither kiss nor be married to such a beast. She wished only for the handsome man she had married."

"She left?" Eliza gasped.

Silas continued without pause. "Barreling into a meadow, the wife found the image of her husband. It was only a ghost, unable to even speak, and an elder pixie warned her it was a trick of magic. If she returned to the donkey, she could save her beloved, but if she chose the illusion, her husband would be forever cursed.

"'My husband is here,' said the woman, embracing the illusion.

"From a distance, the donkey watched, and he wept."

Silas closed the book.

Eliza glared at him.

"What?" he finally asked. "That's the real story. *The Advent Moon.*"

"Mine was better," she said.

"Yours was senseless. Everyone helped each other, and everyone ended up happy. When have you ever known that to happen in real life?"

"It could," insisted Eliza, but her heart ached. More quietly, she said, "It *should*."

"Besides, your version was as inconsiderate as the couple's intrusion on the pixies."

She gaped. "How do you mean?"

"Your version ignored the husband's suffering. The real story honors it."

"I think he would have preferred not to suffer!"

"But he did." Silas tapped the book. "It's right there on the page. The least we can do is not look away."

Seizing the book, Eliza held it to her chest, as if she could protect fictional characters from a real threat. "How *dare* you. You ignored my plight and Henry's. Every time we're in the city, you walk past the beggars and the starving people along with everyone else. You don't care about suffering!"

Silas shot back, too quickly to be anything but defensive. "The real question isn't about caring. It's about whether you're holding to an illusion at the expense of reality."

Eliza stood with such force she overturned her chair. She fumbled and righted it, still clutching the book.

"We're searching again tomorrow," she snapped, "and we're finding him. Then you'll see what's real."

But the search the next day ended just as all the others had.

With nothing.

CHAPTER 18

Eliza held it together as long as she could, but the storm drowned her at last.

She sat in the earthquake dorm, curled on a cushion with a blanket over her shoulders, swallowed by shadows. Silas had already settled into bed and put out the lantern.

Eliza ordered herself to sleep. To stop thinking. To stop feeling.

She ordered the tears to stop leaking from her eyes.

Then, when it became clear she was no longer captain of her emotions, she pressed a hand to her mouth and simply tried to cry without sound, drawing her breaths with all the care of tracing lines on parchment. She didn't know why she bothered, since Silas had proven he could sleep through the end of the world.

But then the dark shape on the bed moved, and his quiet voice echoed in the room.

"You don't have to cry silently."

She jolted.

He sat up, highlighted in the soft moonlight from the window. "I can smell the tears," he said, as if that explained it all. "Not exactly, I suppose. A snake's sense of smell is different from—"

"I'm so sorry," she interrupted harshly, "for disturbing your sleep. For invading your little university paradise and making your perfect life so wretched."

He didn't deserve her anger. Distantly, she knew that. Since being linked together, Silas had been more than reasonable. He'd provided meals, taught her Pravish, helped her search. He'd been the opposite of everything a shapeshifter was meant to be.

But everything was falling apart, and what could she do?

"You're upset," Silas finally said, and even though it was nothing but the truth, Eliza felt that same desire to lash out.

"I don't need pity from a shapeshifter," she spat. "And if you're going to devour me in the end, then just get it over with. As long as I don't have to hear you say another condescending word."

Though she wiped her jaw, the tears kept dripping. An angry, desperate, despairing rain.

Maybe Silas really would devour her.

Maybe she deserved it.

Instead, he yawned. "Pity? If you're sad, be sad. Why should I care?"

Eliza's chest tightened. "How comforting."

Still, there was something about his permission that loosened the floodgates, and after a moment, Eliza found her breath hitching in sobs. She sounded like a choking animal. He could have made fun of her, could have laughed or gloated, but he didn't say anything at all, and slowly, the storm inside tempered. It didn't disappear, but the worst of the waves had crashed and receded.

"There's something wrong with me," she whispered, her voice thick with tears.

She willed herself to stop talking, because this was not the sort of thing she wanted to admit to anyone but Aria. Even if Henry had been with her, she couldn't have told him; he would never look at her the same.

He could never love her if he knew just how unbalanced she was.

The bed creaked as Silas shifted, resting his arm on the bedpost. With all the casual confidence he used to address everything, he said, "Not possible. Morality as a judgment system only functions when applied to actions and behaviors. You can *do* something wrong, but there can't *be* something wrong with you. You aren't a garden with weeds crowding the vegetables, a collection of right and wrong things. Rather, you're a person, and any of your attributes are simply attributes, without right or wrong until you put them into application."

Eliza puffed an incredulous laugh. She'd never met anyone who talked like Silas did.

She'd never met anyone like Silas.

"Well, *you're* wrong," she insisted, "because there's definitely something wrong with me. And it's not weeds. Weeds could be pulled out."

"Do you believe crying is wrong?"

"No." Eliza sighed. She pulled the pillow to her chest and wrapped her arms around it. "Just . . . crying when I have nothing to . . . to cry about."

"Define 'nothing,'" he said.

She groaned. "You're awful. I can't put this into words! I can't . . . I . . ." But when she looked up at him and found him watching her with dark, steady eyes, the angle of his cheekbone highlighted in moonlight, the words just spilled out. "I was cursed by a Fluid Caster, and after it was broken, I thought I'd be normal again. Thought I'd be *myself* again. But everything's felt different since. Like I'm myself, but I'm some . . . slanted version. Like sometimes I'm the best version of myself, and other times, I'm the worst. But I don't get to choose which one I'll be."

No, that wasn't quite right. If she was really the best version of herself, she wouldn't make the mistakes she did. She wouldn't chase every reckless impulse without realizing just how reckless it was. Running away from home. Spending all her money on magic she didn't understand.

She swallowed hard. "It's like . . . it's like I'm captaining a ship through a storm, all by myself. I'm managing the helm and the rigging and the sails, all at once, and sometimes I'm *awed* by how *well* I'm doing. I know my course couldn't possibly be wrong. Then . . .

then there's a lightning flash, and I can see clearly, and I *realize*—I don't even *have* a ship! Or my ship's already been destroyed, and all I have is this wreckage, floating all around, and I'm swimming desperately; I'm grabbing pieces to drag and hold it all together. And the worst part is, I realize there *were* other people—people all around me—and while I'm flailing, trying to control what's already sinking, I'm hurting them. I'm drowning them."

"In this scenario, you're drowning me?" Silas asked, and she could practically hear his smirk.

Absently, Eliza rubbed the bracelet on her wrist. She muttered, "Maybe. The point is—"

"The point is there's still nothing wrong with you."

"How can you say that?"

"Because I'm an advocate of facts. Look." Silas slid off the edge of the bed and crouched in front of her, holding her gaze even when she shifted. "Stone Casting applied to a person uses bones, the way this Cast of ours connects to a jawbone and a wrist bone. Bones are a solid anchor, hard to alter unless you break one, and even if you do, healing is straightforward. Fluid Casting applied to a person uses *blood*, and blood, as you might expect, is a much more *fluid* anchor. It's easy to alter, and it's easy to break in a way without straightforward healing. After you've suffered a blood curse, it's natural to see side effects. Sometimes severe ones."

Natural, he said. Something about that brought tears back to Eliza's eyes. It didn't make sense; he was still saying she was broken. Something *inside* her was broken.

But he didn't seem to think it was her fault.

"I know a little about your curse," he went on. "At least, the little I picked up while talking to your sister. It was meant to *end* the king's line. A curse Cast with the intention of rewriting an entire country into something new. The fact that you outlived such powerful magic says something about you, and it isn't in the direction of weeds that need pulling. Quite the opposite. It says something about your stubbornness, your willpower, your passion for life, and your reckless disregard for any obstacle in your way."

He smiled hesitantly, tilting his head in a way that cast shadows from his unruly bangs across the bridge of his nose. "*Apta*."

Reckless girl. For the first time, Eliza found she liked the moniker. It sounded like a compliment.

"Tomorrow, we can go to the library," Silas said, his voice gaining enthusiasm. It almost made her laugh with what a *Silas* solution that was. "I'll show you the compilations from Nikolai Sidorov and Ahmet Khatib on their Fluid Casting research as it relates to lasting effects from blood curses. It's fascinating."

"I'll prepare to be fascinated," Eliza said dryly.

He had the self-awareness to chuckle, and he held his hands up. After a moment, he spoke again, softer. "I know this isn't research for you. It's real. So deal with it in whatever real way you need. Just . . . don't feel like you need to hide. No one should ever have to hide who they are."

Her throat tightened, but she managed a nod.

"Perhaps the effects will fade in time," he added, "or perhaps you'll just get better at navigating them. You'll sail more confidently, so to speak. But every life change is overwhelming when it's fresh. Trust me, I know something about that." His shoulders tensed, and he hesitated before he said, "The first time I transformed into a snake happened without warning, and it changed everything for me."

She'd always been told shapeshifters were demonic creatures with no conscience. But the way he described it sounded like he'd been cursed.

Her eyes flickered to his scar. Her first response upon hearing the story behind it had been to think how monstrous a creature Silas must have been for his father to need to kill him. Now she had a sinking feeling that she'd ignorantly switched the roles of man and monster.

Silas cleared his throat, looking away. "The point is, I learned to navigate. So will you."

"Why don't you hate me?" Eliza whispered. It wasn't what she'd meant to ask, but she couldn't take it back.

Silas's gaze returned to hers. He raised his eyebrows. "Why don't you hate me?"

Maybe she should have.

She remembered his red eyes, fierce and terrifying, remembered the moment he'd transformed into a venomous snake. But she could also see his eyes now, tender and focused on hers. He looked like a boy a little older than she was, crouching in front of her with his hair shadowing his forehead, his arms resting loosely on his knees. Her eyes darted to the yellow band on his wrist. *She'd* done that to him, not the other way around.

In her flailing, she'd pulled someone else under. But maybe she could still do something to fix that.

Eliza swallowed. She hugged the pillow tighter, and she wiped the most recent tears from her cheeks. With her foot, she felt around on the floor until her toes knocked against the sheathed dagger beside the cushion.

Silas tensed, but before he could retreat, she gave the dagger a decisive kick, sending it spinning across the floor. It disappeared beneath the bed.

For a long moment, Silas stared after it. Then he said, "I can't do the same with my fangs, sorry."

Eliza puffed a laugh. She shook her head, because it didn't matter. She was choosing to trust.

"What's the word?" she asked. "The one for you. Not shapeshifter. It's . . ."

"Affiliate," he said. "Animal Affiliate."

"Affiliate," she repeated, like she was practicing Pravish again. She managed a faint smile.

In return, Silas gave her a smirk and settled back onto the bed.

They didn't speak again, but Eliza's tears dried, giving way to a calming sleep.

CHAPTER 19

Rather than heading directly to the library the next morning, Silas introduced the princess to the campus bathhouse. And he enjoyed the way she blushed once she realized the function of the building.

When had he started enjoying her easy blush?

Unlike most of the buildings on campus, the bathhouse carried accents of color reminiscent of Izili proper—stripes of warm pink on the pillars and cheerful orange on the sloping roof. A few exquisitely detailed mermaid statues pointed the way to the entrance. Inside was a central corridor of polished wood, gleaming in the light of a large fireplace at the end of the hall. The rest of the space was sectioned into private areas, curtained off from one another.

"I've never been to a public bathhouse!" Eliza hissed.

"If you wanted to be treated like a royal," Silas drawled, "then I suppose you shouldn't have left the palace."

She'd realize soon enough—the university bathhouse practically was royal treatment. The stalls were private, and at the moment, Silas desperately needed some privacy. As much as he could get with the Cast in place.

The previous night was still haunting him. He'd told himself to ignore the princess's plight, but instead, he'd grown more tangled in it. He could still see her tears in the moonlight, could hear himself confessing things he'd never intended to tell *her*. He'd been a fool to talk about his first transformation.

And yet, he was still thinking about the way she'd looked at him. The way she'd surrendered her weapon even when he couldn't do the same.

He was still thinking about her soft voice whispering, *Affiliate.* Like a truce. Like a peace offering.

"Two baths?" asked the woman at the front desk, leaning forward in her cushioned chair.

Silas shook himself back to the moment. He paid for two stalls, which the woman recorded in her ledger before ringing one silver bell and one golden, the chimes harmonizing as they echoed down the hallway.

One male attendant and one female opened stalls, and Silas ducked into his without a backward glance at Eliza. Warm steam swirled against his skin with a sleepy, comforting weight, and a light floral scent wafted through the air.

The stall interior was small enough he didn't have to worry about being yanked around by his bracelet, but all the same, he was annoyingly aware of Eliza's presence just one stall over, like a ghost he couldn't be rid of. It didn't help that she whispered in awe at every feature, asking questions about the pipes and the domed ceiling dotted with holes to let in the sunlight.

His attendant stepped around the tub—a hollow depression cut into the floor itself—and crouched by the wall. He was a Fluid Casting student, as they all were in the bathhouse, and would be on rotation, offering volunteer hours to practice Casting. Within moments, he'd called steaming water from a pipe in the wall, filling the bath. He left a basket of soaps and a bell Silas could ring if he needed a temperature adjustment or anything else.

Alone at last, Silas breathed for a few moments. It felt like so long since he'd had solitude.

Yet, even now, *someone* kept intruding on his thoughts.

"This is amazing!" Eliza was still loud and energetic even in a whisper.

Her attendant giggled, her reply an indistinct murmur.

Silas ordered his thoughts to his research. He stripped, climbed in the tub, and dunked his head underwater to plug his ears.

Truthfully, the research was half his frustration. His discovery at the Sarazan tabernacle should have thrilled him—he'd found evidence of his magic stealer. But it was only unnerving, because it wasn't as if he'd caught a glimpse of her on a city street. She'd been in the company of another Loegrian. *Shipwrecked* with one.

After trying to steal Silas's magic, had she followed him back to Loegria? If so, why hadn't she finished the theft she'd begun?

Perhaps she'd been unable to find him in his homeland. Most of his brief trip had been spent either with Maggie or Gill. Perhaps the strict regulations had made her realize Loegria was the most unideal hunting grounds for magic stealing, and she'd returned home.

Where she'd just *happened* to share a boat with Henry Wycliff.

Or had he been a target?

Too many questions, not enough answers. It made Silas's skin itch. He surfaced in the bath, snatched a bar of soap, and scrubbed away the faint pattern of scales on his arms.

He'd thought himself a random target. *Hoped* he was a random target. Hoped the ocean-eyed girl had come to campus—a place crawling with magic—and just happened to light on him as the first magic user in her path. Now he believed she'd targeted him specifically, even if he had no idea why.

And he couldn't explain her interest in Henry. Though they were both members of court, Henry and Silas shared no connection beyond passing acquaintance, if that, and Eliza had been insistent the other boy didn't possess magic.

Unless Henry was also an Affiliate. If so, he'd been the biggest of fools to pursue a Loegrian princess; he'd been courting death.

Silas raked his fingers through his hair, leaning back with a sigh.

Above him, the ceiling let in a thousand pinpricks of sunlight through minuscule holes. A sky of daylight stars. It was beautiful, he supposed, but stars belonged to the night. It felt *wrong*.

Everything about the world felt wrong.

Each time he went out in the city, he wasn't searching alone; he had a network of snake spies. But just as he and Eliza had hit nothing but dead ends, his snakes had brought back a hundred failed reports through magic. There was no sign of the ocean-eyed girl or of Henry, not in any corner of Izili.

He'd told Eliza they might have left the country. It was a possibility. Silas was convinced the symbols on the magic stealer's box were Cronese. But did that mean she was Cronese herself, or was this another invasion of Cronith into Pravusat?

He'd found research on using written language to shape Artifacts, so he'd experimented with words painted on snakeskin, testing his native Loegrian along with Pravish and Cronese.

The Artifact effects were strongest if he used Cronese. Why was that?

It couldn't be the language's cultural attitude toward magic, because Cronith and Pravusat both had comparable freedom of magic compared to Loegria's discrimination.

There was something unique about the language itself, something the magic stealer had discovered and harnessed.

If I had another ten years to study, he thought. But he had to scrape results together in the next two months. If he wanted to learn anything further down this path, he needed to know exactly what words had been inscribed on the magic stealer's box. He needed to study it up close.

If the ocean-eyed girl couldn't be found, could Silas lure her out?

While he tried to construct plans for that, he finished his bath, toweling dry before dressing and exiting the stall. He was so caught up in his thoughts that he was shocked when he came to a lurching stop in the hallway.

From inside her stall, Eliza shouted in protest. He heard water sloshing, and he retreated a few steps to give her freedom of movement again.

"Sorry," Silas called, rubbing a hand across his face. Whatever fledgling plans he'd had in mind vanished in the wake of a returning princess, who always crowded out all his other thoughts.

He was never going to solve anything with her around as a distraction.

While they finished drying by the bathhouse fireplace, the princess surprised him by saying, "You tried to tell me about the girl with Henry. I wasn't listening."

Silas waited, trying to gauge if that was an invitation or a trap.

"You said she was dangerous." Eliza's voice had grown small, and she drew her knees up on the cushion, wrapping her arms around them. "Do you think she's . . . hurt Henry?"

"I don't know what to think," Silas said honestly.

"Could you tell me how you met her?"

That *was* an invitation. Not an order.

Silas found himself torn. He hadn't shared his research goals with anyone but Afshin, and even the dean wasn't interested in his process, only his result. This was something Silas had to accomplish by himself.

But he couldn't do much of *anything* by himself while chained to a princess. Thus far, they'd been pulling each other in different directions, even after finding out the two people they were trying to find were somehow linked. They needed to collaborate.

Yet Silas couldn't help dreading the result. If he told the princess what he was fighting for, what his future hinged on, it would mean she could sabotage it.

"Please, Silas?" Eliza whispered. The firelight brought out the copper tint in her eyes, and she looked both earnest and downtrodden, sitting with her damp hair loose over her shoulders. Her fine silk clothing was ragged, marked by snags and holes gathered in her desperate search, and her fair skin bore splotches of red from their days out in the sun.

You cast the same shadow, said Yvette's voice in his memory. He and Eliza were both frustrated in their goals, but she was open about hers.

"She has a way to steal magic," Silas found himself saying. He swallowed heavily.

And he prayed he wouldn't regret this.

Once committed, he told her everything: his first encounter with the ocean-eyed girl, his agreement with Afshin, and his research thus far. Eliza listened with wide eyes and appropriately timed gasps, but she never interrupted.

Saying it all out loud didn't give him any more clarity than he'd found in the bath, but it carried a kind of comfort. Most of that came from the girl sitting beside him, focused and nodding along, like she wanted to see him solve this problem.

"One of the experiments I studied used composition warlockry," Silas said. "The hypothesis was that a Fluid Caster can draw out magic like they can draw out blood, and a Stone Caster can contain it in stasis the way they can hold a person in sleep. It was extremely promising, but it failed like all the others, and no one is sure why.

"Maybe if I had years to work, I could find my way to this discovery through experimentation alone, but I have *weeks*. I have to get my hands on the magic stealer's Artifact and reverse engineer it. That's the only way."

"Except we can't find her," Eliza said, speaking for the first time.

"Except we can't find her," he agreed.

To his surprise, the princess laughed. Silas raised an eyebrow. She started sectioning and braiding her hair, a faint smile on her face.

"I'm looking for the boy I want to kiss," she said. "You're looking for the girl who kissed you. They're together. We're together. You know what this is, right?"

"The third-worst day of my life?" Silas drawled.

"*Fate*," said Eliza, grinning.

"There's no such thing."

"Obviously you'd say that, because you're you."

It was mildly offensive, but at the same time, it summoned a strange tingle in his chest. He wasn't certain whether she was calling him cynical or delusional or something else, but whatever it was, it wasn't snake or shapeshifter. She was defining him by some human characteristic.

"And obviously you'd believe in fate," he returned. "Because you're you."

"Because I'm right," she said primly, pinning her braid with finality. She lowered her arms. "Well, I know one thing—we won't find either Henry or Lady Magic Stealer lurking in the university library. I think we should go to the market."

"I have snakes looking," Silas countered. "And in the meantime, I can still research. Two tasks at once."

"But your snakes can't interrogate merchants to find out if any of them have seen a strange white box with markings. That sounds like something a sharp merchant eye would notice, right? Out of place, possibly valuable?"

In response to Silas's pause, she grinned, obviously knowing she'd said the right thing.

Perhaps this collaboration could work after all.

"Get your shoes," Silas said.

CHAPTER

20

Before they went out in the sun again, Silas gave Eliza one of his Artifacts: a square of tanned snakeskin affixed to a leather backing.

"It'll keep the heat off," he said.

Half of him expected her to reject it—and she did shiver when touching the snakeskin—but she slipped it in her pocket. When she thanked him, her smile was warm. Although he tried to shrug it off, his steps felt lighter.

They spent all morning interrogating merchants. Most were curt but honest, though a few grew offended when it became clear Silas and Eliza had no intention of purchasing anything. One wrinkled old woman threw her shoe at Silas and then thanked Eliza for retrieving it, leaving the princess laughing.

But none of them claimed to have seen the white box.

Come midday, Silas purchased food at one of the stalls, a bean mash wrapped in flatbread that sent Eliza into a coughing fit. He smirked, warning her too late about the heavy spice. In response, she threatened to throw her shoe at him.

Eliza finished first, wandering the neighboring stalls while Silas purchased and consumed a second flatbread. Just as he was ready to resume their search, he saw the princess take off running through the crowd.

"Seriously?" No sooner had he voiced the protest than the Cast yanked him forward.

At the same moment, it collared Eliza, sending them both plowing into people on the street. Silas waved off the irritated shouts, catching up to the princess while she was still offering bowing apologies to the people around her.

"Silas, look!" Eliza grabbed his arm, pointing with her other hand.

All he saw was a man gathering stoneware from a striped rug and loading it into a small cart.

"He must be done for the day," he said. "What's so—"

"That's the stall where I bought the Cast!"

Now she had his attention. "That's the Stone Caster?"

"No, that's what I'm saying! I recognize the rug, but she isn't here. That man is stealing her things!"

With a frown, Silas hurried toward the stall, Eliza beating him to it.

"Stop!" she shouted in Pravish, planting herself on the rug, blocking the man from the next statue he'd been about to grab. "This isn't yours!"

"*Senen*, not *sizen*," Silas corrected in Loegrian. "He's a singular 'you,' not a plural."

"Why is there a plural 'you'?" Eliza hissed. "*Why* would there *ever* be a plural '*you*'?"

"Who are you?" the man demanded, demonstrating a correct usage of the plural.

Switching between Loegrian and Pravish so often gave Silas a headache. He didn't stumble on the transitions, since he spoke both fluently, but the effect on his mind was undeniable. Splitting it in two. He was meant to be immersed in a new life in Pravusat, but speaking Loegrian dragged his old life through in patches, made it impossible to keep his focus in one place while his tongue was divided.

Silas straightened his posture, towering over the man and looking down with cold eyes. "Where is the Stone Caster who owns this stall?"

"I claimed it first!" the man said, making a grab for the next statue. Eliza slapped his hand away, and the man pulled back, cradling red knuckles. "She's gone! I had nothing to do with it."

"Gone where?" Silas pressed.

"Kuveti took her. Look, we can split the raw stone, but I get the statues!"

"Why was she arrested?"

"I don't know! Sold bad Casts, maybe. But good statues. You can't have them." After feinting one way, he snatched another statue before Eliza could intercept him, then placed it with care in his cart.

"She will come back," Eliza said fiercely.

Despite her Loegrian accent, the words were clear enough, and the man shook his head. "Not from the kuveti. You want to waste good limestone? Foreigner with no sense. Get out of my way."

Before she could get shoved aside, Silas drew her off the rug, ignoring her protests.

"Most people don't return from a kuveti arrest," he said quietly. "Not unless they're rich enough to bribe their way out."

"Then we have to help her!" The copper flecks in Eliza's eyes caught the sun, sparks ready to start a fire.

"It's not our problem."

Eliza gaped like he'd revealed himself as an Affiliate all over again. She turned to watch the man greedily loading stoneware into his cart.

"What is wrong with this place?" she asked softly, and somehow, the gentleness of her tone pierced more than if she'd shouted. "No one cares about the holes in their wall. No one cares about the beggars. No one cares about innocent people getting arrested. No one . . . cares."

"As if Loegrians are so compassionate," Silas said bitterly.

She opened her mouth, her eyes sparking again, but then her gaze dropped to the scar on his neck. They looked at each other in silence.

The man finished loading up his cart and hurried away with a spring in his step, leaving an empty rug behind. The skeleton of a stall.

"Come on," Silas muttered. "We can ask—"

"I want to know why she was arrested." Eliza straightened, lifting her head. "That man said it might have been for a bad Cast. *We* have a Cast from her. It is our problem."

She was trying to manipulate him again.

"Yvette read our Cast," said Silas. "She would have seen anything wrong with it. You just want to help."

Eliza stared him down. "And what's so wrong with that?"

After a moment, Silas groaned, throwing his hands up. "What do you suggest, Highness? Do you have a royal treasury stash to bribe the kuveti?"

"I can write to Aria. She'll send—"

"Loegria's in turmoil, and you want your sister's focus to be on relief for a single foreign stranger? By the time she could arrange and send anything, it would be weeks."

Eliza bit her lip, looking down at the empty rug.

"What if the kuveti have Henry?" she whispered at last.

Silas frowned.

"They arrested *me*. What if the reason we haven't been able to find Henry is because he's in prison?"

"You have a royal ransom. Why would they target him?"

"Maybe it wasn't Henry." She met his eyes again, her face pale. "Maybe someone would pay for the capture of the magic stealer with him."

It was a possibility. A strong one. Silas cursed to himself, rubbing his face. Perhaps he could ask Iyal Afshin . . .

Ask him what? The kuveti hated the university for having its own guard force rather than using their services. Even if they were willing to negotiate with the dean, the prices would be enormous. University funding was stretched thin already, and Silas didn't even have an official research budget.

"I need to think," he said.

—·✸·—

Silas led Eliza to a tailor's stall, hung with brightly colored shirts and sashes.

"Pick two outfits," he told her.

She looked at him like he'd dropped his senses somewhere along the path. "Is this part of your thinking process?"

"Don't question my process." He smirked. But when she continued looking suspicious, he rolled his eyes. "If we're going anywhere near the kuveti, you can't look like a Loegrian. They're on the hunt for a princess-shaped one, if you remember."

Her hesitation melted to eagerness, and she took a step toward the stall.

Then she halted.

"I don't have any money left," she admitted, clearly trying to make the statement casual. Her forced shrug fooled no one. "Maybe I can borrow something from Yvette."

"'Pick two outfits,' I said. That's what *I* can afford."

She looked up at him, and the wide smile growing on her face tugged at his heart in a discomforting way. Without another protest, she scurried over to admire the options. None of them were fit for a princess, at least by Loegrian standards, but she gushed over the bright colors and told the merchant they were all beautiful.

Silas moved to stand just behind her. "If you're calling an inanimate object beautiful, it's *muhetsem. Tatli al* is only for people."

"Why are there two words for that?" Eliza laughed, glancing over her shoulder at him. "Pravish makes no sense!"

In the muggy heat, strands of her brown hair stuck to her forehead and neck, and beads of sweat glistened along her hairline. Somehow, she looked radiant despite that. It was her beaming smile. For as fiery as she got in her irritation, she showed the same amount of enthusiasm in her joy.

He looked away, shrugging, the gesture as forced as hers had been a moment earlier.

Eliza picked her way through the options, finally choosing a bright magenta shirt embroidered down the front with swirls of sunshine yellow. After another moment of indecision, she added a green shirt hemmed in pink.

Spouting praises of her taste, the merchant pulled the magenta shirt over Eliza's head and showed her how to fold it at the waist and fasten it with the sash to make it the right length. Then she fetched matching scarves.

"Turn around," Eliza ordered Silas.

He raised an eyebrow. "You're changing here? In the middle of the market?"

"I'm just going to wiggle out of my shirt with this over the top. I'll be modest."

"Then why do I need to turn around?"

She glared at him until he rolled his eyes and turned, placing himself between her and the other marketgoers. If anyone tried to approach the booth, he gave them a flat stare with the clear message to move on.

"I'm ready," said Eliza.

Silas turned to find her grinning at him, looking much more Pravish than before. The merchant had helped her wrap a yellow scarf loosely over her hair, the cloth hanging like a hood, the loose end dangling in front of her left shoulder. Her former silk shirt, soiled and battered, lay rumpled on the merchant's rug.

"Not bad," he said.

Eliza scoffed. "I believe the term you're looking for is *tatli al.*" She leaned in, pressing her hand to the edge of her mouth for a loud whisper. "That's the way to say *beautiful* for people."

Raising an eyebrow, Silas said, "*Sen tatli al gozumek.*" *You look beautiful.*

She lowered her hand slowly, pink rising in her cheeks. Clearly, she hadn't expected him to say it, but he'd taken it as a challenge.

"*Apta*," he added with a smirk and was rewarded by her scowl. Then, drawing in a deep breath, he said, "I have one idea regarding the kuveti."

CHAPTER

21

The kuveti were notoriously organized, keeping records of every arrest. Eliza had said she wanted to know why the Stone Caster was arrested, and Silas felt fairly confident they could at least get that information. And, if they were lucky, they could find out if Henry and the magic stealer had actually been arrested. Getting anyone *out* of prison was a demand he couldn't meet, but this was a place to start, and before they planned anything, they needed to know if they were even on the right path.

With Eliza as disguised as he could hope for, he led them through the streets to the kuveti prison house near the Nephew King's palace, an area of Izili he had previously avoided.

The prison looked as oppressive as the purpose implied. There were no splashes of color common to Izili architecture, only dull stone, bricked in hard lines. An iron portcullis blocked the entryway, and on either side, the structure rose in spikes, like the overturned fangs of a dead serpent.

"This is a terrible idea," Silas muttered.

"It's not as if you're spending all your money on unknown magic," Eliza said with a self-deprecating smile. "The worst they can do is turn us away."

That was not even *close* to the worst. But sometimes information was only gained by risk.

She slipped her hand into his, jolting awareness up his arm, and in answer to his sharp look, she said, "I can't just cower in your shadow. That would draw attention. No one cowers in this country."

She wasn't wrong. Still, she was wildly distracting. Silas tried to ignore the sensation of her soft fingers threaded through his as he led the way to the front guardhouse, tensing under the eyes of a half dozen veiled men at the gate.

A barrel-chested man came to greet them, his hooked nose holding his black veil a full inch away from the rest of his face. He had the eyes of a predatory wildcat.

Silas wished he had a veil of his own, wished he had a reason to reveal his snake form so he could experience bows of reverence rather than hard stares of evaluation.

"You arrested a female Stone Caster in the market," he said, making his voice as commanding as possible. "I want to know what for and when she'll be out. She owes me for this false Cast!"

He brandished his wrist, and the guard's eyes flickered to the gold bracelet.

Silas was prepared for pushback or bartering. What he wasn't prepared for was—

"No such arrest," said the guard shortly.

Silas blinked, then frowned. Finally, he said, "The arrest was witnessed."

The guard took a threatening step forward. "Are you a captain? Do you command the kuveti? There has been no arrest in the outer market in a week. Shall I arrange for yours?"

In response, Silas bared his fangs, both because he was scared and because, in Pravusat, it was better to be aggressive than afraid.

The guard's predatory eyes crinkled approvingly in response, and he waved them on their way.

With no other option, Silas turned away. He would have to think of a different approach, though he couldn't imagine—

"Don't lie!" Eliza burst out. "You took her! Tell us why!"

If her accent wasn't bad enough, she used the noun form of *lie* instead of the verb form, meaning she'd shouted *don't liar.*

Silas clutched her hand, trying to pull her away before she could do any more damage. But he saw a whisper pass between the guards at the gate, the pointed attention on Eliza.

Clothes could only do so much. She was too pale for Pravusat, her hair too light, and she'd just revealed the voice of a foreigner.

"For future reference," he snarled quietly, "it's *yalan* for *lie*. And, here in a moment, you'll want to know *gravmak*."

The shortened form of *gravdan kazmak*, which meant *outrun the strike*. Run faster than the snake could bite.

"Stop them!" barked one of the guards. "That's the island's runaway princess!"

Eliza paled. But she broke into a run, and Silas ran with her, ducking beneath the iron portcullis before it could be dropped. Shouts of pursuit came from behind as they spilled into Izili's main thoroughfare. No one parted for the kuveti, choosing instead to pretend they saw nothing. Of course, no one parted for Silas and Eliza either.

Eliza kept surging ahead, dragging his hand, then slowing her pace, looking back. Silas almost suggested splitting up, then bit his tongue on the impossibility. Had she been on her own, she would have lost the guards as quickly as she had in the market, winding between houses and people in a mousy flash until she'd scurried away entirely. Silas wasn't a runner, and his tall build wasn't meant for slipping between people. He was going to get her captured.

He thought of calling for snakes, but that worked best if he could corner an enemy, not while he was on the run from one. If he'd laid a trap, maybe, but he couldn't manage that now.

So he focused on the roads that led toward the university. If they could get back on campus, they'd be safe. The kuveti wouldn't cross the campus guard.

"This way!" Eliza yanked him the opposite direction, ducking into the narrow opening between two buildings. Silas hissed as he scraped the skin off his elbow. The moment they burst into open air again, she found another narrow alley and dragged him through that one, too, until finally stopping in a sheltered alcove where they stood with thundering hearts, listening as the shouts of the kuveti faded away.

Sagging in relief, Eliza released his hand and doubled over, gasping in air. Silas wiped the sweat from his brow and prodded at his bloodied elbow.

"You were worried about drawing attention by *cowering*," he snapped. "Then you go and—"

"*You* were about to walk away!" she shot back. "You hadn't even asked about Henry or the girl!"

"Because I was threatened with arrest! You don't poke a cobra with its hood flared."

"It was just blustering. Like all the merchants."

"One of those merchants actually made good on her threat, and prison is a lot more dangerous than a shoe."

"You still should have taken the risk."

"If I didn't have *this*"—he shook his wrist at her—"there wouldn't have been a risk at all! I could have slithered into the guardhouse and looked at their records myself."

"Of course. No matter how you look at it, *I'm* the problem." She gave a dry laugh.

"I didn't say that." Though he basically had. "I said—"

"I heard you. And thanks to *this*"—she shook her wrist at him—"I understand the venom in any language."

Silas clenched his jaw.

"You know what? I'm tired of your sanctimonious attitude." Eliza stepped closer, though there was hardly any space in their shadowed hollow, and she jabbed a finger in his chest. "You think you're so smart, Silas Bennett, with your magic and your linguistics and your grand university education, but you don't know anything about the most important things!"

"What," he drawled, "like love sonnets?"

"Yes, like love. Like caring about other people. Like fighting to help because you can, because it's *right.*"

"Well, I'm sorry I'm not a knight," he said coldly.

Eliza's face paled, her freckles stark against her skin, and he wished he could take it back. For all his accusations that the princess was reckless, he was just as bad—lured by different bait. Her by love and him by . . .

He didn't know. Something made him lash out, strike first. The feeling of being cornered, perhaps. No snake in history managed that feeling well.

"I'm sorry," he said.

She gave a sharp nod. "Me too—because you're right. This Cast is the problem. We are irreconcilable opposites, and as long as we're stuck together, neither of us is going to get what we want."

She stalked out of the alcove and rummaged in the alley, producing a small crate missing one of its boards. He thought she might pry another off and threaten to club him with it, but she marched the whole thing back to him, set it on the ground, and stepped up on it. For the first time, they were truly eye to eye. The better to yell at him, he supposed.

"Look, Highness—"

That was as far as he got. Eliza seized him by the face and yanked him forward. For just a moment, Silas flashed back to the last time he'd been kissed. A magic stealer with eyes of blue.

This time, it was a princess with eyes of brown.

CHAPTER

22

Eliza kissed him as if committing to a leap from Izili's cliffs. A quick smash of her lips into his, rough and unpleasant, and then a retreat as if she could not get away fast enough. Silas ran his tongue over his teeth, checking she hadn't chipped one in the violence.

"There!" she said triumphantly. "I fixed my mistake, so you don't have to worry about me as a setback anymore. Now . . . we . . ."

Her triumphant expression faltered as she looked down at her still-attached bracelet. Silas glanced at his, more out of reflex than anything. His mind was still processing what had just happened, and in annoyance, he was wondering if he'd donned some kind of invisible sign, inviting women to shock him with unwarned acts of intimacy.

Eliza's shoulders drooped. "It didn't work."

Silas snorted. "Well, in the Cast's defense, that was hardly a kiss."

"Yvette just said I had to mean it!" she shot back. "I want the Cast gone. I meant that."

"There's meaning in the sense of emotional significance and then there's pure definition. I'm not sure if you were trying to kiss me or headbutt me. You must have confused the magic as well."

Eliza's face flared brilliant red. She folded her arms. "Fine. If you know so much, then you show me how it's done."

In that moment, she was suddenly attractive. Not in any way related to love, but rather in the way an opponent on a debate floor became attractive when they opened themselves up to brutal counterargument. Silas loved to prove the opposition wrong, and he loved it more when they underestimated his ability and invited the attack.

Show me how it's done. There was no better invitation, and Silas never failed a challenge.

With a smirk, he closed the short distance between them again and rested one hand along the princess's jaw. Her stubborn expression softened, her arms loosening across her chest. He wrapped his other arm around her waist and pulled her close, the crate rattling as she stepped forward on it.

Silas brought his lips to hers. Not as a violent snake strike, but as a gentle, teasing movement, barely a touch before lifting. Her eyes slid closed. He shifted his hand away from her jaw, sinking his fingers into her soft hair, loose in its braiding, and then he kissed her again. A bit more pressure, a bit more intent, all of it calculated. His mind was caught up in the triumph of proving a point, and he was ready to pull back and say something like, *There. That was a kiss.*

But there was something he hadn't counted on, something about the secluded shadow of the alcove, both of them tucked away from the noise of the city in a world of their own, something about the adrenaline still speeding his heart with the memory of a chase when he'd almost lost her, something about the way she fit perfectly in his arms. The world was alive in an uncalculated way.

And then Eliza pressed her palms to his chest, curling her fingers in his shirt, and despite the layers of clothing and muscle and bone between them, he felt a jolt in his heart as if she'd pressed her hand right to it.

Rather than stepping back, he held her tighter. His mouth moved against hers with a sudden desperation, like she was a breakthrough he'd been searching for. Distantly, his mind wondered what he was doing, but he didn't care to hear the logic. All he could hear was the pounding of his heart, which had completely taken over after whatever she'd done to it.

Eliza pulled back first, and Silas felt cold at the loss, like a reptile deprived of the sun's warmth.

Then he cleared his throat, trying to speak as confidently as if he'd followed his plan to the letter. "There. That was a kiss."

"That was a kiss," she repeated softly, her jaw slack and her eyes wide.

He'd thought her expressions easy to read, but that was an oversimplification, because although he could read the current shock, he couldn't tell if it was because he'd outperformed her expectations or if the world had tilted for her the way it had for him.

He'd made a terrible mistake.

Swallowing, Silas looked down, glad at least to be rid of—

His bracelet was still attached.

The silence stretched until it was broken by the cry of an overhead gull, heading out to sea. Silas ran one hand through his hair, drawing it away from his forehead only to have it fall right back.

"Maybe Yvette was wrong," Eliza said in a small voice.

"She wouldn't be wrong about this," Silas muttered. Had she left something out? He should have asked her for more details. Obviously, she wouldn't have expected him to *actually* go through with a kiss.

He shouldn't have. He'd carelessly redefined the terms without considering the consequences. Now, instead of being a princess he was stuck with, he'd made Eliza a princess he'd kissed.

Worse, a princess he'd *enjoyed* kissing.

What was he to make of that?

Trying to reorient himself, he looked out at the street and saw the slope of the city leading to the university. The white buildings called to him like a haven. Clear and focused and familiar.

Without looking back at the princess, he said, "Let's go."

Eliza had made a terrible mistake. She'd actually believed that rotten snake when he'd said a kiss could be without meaning. But the way Silas had kissed her . . . Her lips still tingled from the pressure of his mouth, and she felt a little jittering dance across her scalp where his phantom fingers still teased her hair. His kiss was not a fleeting, insignificant moment; it was a flaming brand that had left a mark she was certain would never fade.

No one could kiss like that and not mean it.

So what exactly had he meant?

She followed him numbly through the winding streets climbing steadily higher. The lowering sun cast her shadow out wide, like a giant version of herself, stomping along beside her and demanding answers she couldn't offer. What had she been thinking? Nothing. She'd been impulsive, as always, steering a ship without any clear heading.

Her first kiss.

It was not the sun's heat that made Eliza's cheeks burn; it was her own recklessness. For so many years, she'd imagined her first kiss, imagined the romance of it, the beginning of an epic love story that would last forever. When she'd wished Henry good luck in his big tournament, he'd kissed her cheek, a brush so light it might have been a butterfly's wing against her skin. He'd whispered his intention to court her. Eliza had nearly broken her cheeks from smiling. She'd swooned all the way to her seat in the stands, and she'd imagined all the soaring moments to come, imagined romantic picnics and evenings beneath the stars, imagined teasing laughter and dizzying flirtation. She'd imagined a first kiss—a real kiss—that would have shaken the palace walls. But their love story had been halted by his banishment.

And now she'd given her first kiss away for what—spite? Goading? Because Silas drove her mad, and for a moment, all she'd wanted was to have the upper hand, to leave him speechless the way he always seemed to leave her. But he hadn't been speechless. He'd been just as smug as ever.

There. That was a kiss. His low voice still echoed in her ears, and she could still taste him on her lips.

She'd kissed a snake!

She was insane!

Eliza shook her head fiercely, squeezing her eyes shut until she tripped over a raised stone in the path and had to limp quickly to catch up with Silas's back. He never glanced over his shoulder, so all she had was a view of the red sash crossing his vibrant blue shirt. Sunlight tangled in his dark hair, fighting to shine through the black. Anything would struggle to shine next to Silas. He was the boldest presence she'd ever met.

And he *really* knew how to kiss.

Of course he did. He knew everything. He lived and breathed university, where he'd apparently developed a bond with every professor and read every book in the library and learned every language in the world and probably swallowed some forbidden Cast that gave him more knowledge than was right for any one person to hold.

It wasn't *right*. Someone who didn't believe in love shouldn't be able to kiss like that. It wasn't *fair*.

He shouldn't be able to walk away without looking back.

When they reached the dorm, Silas didn't go directly to his room. Instead, he picked the lock of the room next door and waved Eliza toward it.

"There's enough length on our tether for privacy," he said.

Eliza should have been thrilled. Instead, she was furious.

"When we were *first* bound together, I asked about my own room, and you had a smug answer about impressing faculty and research and whatever else. Why now?"

"Feeling generous," he said flippantly, but the way he wouldn't meet her eyes betrayed him. Something had changed, and there was only one thing it could be.

Now that they'd kissed, he wanted her as far away as possible.

Stiffly, she said, "I owe you an apology. My actions earlier were solely to get us both out of the Cast, but clearly I overstepped, so I'm sorry for kissing you."

That got him to look at her, but she couldn't read his expression, at least not until he smirked. "I don't recall you ever kissing me. If memory serves, you headbutted me like a goat, and then, for some unfathomable reason, I kissed you. Regardless, we both failed to break the Cast, so we can put the momentary lapse of judgment behind us."

Unfathomable reason. Lapse of judgment. Why had she expected any more of a snake?

Eliza forced a prim smile. "Consider the horrible event forgotten. Good night, Mr. Bennett."

She slipped into the new room and slammed the door behind her.

CHAPTER

23

Silas threw himself back into research, trying to puzzle out why the most promising experiments for magic stealing all failed and what could be done differently. Eliza must have been boiling mad, because her boredom usually overcame her attempts to ignore him. He kept waiting for her to burst out with a question she couldn't help asking, but she never did. She kept her eyes on her sonnets, and, later, he heard her using broken Pravish to ask the librarians for information on the kuveti.

Come evening, they went to the dining hall, only for one of the servers to stop Silas before he could claim a plate.

Was everyone in the world mad at him?

"Silas Bennett? Iyl Yvette's sent for you."

After being unable to break the Cast with a kiss, he'd suspected there was something wrong with it, but when he'd tried to visit Yvette before going to the library that morning, she'd been off campus, so he'd been forced to leave a note.

"She specified I couldn't eat first?" Silas asked.

The server gave an apologetic smile. "Very specific, Mr. Bennett."

That worried him.

"Follow me," he told Eliza, though it was hardly necessary. After all, they were chained together. Maybe for life.

But when they reached Iyl Yvette's office, she wasn't pacing or showing any signs of worry over a horribly skewed Cast. Quite the opposite—she was laughing with her husband, both of them bent over some kind of project on her desk.

"Silas the student!" Baris called out, straightening with a two-handed wave. "*Nirhaba* and happy birthday, you blessed snake!"

Silas blinked.

Eliza gasped, finally breaking her vow of silence. "It's your *birthday*?"

"Is it?" he asked.

Yvette playfully slapped Baris's shoulder. "I told you. Oblivious." She leaned toward Eliza, despite the fact they were still a room apart, and confided, "My darling *erkek* can't imagine the single-mindedness of my students. And no one's more single-minded than this one." She pointed at Silas.

He had the childish—snakish?—urge to stick his tongue out, but he resisted.

"What a waste!" Baris griped. "To be born under the fortune of the advent moon and not even remember!"

"That's your holiday," Silas pointed out, "not mine."

Baris slapped his three-fingered hand to his heart. "He wounds me! He speaks Pravish like a son, yet he wounds me."

"I can't believe you didn't tell me it was your *birthday*!" said Eliza. She spoke Loegrian, but for the sake of everyone's understanding, Silas chose to speak Pravish along with Baris and Yvette.

He shrugged. "I wasn't secret-keeping, *apta*. I just don't care to keep track."

If anything, she looked even more aghast. "Do you even know how old you are?"

Just to irritate her, he made a show of frowning in thought. "Thirty-eight? Fifty-two? Once you're old enough to attend school, the numbers don't matter, do they?"

At least Baris laughed.

Yvette called out, "He's freshly twenty, Your Highness, and if you don't both get in here, we'll eat the food without you."

As it turned out, the project they'd been bent over was a traditional Pravish birthday meal. It was unnecessary of them, but generous, and it made Silas smile. Yvette divided portions for everyone and shooed them all into the corner to sit on cushions. Baris happily explained each dish and its significance to Eliza—rabbit kebabs for the energy to leap into a new year of life, rolled *meze* dumplings because the concerns of the previous year should be bundled up and swallowed, and, most delicious of all, *balimav*, a sweet pastry baked with honey and nuts.

"Because life is delicious!" Baris roared, filling his mouth with a huge square of *balimav*.

Yvette brought out a set of wooden cups and poured a ginger drink that had Eliza doubled up and coughing at the first sip. Silas laughed, but even knowing what to expect, the *zenzil* still made his eyes water. Eliza caught his gaze and lifted her glass, wiping her nose as she did so. When she spoke, her voice had a raspy edge, but she was grinning.

"What's the right toast in Pravish?" she asked Yvette.

Yvette smiled, hair beads clacking as she tilted her head. "*Yeni basi, yeni cilt*—that's best."

New year, new skin. The shedding of the old to make way for the new. Pravish really did have the best meanings.

Eliza sat straighter on her cushion and pointed her glass toward Silas. Loudly, she said, "*Yeni basi, yeni cilt*!"

She stressed the wrong syllables, but Silas smiled anyway. Yvette and Baris echoed the toast, and Silas raised his cup in return, though he was smart enough not to drain his all at once, the way they did. Eliza took the smallest sip possible, with all the dignity of a princess.

"Now," boomed Baris. "Time for the advent story!"

"Eliza can tell it." Silas waved his cup in her direction. "Her favorite part is the very helpful donkey."

The princess frowned, then gasped. "That book from the library?"

"Oh, he showed you?" Yvette grinned. "When I was teaching Silas Pravish, I made him read *The Advent Moon* six times, and he swore he'd never look at it again."

"That's how you knew all the pictures!" Eliza jabbed her finger in his direction.

"It was fun," he admitted, "letting you think I had every book in the library memorized."

She shoved him, almost falling off her own cushion in the process. He laughed.

"I will tell it," Baris declared. "My version is best. Everyone quiet now." He paused dramatically, and when he began again, he'd deepened his already rumbling voice. "Far away and yonder, the pixies danced beneath the sacred moon. The new lunar year is heralded, and under its light, no creature can be the same."

Silas settled into his cushion, sipping his biting *zenzil* and listening to the familiar story. Baris gave it some colorful embellishments—a few sassy pixies, an appearance from a wild boar "to add danger"—but the heart was the same. An arrogant human couple, a string of fatal mistakes, a tragic end.

"I don't think I like that story," Eliza admitted. "I wish it could have been happy."

Yvette sat forward with an instructor's gleam in her eyes.

"Brace yourself," Silas muttered to the princess, taking the final sip of his drink.

"Happiness is the entire point of it," Yvette said. "In fact, *The Advent Moon* is the most important romance ever told."

Baris nodded sagely while Eliza sputtered.

"But it isn't romantic!" she protested.

"Of course not!" Yvette smiled. "Had the couple been pleasant and the husband done no wrong and the wife loved him deeply, the story wouldn't be memorable. As it is, it stirs feelings! Anger motivates us toward defiance, so our anger at the couple's decisions leads us to say, 'I will never make that mistake.' We understand what romance should be, because the story shows us what it isn't, and in the end, we use it as a map to find our own happiness."

"Or," Silas added, "we heed the story's warning, and we avoid relationships so that we never wind up as a grieving donkey."

"And we are never happy," Yvette countered. She reached out to squeeze her husband's hand, and he kissed her cheek.

Eliza looked as though it was suddenly *her* birthday. She beamed in Silas's direction, and he rolled his eyes.

"I've tried telling him the only real happiness is in love," Eliza said.

"A girl after my own heart," said Yvette. "Yet I wouldn't completely agree. There's plenty of real happiness in the world. Romance is only a *unique* happiness, one I find worth pursuing, no matter how difficult the path."

Eliza frowned. "Love isn't difficult. It's just something you feel."

Yvette raised her eyebrows, the same pitying look she gave to students spouting off in lecture hall.

"Love is not an emotion," she said. "It is a choice built on emotion. Attraction, appreciation, admiration. *The Advent Moon* may be worth another look from you."

"But they did it wrong," Eliza protested. "You said that yourself."

"They gave poor responses to very real difficulties, my dear. Indulging vices, acting without thinking, performing tiny acorn-cupfuls of betrayal—these are all inevitable in a relationship, and what we see in the story is a love that could not last because it was built on the shallow ground of attraction without full appreciation.

"Had the wife fully appreciated her husband, his strengths and his weaknesses, she could have forgiven his error, she could have loved him even when he was not in his best form, and she could have helped him back to his best. But she preferred the ghost of the image she'd crafted for herself, a handsome representation without the depth of a real person."

Yvette leaned forward, the ends of her red scarf trailing in her lap. "Real love is difficult, because it requires the most vulnerability two people can ever give, and the most forgiveness."

Silas rolled his empty cup back and forth in his hand. He thought of one of the last conversations he'd had with Gill, when his best friend had told him he was in love with the future queen.

If she cares enough to change an entire kingdom for you, Silas had said, *then take my blessing. It's just an awfully big gamble to make, Gilly.*

And for what? Silas had never seen any evidence that love was worth the risk. Yvette and Baris seemed happy, but they were both good people, and he couldn't imagine them being any different if they were just a merchant and a professor in separate worlds.

One thing was certain: Silas was happy on his own. A relationship was an invitation for pain, and he already bore the scar of one betrayal.

Never again.

CHAPTER

24

The evening came to an inevitable end, no matter how Eliza wished otherwise. It had been so long since she'd laughed freely, relishing the company of other people. It was also surprising to see how Yvette and Baris both doted on Silas—they really loved him. She'd never seen Silas as happy as he was around them. Smiling easily, listening without lecturing. Like he was a different person.

Or maybe, a little voice within her said, *he's finally himself.*

But even in this setting, he was still the academic, and as soon as the *balimav* had been eaten and the drinks drained, he had questions for Yvette. The two of them stood next to her desk, discussing scholarly whatsits, while Eliza fiddled with her sonnet book and wished she could have made the dinner conversation last forever.

"Good book?" Baris asked in a booming voice.

He dropped heavily onto the cushion beside her and plucked her red book from her hands, turning the pages with his eyes sparkling. "Ha! All Loegrian. I cannot read a word." He squinted closer. "No, this is Pravish here. You write Pravish in your books?"

Eliza had started keeping a list of Pravish words on folded parchment, but she'd gotten tired of the sheet slipping out whenever she opened her book, so she'd been writing new vocabulary words directly on the pages. Wherever possible, she matched them to a Loegrian counterpart in a sonnet.

"I'm learning," she stammered out in Pravish.

"Very good!" Baris thumped her on the back with his three-fingered hand, and what it was missing in digits, it certainly made up for in power. Eliza had to catch herself before she overbalanced on her cushion. "Learning is very good. That is why I married a university professor. Here, practice your Pravish with me."

Haltingly, she asked, "How you . . . meet your . . . Iyl Yvette?"

"Wife," he supplied for her. *Hana.* Eliza repeated it a few times in her mind to write down later. Then he went on, "The best story! Even better than *The Advent Moon.*"

He launched into a tale about a beautiful Stone Caster who loved papayas, and before long, Eliza found herself smiling and laughing along with him—though she was certain it had not actually taken *ten years* of asking before Yvette agreed to meet his parents.

A corner of her heart ached, because she'd always imagined telling her own story like this. The story of meeting Henry.

"Do you know . . . about . . . kuveti?"

Baris waited patiently for her to piece the question. When she finished, his expression turned grim.

"Know what of them?" he asked. "Beyond their greedy, brutal ways."

"My friend . . . maybe prison . . . person."

He gave her the word for *prisoner*, then nodded toward Yvette. "My wife helped build their prison. Ask. If she can find out, she will."

Hope lifted Eliza's chest, and just then, Yvette spoke from behind her.

"Highness, you'll want to hear this."

Eliza scurried over to the desk, only to be met with Yvette's grin.

"Silas was just telling me about your very romantic kiss."

Flushing red, Eliza glared at Silas, but he was busy glaring at his professor.

"This is your fault," he said. "The only reason I kissed her was to break the Cast, but it accomplished nothing."

Yvette waved a hand. "You know as well as I that magic is as much about emotion and intention as it is about action. If you aren't both in love with each other, then the kiss won't strike the right chord for the Cast."

"You could have told me that to begin with," he griped.

"You didn't seem interested in the details. As I recall, you were adamantly against any relationship with Her Highness, even one as simple as translator."

Before she could talk any more about relationships, Eliza cut in. "You had something for me to hear?"

Sobering, Yvette touched Eliza's bracelet, leaving a faint glow, a moment of light capturing a fingerprint. "I examined Silas's bracelet again, at his request. There has been a change in the Cast." After Eliza's panicked gasp, she hurried to say, "Nothing *wrong* with it, only a sad reality—the Caster behind it is gone."

It took Eliza a moment to sort that out. "You mean she's . . . Are you saying she's dead?"

"Casts remain upon death, but there is a ripple in the magic, as if it mourns the creator." Yvette shook her head. "It means you can't seek her out to end the Cast, and she would've had the easiest time doing so."

"But you can do it," Silas pressed.

"With a great deal of effort, and I have expended too much today." Yvette's faint smile betrayed her words. "Besides, I believe I made my own terms clear when you first sought my help."

"I think the kuveti took Henry!" Eliza burst out. "We've searched, but . . . Is there any way you can find out if he's in the prison? Baris said you have connections there."

Yvette squinted at her husband, who whistled innocently.

"*Connections* . . . is not what I would call it." The professor sighed. "Finding out if there's a Loegrian prisoner shouldn't be impossible. I'll look into it. Give me a few days."

Impulsively, Eliza hugged Yvette, regretting her boldness for only a moment before the Stone Caster gave her a return squeeze that may have bruised a rib.

"Thank you," Eliza whispered, glancing up to include Baris in the gratitude as he approached.

When Yvette stepped back, Baris slung an arm around her shoulders and kissed her temple before pointing at Silas. "If you are grateful, soft-bellied snake, then you buy papayas!"

"Maybe," said Silas.

"And you!"

Eliza jumped as Baris's thick finger pointed close to her face. The merchant grinned.

"When you need more Pravish words, you come to my stall." He lowered his voice and leaned in like a conspirator. "And make him buy more papayas."

Eliza laughed.

They walked back to the earthquake dorm in a gray dusk. Silas's posture was relaxed, his hands in his pockets, his hair ruffling in the gentle evening breeze. Eliza breathed in the salt from the ocean and smiled.

When they reached the dorm hallway, she found herself reluctant to go in her room. She paused, playing with a loose strand of hair behind her ear.

"I'm sorry I don't have a birthday gift for you," she said. "I'd get you a book, but odds are you've already read it."

Silas leaned on the wall beside his door, shrugging. "It doesn't matter." He tilted his head. "When I was growing up, my sister, Maggie, would always try to make a fuss. She'd drag me out on horseback to some little clearing for a picnic."

Eliza raised her eyebrows. "Don't horses hate snakes?"

"I'm not *actually* a snake, you know." After a moment, he admitted, begrudgingly, "They are skittish. It takes a mild-tempered gelding to tolerate me as a rider."

Eliza laughed.

"Anyway, Maggie would lay out a feast of whatever she'd smuggled from the kitchen, and she'd force me to play hacky sack with her, and she'd give me a new book. She always got me a book, but she only picked the ones that looked interesting to her. She's the reason I've read half the pastoral poetry I have, or that author you carry around in your pocket."

He'd been smiling, but it faded slowly, leaving behind something that looked like aching pain. Eliza's heart twisted.

"You miss her?" she asked.

He nodded, and since she couldn't let him be gloomy on his birthday, she launched into speech without thinking.

"Aria never made a fuss on her birthdays. She went along with whatever our parents planned. The thing is, I think she was *actually* happy with that. I think she just appreciated that people cared, however they showed it." Eliza winced, leaning against the wall to mirror his pose. "It always made me feel selfish when I had specific plans—when I didn't want Father's falconry exhibition or Mother's recital."

"That's not selfish," he said. "Just honest."

"You seem to value honesty."

He frowned. "Doesn't everyone?"

Eliza ducked her head in another laugh, shifting slightly. He'd clearly never been to court. Or spent time in her home. She couldn't count the number of times she'd upset her family by being *too honest.* Her parents were both masters of stepping around distasteful truths, and while Aria preferred honesty, if that honesty revealed any problems, she usually blamed herself for them.

Silas didn't deflect Eliza's opinions *or* internalize them; he met them head-on with his own. While that made him frustrating, it also made her feel like she could tell him *anything* without worrying about how it might affect him. Like she could be herself without apology. He'd already seen her at her worst, both insult-flinging anger and racking-sob despair, and he'd taken both without flinching.

Hesitantly, Eliza smiled. They were both leaning against the wall, facing each other. She'd shifted closer to him without meaning to.

He brushed his hair back, but it almost immediately fell into his eyes again. His dark, captivating eyes. The sensations of their kiss came flooding back—the tingle of his fingers through her hair, the dizzying pressure of his lips against hers. The way he'd responded to her touch, pulling her closer, wrapping her in his embrace.

Was she blushing? She was certainly blushing.

Yet she couldn't pull her gaze from his.

In the interest of honesty, she admitted the truth to herself: *I want him to kiss me again.*

But the moment she had the thought, she heard her father's accusing voice: *Another of your romantic whims?*

Her momentary flush of desire sank in the depths of shame, and she shoved away from the wall.

"Good night," she said abruptly, fleeing into the safety of her room. She pressed her back to the closed door and dropped her burning face in her hands.

She'd crossed an *ocean* for Henry, and now she was acting like this? Flirting with another boy? Hoping to be kissed? She was proving her father right.

She prayed Yvette came back with news about Henry soon. In the meantime, Eliza would work with Silas because she had to, but she would *not* think of kissing him again.

CHAPTER

25

The news about the dead Stone Caster churned in Silas's mind. While waiting to hear from Yvette again, he tried to conduct his experiments, tried to find any evidence of magic being stolen in the city, but he couldn't focus.

Half of that was Eliza's fault. Every time she opened her mouth, she spilled a bucket of *Henry*, as if determined to wash away every other topic with praise of *the most charming knight in existence.*

Silas tried to tune it out, but her voice pierced his thoughts in a way nothing else could.

So, finally, he dragged her out into the city, backtracking a few streets because he had only a vague idea how to reach his destination, until, at last, they came to a low fence sectioning off a gloomy, oft-avoided part of Izili.

The public graveyard.

With its history of bloodshed, Pravusat had its share of bodies, and most of them were interred in public graveyards. Pravish culture—so bold in so many areas—held grief as a quiet thing. Those who lost loved ones kept a stick of incense burning, and they said silent, private prayers. Graves were not visited, because no one believed a spirit was tied to the resting place of its body, and no one believed a body meant anything after decay.

So the graveyard was silent.

Absently, Silas rubbed the gold bracelet on his wrist. He could sense the magic within it, but he couldn't read it, couldn't discern if it carried any faint connection to one of the unadorned markers in the yard.

"I wonder which grave is yours," he murmured, thinking of a woman he'd never met.

Arrested by the kuveti and dead a few days later, all while they claimed it never happened. If she'd been executed for a crime, the guards would have had no qualms admitting such. They executed plenty of people.

No. They were hiding something.

Who killed you? And why?

Eliza stepped up beside him, a reverence in her careful footfalls. She cast her eyes along the fence, then moved to a stubborn clump of maiden's weed sprouting around a post and pulled a handful of blossoms. She stacked them on the fence.

Rather than telling her about Pravish mourning traditions, Silas kept silent. They were both from a culture where graves were visited, where flowers and offerings were left and prayers were spoken aloud as messages given to people who could perhaps still hear them.

"I liked her," Eliza whispered. "She was kind."

Silas couldn't help a wry smile. "She took all your money and left you chained to a snake."

"Not on purpose! Besides, I was an equal partner in that." Eliza blushed.

Without thinking, Silas reached out. With a jolt, he realized he was about to brush his hand over her cheek, and he gripped the fence instead.

Focus, he ordered himself.

Jerking his head for Eliza to follow, he circled the fence and headed for the council house in charge of the graveyard. Most of the building provided living space for the gravediggers, but there was a front office in charge of making arrangements for new graves.

Silas asked the caretaker if he kept a list of bodies delivered by the kuveti.

"Sure do. Keep track of the services, since it's government work charged to the palace." With a grunt, the thin man pulled one log out from under a few others. But rather than handing it to Silas, he drummed his fingers across it.

"What kind of business have you got with this?" he asked, glancing between Silas and Eliza.

Research, was Silas's first instinct, but a greedy spark in the man's eye said he was looking for payment, and the university *did* pay for its research.

Eliza startled him by grabbing his arm, leaning on him as if suddenly overcome. When he glanced down, he saw tears glittering in her eyes.

"M-my aunt," she said in Pravish, using the tearful quaver to hide her accent. As if she simply couldn't speak any more, she hid her face in Silas's sleeve, giving a muffled sob.

Clever little mouse.

It took all his willpower to keep his face blank and give a serious nod.

The caretaker sighed and pushed the ledger forward.

Silas scanned the latest entries quickly. They listed the names of the dead, a few details of their arrest and sentencing, then any trouble or extra expense from the gravediggers interring the body. Without a name to search for, he expected disappointment.

What he found was a pattern.

Silas's eyes widened, and he pulled his journal from his bag, copying over information.

Eliza stepped back when he grabbed his writing materials, and though she rubbed at her eyes and kept up a sniffly act, the caretaker's expression grew more and more suspicious.

"This aunt of yours—"

That was as far as he got before Silas closed the ledger, pushed it back, and thanked him for his time. He guided Eliza out the door with an arm around her shoulders, as if consoling her, but as soon as they were out of the council house, she grabbed for his journal.

"What did you find?"

His mind was still racing too much to talk, so he surrendered it, let her read. His eyes wandered the graveyard.

The pattern had been in the notes of arrest. While most of the crimes varied greatly—everything from stealing market wares to murdering a neighbor—there had been one crime listed repeatedly, always with the same phrasing. *Causing magical disturbance.*

None of the entries had details of a trial or sentencing. And the latest, Remzi Pelin, interred just yesterday, carried a gravedigger's note of trouble laying the body to rest.

Used linen and boards to wrap the remains, it said. *Body, such as it was, had no bones.*

No bones in a Stone Caster. Just like Iyal Havva.

Eliza looked up in horror. "What does it mean 'no bones'? People have bones, I'm certain. Even magic users."

"Why is she different?" Silas murmured. The other listed names had the same arrest reason but no notes about difficulty burying the bodies.

Eliza ran her finger across the lines. "*Causing magical disturbance*—is that a tactful way of saying *killing people*? The Affiliate I saw outside the inn killed people before the kuveti took him."

Silas spun to focus on her. "What did you say?"

Quickly, she recounted the story of a dark night and an Eagle Affiliate. Silas wished he had a name to put to the story. Even linking Remzi Pelin to the Stone Caster in the market was an assumption—one he felt he was making on solid ground, but an assumption nonetheless. He needed more than that.

If someone was using the kuveti to target certain magic users, Silas wanted to know why. And he wanted to know what it had to do with a dead professor at the university who'd supposedly succumbed to his own experiment.

Careful, he warned himself. *No conclusions, just observations.*

Iyal Kerem had taught him that, early in his university days. A good researcher kept his eyes open to everything and recorded loose ends without trying to tie them, because if he jumped to conclusions too soon, he'd inevitably miss the thread that actually tied it all together.

What thread was Silas missing?

Eliza had resolved to speak only of Henry, but after the graveyard, her mind was buzzing. For the next two days, Silas immersed himself in researching Stone Casting and bones, and she immediately made a nuisance of herself, asking questions about magic instead of offering helpful insights. There was so much she didn't know.

She was definitely distracting him from his purpose. But when she yet again tried and failed to keep her mouth closed, Silas only chuckled.

"In case you haven't noticed," he said, "I don't mind educating people. In fact, I'm trying to do it for a living."

That made her feel a little better.

She couldn't understand everything he told her, since he loved to get technical or discuss specific experiments that went far beyond basics, but she gathered snippets. Details about Artifact creation and Casting limitations. Truths about Affiliate powers that dispelled shapeshifter myths.

Magic was more interesting than she'd realized. And much, *much* more complicated.

So she expected a complex answer when she asked, "Why does Kerem need your venom? What does yours do that his can't?"

She'd watched Silas be milked again, a process that was still unsettling. But although he clearly despised it, he endured it anyway.

"He doesn't have any," Silas said shortly, packing his bag on Kerem's desk. The professor had already left, and, honestly, Eliza preferred it that way. Despite his relaxed demeanor, Kerem had an unsettling gaze—like a predator's. She could never quite escape the feeling that he was evaluating her for weakness, and she pitied the students who performed poorly on any of his exams.

"No venom? So he's not a . . . viper, then? Like you?"

Seeing the gleam in Silas's eye, she knew she'd stepped into lecture territory, and she inwardly groaned. She spread both arms in a sweeping gesture. "Go on. Tell me all the ways I'm wrong."

"You're not wrong; my link is a viper." But he was smirking as he held the door for her.

Then, on their way down the stairs, he proceeded to tell her all the characteristics that made a snake a viper versus other groups like elapid and colubrid. She heard more about snake fangs than anyone should know.

"*Rear* fangs?" she muttered. "I'm going to have nightmares."

Silas was unrepentant. "We have a vine snake native to Loegria that fully *chews* its prey. You should look for it; it's fascinating."

"I absolutely will not look for that snake ever, thank you."

He snorted. Then, after a pause, he said, "Kerem's link *is* a viper. Horned viper, which looks a lot more impressive than my transformed state. I'm just a common adder."

Eliza frowned. "You said vipers are always venomous."

"Vipers are. Kerem isn't."

He held the door for her again as they exited the Yamakaz, and she waited for the rest, but, for once, he hesitated to elaborate.

Finally, he said, "When Kerem was around our age, he was sold to slavers in Cronith. They kept him as a snake on display. An exotic pet. Whatever they used to control his magic damaged it, so now some of his Affiliate abilities are limited—for example, he can still transform, but he can no longer produce venom."

Just weeks ago, Eliza never could have imagined pitying a shape-shifter, but thinking about anyone being enslaved made her ill. And she knew well enough how it felt to walk away from a captivity forever changed, even if she was physically unharmed.

"He doesn't like to talk about it," Silas said, the request clear.

"I won't ask," Eliza promised. But she resolved to think of the professor more kindly.

Yvette finally sent word, and Eliza couldn't say whether she felt better or worse for it.

There were no Loegrian prisoners being held by the kuveti.

Which meant Henry was still missing, and she didn't have the first clue what to try next.

CHAPTER

26

While Eliza felt the storm inside threatening again, it was Silas who gave her focus. Rather than seeming discouraged by Yvette's news, he seemed bolstered by it.

"Every eliminated possibility makes it easier to see the truth," he said.

"What does that even *mean*?" Eliza asked.

"It means as soon as I finish my tasks for Kerem, we're going to the map room."

He led her to a new building on campus. This one had a single large dome, surrounded by peaks and steeples. The statues adorning the walls were all engaged in performances of some kind. Eliza would have loved to explore the interior, which had been decorated with maroon tapestries and velvet upholstery, encouraging a rich reverence, but Silas shot straight for the map room like an arrow, speaking only briefly to the archivist before pulling the maps he wanted from various shelves and spreading them over the central table.

"What are you looking for?" she asked.

"Your beloved Henry," he said. "And the box-holding girl he was last seen with."

Eliza raised her eyebrows. "If I'd only known they'd be generous enough to mark their position on a map, I'd never have needed you at all."

She caught his lips twitching, though he tried to conceal it.

Standing on tiptoe, she peered over his arm at the ivory-colored maps. One showed a detailed view of Izili with the largest streets and buildings labeled. The remaining two explored layouts for the palace and the kuveti prison house.

"Yvette said they weren't in the prison," she pointed out.

"*In*," he repeated, as if that made any sense.

He shifted the maps so the palace rested on top, and Eliza almost barked a laugh. It could hardly be called a map at all. If anything, it was the outline of a building and nothing else.

"Did the king throw the cartographer out?" she asked.

"He doesn't want anyone too familiar with the layout of his palace."

"I've heard the Pravish kings are paranoid and unreasonable."

"Oh, I wouldn't give them too much credit. Kings everywhere are much the same." Silas glanced at her in challenge, clearly expecting her to deny it.

"At least in Loegria," she agreed.

Sorry, Father, she added silently, *but it's true.*

Silas blinked, and for once, she enjoyed catching him off guard.

"My father set an impossible challenge," she said. "He forced Henry to take it, pretending it was an honor, and then banished him for failing. I could write Father's name in the dictionary next to 'unreasonable.'" Her voice softened. "What's worse is that the challenge's reward was marrying Aria, and Father knew how I felt about Henry, but he still went forward."

Her father's dismissal rang in her ears. *Eliza's romantic whims are such that she'll find a new boy within the week.*

That accusation permeated her dreams, along with a fear that *she* was to blame for Henry's fate more than her father was. If she hadn't spent all her time dancing through the palace, spouting love poems and ignoring duties, perhaps her father wouldn't have dismissed her feelings. Perhaps her love could have saved Henry.

"My father shaped himself in the image of yours, so they can share the dictionary page," Silas said, shifting the maps again. He set out a few weights to hold the map corners in place. "In fact, my father forced me to take that same challenge, all for the prestige of marrying a crown princess, no matter the impossibility of the test or my disinterest in the reward. I was the third challenger."

Eliza stared at him, jaw gaping. Finally, she managed, "That's why you're in Pravusat."

"I'm in Pravusat because this is my home."

"So you didn't want to marry Aria?" Most men did, although more for political than romantic reasons. Eliza didn't envy her crown-carrying sister for that.

Silas snorted. "I have no interest in marrying anyone."

Eliza rolled her eyes and muttered, "*Sarazan kurta beni.*"

Sarazan save me. She'd been waiting to use it on him ever since he'd drawled it at her in the desert after she had admitted to never courting Henry.

"Something to say, *apta*? It must be dramatic if you're swearing by snakes now." Without looking at her, Silas opened his journal on the table and began making notes, his eyes flickering between the journal pages and the maps.

Eliza tossed her hands dramatically to irk him. "*Anyone*, Silas? Really? You have no interest in marrying *anyone*? You're saying if you met a gorgeous, book- and university-obsessed student right here on this campus, you'd walk away to be a grumpy old hermit?"

"And *you're* saying I should look for my perfect match in a mirror?" He scratched something out and wrote beneath it.

"Well, you're arrogant enough."

He looked up with a flat glare, but his twitching lips betrayed him again, and Eliza grinned.

"Admit it!" She wagged her finger at him. "There's a girl out there who could tempt you."

The mirth faded from his expression, leaving behind an intensity boring straight through her. Her mouth went dry under the force of his gaze.

Until he finally looked away, pausing as if he'd forgotten what he meant to write. She was distracting him again. Well, she couldn't help it; he was a constant distraction for her. Even now, she had to struggle to keep her eyes from tracing the curve of his wide shoulders, the long line of his throat, all the hundred distracting details of him.

"Doesn't everyone . . ." Eliza swallowed to clear the rasp from her voice. She looked down at the maps, and her thoughts tumbled free without control, gaining reckless speed. "Doesn't everyone want to be in love? Doesn't everyone yearn to hear someone else say, 'You matter to me more than anything in life. More than my *own* life. I would give everything for you—what's mine to give and what isn't. I would pull down the stars and leave the sky an empty black space. I would flatten the mountains and leave the earth an empty green plain. I would reshape the entire world for you.'"

Eliza's longing to hear such passion was a fierce ache in her chest. It was as if the imaginary words had hooks in her heart, and either she would pull them to her, or they would pull the heart right from her body.

But Silas only scoffed. "I certainly don't."

He was unfathomable.

"Are you so cold-blooded that you don't care about being cared about?"

"Cared about is one thing." He waved his pen dismissively. "*Obsessed over* is another. It's unsustainable, because in the end, you're just a person, and so are they. You'll inevitably disappoint and irritate each other, and then you'll be bitter about all the star-stealing, mountain-flattening nonsense, because it was just wasted effort to make a world that really benefits no one. The stars serve a purpose, you know."

Uncomfortably, Eliza thought of *The Advent Moon*, of a woman fawning over the image of a perfect husband while leaving the imperfect but real one behind.

She swallowed. "Fine, then. What do you imagine a real love would be? If it existed. If it wasn't pulling down stars."

To her surprise, Silas thought about it. He shifted one of his maps, but his eyes looked past it, and the way he tapped his pen without seeming to care that it was leaving tiny ink dots on his page told her he was deep in contemplation.

She found her heart beating faster, driven by a building curiosity. Maybe even a need.

"A simple thing," he said at last, his voice quiet. "Someone saying, 'I like you as you are. I want you to succeed. I won't ever harm you, not on purpose. Don't sacrifice the stars for me; watch them beside me.' In Pravish, the way to propose marriage translates as 'I want to be your equal.' If love does exist, I think it must be like that."

He glanced up, and sudden panic flashed across his face, like he'd said too much. In an instant, his scholarly focus was back, jotting notes, moving maps with purpose.

Without giving Eliza a chance to respond, he said, "You had a good intuition about the prison. It isn't easy to avoid a snake in Pravusat, so a prison cell was one option. Another is the palace. And here's a third—when we went to the kuveti, I sensed a snake underground, deeper than a burrow would have been. I suspect there are underground tunnels, maybe beneath the prison or maybe throughout the city. They would have to be constructed by Stone Casters, since regular delving this close to the ocean risks flooding."

Eliza nodded woodenly, her mind still replaying his words about love. Once out, he couldn't take them back, which he'd seemed to realize. Silas the love-hater had at least one romantic bone in his body, and the expression of it was more poignant than any poem Eliza had ever read, more real in its rawness and honesty.

Don't sacrifice the stars for me; watch them beside me.

Silas waved the archivist over and asked about tunnels beneath the university. The man talked about caves at the foot of the cliffs but denied any tunnels, though he was quick to point out other architectural marvels at the university, starting with the Yamakaz and making special mention of the music hall "right here in this building."

"If you haven't seen it, you simply must," he said.

Even distracted as she was, Eliza brightened at the thought of music. Then she forced herself to focus on the task at hand.

But Silas had already moved his weights and rolled the maps. "I know you want to see the music hall. I'm done here anyway, and we can't manage anything else tonight."

"It's not important," Eliza protested. "We can't afford to be distracted by . . . whims."

Silas blinked like she'd said something foolish. "You'd rather go back to the dorm and sit in the dark? Neither one will find tunnels, but at least music is said to spark ideas."

How did he manage to make anything sound reasonable?

"A quick peek," Eliza said, breaking into a grin.

Silas had been to the music hall before. It was an impressive, domed room, built without pillars to allow the most rhapsodic sound possible. The one performance he'd watched had been enchanting, but Silas didn't have time to sit through three hours of music when he could be studying instead.

Music echoed from the chamber, the distinct twang of strings belonging to the Pravish *kiyum*—a small harp with a backing board that rested on the musician's lap.

Eliza rushed through the doors, and Silas had to jog so he didn't get yanked along behind.

Once inside, the music swelled in volume, filling the domed room. Six students sat onstage, without instructor or audience. Merely a practice session. All the same, Eliza flew to the stage as if drawn by the most wondrous thing she'd ever heard.

One of the boys saw her and broke into a grin. His playing grew obviously flamboyant, full of unnecessary trills and showy gestures as he dragged his right hand rapidly down the strings and plucked with his left. Silas rolled his eyes.

When the music faded, Eliza applauded. "That was beautiful!"

"Would you like to try?" the boy offered, gesturing at his *kiyum*.

Eliza was in his seat almost before he could vacate it. The boy fitted tortoiseshell picks to her pointer fingers, then showed her how to brace her thumb and middle finger around them while holding her other fingers out of the way. Eliza listened, concentration knitting her brow, imitating each gesture he made. He kept his hands around hers while demonstrating how to pluck the seventy-plus strings, and then he stepped back, leaving Eliza to pluck notes on her own. She drew slow but strong notes that rang out over the stage, and the other musicians exchanged approving smiles.

"You're a natural!" said the boy. He tapped his chest. "Born with *kiyum* strings in the heart."

Eliza grinned. In Loegrian, she said, "I always loved the harp, but this is even better. Listen to the tones!"

It took Silas a moment to realize she was speaking directly to him. He managed a nod, a pleasant warmth spreading through his chest at her individualized attention.

She felt her way up and down the notes, falling into a rhythm that even Silas could hear. Soon enough, it transformed into a familiar song, a Loegrian children's rhyme.

Then Eliza started singing.

Silas blinked. He'd known the royal family was musically inclined—at least the queen was. He'd often heard his father complain about yet *another* musical exhibition at court. But Silas had spent more time in school than at court events, and if he'd ever attended an exhibition where Eliza had performed, he'd no doubt snuck a book in and read through it.

But he was focused now, listening to music pour like a waterfall from a girl who sparkled in the spray of it. The music itself was simple, yet her passion was the opposite, filled with depth and complexity.

She had all the other musicians beaming, and by the time she reluctantly returned the *kiyum* to its owner, he'd obviously assumed she was a new student in the music department.

"We'll see you in class," he said. "I look forward to it!"

Eliza blushed, ducking her head.

When she and Silas exited the building onto campus, the evening air had softened the sun's heat, and the university buildings carried the warm glow of sunset. From the corner of his eye, Silas noticed Eliza's fingers moving in front of her, still plucking notes.

"You should attend the university," he told her. "Study music. Clearly you have a talent for it."

She shook her head, scuffing her shoe against the ground. "Oh, I couldn't."

"Why not?"

"I just—I don't belong here."

He raised an eyebrow, glancing back at the arts building growing smaller on the path behind them, the dome of the music hall its most prominent feature. "You certainly belonged in there."

"Princesses don't attend university," she insisted.

"Oh, well, if it isn't what princesses do, then I see the problem. After all, princesses don't run away from home, travel across oceans, hide in foreign countries—"

"You are insufferable!" Eliza pushed him on the shoulder, laughing. Then she sobered. "It isn't what I want, Silas. It isn't my plan."

His shoulder tingled from the brief contact. Distracting. It took him a moment to find his words. "Plans can change, Eliza."

She stared at him until he realized he'd addressed her by name rather than by title.

Gripping his bag, he looked away. "Just think about it."

After a moment's pause, she whispered, "All right. I will."

CHAPTER 27

After looking for evidence of tunnels, Silas announced grimly that he was convinced they existed but his snakes couldn't find an entrance. His best guess was that it was *inside* the prison.

Which was when Eliza suggested sneaking into the prison, and, to her shock, he agreed.

They argued details all afternoon. They'd taken seats at one of the many tables in the Yamakaz, next to a window streaming sunlight, and the warm light on Eliza's skin made her feel confident and daring—though not quite daring enough to agree to some of the insanity Silas had in mind.

"You want *me* to be a snake?" she repeated, her legs tensing to run from the idea.

He lifted his shoulders, palms face-up on the table with his fingers laced. "How do you think I plan to escape the cell? A person can't fit through the bars, but a snake can, and since we're stuck together on everything, you'll need to be one too."

Eliza scooted her chair back until she was out of his reach. "You can turn *other* people into snakes?"

"If I draw their blood. So I'll need to bite you—while in my own viper form, of course."

Of course. It would be ridiculous if he bit her as a human, but it was reasonable if he bit her as a venomous viper. Ridiculous. *So very ridiculous.*

She opened her mouth, but he beat her to it.

"Before you start panicking about venom," he said, "I can control that. I'll dry bite."

"I'm not going to be bitten by you or anyone!" she shot back. "You can pick the lock on the cell. I wouldn't want to deprive you of practice for your special skill with doors."

"Assuming my lockpicks aren't confiscated, assuming my hands aren't bound, and assuming I can even reach the lock at any decent angle, your plan sounds splendid. If not, it'll have to be mine."

Before she could protest again, he cut her off.

"It's a good thing you're willing to do *anything* for your beloved Henry."

Eliza snapped her jaw closed. He was clearly taunting her, but even so.

"I am," she said defiantly.

"Then it's settled." Silas leaned forward with a crooked grin that had never looked so serpentine before. "All that's left is the crime. So how about it, Highness—shall we start a fight or a fire?"

"I knew you were a thug," she muttered.

"Fire it is, then."

"I don't want to risk hurting anyone. The kuveti already want to arrest me, so"—Eliza steeled herself—"I'll be the bait."

Silas raised his eyebrows, apparently impressed, and despite herself, she delighted in that.

Even if she was about to get herself thrown in prison. On purpose.

Clearly, Silas's thoughts followed the same track. "You know there's no guarantee," he said softly, his dark eyes fixed on hers. "We might take all this risk and not find either of them. Something might go wrong, and we won't make it back out."

Leaning forward on the table, Eliza folded her arms, hushing her voice. "You know, I'd almost think you're getting cold feet . . . if vipers had feet."

Silas groaned loudly enough to echo from the domed ceilings. He stood, pushing away from the table, and Eliza scrambled to follow, grinning all the way.

"No, no, you walk over there." He gave her a light push on the shoulder. "I don't want you near me."

She feigned a dramatic gasp. "It was just a joke, Silas."

"The worst joke I've ever heard."

"Maybe it will sound better in Pravish. *Engerek avaklari soguk* . . . uh, *yoktur*—"

"Stop." He groaned again. "It's so much worse. 'Cold feet' is an idiom, so you can't translate it literally. You sound ridiculous."

"Not as ridiculous as you talking about turning decent people into snakes."

She bit her tongue, wondering if she'd taken it too far, if they'd lose the humor, but Silas's shoulders held their easy, relaxed curve, and he kept one hand in his pocket as he walked, the other dangling near her, close enough to reach for.

Eliza forced her eyes back up to his face.

"At least I can translate mine in any language," he said, shooting her a glance with a raised eyebrow. In return, she gave him a smile.

But she'd killed her own mood. Her thoughts spiraled back to his earlier words. *Something might go wrong, and we won't make it back out.*

"I'll write a letter to Aria," she said. "In case everything goes horribly wrong."

She felt a twinge of guilt. When her sister had needed her, she'd fled the country, yet she was depending on Aria's help like always. It wasn't fair to her older sister.

But Silas said, "That's not a bad backup plan. Ransom from a queen."

At the very least, she needed to take that option for his sake, because it wasn't just her own safety on the line. And despite his faults, Eliza had no desire to see Silas trapped in prison.

Especially not a prison that had sent a string of magic users to the graveyard—at least one without *bones*.

"You won't let them know you have magic, right?"

"Obviously not," he said. "I want it to be a surprise when I slip through the bars, and I don't want to risk being slapped with a set of magic-restraining manacles, if they have those. I have enough on my wrist as it is."

Against her better judgment, Eliza reached for his hand. Just for a moment. She gave it a quick squeeze and released.

But her fingers continued to tingle long after she let go.

Silas insisted on scouting the prison more thoroughly and getting a better network of snakes in the area before entering. Since their last encounter with the kuveti had gone awry, he was determined to be careful about this one, and to his pleasant surprise, Eliza agreed. Though she was often reckless, she'd also shown a great capacity for planning and execution. She thrived with a goal to focus on.

The biggest difficulty was contingency planning—if they *didn't* find a tunnel entrance, they would need another escape. Leaving as snakes was better than trying to sneak out as humans, but even then, two adders coming out of the prison depths would be suspicious. The kuveti had experience with magic users, so Silas couldn't expect them to ignore a pair of animals out of place.

He needed help.

While in Kerem's office, Silas worked up the nerve to ask for it.

"I'm doing some . . . field research," he said tentatively, glancing at Eliza in the corner. She had her nose in her sonnet book. "And I need help with one small aspect."

Kerem laughed. He set aside his book and folded his arms on his desk.

"If you tiptoe any more than that," he said, "I'll think you're black-market dealing. What dangerous net are you entangled in? Say it plainly."

Silas sighed. "If a kuveti guard were bitten by a snake, how likely do you think it is they'd send for you to administer an antivenom?"

"Plainer than that."

In the end, Silas had to explain it all—the prison infiltration, the tunnels, Eliza's missing knight, and the magic stealer. Kerem listened with rapt attention.

"You're *certain*?" he asked regarding the magic stealing. "There have been countless experiments—"

"I'm certain," Silas said. "I've never felt anything like it. And if I can prove it, then I can stay here permanently."

Kerem nodded, leaning forward slightly, his expression showing the same eager grimness as when he sensed an upcoming breakthrough in an experiment. "Then let's prove it. I'll prep my antivenom kit."

A heavy weight vanished from Silas's mind. He had his contingency plan.

"Thank you," he said.

Standing, Kerem waved a hand. "Don't thank me. This is entirely selfish. I want to keep my research assistant." He gave a sly smile. "And I'd very much like to see that Artifact."

You and me both, Silas thought.

Eliza had been so impatient to put the plan into action, but when the day finally came, she had the unfair feeling it had ambushed her. Was she ready? Or was she going to make a mistake like she'd made the last time at the prison house?

Silas arranged for someone to tip off the kuveti, and then he waited with Eliza on a busy street between the prison and the market. He looked as calm as a breeze while Eliza couldn't stop fidgeting.

"You know, you could at least protest the idea of me being bait," she said, picking at a loop of embroidery on her shirt.

"Why? It was a clever idea." Silas kept his eyes on the street. They stood in the shadow of a wall, waiting for a signal from a pointy-nosed snake.

Eliza smiled to herself at being called clever. All the same, she said, "It would be the chivalric thing to do, not to let a lady endanger herself."

Silas snorted. "My other option was to get you involved in a fight. How is that more chivalric? Besides, I'm not a knight, and I'm not a lord. I'm just an academic."

For a moment, Eliza was struck by that statement and all its implications—*I'm not a knight.* Henry and Silas could not be more different.

She slid her hand into her pocket, finding it unnervingly empty. If she hadn't left them at the university, there should have been two items. One, the sonnet book with a pressed snowdrop flower inside. The essence of romance. The other, a square of leather-backed snakeskin that made her squirm to touch but protected her from sunburns. Silas had seen a need and addressed it. It was compassionate and thoughtful, just not in a romantic way.

Henry never would have allowed her to be arrested. Silas was going to prison right next to her. Which did she prefer, the romantic protector or the companion in adventure?

She shook her head fiercely, banishing the comparison, because it had no business existing in the first place. Henry was the clear champion in all things. She'd crossed an ocean for him.

And today, she was going to find him.

"Kuveti coming," said Silas.

Eliza tensed. She shouldn't have to do much of anything, really, except not run. A harder impulse to resist than she'd imagined.

Even in the shade, she was sweating. The humid air weighed on her skin, and the chaotic noise of the city buzzed in her ears. She strained to see the veiled guards on the street but couldn't spot them yet.

Silas stepped closer, and his hand brushed her shoulder lightly, spreading a shiver down her arm beneath the fabric. "Drop the wide-eyed stare, Highness. Pretend you don't notice them coming."

"How exactly am I supposed to do that? It's all I can think about." Nevertheless, she fixed her gaze on his, trying to ignore the pounding anticipation of her heart.

"I'd recommend a distraction. What's your favorite topic to discuss?"

"Music."

"Of course you'd choose the one area I'm not knowledgeable in."

"That's not true—you're also unskilled in sailing, or so I've been told. Otherwise you would have already sailed me home." They shared a brief smile, and then Eliza furrowed her brow. "Do snakes carry an aversion to water?"

"Once again, I'm not *actually* a snake. We share some attributes through a magical bond, that's all. And as a matter of fact, snakes enjoy water more than I do. Some even live in it."

Eliza scoffed. "'Some attributes, that's all.' You can transform *into* a snake. You have venom. You . . . you can even talk to them!"

"Nothing as entertaining as this conversation." Silas smirked. "I can give commands, if I'm strong enough, and they give impressions in return. It's magic and sensory input, not rational thought and language. Though I do sometimes use language to direct my own focus. I find it helps."

His smirk was contagious, but Eliza resisted. Instead, she eyed him, making a show of squinting. "What other abilities do you have, Snake Affiliate? Is your skin going to peel off without warning? Do you leave Silas husks behind?"

As she'd hoped, he laughed. He had a higher-pitched laugh than his voice, and it was always short, like it could only be startled out of him. It was delightful.

"No," he said. "No, my skin doesn't . . . In fact, even as a viper, I can't shed. Kerem has done extensive experimentation, and even when he remained in snake form for months, he couldn't shed. We don't grow or sustain damage the same way as natural snakes."

There was a small—very small—part of her that wondered what it would feel like to be something else entirely. To be full of magic that wasn't a curse.

She smiled. "Do you stick your tongue out all the time? Do you like warm rocks?"

"Who doesn't like warm rocks?" Silas stuck his tongue out at her.

It was Eliza's turn for a laugh, and in return, Silas grinned. She was always surprised to see that the venomous snake had a fun, playful side.

He could be charming sometimes. Perhaps more often than she'd likc to admit.

A shout went up nearby, and Eliza jumped. Silas tensed, but he kept his eyes on hers and gave a subtle nod. Neither of them ran as a set of kuveti guards rushed in to surround them. It had only been a pair grabbing Eliza the first time, but this time, there were six guards. Her panic spiked.

Silas brushed her shoulder again gently, and then he turned his attention to the kuveti, shouting at them in Pravish. He took a swing at the closest guard, who caught his arm and declared the arrest for both of them. Eliza was designated, once again, as the "missing island princess." It was humbling to realize that Pravusat didn't think of her home country as anything more than an insignificant island.

She could only hope the promise of a royal ransom would keep them from thinking of her as insignificant too. Otherwise, she didn't look forward to what awaited her in prison.

CHAPTER 28

From the moment the kuveti approached, Silas was careful not to use any magic. He'd warned Eliza about the possibility of magic-suppressing manacles, but he hadn't mentioned his concern that the ocean-eyed girl with her box was somehow one step ahead of him, lying in wait. Nor had he mentioned his deeper fear that he'd end today without any magic at all.

This was the third-worst day of his life. Second-worst, actually, because the reckless princess wasn't as bad as he'd first thought. He still couldn't believe she was accompanying him to prison, all for the slimmest chance she could save the boy she loved.

Maybe it was actually love. Maybe, amid all the recklessness that was *undeniably* recklessness, she was also the bravest person Silas had ever met. Crossing oceans, facing foreign lands, suffering capture—all for someone else.

Maybe the reason he liked to believe love didn't exist was because he was too selfish and cautious to ever brave something like that.

Or maybe he was feeling sentimental because he was being dragged to prison and didn't know if he'd come back out. At least not as himself.

The portcullis closed behind them with iron finality.

Eliza stumbled along with her head down, but Silas swept his gaze over everything, overlaying the real features he observed with the map layout he'd studied, looking for anything that didn't fit. Any oddity at all. He saw kuveti in their gray suits and black veils, and as they passed one room, he caught a glimpse of a few men in gold armor—part of the Nephew King's royal guard.

In a room filled with chests lining the wall, the guards gave them both a rough search. For Eliza's sake, Silas had tried to conceal his lockpicks well, but not well enough. A guard tossed them in a chest, along with the small dagger Eliza had insisted on bringing. She'd left her book of sonnets at the university, so at least that wasn't lost. It would have been a shame to waste a book on the kuveti.

"What do you do with prisoners?" Silas demanded of the guard on his right.

"Depends on the prisoner," the man responded, his eyes narrowing from behind his veil. Even without seeing the rest of the man's face, Silas could read the leer. The guard leaned in slightly and added, "If you'd like to avoid any unpleasantness, honored prisoner, you can always negotiate."

Silas didn't have the money for that—which they already knew from his lack of purse—and when it became apparent he wasn't going to make an offer, the guard huffed, tightened his hold, and resumed a silent march.

Eventually, they reached dividing hallways, and the guards attempted to drag Eliza down the right fork and Silas down the left.

"Careful—" Silas warned.

Both guard groups got yanked along with the prisoners.

"We can't be separated." Silas tugged on his right arm, trying to indicate the bracelet there. "That is, unless you can readily break a Stone Cast."

Two of the guards examined the bracelets, muttering foully.

"It's her fault," Silas added, glancing at Eliza. She rolled her eyes at him, though he could still see her fear in her stiff posture, her trembling arms. "She tried to make me her guard. It didn't work as planned."

"It won't be a problem if I break your wrist," the guard from earlier said, meeting Silas's eyes with his narrowed ones. Like a cobra with hood flared.

Instinct told Silas to retreat, to placate. But this wasn't like the first encounter, where he could walk away.

He drew himself up, puffed snake against puffed snake.

"Two bracelets," he said. "And if you shatter *her* wrist, it'll be your head next. The Nephew King wants to remain on good terms with Loegria, thanks to the new trade agreements. He won't defend a careless kuveti."

After a moment of tense silence, the guard barked an order, and both groups moved to the right.

The hallway they entered was lined with barred iron doors, each leading to a tiny, square cell except the one at the end, which opened into a large, rounded room. Although they were not underground, they may as well have been, since none of the cells had windows and the hallway was lit only by infrequent, shabby lanterns. The guards shoved Silas into the cell first, then Eliza.

"Enjoy the accommodations, Your Majesty," said the leader before locking the door.

Eliza lifted her chin primly. "It's 'Your Royal Highness,' actually."

Silas shook his head with a smile.

At a command from the main guard, the hallway emptied of all but one sentry, who took up his post down the hall, leaving Silas and Eliza essentially alone.

"Did I say it right?" she asked.

"*Lirinal* is a male 'royal highness.' You wanted *lirina et*."

"Rats."

"Oh, you saw those too." Silas pointed at the far side of the cell, where a skinny rat fled through the bars and into the hallway shadows. "This cell could use a snake."

Even in the dim, windowless light, the princess looked green. "Tell me you don't eat rats."

"Not a snake," he reminded her. In snake form, he didn't feel the urge to hunt for prey or to mate or anything else. He was himself just in a different form with new senses and awareness and a widened view of the world.

He walked the length of the cell, stooping beneath the low ceiling. Eliza had no such trouble, striding about as if she didn't even notice the roof pressing down on her head. She hesitantly touched a grimy wall, then shied away, rubbing her fingertips together. The lingering smell was unpleasant, but Silas tried to ignore it. It wasn't as if he'd be here long. They'd timed things to coincide with the shift change, so they only had to wait for the guard in the hallway to be swapped, and then, after removing the new guard, they'd have plenty of time to search before anyone discovered the attack.

Hopefully.

He picked a reasonably clean spot of stone and sat, tucking his legs beneath him. Eliza continued her anxious pacing.

"In Pravusat," he said, his eyes following her from one side of the cell to the other, "sonnets are sung, not recited. Did you know?"

Her steps faltered as she frowned at him.

He shrugged. "You said your favorite distraction is music, and it's taken me all this time to come up with something to say on the topic."

If he wasn't mistaken, she relaxed slightly. After a moment of staring at the hallway with its barely visible guard, she came and sat beside him, her knee brushing his so lightly, he shouldn't have noticed. Except he couldn't help but notice everything she did.

"I'd love to hear a demonstration," she said. A challenge.

"You're out of luck, Highness. I may know the cultural tradition, but that doesn't mean I have a list of sonnets memorized—though I'm sure *you* have several from your book at the ready."

"Eliza." There was something in her tone he couldn't read. "I wish you'd just call me Eliza."

That was dangerous ground. It was much easier to keep her at bay if she was a royal.

Even so, he said, "Eliza," letting each sound roll slowly off his tongue.

Her eyelids fluttered closed, and she drew in a long, slow breath. For a moment, his heart sped, thinking she was savoring the way he'd said her name, until he realized she'd been recalling one of her sonnets.

"*Love, my crown,*" she whispered, "*most precious gems within its settings gold; patience abiding, unceasing hope, and mine endurance bold.*"

Poetry within a prison cell. Idealism and reality colliding, irreconcilable.

Though Silas normally chose reality, he pushed away his awareness of the prison, focusing instead on the girl beside him, on the lilt of her voice as she recited. To better hear, he shifted closer, his leg pressing into hers in a line of thrilling warmth. She opened her eyes and leaned in to match him, imparting a sonnet like a secret.

Love, my armor, gleaming steel, the guard above mine heart;
To pointed axe and hardened falchion, ne'er will it part.
Love, my sword, a sharper blade will ne'erwhere be found;
Which severs lies, defends the truth, and holds me honor bound.
Love, my cup, and to it raised;
Drink deeply now and all my days.
For with thy love, a king I'll be;
And with my love, all's well with me.

Eliza's voice faded into poignant silence. Silas was close enough to count her freckles and the copper threads of her eyes.

"Beautiful," he whispered, the word nearly catching in his throat.

She lowered her eyebrows, taunting him, the smooth curve of her lips puckered in a frown. "But you don't believe in love like that."

"I don't." He allowed a slight smirk. "But I'll admit, a good poet makes it sound enticing."

She filled his passive senses—sight, smell, hearing—leaving his mind to wonder about the ones left out. Touch. Taste.

He swallowed heavily. "What's your favorite line, Eliza?"

She took a moment to think, her eyes studying his face. He wondered what she saw.

"The sword," she said softly. "Which severs lies, defends the truth, and holds me . . . honor bound."

Sword. He should have known. Of course it wouldn't be the crown; she didn't seem to care about being royalty at all. Not the armor, either, because she had no interest in defending herself. The sword, because Eliza fought for what she wanted, because she went on the offensive, even when her plans for doing so were irresponsible. She was a warrior.

Heart pounding, Silas closed the little distance between them, and she tilted her head in response. Her soft lips brushed his, so lightly it might have been another whisper of poetry.

Then something crashed in the hallway, startling them both upright. Silas held rigid, poised to transform, until he heard one guard berate another for carelessness.

The shift change.

Eliza scurried away, rolling to her feet and brushing dirt from her trousers with devoted franticness. No doubt she was grateful for the interruption.

He was too. Or at least he told himself so and refused to look back on the emotions of the last few minutes.

Standing, he peered through the bars at the guard, barely visible past the curve of the hallway. Thirty feet, maybe? Silas grimaced, then waved Eliza over. She approached hesitantly, eyeing him like he might suddenly kiss her again. But reality was back, present in the scent of a rotten cell and the shadows of dim lanterns along a gloomy wall.

Quietly, he said, "You'll have to lure the guard closer. I can't reach him if you're still in here. But wait until I've transformed and gone through the bars."

Eliza's eyes widened, and she whispered back, "What if he steps on you?"

He smirked. "Your concern is noted, but I'm faster than the average adder."

"And how do you expect to . . ." Dawning horror paled her cheeks. "Are you going to bite him?"

"Of course I'm going to bite him. Did you expect me to lick his boots?"

"Just a dry bite, right? You wouldn't . . . poison him?"

"A dry bite *will* get me stepped on, and it will do nothing to solve our problem. The only way I can take him down is with venom."

She grabbed his arm, her grip painful. "But you'll kill him!"

"He'll be sick for a while. Fever, aches, maybe a scar. But, no, I won't kill him. The important thing is paralysis. He can't give chase if he can't feel his legs, and he can't shout for help if his vocal cords are out of commission."

Together with Kerem, Silas had done an exhaustive amount of testing on his own venom. Unlike a natural snake's, Silas's venom could produce different effects, depending on his intention when he struck. Paralysis was the hardest effect to achieve, and when they'd first started, Silas had only been able to make it last a matter of minutes. With practice, he'd grown that to a full hour. It would have to be enough.

Eliza recoiled, pulling her hand back as if he'd bitten *her*. The look in her brown eyes hearkened back to the moment she'd first seen him transform. The moment she'd written him off as a monster.

Silas looked away.

"You can't do that," Eliza whispered. "It isn't right."

He clenched his jaw, thinking of the scar beneath it. Thinking of the way his father had looked at him, drained of color and affection, just before he drew his sword. Though Silas knew his eyes had changed to viper-red, he looked at the princess anyway, and she took another step back.

"Tell me, Highness, how it isn't right. Tell me how it's more unethical than any other option." He struggled to keep his voice low. "If I were to sneak up behind the guard and knock him unconscious by smashing a heavy object into his skull, would that be more humane? You're assigning moral superiority to one type of intentional injury over another. Were your beloved Henry here, in all his glorious knighthood, maybe he could challenge the guard to a duel. Then the guard would shout for help, and the entire prison would come down on us. Would that satisfy your sense of what's *right*?"

Silas flexed his hand, rippling a deep scale pattern across the knuckles, but since he'd spoken his mind, the emotion calmed. Or at least retreated beneath the surface.

Eliza had fallen silent. He could feel her gaze, but he refused to meet it, lest she bring the pain rushing back.

"I'm sorry," she said.

Silas frowned. Before he could stop himself, he was looking at her again, and her sad brown eyes were sincere.

"I didn't mean it like that," she went on. "Or at least, I didn't *mean* to mean it like that. I'm so . . . I'm so new to this, and shapeshifters were always—Affiliates, I mean. I don't . . ." Drawing in a shaky breath, she said, "It's not just the magic. When I was young, I was out in the field with my mother, and a viper killed my horse. That's why they scare me. So it's not *you*, it's just . . . history."

She gave a quiet little grunt, scrunching her freckled nose. It was almost cute. "Can you forgive me?"

Gill was the only person he knew who spoke like that—heartfelt, unguarded. He was the only person who ever asked Silas's forgiveness, and always for things that didn't need forgiving. Minor infractions compared to the rest of their friendship.

Was Silas friends with the princess? He wasn't sure, but somehow he couldn't convince himself to be enemies with her any longer.

"Are we friends?" he asked, trying to maintain a straight face instead of an awkward wince. Heartfelt conversation did *not* come naturally to him.

Eliza blinked. "Yes, obviously. I don't see how we could be anything else considering *this*." She gestured to the grimy prison encasing them, which was a good point.

Silas opened his mouth, then closed it. On a second attempt, he said, "I'm sorry about your past experience with snakes. You have a valid reason to be wary. As for the magic . . . The first rule of academia is learning to challenge your inherent beliefs. You've been raised in a country that taught you magic is evil, so you believe it in your core, regardless of truth."

"I don't mean—"

He cut her off. "I remember what that's like. It's my country too." He looked away. "I hated shapeshifters . . . before I was one."

Funny how a single day changed everything. At the time, he would have considered it the worst day of his life, but now he had enough perspective to regard it as one of the best.

"You've changed already," he said. "That matters. Keep at it." He drew in a quick breath, then added, "And thank you for the apology. That matters too."

Her eyes were shining, and his skin was itching. That was enough heartfelt confessions for now; it was crucial he keep his emotions under control.

Calmly, he said, "Now, if you would kindly offer a distraction, I'm going to bite a guard."

CHAPTER

29

I have money!" Eliza shouted in Pravish. "Please, I can't survive this prison!"

A little dramatic, but she'd panicked trying to remember *endure*, so *survive* was the best she had. She could play the wilting princess in the cage.

Silas had already slithered through the bars and was lurking somewhere in the shadows along the wall. She'd lost sight of his gray-and-black pattern almost immediately, and she shuddered on the guard's behalf.

Booted footsteps echoed down the hallway, approaching.

Eliza decided she was better off not watching what was about to happen, so she squeezed her eyes shut and tried to imagine the moment she would see Henry again. Though they'd only been apart a couple months, she had difficulty picturing him. Rather, she could imagine his adorable smile, his sun-kissed brown hair, his swirling hazel eyes, but there was a distance in it. As if he were someone she'd met long ago rather than the boy she intended to spend the rest of her life with.

She didn't like that distance. If she wasn't careful, she saw a silhouette in it, tall and broad-shouldered, looking an awful lot like Silas.

She'd almost kissed him. Or he'd almost kissed her. She wasn't sure which, but it had happened without either of them trying to break the Cast, without any reason except—

She couldn't finish that thought.

Inside, her heart pounded an accusation. *Whims. Whims.*

From beyond the cell, she heard a sharp grunt. Then a stumble and crash.

After a stretch of tense silence, she dared to peek, finding the guard sprawled across the floor, his limbs at awkward angles. At least she didn't have to see his face, since it was turned toward the wall. Silas was himself again, one hand on his jaw and a grimace on his face like it ached.

She couldn't believe he'd actually *bitten* someone. It felt strangely juvenile, probably because humans stopped employing biting as a reasonable disagreement solution by the time they could form sentences.

Apparently, she'd shifted from thinking him monstrous to thinking him childish. Eliza's lips twitched, picturing his scowl if she told him as much. But she didn't want to prod the subject if it was still sore. The way he'd looked at her before—after she'd said it wasn't *right*—would haunt her forever. It was like she'd driven a dagger through his back.

She would do anything to avoid making him feel like that again.

Silas approached the cell and crouched to peer at the lock.

It was then, with a dreadful, sinking feeling, that Eliza remembered the guards had taken his lockpicks.

"On second thought," she said weakly, her knuckles white as she clutched the bars, "you can just leave me here."

"Would that I could, *apta*." Silas rotated the wrist with his bracelet. Eliza regretted ever purchasing the infernal thing.

He made a valiant effort. The guard hadn't carried keys, but Silas used the man's dagger to prod at the lock, even as each passing second meant less time to find Henry. In the end, that was the tipping point, the thing that gave Eliza enough courage to face a nightmare.

"Just do it," she said, struggling to breathe past the tightness in her chest. "Make me a . . . snake."

She almost choked on the words.

Silas handed her the dagger through the bars. "Hold onto that. And don't stab *me*."

She tucked the leather sheath through her sash and tried to fill her head with thoughts of comforting sonnets, but it was hard to grasp any words past the fear. What if something went wrong and she never changed back? What if she was a snake for the rest of her life?

Tiny black dots fluttered at the edges of her vision as her breathing came faster and faster. She sat heavily, gripping the bars like her only anchor in a storm.

Silas knelt in front of her.

"Eliza, close your eyes." His voice was soft and soothing. He reached through the cage dividing them, resting his hands on her shoulders. "Trust me."

She squeezed her eyes closed, focusing on the sound of her name in his voice, replaying it like a favorite melody.

Silas's hands moved from her shoulders, sliding down her arms. With a light touch, he rolled back her left sleeve, but before she could start panicking about fangs in that arm, his hands moved again, lifting to her face. He tucked a strand of hair behind her ear, then brushed his fingertips like feathers along her cheek. A shiver traveled all the way down her spine.

While she was still tingling from it, his touch disappeared.

A moment later, pain stabbed through her arm, and she released a hiss of air through her teeth. It lasted only a moment before she opened her eyes—or maybe the magic had done that for her. Snakes didn't have eyelids, did they?

The world was bigger than it should have been. Far too big. The ground pressed up like jaws trying to close around her, but when she shrank from it, she could only curl in on herself, not stand. She had no legs. Above her loomed the prison bars and a human Silas. He looked strangely pale, even ill, his skin drained of its usual honey tones, his inky hair missing its rich depth. With gentle hands, he reached through the bars to pick her up.

Eliza squirmed. She opened her jaws, then snapped them shut again because she didn't want to bite him. She wanted to cry at how *wrong* everything felt—the shape of her own mouth, the way her body moved, the lack of any limbs to flail. She was herself, but she was all wrong, wrong, *wrong*.

Then the wrongness vanished, swirled away in a puff of mist. She was human again, kneeling next to Silas outside the cell. She choked on a sob.

Silas pulled her into his arms, rubbing his hands over her back, his touch firm but soothing along the curve of her spine. Eliza clung to him, burying her face in his chest, finding comfort in the steady rhythm of his heart. She realized he was murmuring words in her ear.

Her sonnet.

"Love, my sword," Silas whispered. "A sharper blade will nowhere be found. Which severs lies, defends the truth, and holds me honor bound."

Warmth fluttered through her chest, giddy little butterflies that banished the last vestiges of feeling like a snake. Eliza wriggled back in his arms, smiling up at him.

"Ne'erwhere," she said, pleased to be able to correct him for once. "A sharper blade will ne'erwhere be found."

"That's not a word."

"It's poetry. It's meant to create an impression."

"Well, it clearly made the wrong impression on me." With clear concern, he shifted his hands from her back to her left forearm, examining the spot where he'd bitten her. The twin wounds were smaller than she'd expected, red but not bleeding, barely pinpricks in her skin. "Are you all right?"

Eliza nodded slowly. She'd survived. And Silas had gone out of his way to make the experience as gentle as possible.

"Thank you," she whispered.

He lifted an eyebrow. "If you enjoy being a snake that much, I'll transform you anytime."

She shoved his chest, and he flashed a smug grin. Then he stood, lifting her along with him, his hands steady around hers.

"We don't have much time," he said, serious now. "Look for anything that could be a tunnel entrance—a trapdoor, a seam in a wall. Anything strange."

Eliza nodded again, and together, they crept down the hallway.

They searched without speaking. It was easy at first, since the guard Silas had taken out was the only one posted in this wing of the prison, and the other cells were empty. Clearly the kuveti had put their captured princess in the "luxury" area.

But once they reached the fork where the guards had initially tried to separate them, the prison took on more life, and they had to creep past inhabited cells, trying not to alert anyone who might shout for a rescue. Eliza couldn't look inside the cells; she wanted to throw the doors open, regardless of consequence.

Silas took down another guard—a close call, since the woman spotted Eliza a moment before Silas bit her. Luckily, the guard spent that moment in slack-jawed shock rather than in raising the alarm.

They found no trapdoors or any other signs pointing to an underground entrance.

Eliza saw Silas's lips moving as he murmured something soundless. Counting the minutes since the first guard went down?

If they never found the tunnel entrance, she would have to become a snake again. Silas had warned her briefly of his exit plan involving Kerem—where the professor would be called in by the kuveti to provide antivenom, and the two of them would escape as snakes in his bag. She hadn't allowed herself to think of it. They *would* find the tunnels. They had to.

A rat scurried past her heels, and she clamped down on a startled yelp. As she watched, the rat scampered into an empty cell, then squeezed through a hole in the wall and disappeared. Eliza squinted in the gloom, trying to better make out the space where it had vanished.

Hesitantly, she reached for Silas, but her fingers met air. She turned to find he'd slunk down the hallway, his head tilted as if listening to something.

A moment later, she heard it too. A familiar voice.

She crept with Silas to the corner.

In the next hallway over, standing beneath the greasy light of a dirty lantern, Iyal Kerem was arguing with a kuveti guard. It might have been a whispered argument to begin with, but Kerem's voice had risen.

"I want straight answers regarding his state!" he said sharply.

The professor looked frazzled. His half-tied hair was coming loose, strands of it catching in his spectacles.

Eliza and Silas exchanged a look. Nervous sweat beaded on her forehead. Had the bitten guard been discovered so quickly? If so, why had there been no commotion?

"You'll have to speak to Captain Galip," the guard said, his voice muffled compared to Kerem's.

"I've spoken to Galip, and he clearly intends to turn me in circles. I'm investigating the cells myself. If you don't want me to find anything that contradicts your story, you'd best tell your captain quickly."

Kerem strode forward.

Eliza ducked out of view, pulling Silas with her. A set of hurried footsteps marked the guard's retreat, while a slower, purposeful set approached them until Kerem turned the corner.

"You're early," Silas whispered, barely a breath.

Kerem shook his head, expression grim. "I'm glad I located you quickly. Something's happened. Let's go."

A shiver of despair trembled Eliza's legs. After everything they'd gone through, they couldn't surrender without finding anything!

Silas hesitated along with her, glancing deeper into the prison.

"Silas," said Kerem.

Shoulders drooping, Silas nodded.

Another rat scampered past Eliza's feet, disappearing into the empty cell. In a split-second decision, she caught Silas's arm and pulled him after her, ignoring Kerem's sharp whisper. He could choose to follow or not.

In the empty cell, she pointed out the rat-favored spot in the wall, and Silas felt along the stones before discovering a hidden catch. A door swung open on silent, oiled hinges.

Eliza bounced in place, hands clutched to her chest as she enjoyed a silent victory scream. Silas grinned along with her, then glanced back at Kerem.

"Go quickly," Kerem whispered.

For a moment, she thought that meant he wasn't coming, but when she and Silas slipped through the opening, Kerem followed, pulling the door closed behind them.

Eliza's eyes struggled in the nonexistent light. She reached out a hand, feeling blindly for the wall. She hit Silas instead. Without hesitation, he caught her hand in his, twining their fingers and guiding her forward. Her heart wiggled its way into her throat, putting an odd pressure on her breathing.

She stumbled a few times, but Silas walked with confidence, obviously possessing a better sense of direction in the dark. He led them to where the passageway opened up, and an almost-spent candle burned in a shallow alcove in the wall. Most of the curved ceiling and walls of the stone passageway remained shadowed.

"Did they find the guard?" Silas asked.

Kerem's eyes flickered down, and Eliza quickly dropped Silas's hand, though it left her fingers cold.

"Something else." The professor's voice was tight, and he swallowed before going on. "Iyal Mazhar. He missed our scheduled meeting yesterday. His neighbor saw him arrested by the kuveti—something about 'a magical disturbance.'"

The cold spread as Eliza remembered the names in Silas's journal, each arrested for the same thing.

The dead Stone Caster without bones.

Kerem gripped the strap of his bag, looking more frazzled by dim candlelight than he had in the prison. "I demanded answers of the guard captain, but there aren't any to be had. They insist he was never arrested."

Looking ill, Silas reached one hand down by his side, then halted, flexing his fingers. Reaching for his journal, Eliza realized. But they'd left everything at the university.

"Did you see him in the cells?" Kerem asked.

"No," Silas whispered.

"Well . . . that's a relief." Despite the words, Kerem's brow furrowed.

Silas opened his mouth, then closed it, clearly uncertain how to broach the topic of dead magic users. In his silence, Kerem surveyed the tunnels, adjusting his spectacles and squinting in the dim light.

"Iyl Yvette never mentioned these," he murmured, almost to himself. "She was the lead Stone Caster on the prison construction. Always bragged about the impenetrable spires on the roof, but she made no mention of underground tunnels." He reached out and brushed one hand down the wall, rubbing his fingers together. "These were clearly made by a skilled Stone Caster. I wonder how far they reach."

Likely all the way to the graveyard, Eliza thought with a ghostly chill.

"Let's find out," Silas said quietly.

CHAPTER

30

All of Silas's senses were on alert as they crept through the dark. While facing so many unknowns, he welcomed the addition of Kerem's abilities, but the professor's words had hollowed out a pit of dread deep in Silas's bones.

Iyal Mazhar arrested. A magical disturbance.

The pattern was undeniable. Using the kuveti, someone was targeting magic users. Had it started with Iyal Havva? For so long, Silas had considered the university a haven against Pravusat's darkest dangers, but now two professors had been targeted.

Iyal Mazhar wasn't one of Silas's favorites—too short-tempered with his students, too reminiscent of Silas's own father—but he was a brilliant mind who'd contributed greatly to his field, just like every professor at the university. Silas had worked on venom projects with him alongside Kerem, and the thought of the short, bearded Fluid Caster turning up as a boneless body made his insides slither down to his shoes.

The tunnel twisted gently. After a steep downward slope at the entrance, it had leveled out and remained flat, and thus far, it hadn't branched. Silas wondered if it would empty directly at the graveyard—a way for the kuveti to smuggle bodies they didn't want seen.

Every forty feet or so, a new candle in an alcove lit the path. Silas paused beside one, extending his hand to the wall.

"*Nirhaba,* friend," he said.

Behind him, Eliza jumped, grabbing his arm and looking around wildly, as if expecting to find a guard bearing down on them. Silas nodded toward the wall, and a thin snake wove through his fingers until it wrapped around his hand. Eliza sighed, releasing her death grip, and he wondered if it was the first time she'd ever been relieved it was just a snake.

Silas lifted the tiny snake to eye level. "Tell me what it's like down here."

The serpent flipped its tail back and forth across his pinky before releasing the squeakiest little hiss imaginable. A quick flicker of hazy images and impressions passed through Silas's mind, and he parsed their meaning.

Humans come and go. Scare out the spiders. Loud stomps. Dragging. Body stink. Big, big, big.

"Fascinating." Kerem leaned closer, lifting his spectacles. "It must survive on insects down here. Look at that—eyes so small they're almost nonexistent. You're accustomed to the darkness, little one."

"We're looking for two people." Silas sent an impression of the ocean-eyed girl and Henry. He couldn't hope for much, since Kerem was right about the snake's dim vision.

But the snake flicked its tongue. *Lighter feet. Pitter-patter. That way.*

After releasing the snake, Silas looked up, his nervous eyes meeting Eliza's.

"That way," he rasped.

The trouble was, there *was* no "that way." The tunnel continued forward—north, as far as Silas could tell—but the snake had indicated east. After searching for a moment, Silas found another catch in the wall, another secret door.

"Secrets within secrets," Kerem said, his eyes alight with the thrill of discovery.

"If we find the girl we're looking for," Silas warned, "don't let her . . . touch you."

Kiss you, he amended silently, but it was safe to assume that skin-to-skin contact was the catalyst and she'd only kissed him because it was more distracting and less aggressive than grabbing him by the throat.

Silas led the way into the branching passage. Eliza trailed behind, glancing over her shoulder as if afraid of being closed in.

The new space wasn't an ongoing tunnel but rather a connected set of small hollows, like a storage space, or an oversized snake's burrow. Candles burned in the corners, casting more light than the sparse guides in the main tunnel. There was no furniture aside from a few crates and a pair of thick rugs. A still form lay stretched out on one of the rugs, his back toward them.

"Henry!" shrieked Eliza.

She darted forward before Silas could stop her. He glanced around wildly, spotting a second person crouched in the farthest hollow, watching him from behind a crate. Silas recognized those panicked eyes. Blue as the ocean.

"Come out slowly," he ordered, feeling the itch of scales across his cheeks.

Eliza fell to her knees beside Henry, turning him onto his back. From this distance, Silas couldn't tell if he was breathing, but he could tell Eliza was crying.

The ocean-eyed girl rose slowly to her feet, still standing behind the crate as if it could protect her, even though it only came up to her knee. She held her hands up, palms out. They were empty.

Silas narrowed cold eyes on her. "Where's your box?"

She pressed her lips into a line, apparently determined not to speak.

Eliza whirled to her feet, pointing at the girl. "You! What have you done to him?"

Despite her grief, she managed the demand in understandable Pravish. Her language skills had improved by leaps.

Using magic, Silas reached out for any of the snakes he'd put into place before his arrest. He could sense a cobra overhead, which put them a few streets northeast of the prison. The magic stealer stood in front of a narrow, steep staircase that had been cut directly into the stone, which presumably led up into the city. He pointed the cobra in that direction, ordering it to make a threatening show in case the girl tried to run.

Kerem knelt by Henry, his fingers pressed to the pulse point at his neck. He tested his eyelids, before he declared, "*Tasumak*."

A Stone Caster's coma, a magical hibernation. Henry was alive.

"You're a Stone Caster," Silas said to the ocean-eyed girl.

She gave no answer. For the briefest instant, her eyes flickered toward another crate, shoved back into the deep shadows by the stairs.

"Eliza." Silas pointed at it. "Open that."

Though the princess cast an agonized glance at her fallen knight, she did as instructed. From the depths of the crate, she produced a familiar white box, holding it on her palm. She stood and took a step as if to bring the Artifact to him.

"Don't trust him!" the girl cried, speaking at last. "He killed my father!"

Silas blinked. Of all the various insults shot at him through the years, *murderer* was new, and it was more offensive than shapeshifter. Shapeshifter may have been vulgar, but at least it was accurate.

"What's your name?" Kerem asked gently, addressing the girl with the same calming presence he used on frightened snakes.

She swallowed, her eyes darting frantically between the three of them. "Ceyda Polat."

A shadow of grief crossed the professor's face. "You must be Havva Polat's daughter."

Iyal Havva. The first boneless Stone Caster.

Silas frowned. "I'm sorry for your loss, but I wasn't even in the country when your father died."

Finally, his trip home carried some good with it.

But the girl spat in his direction, her expression and tone dripping venom. "Shedskin!" she accused.

Eliza protested, her own expression fierce on his behalf. "Just because he's a snake—"

"*Shedskin* means liar," Silas explained, though the fact that Eliza would defend him for being an Affiliate meant more than he could say.

"You were in the country." Ceyda's voice cracked, and her hands, still raised, shook with tremors. "Is this a show for your friends? Are you going to pretend we haven't met twice already?"

"We've met *once*, when you—"

"Of course you won't admit the first—when you dumped my father's body."

Silas frowned, looking to Kerem for any kind of explanation.

"From what I heard," the professor said quietly, "Havva was dead long before his body was discovered. Since he was on a research leave, no one was looking."

"I didn't even know him!" Silas protested. "I took my Stone Casting classes from Iyl Yvette. I'd never heard Iyal Havva's name before I saw the memorial at his office door."

Ceyda surged toward him, and despite himself, Silas jumped back a step.

"I saw the vial of venom! It was labeled with your name: *Silas Bennett*. Father said it was part of an experiment, told me not to ask questions . . . and then he didn't come home." She shook her head. "I searched. I waited. *Days* without anything. Then, one night, when I saw the kuveti coming, I hid in Father's study, crouched in a cupboard. I couldn't see clearly, but I *knew*. When they didn't search the house, just silently unloaded a cart, I *knew* what they were unloading. I knew why they'd come to his study, why they carried something heavy to the table. Only someone who was part of his experiment could have led them there."

"I wasn't there!" It was the only objection Silas could offer, his mind spinning with the implications of what Ceyda was saying.

"There was only one person with the kuveti. I may not have seen your face, but I know it was you. And when you set your bag beside the cupboard while you stole whatever you wanted from his study, I saw the Artifact inside. I knew it was made of bone—Stone Casting. I knew it didn't belong to you, so I took it back. It was only after you left and I could see my father that I realized, he . . . he didn't have . . . I realized it was . . ."

Her blue eyes dripped tears, but she only glared with fiercer heat. "You used my father's bones to make your Artifact, and I only wish I could have used it to kill you."

When she turned to run, Silas couldn't react. Kerem stood, reaching as if to catch the girl, but she dodged around him. She lunged at Eliza, clearly trying to retake the Artifact, but the princess was faster, ducking behind the crates, and Ceyda apparently thought it better to escape without the Artifact than not at all.

She dashed up the stairs and out of sight. There was a bang like she'd thrown open a trapdoor.

Too late, Silas remembered the cobra. "Wait—"

A sharp, high-pitched scream echoed down the stairs.

Silas's blood ran cold. He jolted into motion at last, running up the stairs and emerging into a narrow alley crossed with overhead laundry lines. A black cobra sat poised among the cobblestones, hood flared and fangs exposed. Ceyda had fallen to the ground before it. Blood marked a puncture site just above her ankle.

"Don't move," he ordered her.

She curled her lip at him, and then she scrambled away.

Silas swore. Before the cobra could bite her a second time, he stepped forward, focusing on a command to halt the strike.

Unfortunately, a sharp yank on his bracelet interrupted his focus and made him stumble. He'd reached the end of his leash with Eliza.

The cobra struck, pumping venom into his leg.

Eliza had imagined so many reunions with Henry Wycliff. She'd imagined finding him at an inn, watching his hazel eyes widen from across the room as they focused on her, then running to meet him halfway and throwing herself into his arms. She'd even imagined him trapped in a kuveti prison cell, imagined rescuing him from the dark.

She'd never imagined a reunion where she couldn't speak to him. Where he lay unconscious in a dark cave, the victim of a sleeping curse.

Ceyda ran, and Eliza wanted to follow, wanted to wrestle answers from the girl and force her to undo the magic on Henry. But she hesitated, unwilling to leave Henry's side.

She hesitated too long.

The yank on her bracelet finally gave her the push needed, and she staggered up the narrow staircase, only a few steps behind Iyal Kerem. She expected to find Silas with a trapped Ceyda. Silas was so good at everything, it didn't cross her mind that he might fail. That he might get injured.

And never from a snakebite.

With a sharp gesture, Kerem banished the cobra, sending it slithering down the alley. Silas stood with an ashen face, breathing raggedly. Blood stained the cuff of his pants, dripping down into his ankle-high boot. When Kerem told him to sit, he lowered himself slowly, favoring his injured leg. The professor crouched beside him and rolled back his pant leg.

The twin-puncture wound was so much bloodier than the little pricks on Eliza's arm. The skin around it was already beginning to discolor and swell.

She remembered Kerem's comment about venom on skin. *Tissue will rot, even with magic beneath.* She thought of Henry, already unconscious. She didn't know if he would wake up, if he would be all right.

Not you too, she willed Silas.

"You should have let it bite her the second time," Kerem said, exasperated.

"I should have," Silas agreed through clenched teeth.

Fishing in the bag by his side, the professor said, "I'm not prepared with a cobra antivenom, but I have something general for elapids. It will have to do."

"Eliza?" Silas's voice was low.

It took her a moment to shake off the daze, to meet Silas's eyes, and then everything inside her shrank.

"I'm sorry," she said. She'd felt the yank on the bracelet, and she knew this was her fault. There was no way Silas would have gotten himself bitten by a cobra, not without her limiting him.

He waved off the apology, pointing at the Artifact still clenched in her hands. "I want a look at that."

Of course. Even bleeding on the ground, his first priority was research. Eliza was tempted to throw the box at him. Instead, she knelt by his side and handed it over.

Kerem unpacked supplies from his bag. He cleaned the wound with steady hands. "Without a Fluid Caster's help, I can't spread the antivenom through your blood quickly, so it will be a slow battle until the cure wins out. You should avoid fever, thanks to quick treatment, but the wound will continue to burn for several hours, and it will take longer to heal."

"Got it." If anything, Silas focused even more intently on the box, turning it and tracing his fingers over the carved black symbols. Perhaps he was using it as a distraction from the pain.

Eliza couldn't do anything about the wound, but she could help distract him. "Is that Cronese?"

"You remember." Silas glanced up with the faint echo of a smile, which quickly turned to a grimace. He drew in a sharp, pained breath. "I'll have to translate it with a dictionary. I recognize the symbols, but I don't know their meaning. *This* is definitely new since my first glimpse."

He showed her a deep crack in one edge where the box had split, as if someone had taken a hatchet to it.

Kerem finished wrapping Silas's leg and knotted the bandage, eyeing the Artifact carefully.

"Blood," he said, pointing to a set of symbols on one side. "And over there, bone."

"I miss my journal," Silas bemoaned, handing the Artifact off to his teacher. "Any others?"

Rotating it slowly, Kerem listed the rest. "Flesh. Soul. Bind. Unbind."

"Shouldn't the opposites negate?"

"One would assume." Kerem frowned. "I can't sense much from it. Perhaps because I'm not a Stone Caster."

"Or it could be that big split in the side." Silas adjusted himself on the ground, hissing air through his teeth. He shook his head. "Never as many answers as questions."

Kerem smirked. "The first rule of discovery. And you stay off that leg. In fifteen minutes, I can do a second application of antivenom and change the dressing. Then you can walk, with help."

"I don't need a second dose." Silas nodded toward the mouth of the alley, curtained by laundry drifting gently on the overhead lines. "I need you to go after Ceyda. If she keeps running on that leg, she'll kill herself."

"I doubt I can find her." He didn't seem that enthused about making an effort.

"You can try!" protested Eliza. She struggled and failed to find the right words, so she added in Loegrian, "Don't you care that she's your friend's daughter?"

Silas was gracious enough to translate the question for her.

Kerem met her gaze evenly, his dark eyes shadowed behind his spectacles. "When you live in a country of turmoil, you lose friends. And their daughters. That's the reality of it."

"Then change the reality," she shot back.

He looked away, giving a faint, melancholic smile. "I'll see what I can do."

Leaving a few supplies, he packed the rest and stood. Before he left, Silas touched his leg, pausing him.

"Who had access to my venom?" he asked quietly.

"Myself," said Kerem. "Iyal Mazhar, for the dehydration project. Iyal Afshin, for all research approvals."

"Not Iyal Havva?"

"Not to my knowledge. Unless someone broke into my office."

Eliza remembered how easily Silas picked the lock on the door. Based on his frustrated expression, perhaps he was thinking of that too. He sighed.

"Fifteen minutes before you walk," Kerem said sternly.

Then he disappeared through the laundry lines.

CHAPTER

Eliza went back to check on Henry. There was no change, but at least he didn't seem to be in pain. His face was relaxed in a sound sleep, his lips slightly parted. The layer of dark stubble along his jaw looked strange, since Eliza had never seen him in a state other than attending court. She longed to see his hazel eyes open, longed to hear her name in his voice.

A rat scurried from among the crates, coming to sniff at Henry, and Eliza shooed it fiercely away. If only it were so easy to protect him from other things, like magic.

Reaching out, she smoothed his shoulder-length hair where it had splayed on the rug, tucking it against his neck. His clothing was still Loegrian, a buttoned shirt beneath a vest. He always wore his shirt untucked, so she couldn't blame that on travel, but the dirt and grime was a different story. One sleeve was rolled above his elbow; the other had been cut with surgical precision in the same spot. Eliza remembered the sister at the Sarazan tabernacle talking about a wound, and she ran her fingers gently down his forearm, tracing a long mark that had already turned into a fading scar. The sisters must have accelerated the healing.

In a desperate hope, she leaned close to his ear and whispered, "Wake up, Henry. Please."

But he slept on, and finally, she returned up the stairs to Silas.

"How is he?" Silas asked, glancing up from his study of the Artifact. He'd scooted himself to the alley's edge, resting his back against one of the two buildings enclosing their space. A middle-aged laundress gathered hanging sheets into a basket near the alley's entrance, shooting them both suspicious glances and ignoring Eliza's wave.

Eliza sighed, seating herself next to him. "I don't think he's hurt, but he's just . . ."

"*Tasumak*, which is much better than shipwrecked. I can fix it, once I can actually walk. I'm no Stone Caster, of course, but every Cast has a means to unravel it, and some are consistent. Yvette made me memorize a list."

A wave of relief washed away the tension that had knotted her insides since the moment they'd found Henry.

They'd *found* Henry. After all this time, all the effort . . . they'd found him.

She wrapped her arms around herself, feeling a strange tingle from head to toe. It was like her whole body was still trying to process this new reality.

"I'm sorry," she told Silas again, glancing down at his bandaged leg. "If I'd followed you right away, you wouldn't have been hurt."

"I'm the one who poised a cobra to strike. In terms of fault, I carry more than you." He ran one hand over the bracelet, and when he spoke again, his tone sounded strained. Perhaps a result of the pain in his leg. "Now that we've found your beloved Henry, Yvette can take care of the leash between us."

Eliza didn't know what to say, so she just nodded. She'd achieved her goal, but it still didn't feel real.

It wouldn't feel real until Henry was awake.

Silas set the Artifact down at last. It looked out of place—stark black symbols and clean white edges against the battered sandstone cobbling the ground. Without knowing it was a thing of magic, Eliza could have guessed.

"She said this was made from her father's bones," Silas murmured.

Eliza inched back from it. The polished white took on a different shade, unnerving to look at. "Do you think it is?"

"Why not? Magic works in blood, bone, flesh, and soul. Four words on the box."

"Who would . . ." Eliza couldn't finish the thought.

Silas looked up at her, his bangs shadowing his dark eyes. "I didn't kill Iyal Havva. I've never killed anyone."

He said it with a quiet desperation, like he worried she believed differently, but it had been a long time since Eliza had thought of the boy at her side as a murderous shapeshifter. She knew him better now.

"I know." She gave his hand a quick squeeze that left her fingers warm. To distract herself, and to tease him, she raised her eyebrows and added, "Just be careful when you become a professor. There's a very real chance you might bore some poor student to death with a lecture about the influence of Stone Casters on Pravish architecture."

He scoffed, clearly trying to appear more offended than his twitching lips allowed. "I'll have you know I intend to be a greatly sought-after professor, with every lecture hall filled and a long wait list for my classes."

"Oh dear, oh dear." Eliza shook her head, clucking her tongue. "So many students, gone so young. May they rest in peace."

"How dare you."

"Iyal Gravestone, they'll call you. Or Iyal Deathsgate. Iyal—"

He took a swipe at her, and she leaned away, giggling. But he hissed at his own movement, scrunching his face in pain and straightening again. A slow, deep breath lifted his chest.

"Are you—?"

He cut her guilty question short. "It'll heal. That's what wounds do."

She couldn't help glancing at the scar on his neck. A murder attempt from his own father—could such a wound really heal? Or was it a surface illusion with pain still aching beneath?

Eliza tried to find the words to tell him how strong he was, how much he inspired her, how sorry she was for misjudging him in their first days together. But in the end, she only said, "If you transform, would that heal it?"

He snorted. "If only. I wouldn't have a wound in my snake form, which would be helpful for pausing blood loss, but I'd still feel the physical strain, and injuries are taxing on my magic. I wouldn't be able to transform for as long. With a more severe injury, I wouldn't be able to transform at all."

"Guess we'll have to heal it the regular way, then."

Eliza grabbed the supplies Iyal Kerem had left behind, and she set to work changing the wrapping on Silas's leg. He grabbed her wrist, protesting, but she shook him off.

"Sit back, Iyal Deathsgate. I may be an uneducated princess, but I at least know the basics."

Silas tried to think of what to say to Eliza, but for once, his mind failed him. There was too *much* to say, all of it tangled ideas and feelings that couldn't find their way into a proper language. As a result, he sat stiffly while her soft, gentle hands wrapped his wound. His leg burned like someone had stabbed a hot poker through his calf, though Eliza's cool fingers against his skin and her fierce concentration wrinkling the freckles across her nose made a decent distraction.

Until, at last, she finished, and Silas picked up the Artifact and pushed his way up the alley wall, testing his weight on his injured leg to stand.

"How is it?" She held her hands slightly raised, like she was ready to catch him if needed. The mouse catching a falling viper was comical enough to make Silas smile.

"Stings like Sarazan's fangs," he said. "But I'll live."

He knew what she'd want him to turn his attention to. Slowly, he limped his way back down the stairs to Henry Wycliff.

"Still have your dagger?" Silas extended his hand, and, in response to Eliza's sharp glare, he added, "Don't worry. I'm not going to stab your beloved."

He pricked the small outer hollow where Henry's hand met his wrist, squeezing out a drop of blood. The fascinating thing about Casting was that the types were intertwined: Stone Casting rested in the bones but could often be undone by blood drawn in the right way, and Fluid Casting rested in the blood but could sometimes be undone by breaking the right bone.

Understandably, not many people tried undoing Fluid Casts without the assistance of an actual Caster.

Henry stirred, and Silas backed away, resting on a crate with his injured leg stretched out in front of him. Eliza knelt by Henry's side, her hand hovering above his shoulder, as if afraid to touch him.

"Henry?" she whispered.

Slowly, the knight blinked his eyes open, and his gaze wandered a hazy path before landing on Eliza. Then he stared. Mouthing wordlessly, he pushed himself up on his elbows.

Only to be knocked back down by Eliza throwing her arms around him with a delighted shriek.

Despite himself, Silas remembered the morning she'd climbed into his bed, afraid of earthquakes. If he could relive it now, he wouldn't sleep, wouldn't miss a moment of having her that close to him.

To what end? he asked himself.

Henry managed to sit up again, pulling Eliza with him, and his return hug was so forceful, Silas could see the strain of knuckles through skin. A decent person would give them a moment of privacy for this reunion, but he was trapped by both his leg and his bracelet. He tried to study the Artifact again, but the black symbols slid together as his vision refused to focus.

"Eliza, what are you doing here?" Henry asked hoarsely.

Eliza was crying, clutching his face with both hands. "I thought you were dead. As soon as I reached Pravusat, the first news I heard was your shipwreck. They said there were no survivors. Then I went to the tabernacle, and they'd seen you, but I wasn't certain. Everything was so confusing and overwhelming. We searched *everywhere* and—what are you doing here? Who was that girl? How did you—"

Every word tumbled faster until she was scarcely coherent. A few scattered words even came out in Pravish, and Silas wondered idly if she was dreaming in it. Yvette had once told him the mark of absorbing a language was when it bled into dreams.

"I—" Henry stammered, clearly trying to parse the barrage. His eyes moved from Eliza for the first time, landing on Silas.

Silas lifted his fingers from the Artifact in a half-hearted wave.

"Lord Silas? You're here too?" The knight blinked hard, as if expecting what he saw to change.

"Lord?" Eliza repeated with a frown.

"Just Silas." Now wasn't the time to discuss the details of his disinheritance, so he said only, "I live here. Here in Izili, not here in the dank, underground tunnels, obviously."

Perhaps he should have explained more. Perhaps it would have erased the betrayal in Eliza's eyes.

"You know each other?" She directed the question at Henry, her gaze cutting sharply back to him.

"We've crossed paths at the Reeves estate." Henry shook his head, still looking dazed. "He was always reading. For the longest time, I thought he was Baron Reeves's brother. Until Baron said they were friends."

Brothers was accurate enough, at least in an emotional sense. Even at the mention of Gill, Silas felt a stab of longing for what he'd left behind, what he'd never have again. Plenty of things could be replaced in life, but not people. That was why it was so dangerous to forge relationships in the first place.

He looked down at the flat yellow band encircling his wrist, binding him to a girl who had her attention on someone else.

"It isn't safe here," he said abruptly. "We don't know who else Ceyda is in league with or who else knows about this place, and the main tunnel is a highway for the kuveti. We can talk at the university."

With more effort than it should have taken, he managed to stand and maneuver himself back up the stairs. Eliza fretted over Henry, who kept assuring her he was uninjured, just weakened. He must have been under the *tasumak* for an extended period. Once he came back to his full senses, he'd be ravenous.

Out on the street, Silas flagged down a cart puller to take them to the university. The three of them piled into the back of the wooden cart, and Silas clenched his teeth, bracing himself for the long, bumpy ride over uneven streets.

Though, somehow, it wasn't as uncomfortable as watching Eliza snuggle up to Henry's side, resting her head on the knight's shoulder.

Under Silas's directions, the cart puller left them at the healing hall, one of the outermost buildings on campus. Both a Fluid Caster and a non-magical physician looked him and Henry over, though the knight remained tense the entire time. Based on his comfortable mention of Gill—"Baron," as most people called him—Silas hadn't expected Henry to be wary of Fluid Casters. Perhaps he was still disoriented from the sleeping Cast.

"I'm sorry I can't do anything to speed the antivenom," said the Caster on duty after she finished examining Silas. "Circulation Casts cause harm if not done right, and I'm a first-year student. Once Iyal Mazhar or Iyl Daria come in for a shift, I could send for you."

Silas declined. Given enough time, his body would reach the point where it had to heal on its own anyway, and the tea she had given him had eased the pain.

He hesitated, then asked, "Has there been any word on Iyal Mazhar? I'd heard he was . . . missing."

The girl frowned. "He skipped his morning shift, but no one's told me more than that."

"Never mind." Silas thanked her again and exited.

He took Henry and Eliza to the dining hall, where they managed to catch the last scraps of the evening meal. As predicted, Henry inhaled everything available, including half of Eliza's plate after she insisted for the third time that she was full. But he acted strangely while he ate, hunching his shoulders as if trying to ignore everyone else in the room, flinching when the staff turned any attention on him. He'd acted the same way with the healers.

Silas had a sneaking suspicion why, but he wasn't about to address it in public.

The dorm had never felt farther away, and though the Caster's tea had eased the burn in Silas's leg, he still limped. He tried to focus on the light fading from the sky, the layers of gray clouds painting long streaks across the darkening ocean in the distance. It was almost unbelievable how much had happened in a single day—their planned arrest, the torturous search in prison, everything in the tunnels.

He'd transformed Eliza into a snake only hours ago. The memory of her trembling in his arms was sharp and fresh, as was her smug expression when she corrected his sonnet and the warmth in her voice when she thanked him.

Now that she had her beloved Henry back, how long would she stay? Probably not a moment longer than it took Yvette to break the Cast.

Silas found himself suddenly hoping Yvette would take an immediate, possibly indefinite research leave.

CHAPTER

32

The tiny dorm had felt cramped with two people, but three made it so they couldn't close the door without shifting someone out of the way. Henry sank onto the cushion, pressing his back to the wall. Eliza stepped over his legs and wedged herself into the space between him and the dresser while Silas perched carefully at the end of the bed.

An awkward silence fell. Eliza fidgeted. Should she talk? Or wait? Her self-restraint finally cracked.

"Henry, what happened to you?"

Henry picked at his healed arm. He gave a small toss of his head, moving his hair back only for it to slide across his shoulder again.

Silas sat without moving, legs stretched out in front of him, crossed at the ankles with his injured leg propped up. There was no tension in the gentle slope of his shoulders. He didn't ever seem bothered by silence or emotion.

It took an eternity for Henry to speak, and Eliza clenched her jaw tightly to give him that time. She remembered his overwhelmed face when she'd first spoken to him in the tunnel.

"Well, you know the first bit." Henry tried for a smile that quickly faded. "I was banished from Loegria, and I got on a ship to Pravusat."

"A ship that sank." Eliza's chest tightened, making it difficult to breathe.

Henry flinched. "Yeah."

He continued picking at his faint scar, his worn clothes, his growing stubble, until Eliza felt the need for more information like snakes crawling across her skin.

Finally, she prompted, "You washed up at the tabernacle?"

Silas shot her a disapproving frown, and she glared back. What did he even care about Henry's situation? He'd had to be chained into helping her—even though he was a member of court who'd actually *known* Henry, spent time with him.

She couldn't fight the sting of that revelation. She'd asked Silas if he had any relation to Viscount Bennett, and he'd claimed he wasn't the man's son. Was his disdain for royalty so great that he'd also sworn off the entire court? Was that why he'd refused to help Henry until forced into it?

Henry nodded. "It's sort of a blur. Anyway, um, thanks for—"

"You don't have to lie," Silas said quietly, his dark eyes piercing. "You have nothing to be ashamed of."

Eliza looked between the two of them, trying to read the unspoken. Silas clearly knew something, or thought he knew something. He always thought he knew something.

"I don't know what you mean," said Henry. But his fingers were shaking, and he folded his arms across his chest, pulling one knee up like a shield.

"Here's my theory." As Silas spoke, he kept his relentless gaze pinned on Henry. "Ceyda blamed me for her father's death. She came after me but failed. So she followed me back to Loegria only to lose me there, a blessing I'll ascribe to my antisocial tendencies and her ignorance of the country. Discouraged, she returned home on a ship that happened to be carrying you. Something happened on that ship—either to cause the shipwreck or in response to it. Whatever it was made you interesting enough to her that she took you to the Sarazan healers rather than walking away."

After a meaningful pause, he added, "I can guess what made you so interesting to a girl who can steal magic. Should I go on, or would you rather say it yourself?"

Henry stared down at his lap, shoulders curled in, all of him closed off like a shuttered window. Eliza wanted to tell Silas to back down, but before she could, he spoke again.

"Maybe this will help." Gripping the bedpost, he pushed himself to his feet, weight on his good leg.

And then he puffed into a cloud of gray mist, dissipating around a black-patterned viper, its red eyes trained on Henry.

Eliza remembered screaming when she'd first seen that transformation, how terror had iced every bone, freezing her in place. She wanted to smack Silas for inflicting it on Henry without warning.

Except Henry didn't scream.

He was pale and wide-eyed, but it didn't seem to be from terror. If anything, he released a gusting breath . . . of relief?

Turning human again, Silas eased himself back onto the mattress. He crooked his fingers in Henry's direction, encouraging him to speak.

Henry opened his mouth but closed it again, like whatever it was couldn't get past his throat.

Eliza's insides slunk behind her spine, trying to avoid where she finally realized this conversation might be going.

"You had a rage transformation on the ship," Silas said quietly. "Right?"

Henry swallowed. Finally, he rasped out, "Is that what they're called?"

"Well, if you want the Pravish term, it's *kemik kirmasi*—the flesh rip. Makes it sound a lot more gruesome than it is. I'd say 'rage transformation' makes the point well enough. I adopted the phrase from a Cat Affiliate I know."

Henry shook his head, rubbing his arms like he was trying to find warmth. "You're so calm. You're . . ."

"Six years into this," said Silas. He lifted an eyebrow. "And you're—let me guess—one single transformation?"

Eliza licked her lips. She waited for Henry to deny it, but he looked down and away, his hair shadowing his eyes.

When he spoke, his voice was fragile, wavering. "While we were on the ship, I kept thinking about . . . my family, my future, my . . . and then, suddenly, I wasn't . . . myself."

He shot one fleeting glimpse at Eliza, and she tried too late to look comforting, but he'd already turned away. Did he see anger in her face?

She'd come to accept Affiliates through Silas, and there wasn't any magic in the world that could make her love Henry less, but all the same, it felt *unfair*. Just months earlier, Henry had been a normal knight, winning a tournament, grinning for the world to see. Even if magic didn't make someone a monster, it still changed them.

Seeing Henry now, small and ashamed, obviously hurting, how could she not feel upset for him?

Silas nodded. "Animal Affiliates are driven by emotion. When we feel too much, it triggers a transformation. You'll get better at controlling that, but to a certain extent, you also have to learn to live with it."

"Were you one all along?" Henry stared at Silas in awe. "All those times at the Reeves estate when you sat on the sofa reading a book and eating Leon's pastries like . . . like . . ."

"Like a regular person?" Silas asked dryly. "I *am* a regular person, and so are you."

Henry laughed. A harsh, cracked sound, devoid of any actual humor. "I'm a *shapeshifter*. I can't— Even without the banishment, I can't ever go home. My brothers, my parents . . . they'd . . ."

Eliza's heart twisted at the raw pain in his voice, and she reached for his hand, but he flinched at her touch. Slowly, she withdrew, resting her hands in her lap.

She glanced at Silas and caught him touching the scar on his neck before he lowered his hand in the same way.

Silas's father had tried to kill him. Would Henry's father do the same if he knew the truth?

She couldn't imagine that. Lord Wycliff was part of her father's Upper Court, and she often saw him at the castle. He dressed brightly and laughed easily. Aria said he had a level head when offering suggestions in the king's council. When Henry had won the tournament all those weeks ago, Lord Wycliff had come right out of his seat cheering his second-youngest son.

Would all of that vanish just because of magic?

Had it vanished for Silas?

Eliza swallowed. The tiny dorm felt smaller than ever, her legs cramped, the dresser pressing from behind.

Silas's voice broke the silence. "My first transformation happened at Fairfax."

Henry lifted his head, blinking.

"That's where you went to school, too, isn't it? If you're eighteen, you and I would have overlapped a year. I was arguing with Professor Harrison—you remember him?"

The smallest twitch moved Henry's lips. "Impossible to please."

Silas scoffed. "Stone-headed is a better term, and wrong about most of what he teaches. So you can see why we were arguing."

Eliza couldn't help teasing, "Are you sure you don't think that about all your professors?"

"Hush," said Silas. The gloom in the dorm lifted a little. "Professor Harrison was trying to claim that Loegria's biggest export was precious metals, even though Patriamere has twice as many mines as we do. It's actually wool, just so you know—Loegria is full of sheep. Take all the meaning from that you'd like."

Eliza reached up to jab him in the arm, and he cracked a smile.

"Anyway, it got heated," he said, "because he was wrong and wouldn't rescind, and I was right and wouldn't let the falsehood stand. My anger rose, and my skin started itching. I ignored it; I was too focused on the argument."

Henry stared in horror. "You transformed in front of Professor Harrison?"

"I didn't, actually." Silas's voice quieted, and he drew in a breath like he was gathering details of a memory he didn't often revisit. "You only ever saw me at the Reeves estate. I practically lived there during the summers, because Gill was my best friend. We met at Fairfax, months before this event. *He* noticed what was happening to me. He knew the signs. So he strong-armed me out of the room just in time, shoved me into a closet, and then locked himself in with a hissing viper."

When Eliza had first suspected her sister was in love, she'd known it had to be someone special. Even more so when she found out he was a Caster. But apparently Guillaume Reeves—or *Baron*, as Aria said was his preferred nickname—was even more impressive than Eliza had imagined.

"I'm not surprised," Henry said softly. "I mean, I am, but . . . if anyone could be fearless around shapeshifters, it's Baron."

Silas shook his head. "No. He's more afraid than most, because he knows several Affiliates, and he knows what happens if they get revealed. He wasn't afraid *of* me; he was afraid *for* me. And I was so overwhelmed that I couldn't even hear what he was saying. Maybe he could have calmed me down if I'd listened. Instead . . ." He looked away. "I bit him."

Eliza flinched, remembering the sharp prick of Silas's fangs in her own arm.

But she also remembered being a snake. Remembered how the world had doubled in size around her, trying to swallow her, how her body no longer felt like her own and everything seemed wrong and she was trapped in a nightmare. At least she'd had a warning. At least she'd known what was happening. Even so, she'd still almost bitten Silas.

She could only imagine how much Silas would have blamed himself after biting his friend, but she would have done the same. Even without being an Affiliate, she knew how it felt to lash out and then regret it. She knew what it was like to be overwhelmed with emotions, trying to sail in a storm.

Silas had sat with her through moments like that. Without judgment. Comforting.

Now he was sitting with Henry in the same way.

You don't care about suffering! She'd shouted that accusation at him once. Her cheeks heated now to think of it.

"I gave him a scar," Silas said quietly. "I thought he'd hate me for being an Affiliate—Affiliate, by the way, not shapeshifter; better start adjusting—and if he miraculously didn't, then he'd hate me for hurting him when he was trying to help. But he never did. He insisted we were still friends. He said there was nothing wrong with me. During our next school break, he introduced me to the other Affiliates in his life."

Silas nudged his good leg against Henry's, pausing until Henry looked up to meet his gaze. "I'm going to tell you something. You don't have to believe it yet if you can't, but I want you to remember it."

He let the silence stretch, a net of anticipation waiting to catch his next words.

"There is nothing wrong with you, Henry. You are not broken. You are not cursed. You are not lesser. All you are is a person. Some of what you can do, like jousting, is a skill shared by many other people. And some of what you can do, like transforming into an animal, is a skill shared by very few. The unique combination of traits is what makes you the person you are, but there's not a single trait in itself that isn't shared by some other human. If you need time to adjust to this new trait, that's fine, but don't waste time mourning that you're different from everyone else. You aren't. You're just an ordinary person, now and always."

Eliza couldn't read Henry's reaction because her own eyes had blurred with tears. Only Silas could say, *You're nothing special,* but in such a way that it was empowering rather than an insult. And although the message was meant for Henry, she selfishly tucked it into her own heart.

You are not broken. You are not lesser. All you are is a person.

CHAPTER

33

Baring his soul left Silas feeling drained and empty. More than that, it left him aching for home.

He'd willingly dredged up the past, and now he was mired in it. Remembering his years at Fairfax and his first visits to Gill's house. Remembering being mobbed with hugs by Gill's younger twin brothers as soon as they found out he was an Affiliate too. Corvin coaching him through his first Artifact creation. Leon hissing about the professor who'd triggered Silas's rage transformation and telling him he should go bite the idiot after all. Gill sternly forbidding animal attacks from anyone under his watch.

Silas had never been ashamed of himself or his abilities at the Reeves estate. Only in his own house. Only in the presence of his father.

His father's reaction to the truth was a story Silas didn't share with Henry, because the knight needed hope, not more despair. He swallowed that story, and it weighed heavily on his throat in the form of a scar.

He needed something else to focus on.

"What can you tell me about Ceyda?" he asked.

Although Henry looked as drained as Silas felt, he nodded. "She was just a passenger on the ship. Kept to herself, didn't speak to anyone. I was so caught up in my own situation, I didn't take much notice of her, except that she was always holding a white box.

"Every day on the ship got worse. We were farther from home, and things kept becoming more real, things like, 'I'll never see my family again.' When they finally made the call for land, I . . . lost it."

"You transformed," Silas said, sparing him from having to recount the details. "On a ship with a Loegrian crew and captain. I can imagine how they responded."

"Torches and pitchforks." Henry grimaced. "Or swords, rope, and crossbows, as it were. They would have killed me if not for Ceyda. She, uh . . . she made that box glow, and then an enormous wave overturned the ship."

Eliza gasped. "*She* sank the ship?"

Creating an ocean wave big enough to sink a merchant galley would require an *enormous* Fluid Casting effort. Even Gill would struggle with the task.

"Was she unconscious after?" Silas asked.

"No, but I was. I think I hit my head on the mast when the ship went over. She got me out of the water and all the way to shore." Henry's voice quieted, nearly inaudible. "I don't know why it was just me."

There certainly should have been other survivors. Any of the seafaring crew would have been strong swimmers, with knowledge of how to respond to a shipwreck.

Unless someone made sure they didn't survive.

Silas drummed his fingers on the bedpost, frowning to himself. In his first encounter with Ceyda, she'd been frightened of him, retreating as soon as he showed resistance. In their second encounter, she'd been much the same, sheltering behind crates, fleeing at the first opportunity. Hardly the battle-hardened killer he would expect capable of taking down an entire ship's crew.

Then there was the matter of Henry's sleeping Cast and the tidal wave. Ceyda could not be both Fluid Caster and Stone Caster, not through her own abilities.

He glanced at the bone-box Artifact, sitting innocuously on his desk. *Unbind. Bind.* Unbinding magic from an original host and then binding it to the box to be used by someone else. It was unfathomable. It was groundbreaking.

Silas itched to experiment on it right away, to see if it was broken beyond use or if he could glean anything from its depths.

Later, he ordered himself sternly, refocusing on Henry's story.

"I woke in a large tent with physicians, I assume. I couldn't understand any of them. Ceyda was still there. She told me her name, but that was the extent of how much we could communicate. She seemed . . . scared. Looking over her shoulder, flinching. She was still protecting that box."

"I assume the crack happened during the shipwreck?" Silas asked.

Perhaps when a normal person would be rendered unconscious for overtaxing their mind and magic, the Artifact failed instead.

But to his surprise, Henry shook his head. "No, it was intact."

Silas squinted at the knight, trying to make sense of all the pieces. "Why didn't she steal your magic? Why put you to sleep instead—and why for so long?"

"It couldn't have been more than a day," said Henry, although he rubbed self-consciously at his beard.

Looking at Eliza, Silas left that one open for her to address. She sat with her knees pulled up to her chest, playing with the ends of her scarf, and judging by her drooping eyelids, she was using the movement to stay awake. Silas felt a twinge of guilt.

"I've been in Pravusat for weeks," she whispered. "Looking for you."

Henry made a strangled sound. "No, I . . . it . . . it wasn't like she *discussed* things with me. We couldn't understand each other. I just knew she was scared, and I figured . . . she'd saved my life, the least I could do was try to help."

Silas gave him a flat stare. "Not the best idea to trust a stranger who has a mysterious, magical box."

"I'm a knight, and we vow to protect even . . . questionable people."

He and Eliza were certainly perfect for each other. Silas's chest tightened at the thought.

"I followed her into the city," Henry went on, "and she led me to that underground hiding spot. I couldn't sleep—my arm hurt. She brought that box over, and the next thing I knew, I couldn't feel any pain. Then I woke to . . . Eliza."

He glanced over, and Eliza gave a tired smile.

"Anything else you remember?" Silas asked.

Henry shook his head. "I'm sorry. She tried to speak to me, but I never learned any Pravish. I was planning on crossing the border into Thesland to find work there. My father traveled there when he was young, and I always loved the stories."

"It's beautiful, so I've heard." Silas shrugged. Thesland was a small country of mountains and rivers, where people lived in roving groups rather than in cities. He'd met only a few Thesan students at university.

"I guess my plans are different now," Henry murmured.

"Well, you don't have to figure them out tonight. It's late. We should all get some rest."

Although it was dishonest to the university, Silas picked yet another lock—on the door across the hall—and offered the room to Henry. It wasn't as if anyone else was using the earthquake dorm, and Silas hoped to pay the deficit once he had a real salary.

Henry thanked him and closed the door, but Eliza hovered in the hallway, rubbing her eyes.

"We've filled three out of the four rooms," she joked. "I guess that means we need to add one more person to the group. Maybe Tulip's looking for a place to stay."

Silas stared at her with raised eyebrows, and he couldn't decide whether to laugh or not. She always put him off-balance.

She ducked her head. "I'm sorry for snapping at you earlier."

Had she? Silas cast his mind back but couldn't recall an offense.

"It's been a stressful day," he finally said.

"Can you believe only this morning, we were in prison?"

He remembered the cell all too vividly, sitting in the dim light next to her, thinking of her as a warrior and leaning in for a kiss.

Just how much power did she have over him, and how had she gained it without him even realizing?

"I know I've already said thank you," she went on, "but it can't cover everything you've done for me. I guess I could say it again in Pravish." She flashed a smile that quickly died. "What I mean is, I really . . . appreciate you."

She glanced up at him through her lashes, then looked down again, and Silas hated the way this felt like a goodbye.

When he didn't speak, she rushed to add more. "The way you've helped Henry is wonderful too. You're a good person, Silas."

"Funny," he managed. "I seem to recall you saying I might kill all my students."

It was a pitiful attempt to resurrect their banter from the alley, a moment when he'd felt like she knew him completely.

But that moment was gone.

"I was wrong," she said, as if he'd been fishing for an apology. Her cheeks burned pink in the light from the hallway lantern. "I can't help thinking if I'd found Henry on my own, back when I first arrived, I would have been awful. I would have said all the wrong things about magic and *shapeshifters*. Henry's already doubting himself, and I would have made it so much worse. I thought I was perfect for him. I thought we were perfect together."

Ironic that Silas had been thinking along the same lines since meeting the knight.

"No one's perfect," he said softly. "We're all just people."

Her expression bloomed into a wide, stunning smile, and she reached out to squeeze his arm. "I'm a better one, because of you."

Her words filled his chest, laboring his breathing.

When she turned to leave, he caught her arm, and she looked

back. He was drowning in her gaze, but he didn't care about the pain in his lungs if it meant he could just stay in the water. If he could just capture this moment and make it so she would never leave. The scent of her filled the hallway and threatened to overcome his sense of reason.

But he couldn't rid his mind of an echo: *The way you've helped Henry.*

That was where her affections centered. If she felt anything toward him, it was because he'd helped Henry.

Silas released her arm. He couldn't bring himself to speak. What could he say? Certainly not *you're welcome*. He wasn't feeling very welcoming about anything at the moment.

So without a word, he entered his room and closed the door, using it as a barrier to divide him from every confusing, aching emotion out there in the hallway.

Silas couldn't sleep, so he spent the night writing. He filled pages in his journal with all his disjointed thoughts about Ceyda and Iyal Havva, about an unknown experiment using his own venom, about Casting types and a bone box with Cronese writing, about the kuveti and the tunnels and the magic users "causing disturbances."

He willed his mind to focus, to see the big picture he was missing, but his traitorous thoughts kept drifting through the wall to the girl sleeping in the room next to his.

Tasumak, the Stone Caster's sleep, was used to accelerate a body's natural healing process. Henry said his arm was hurting, and then Ceyda used the Artifact to put him to sleep. Rather than stealing his magic, she'd healed him. But why not wake him?

Unless she couldn't because the Artifact was broken. Unless she wasn't a Caster at all and her abilities had come from the bone box.

How had it broken?

And who had worked with her father to make it in the first place?

Silas tore out a page just to have something to crumple between his hands. He threw it across the room, satisfied with the way it bounced hard yet soundlessly against the wall. He should give up his university work after all, go pick papayas for Baris. Nice and simple, twist-twist and done.

Then he sighed, picked up his pen, and returned to work.

CHAPTER

34

Eliza heard movement in the hallway, but it couldn't be Silas. It was too early for him to be up. She cracked open her door and peeked out to see Henry with his back to her, stretching his arms and legs, perhaps going through a morning exercise.

Quickly, she ducked back into her room. She rebraided her hair and changed her clothes, almost strangling herself as she wrapped her scarf with shaking hands and wound up all tangled in the fabric. Should she even wear a scarf? Would Henry prefer to see her looking more Loegrian than Pravish? Secretly, she'd come to love the bright, flowing fashion.

Without permission, her mind summoned the memory of when Silas had purchased her clothing in the market, his low voice saying, *You look beautiful.*

He'd been teasing her, nothing more. And she had nothing else to wear, so debating was pointless.

She scrubbed her face with a bar of lemongrass soap and water from the basin on her dresser. It was a day old now, since she and Silas had to go to the outside well together to draw anything fresh, but it was better than nothing. At least there hadn't been any earthquakes to spill it all over her floor. She'd woken to that more than once.

When she was finished, she paused with her hand on the door. Her nerves unsettled her stomach. What could she say?

What if she said all the wrong things?

Even while her mind fretted, her body struck out on its own, turning the handle, marching her into the hallway with purpose, as if she knew what she was doing.

Henry turned, smiling when he saw her. That smile brought back a rush of memories—dancing with him on her birthday, pressing a flower he'd given her into her book of sonnets—and she smiled back, her insides aflutter. Even with the short beard and the travel-worn weariness, he was as handsome as ever.

He offered his arm. "Care for a morning walk?"

Eliza's heart leapt to take the offer, but she hesitated, her arm halfway to his. The golden bracelet hung heavy on her wrist, and she thought of Silas, asleep and immobile in his room.

"It's better if we speak here." She gave a weak smile.

"We could at least sit on the front steps. Surely watching the dawn will be more enjoyable than sitting in this gloomy hallway."

Heat rose in Eliza's cheeks. She showed him her bracelet. "Truthfully, I'm . . . That is, Silas and I are, um, stuck together? I made this mistake, buying magic, and now we can't stray more than twenty feet from each other. But that will be fixed today, I swear!"

Henry's eyebrows lifted, and he floundered a moment before saying, "It seems you've had adventures of your own."

"*Adventure* is not the word I'd use. *Headache* would be more accurate." Though that didn't entirely describe the complicated tangle inside her. If there was a good word for that, she hadn't learned it in either Loegrian or Pravish.

"Really? Lord Silas is that bad?"

She bit her lip, not wanting to give the wrong impression. "It's not him. Well, it's partly him. He's so bullheaded in his opinions. Not that I can't be the same way. I—what I mean is, the heat and the snakes and the language, you know?"

Henry clearly did not know. He blinked at her like a poor lost owl.

Was he an owl? She wanted to ask about his Affiliate type, but instead, she found herself saying, "And *lord.* That's another thing. He never told me he was part of court. In fact, he said . . ."

Her voice trailed off as she remembered the first time she'd mentioned Lord Bennett, saying she thought Silas might be his heir.

He wouldn't claim me as such.

Now, looking back, she could hear the meaning in that. Silas was always honest, but he sometimes hid from pain in nuance.

"Oh," she said softly, feeling foolish. Of course the father willing to go after his son with a sword would have disinherited him as well. So, no, Silas wasn't a lord. At least, not anymore.

Henry shifted restlessly, and Eliza gave herself a mental kick. After all this time, she was finally alone with the boy she loved, and yet her mind and conversation were still filled with Silas Bennett. What was the matter with her?

"I've missed you!" she blurted, too loudly for the narrow hallway. She winced.

But Henry smiled again, the soft, tender smile she'd missed so dearly. "I can't believe you're here. Things happened so quickly yesterday, I never had the chance to ask what brought you to Pravusat—although, no matter the reason, I'm grateful to see you."

Eliza blinked. Her ribs seemed to sharpen into points, pricking at her insides. "I came after you. Obviously."

His eyes widened in what she hoped was awe rather than bafflement. "But your family, your—"

"None of it mattered." Instantly, she realized how petty that sounded. He probably would have given anything to see his family again, and she'd left hers behind with only a note to explain her absence. "What I mean is . . . you mattered most."

"Oh." He didn't seem to know how to take that. "I . . . I mean that much to you?"

"Of course." She stepped forward, clasping his hands in her own.

"And I'm so sorry about everything that happened with my father. I—"

"That wasn't your doing." He squeezed her hands. "You can't control the king."

She looked up hopefully. "Aria's queen now. I'm not certain of the details, since I've been away, but I *know* she'll grant you a pardon. She was so angry at Father for everything surrounding the challenge that I know she'll set it right. We can go home together."

He pulled away, a deep furrow on his brow. Though she tried not to be hurt, the withdrawal stung. This wasn't the reunion Eliza had hoped for.

When Henry had first been banished, she could think only of seeing him again. When she'd packed her bag and written a farewell letter to Aria, she'd been filled with purpose, with certainty. She'd imagined sailing across the ocean like a maiden in an inspiring fable, imagined the moment she would surprise Henry and watch his expression melt into adoration. The moment she would feel his arms around her. The moment they would kiss.

In her mind, everything had been warm and glowing and romantic, just the way love should be.

In reality, the slight draft in the hallway made her shiver. The dim light made it hard to see, and the floorboards creaked when she shifted. Nothing felt warm or glowing at all.

Then, just to crown her disappointment, the ground began shaking.

Henry stumbled, grabbing the doorframe with one hand to catch himself. His startled eyes found hers.

"It's just the Stone Casters practicing in the yard," she said with a heavy sigh. "Give it an hour."

"An *hour*?" Henry repeated as another tremor rolled through.

Eliza should have found humor in his reaction, but she couldn't. Rather than trying to hold herself upright, she sank to the floor, bracing her palms on the wood. She thought of that long-ago morning with Silas, when she'd fallen into his bed, elbowing him in the stomach. When he'd looked at her with irritated eyes and disheveled hair and asked, *What is the matter with you*?

There *was* something the matter with her. She could not banish a snake from her mind.

Silas was clever and softhearted as well as irritating and abrasive. He wasn't like any of the men in the romantic stories that had filled her dreams. Silas would never go charging on a stallion to save a lady. He would quote an essay about why she didn't need saving at all because, contrary to popular opinion, ladies preferred to save themselves, and so the best course of action would be to send the stallion along as a gift, along with any supplies that might aid the lady in question. Meanwhile, he'd be reading his book in the corner.

The world rumbled around her, and the shaking reached all the way to her core with a dreadful, waking truth.

Eliza was in dangerous territory. If she did not separate herself from Silas *right now*, she risked something terrible, something that would end in heartbreak.

How else could loving someone who didn't believe in love end?

Her reunion with Henry was not as she'd pictured, but Henry was a *knight*. He believed in romantic gestures like flowers and dances. She could be happy with him eternally. He would never shatter her heart. Besides that, if she allowed herself to feel things for Silas, if she allowed the object of her affections to change, she would become everything her father had always claimed she was. A girl of romantic whims. Perhaps she'd move right on from Silas to another boy on campus, or a sailor, or whoever next managed to catch her eye. Perhaps it would never end, and she'd be drifting forever.

She had to be steady. If she could not control the swells and tides of the storm inside, she could at least control those of her heart.

With a desperation she'd never felt before, Eliza stumbled to her feet, clinging to the wall as it bucked beneath her hands. She walked slowly, tripping once without falling, until she slammed her hands against Silas's door. She pounded loudly enough to wake the dead—necessary for the way he slept through the tremors.

"Silas, get up!" she shouted. "We have to see Yvette!"

She could not live another day with the Cast in place. She had to be free of it. Free of *him*, with all his contradictions and irritating charms.

Before it was too late.

Silas told himself this was just one more duty to complete, just the next item on a work list. As soon as it was done, he could find Kerem and see how things had turned out with Ceyda. He could experiment with the Artifact. He could move on.

He knocked with purpose at Yvette's door, and the Stone Caster opened it to admit them.

"This must be Henry," she said, raising her eyebrows as she evaluated the knight like she was fitting him for his next suit of armor.

Henry startled at the sound of his name and gave a hurried bow.

"He doesn't speak Pravish," Silas said.

Smoothly, she switched to Loegrian. "Pleasure to meet you at last."

Henry grabbed her hand in an enthusiastic handshake, grinning all the while.

Yvette gave an indulgent laugh before freeing her hand. Then she glanced at Eliza. "You must be relieved."

"I am." Eliza looped her arm through Henry's.

Silas stepped into the office first. He tapped his bracelet. "I finished my homework. I'd appreciate the grade."

Yvette gave a sly grin. "Not so fast. What did you learn?"

"You were right."

"Ooh, flattery. I love it. Tell me more, and then tell me the real answer."

She gestured them into her seating area, and then she handed Henry a bowl of roasted, shelled *hirk* nuts, as if warning him to settle in. He thanked her and tucked in with delight. Silas shook his head. He'd find the pepper flakes soon enough.

Yvette settled on a cushion between Eliza and Silas, arranging the ends of her red scarf in her lap and then placing her hands on her knees. "Second try. What did you learn?"

"I wasn't warned there'd be a test," he drawled.

"Ah, but I trust you studied anyway."

Eliza watched smugly, as if enjoying his torture. She didn't realize it would be her turn soon enough. Yvette was never one to let an evaluation slide.

Best to get it over with.

"You were right about compassion," Silas said, trying not to squirm. "I should have had more. In the end, it felt rewarding to help, and I gained an appreciation for Eliza's strengths. I'll miss her when she's gone."

He could admit that. It stung, but honesty had a better burn than dishonesty. Besides, he'd never given a dishonest report to a teacher, and he wasn't about to start.

Yvette patted his knee. Then she looked expectantly at Eliza.

"Your turn," she said when the princess didn't speak.

Eliza's jaw dropped. "What, me? What am I meant to say?"

"Tell me what you learned from this experience."

It was Silas's turn to look smug, and he indulged it wholeheartedly.

"I didn't learn anything," Eliza protested. "I just . . . we just—it was just something that happened. It's not as though we were on trial."

Henry started coughing, pounding his chest. He'd found the pepper at last. Without missing a beat, Yvette handed him a cup that Silas hoped wasn't *zenzil*.

"Not on trial, no," said the professor, resettling on her cushion.

"But you returned to me now because you want me to break the Cast, don't you? Did you expect that service for free?"

Eliza's face reddened. Weakly, she protested, "But what kind of payment is this?"

"It's not a very good one, true. It benefits you far more than it does me." Yvette smiled. "Highness, you will have all kinds of experiences in life. Things that *just happen*. If you never pause to evaluate any of them, to look back and ask what they've taught you and how you intend to direct yourself as a result, then what is the purpose? Imagine if captains sailed with their eyes shut; they would never make harbor. If you wish to direct your life, then I'm asking you to sail with your eyes open. Tell me what you've learned from your time with Silas."

The room fell silent save for the crack and crunch of nuts as Henry chewed, which quieted as he clearly grew self-conscious, hunching over the bowl. Silas stole a handful of nuts—not really to make the knight feel better but because roasted *hirk* was an indulgence.

Or maybe because he needed something to occupy his attention while he waited to hear what Eliza would say about him.

"Silas isn't who I thought," Eliza finally said, her voice quiet and a bit raspy. "At first, I thought he was a thug. Then I thought he was a monster."

Silas kept his eyes focused on the nuts, wishing they had shells to crack.

"Now I know he's . . . just a person. A frustrating one, sometimes. And inspiring sometimes too. And he's wrong more often than he'll admit. For example, he's wrong about love, because it definitely exists. And he's wrong about compassion, because he says he should have more, but truthfully, no one has ever shown me more compassion than he has, from the moment I first trapped him in this Cast and he sat with me while I cried. I think he's just careful where he spends it. And maybe that's for good reason."

Silas lifted his eyes to see Eliza looking at him, her cheeks pink but her expression earnest.

Maybe he *was* wrong more often than he cared to admit.

He'd certainly been wrong about her.

Eliza wasn't an entitled royal who expected life to bow for her. She was a brave, stubborn girl who loved with her whole heart and fought for what she believed in, even when it appeared impossible. She soared high and crashed low, and through it all, she never surrendered. She'd changed his life just by being in it.

And he'd been honest when he'd said he would miss her, but maybe he hadn't been honest about just *how much*. That truth might crack something in his soul.

"He's been hurt before," Eliza whispered, her eyes fixed on his. "But I would never hurt him. At least, I'd never want to."

The itch of scales rippled across his hands. His body didn't know what to do with all the emotion bubbling up inside, and he fought to keep the confusing surge at bay. He wanted to kiss Eliza, to crawl the distance between them on hands and knees, plead for her to stay. But the distance between them couldn't be crossed so easily.

She was right. Silas had felt the sharp bite of a loved one's sword at his neck. He knew that loving only led to betrayal and pain. The longer it took, the worse it would hurt. And he'd promised himself he'd never be in that situation again.

He looked away first, breaking the connection.

"Lessons in droves," Yvette said softly, "and, Highness, I do believe you'll navigate far better after acknowledging them. As for the Cast—"

The door to her office banged open, startling all of them.

CHAPTER 35

As the university guard filed into the room, surrounding the seating area, Henry leapt to his feet, battle-ready and clearly wishing he had a sword in his hand. Silas didn't move, trying to absorb the transition from evaluation to what seemed to be an interrogation.

Yvette rose slowly, facing the guard marked with a silver rope at his shoulder. "Your reason for entering so dramatically, Captain?"

The captain grimaced, clearly unhappy with the task at hand. "Yvette Sahin, we will escort you to the dean's office for questioning in connection with the death of Havva Polat."

Silas's heart stopped.

Eliza jumped up, stumbling as her foot caught on the cushion. "That's ridiculous! Yvette would never—"

Silencing her with a raised hand, Yvette kept her attention on the guard. "My accuser?"

"Kerem Aytac, supporting a witness from Polat's daughter."

"He can't face me himself? Unworthy to be called a snake." She scoffed. "What evidence is set against me?"

The captain shifted uneasily. "I'm to escort you to Iyal Afshin. Further questions can be asked of him."

Yvette's expression had never looked stonier. Straightening, she composed her red scarf, smoothing the twin tails against her shirt, and then she marched from the room as if she were escorting the guards instead of the other way around.

Half the guards remained behind, beginning a search of the room, examining every paper on the desk and every book on the shelves.

Silas couldn't move. His mind kept replaying the sharp *bang* of the door, as if he'd yet to process anything beyond the entrance of the guards.

"Silas, *do* something!" Eliza said sharply, kicking her shoe into his.

He scowled up at her. "What do you expect me to do, *apta*?"

"Tell the guards she's innocent and this is nonsense!"

He wanted to.

But what if she wasn't?

In the shadow of every bookshelf, Silas saw the image of his father drawing a sword. His mouth went dry, and his hands grew cold in his lap.

He looked away. "I don't know anything about Yvette's private life. For all I know—"

"For all you know, she's secretly murdering colleagues? Have you lost your mind? She's your friend! She remembered your birthday even when you didn't."

Provoked, Silas finally climbed to his feet, staring Eliza down from his superior height. "And that *means* something? Do you know how many times I looked at my father and thought, 'He loves me. He gave me a horse, or he boasted to Lord Brightwood about my early acceptance to Fairfax, or he took me on a trip, just the two of us.' That didn't stop him from cutting my throat the minute I grew fangs."

Behind Eliza, Henry grew deathly pale. Silas gave a silent curse.

But maybe he'd been wrong to try to spare the knight this truth. Maybe it was better to warn him about inevitable outcomes.

"That's what this is about," Eliza said softly, her coppery eyes full of pain. "Silas, not everyone is your father."

"No one is," he said coldly. "Everyone's their own unique flavor of betrayal."

Her expression hardened, and she stepped right up to him, forcing him to retreat a pace. "*Everyone*? Your best friend, who stood by you even as a shapeshifter in Loegria? Your sister, who you said you missed? *Me*?"

He wavered, then clenched his jaw. She never lowered her challenging gaze.

"After everything we've been through," she said, "do you really think I'd betray you?"

Yes.

Even if her opinion of him had softened over time, he had always been a means to an end, and she had her end now. As soon as the bracelet was off, he would never see her again.

The flavor of that betrayal was particularly bitter.

Scales itched across his cheekbones, and he closed his eyes before they could turn red. After all the years he'd spent fighting for control, learning to live with things pushed beneath the surface, Eliza swept in like a hurricane to undo it all. She blew away all his certainties and washed the ground from under his feet.

"Looks like they found what they were searching for," Henry's voice cut in, grim and low.

Silas blinked, reorienting himself in the room to see the guards filing out. One guard held a leatherbound journal, similar to the one Silas carried in his own bag.

"Excuse me"—he stepped into the guard's path—"what is that?"

The guard opened the cover, displaying the first page with its messy, uneven scrawl. It wasn't Iyl Yvette's handwriting.

In the top left corner was the name *Havva Polat.*

The guards left, and Silas remained in place, his insides twisted like a serpent around his spine.

As usual, Eliza broke the silence, hands on her hips and a stubborn frown on her face. "It's possible they did a research project together. Or someone slipped into her office while she was at lecture, knowing the guards would arrive soon, and left that journal."

"Eliza . . ." Silas whispered, rubbing his hand over his face. He sighed.

"Yvette has always helped you!"

"Like how she helped us know whether Henry was in prison."

"Yes, exactly! She—"

"With her connections to the kuveti."

Eliza stopped short, and he could see her mind working frantically to explain it. His own mind was doing the same thing. Because this was *Yvette*—the woman who'd taught him everything about Pravusat and everything about Stone Casting. The friend who'd always kept an open office door, no matter what he needed, from helping with an experiment to kindness on his birthday.

Could she *really* be a killer?

Silas wanted to say no.

Yvette knew about the venom experiments he did with Iyal Kerem. When they'd found the tunnels, Kerem had recalled her hand in the prison construction. Since Ceyda had known about the tunnels as well, perhaps her father had worked on the prison along with Yvette. Perhaps they'd crafted the tunnels together, the beginning of a collaboration that turned much darker.

In every shadow, he saw a sword.

"I won't believe it." Eliza's chin trembled, but her voice remained fierce. "We have to investigate."

Silas turned away. "The university guard will conduct an investigation, overseen by Afshin. If she's guilty, she'll be removed from the faculty and turned over to the king. If she's innocent, she'll be released."

"Since when is Silas Bennett content to let other people do the research?"

He threw his hands up, displaying a bracelet still attached. "What do you want from me, *apta*?"

"I want you to be better than this. Be braver. I want you to realize that not everyone betrays—or that, if they do, not all betrayals are the same. Some can be forgiven. Maybe Yvette built secret tunnels, and it was a bad decision someone is taking advantage of. Maybe she has kuveti connections she's trying to sever. Maybe she's got secrets that don't make her a murderer."

Silas flinched from her words, but inside, they resonated.

No conclusions, his academic side whispered. *Just observations.*

He didn't know what the truth was, and that was key. He didn't *know*. Not yet.

But he had the power to find out.

"I can't go home," Henry said quietly, breaking the silence. He looked at Eliza, and his furrowed brow spoke to both pain and apology. "Not yet, at least. Not until I figure out . . . who I am now. If there's something to be done here, especially to help someone, I'd like to be part of it."

An echo of his pain flashed through Eliza's expression, and she gave a barely perceptible nod.

Then she cleared her throat. "Well, *I* believe Yvette is innocent, and I'm going to do something to prove it. Silas can be dragged along on a tether. If we need a real snake's help, I'll enlist Tulip."

"*Disi dokmek*," Silas muttered, then set his jaw. "If we want the truth, we need to figure out how the bone-box Artifact was made, and we need to find where Iyal Havva died."

CHAPTER

36

From the moment of Yvette's arrest, Eliza had felt a threat brewing inside, like gray clouds gathering on the horizon. She ordered herself to focus on the task at hand. With the uncontrollable all around, she had to seize what she *could* control.

They couldn't speak to Kerem yet because he was with the dean and Yvette. Although Eliza wanted to storm right into that meeting, she realized the best approach to proving Yvette's innocence was not pleading an impassioned case hinged on, "But, sir, Yvette has always been kind!"

Silas's approach to proving it was a little more . . . terrifying. He dragged her and Henry all over campus, experimenting on the bone-box Artifact like he was determined to destroy it: He submerged it in bubbling liquids, stabbed it with sharp objects, even doused it in oil and set it on fire.

"Is this what magic normally looks like?" Henry asked, pale in the orange light.

With a long iron poker, Silas prodded at the mass on the stone table, turning the box onto its side.

"Magic in a research setting," he said, flashing a wide, serpentine smile.

The flames burned down quickly, leaving the white box untouched. Silas muttered about a lack of heat retention and made more notes in his journal.

"Your leg's going to give out before you learn anything," Eliza scolded, noticing his limp had grown more pronounced and that he leaned heavily into his uninjured side.

He waved her comment off like a gnat.

"I've already learned things, *apta*." He gestured at his journal as if she could read it from ten feet away. "This test confirmed that this *is* composition warlockry."

He said it with a sense of triumph, and when he made his final note, he flourished his pen.

"Composition warlockry," Henry deadpanned. "Just as I suspected."

Eliza laughed, and although Silas huffed, he didn't seem genuinely annoyed. The excitement of discovery brightened his dark eyes.

"Composition warlockry," he said, "means the involvement of more than one magical person. The easiest compositions are made by Casters of the same type—for example, a triplet of Fluid Casters working together to direct water in the university pipes. Much harder is the coordination of non-identical magic types, like a Fluid Caster and a Stone Caster manipulating water and silt to create quicksand. Based on the box's resistance to fire, this is one of those trickier compositions."

Eliza stepped forward, pressing her hands to the soot-streaked table. "Havva and Yvette are both Stone Casters, so you're saying this couldn't have been made by just them."

But he dashed her hopes. "Ceyda was right about the venom; I can sense my own magic, however faintly. That could be the factor creating a composition." He paused, hefting the Artifact almost reverently. "This might be the first of its kind—Affiliate and Caster magic."

"Affiliates have never worked with Casters before?" she asked.

"We've tried. We're incompatible, or so the research has always shown." His voice quieted. "Until now."

"If you can tell it's *your* magic, can't you tell if it's Yvette's too?"

Silas shook his head. "It doesn't work that way, although I have confirmed the presence of Stone Casting. That was fairly evident from the use of bone, but I tested it to be sure. At least this explains how the *bind* and *unbind* don't negate—they must be linked to different magic sources."

Pushing back from the table, Eliza tried and failed to wipe the soot from her palm. She felt that same dark streak marring her hopes. Why couldn't magic just have a voice? If the box piped up and said, "I wasn't made by Yvette," that would be that.

Unless magic voices could lie like human ones.

She shook her head, frustrated that she couldn't help with this. Silas would figure it out, but she needed a task for herself. Something she could do.

The storm inside rumbled with distant thunder, and she willed herself to hold it back. Now that she'd found Henry, she wasn't about to lose control in front of him.

"I wonder . . ." Silas pursed his lips, then pressed on. "I've tried to identify Fluid Casting, but that's harder to test than Stone Casting, and I can't tell for certain. I need a strong Fluid Caster to read the Artifact. Unfortunately, the strongest we had on campus was Iyal Mazhar. But if this is a composition between all known magic types, it might be more groundbreaking than I ever imagined."

Something about the way he said it made her shiver, like he'd awakened to a new, dangerous ambition.

"And deadly," she added, in case he'd forgotten the boneless bodies.

"And deadly," he agreed, though it didn't seem to deter his enthusiasm.

He tucked both Artifact and journal in his bag, but when he took a step away from the table, he hissed sharply, pressing his hand to his thigh.

"Time for a break?" Henry suggested.

Silas shook his head, speaking through gritted teeth. "We have to find where Iyal Havva was killed."

"What's your plan for that?" Eliza folded her arms, staring him down. "Are you going to wander the city, knocking on doors and asking, 'Was anyone killed here lately?'"

"Think we'll have more success searching for murders in the inns and *birahans*? Or should we skip straight to underground tunnels?"

"First, you sit. Then we figure out the rest."

Aided by Henry, who made himself a nonnegotiable crutch, Silas limped out of the building and onto a bench beneath a shady tree. They were on the south side of campus, looking down the hill over the bustling spread of Izili. In the distance, a ship left the harbor, pointed toward the horizon. Eliza tried not to think of home, but Henry's words stuck like sap in her mind.

I can't go home. Not yet.

Eliza hadn't intended to stay away forever . . . had she?

She'd declared as much in her runaway note to Aria—*If exile is to be Henry's sentence, I choose to bear it as well*—but she'd always known her sister would grant him a pardon as soon as she could. Not only that, but as soon as Eliza had arrived in Pravusat, she'd missed home. She missed the shadow of the mountain and the crisp winter cold. She missed her sister and her mother.

There was the matter of duty as well. Eliza was crown princess now, though she'd never wanted to be, and it was her responsibility to share some of the burden Aria was currently carrying alone. She'd let her sister down in so many other ways, and while the search for Henry had kept that guilt at bay, now it pulled on her like a rope, trying to drag her where she belonged.

If Henry decided to stay, would she return home alone? Was that the right thing to do, and was she even strong enough to do it?

Not so long ago, she would have said the right thing was always choosing love.

But matters didn't feel simple anymore.

"We need to speak to Ceyda again," Eliza said. "She has the best chance of knowing something that can help us retrace Iyal Havva's steps."

Silas started to rise, but she ordered him sternly back down.

"You're going to have to climb all the stairs in the Yamakaz," she said, "so take ten minutes to rest first. Besides, I need to speak to Henry. In private."

"I'll plug my ears," Silas drawled, settling back on the bench.

Eliza drew Henry off as far as her bracelet would allow. He tensed, as if expecting an accusation. Honestly, she wasn't certain what she wanted to say. It only felt like the storm was growing, and she needed to find a clear heading before the waves turned unmanageable.

"Do you think your horse misses you?" she blurted.

She winced as soon as the question was out of her mouth. In lunging to avoid any uncomfortable topics, she'd instead landed on a silly one.

But Henry relaxed, breaking into his warm smile.

"Tidalwave?" He gave a small laugh. "To be honest, he was never particularly loyal. Downright grumpy, too, if he's not in the arena at least once a week. I'd be delighted to know how many times he's thrown Hugh by now. I'm sure between all the Wycliff boys, Tides is well taken care of and has never given my absence a second thought."

Eliza smiled but shook her head. "I highly doubt that. I find it unthinkable that you could disappear from anyone's life without them feeling a profound absence, even if that person was a grumpy horse."

"He certainly didn't carry enough concern to chase me." Henry came a step closer, then halted, scuffing his boot across the dirt path. "What I mean is, I still haven't found a way to properly thank you, Eliza. I doubt I ever could."

She could think of a few romantic gestures, and yet he made none of them, just slid his hands in his pockets and continued shuffling his feet.

A dangerous question tumbled from her lips. "Henry, what are we to each other?"

He lifted his shoulders, more shield than shrug. "I don't know."

Inside, she felt the helm slipping from her fingers. She gripped tighter.

"Well, you could make a few guesses, at least," she said hotly.

If anything, he looked more pained. "I know I made promises, and I meant all of them at the time, I swear. I still mean them. Or at least I . . . I want to. Eliza, you deserve so much, but the truth is—right now, I don't know who *I* am. Do you understand?"

She wanted to, really, but her heart was all tangled up in the weeks without him, and the dreams she'd created crashed around her like thunder on the deck. Not just the romantic dreams—Eliza had convinced herself that whatever was broken inside from the curse would be fixed when she found Henry. But she wasn't fixed.

Did that mean she never would be?

She was lost in uncertainty, and while it wasn't his fault, she couldn't help blaming him anyway.

"I left *home* for you," she snapped.

He never asked you to, said a voice inside.

But that only made the storm worse, because she felt foolish. Because she saw her father's looming shadow in the clouds, and she heard his mocking voice. *Romantic whims.*

Had she imagined everything from the start? Had she taken a few flowers and turned them into an entire future?

Yes, said the voice inside.

Eliza willed it to drown.

"You left home for the old me," Henry whispered. "The knight."

Eliza threw her hands in the air. "So that's what this is about. Well, I don't *care* that you're an Affiliate. It doesn't change anything for me."

He looked away. "You don't even know what I am."

"Your animal link, you mean? I don't care! You could be a hog or a skunk or even a ravenous wolf, and *I'd still love you*!"

She let the words hang like a sunbeam through the storm. It was her first time confessing to him, and she'd always imagined a romantic whisper rather than a hurled accusation, but she was who she was. Maybe she needed to accept that the storm was a part of her now. It changed how she had to navigate, but it didn't change her heart or the things she wanted.

And if he could just feel the same, she could navigate any storm or shipwreck. If he could just say—

Henry winced.

Eliza felt it like a slap.

"You say that like it doesn't matter," he said, oblivious to the way her mast had cracked in a lightning strike, the way it was plunging into the water. He swallowed. "But what does it say about a person if they share a magical link to a wolf? Does it mean they're aggressive? And did the magic activate because they were innately like a wolf, or is the magic going to *make them* like a wolf?"

"I said I love you!" she shouted. "Did you even hear? No, you're too caught up in self-pity. Some chivalrous knight."

She meant it as a return slap, and the blow succeeded, obvious in his sharp flinch. She simultaneously hated herself for it and wished to throw another. She was just trying to hold her ship together.

For a moment, Henry met her eyes, his a tortured swirl of brown and green.

Then he walked away.

"Come back here!" Eliza shouted desperately, catching his arm. But she had a tether and he didn't. He pulled away, disappearing down a campus footpath that wound between the trees, and no matter how she strained, she couldn't pull Silas from his bench.

Glaring over her shoulder, she found the snake's black eyes resting directly on her.

"Let me go!" she shouted.

Without a word, he gestured at his leg, stretched out before him. She wanted to yell at him for a convenient injury, for holding her back on purpose, but her eyes followed Henry's empty path, and she suddenly thought of how long she'd searched, *praying* to see him again.

Only to chase him away.

Eliza hit her knees, scraping her fingernails in the dirt. This was everything she'd feared. The worst side of her, exposed to the boy she loved. She pounded her fists twice, a scream held silent behind her tight throat.

"He'll come back," Silas said. "Give him time."

She cast a hateful glance over her shoulder at the snake. "I don't want to hear your opinion when you've made all of this so much worse!"

If Silas had never kissed her, never made her question everything, then she could have been more devoted. Maybe Henry had noticed how she couldn't keep Silas from her mind no matter how she tried. Maybe he hated her for it.

Whims.

She clenched her teeth, straining against a Cast that held her in place. It was like trying to tear a stone foundation from the ground with her bare hands. She slipped in the dirt.

"Breathe," said Silas with his infuriating steadiness.

"Choke," she snarled back.

But she dragged in a long, slow breath, abandoning her struggle against the magic. She remained kneeling on the path.

"It always takes time for me to find the calm again," he said. "To transform back. It's always a struggle."

Slowly, Eliza's anger deflated, leaving behind an awful emptiness. Her feet prickled beneath her, then went numb. She didn't move. She floated among wreckage, just jagged pieces of wood she'd been flailing to hold together, trying to pretend they were a ship.

"Are you all right?" Silas finally asked, his voice gentle.

Like he hadn't witnessed her attacking the boy she claimed to love. He should have been asking what was wrong with her.

Even as she had the thought, his voice echoed from memory. *You can* do *something wrong, but there can't* be *something wrong with you.*

"I hurt him on purpose," she whispered. "*Why*? Why can't I just . . ."

"Control it?" he supplied.

She turned, meeting his unwavering gaze.

"Sometimes, in a rage transformation," he said, "we bite friends."

She didn't deserve the empathy, but it wrapped her anyway, removing the weight from her shoulders like someone taking a burden. Eliza looked away, squeezing her eyes shut against tears.

All she wanted was to be *herself*. The girl she'd been for seventeen years. The curse had taken that from her, like a pirate stealing her from home and dragging her out to the ocean. She could sail or drown, but she couldn't undo what had happened, not with any amount of wishing.

"How did you adapt?" she asked Silas, voice trembling. "How did you accept being someone new?"

"I'm still me." He smirked. "Just with fangs."

She rolled her eyes, denying the little smile that almost broke through. She couldn't smile after hurting Henry. Not when he was struggling with the same thing she was—something that had altered his life.

One more chance, she prayed silently. *Please*.

When Henry returned, she leapt to her feet, stumbling as the blood needled back into them. "Henry, I'm so sorry—"

But he interrupted with a strained smile. "We need to find Ceyda, right?"

She didn't want to force her feelings on him again, even to explain herself, so she swallowed hard, and she managed a nod.

CHAPTER 37

Feeling any better?" Henry asked, clearly anxious to be on their way. He stood with tense shoulders and a clenched jaw while Eliza hung back, her eyes on the ground.

As a fellow Affiliate, Silas's sympathy should have rested with Henry, but he was too caught up in the echo of Eliza's breaking voice.

I said I love you! Did you even hear?

The most foolish part of himself wished he knew a Pravish sonnet, wished he could offer something to lift her eyes and restore her smile.

But she didn't want to hear such things from him anyway.

Gripping the bench, he pushed himself up. His stiff leg ached, but that wasn't going to fix itself in a day. So he nodded his readiness, and even though Henry offered assistance, he walked on his own.

As they entered the Yamakaz, Silas turned his attention to the stairs, but Henry fixed on the front desk, coming to a startled halt.

"Baron!" he shouted.

Silas blinked, certain he was mistaken. The librarians at the desk scowled at the loud shout, and it also drew the attention of the man they'd been conversing with.

He wore a dark, tailored suit, evident of Loegrian nobility, though the gentlemanly demeanor was tempered by both the sword at his side and the Caster's brand on his neck. His reddish hair looked windblown, as if he'd shown up in a hurry, and when his green eyes locked on Silas, his expression split in a grin.

In quick strides, he crossed the distance, and before Silas could protest, Gill pulled him into a crushing hug.

"Let me up for air," Silas complained, thumping him on the back. But when he pulled away, he wore a grin of his own. "Guillaume Reeves on Pravish shores. I'm not one to doubt my senses, but . . ."

"I'm here on Her Majesty's business." Gill's eyes flickered toward Eliza as he added, "Aria's concerned about her sister."

Eliza flushed pink from her neck to her ears, as if she'd been caught in something scandalous.

Silas huffed. "I sent word she was safe."

"That was before Eliza's letter about Henry's disappearance. After that, Aria's worry wasn't so much for Eliza's safety as it was for the people of Pravusat if they stood in her sister's way—or so she told me."

He gave a mischievous smile, and Eliza's coloring darkened.

"I didn't tear the country apart," she mumbled.

"Much," Silas couldn't help adding.

She wrinkled her freckled nose at him.

Gill turned his attention to Henry, extending a handshake and gripping the knight's shoulder. "Glad to see you've been found after all."

"It's a long story," Henry said weakly.

Ever courteous, Gill didn't press for details. Instead, he produced a signed, stamped document from an inner pocket of his vest. "Your official pardon." He leaned in slightly, lowering his voice. "And I've been warned by your father that if I'm unable to bring you home, he'll come for the rescue himself."

Henry paled, his brow furrowing as if torn between fear and gratitude. Even so, he grasped the parchment with steady fingers. His control was admirable; it would serve him well as an Animal Affiliate.

Finally, Gill swept a deep bow in Eliza's direction. "Your Royal

Highness, I'm pleased to see you safe as well, and I'm sorry we didn't have the chance to be acquainted earlier."

"Before I ran away from home, you mean?" Eliza gave a nervous laugh, shaking her head. "So you're Aria's Baron—er, Guillaume. I . . . would you—um, can I call you Gill?"

Shooting a quick glance at Silas, as if trying to discern what had already been said about him, Gill nodded. "I know 'Baron' is an unorthodox nickname. If you'd prefer 'Gill,' it doesn't bother me."

"Unorthodox nickname, perhaps, but a clever secret identity." Eliza smiled ruefully. "I tried for weeks to discover where all of Aria's secret love letters were coming from—which baron in the kingdom might have caught my sister's attention. She was wholeheartedly smitten, you know. I even caught her *daydreaming*. My sister, the practical crown princess who always saw courting as just one more duty on the list."

Her smile widened. "Maybe we hadn't met before now, but I always knew what mattered. You make Aria happy."

Gill seemed stunned. Slowly, he dipped another bow, his hand pressed to his heart. "I'll try all my life to continue to do so, Highness. You have my word."

"Thank you for not getting married before I could be there." She squinted. "You haven't, right?"

"Aria wouldn't dream of it. To be honest, there are people I'd like present as well."

Gill's gaze returned to Silas, settling on him like a heavy weight. He extended a second pardon identical to Henry's, and Silas eyed the official document in the manner of evaluating a frozen lake for stability.

Rather than accepting it, he handed Gill the bone-box Artifact. "What do you make of that?" he asked quietly.

His friend hovered a moment longer, then tucked away the pardon, removed his gloves, and set to examining the box. After only a moment in his hands, the symbols took on a faint, hazy glow.

Silas felt a flash of triumph. He could always count on Gilly.

The Caster gave a disquieted hum. "This is human blood"—he indicated the symbols—"embedded in the bone. Some kind of Fluid Casting. I've never seen anything like it, but I'm sure you assumed that."

"It's a triple composition," Silas said. "The first of its kind."

Three magic types combined in one Artifact. Only the loftiest dreamers would have dared imagine it, and here it was, made real.

Gill's fingers brushed the deep gash in the Artifact's edge, and his brow furrowed. "The damage makes it hard to read the Cast, but as far as I can tell, it's meant to siphon and hold magic. If the reservoir is ever fully depleted, the Artifact will cease functioning." Tapping the gash again, he concluded, "I'd assume that's what happened here. Someone took the full magic supply without leaving any reserve."

Someone like Ceyda, using it without knowing the Artifact's limitations.

Not for the first time, Silas mourned all the achievements his best friend could have made had he been born anywhere but Loegria.

"Thanks, Gilly," he said, his mind already racing through implications. Dazed, he added, "I need a place to write."

He limped to the nearest empty table and dumped out the contents of his bag, snatching up his pen and journal. Faintly, he heard Gill express concern and Eliza explain the cobra bite. Silas tuned them out and poured his thoughts in ink over the page.

Sketching furiously, he drew a triangle with three types of magic. He added the names of everyone tangled in this mystery—Havva, Ceyda, Mazhar, Yvette, himself.

If Iyal Havva had died in the experiment, perhaps he'd been betrayed by his Fluid Caster, or perhaps he'd been sabotaged by another Stone Caster who didn't want to contribute their own bones to the Artifact.

He circled *Silas Bennett, venom*, then wrote, *WHY?*

Affiliates could only create Artifacts from a piece of their animal link. Casters had to use something related to the purpose of their Cast. Historically, the two branches of warlockry couldn't work together because there were no Casts that coordinated with snakeskin or hawk feathers or ferret pelts.

This Artifact was made of human bone. It couldn't hold any Affiliate power.

Except . . .

This is human blood, Gill had said, *embedded in the bone.*

When Kerem had first brought Iyal Mazhar into their venom research, the Fluid Caster had talked animatedly about the possible benefits of their joint research in the medical field, including use in pain treatment and blood clotting.

"You snakes are remarkable!" Mazhar had declared. "I always thought Affiliates weren't that useful, no offense. Turn animal, sure, and you're quicker or stronger than the original. You can transform someone else if you get a good bite off. That's all. This venom is different. Paralysis, sleep, hallucinations—the effects go on, and so do the possibilities!"

As a liquid, venom could be manipulated by a Fluid Caster; that was how Mazhar had been able to dehydrate it. It could also infect blood.

Had Iyal Mazhar discovered new applications using venom-infected blood? Had the Fluid Caster's famous impatience led him to reckless experimentation?

Silas should have searched harder for Mazhar. If they used the tunnels to get back into the prison—

"Silas," said Eliza's quiet voice at his shoulder.

His hand jumped, adding a tail to one of his letters, but he continued scribbling out thoughts. They became harder to grasp with her nearness.

"Silas." She gripped his arm, pointing up with her other hand. "Look."

Kerem was on the first landing, speaking with Afshin. Then

Afshin turned away, climbing back up the stairs toward his office, while Kerem continued down, as if headed for the library.

In a snap, Silas closed his journal and met his professor at the bottom of the stairs, ignoring the throbbing protests of his leg.

"Silas! You're walking well." Kerem glanced down at the injured leg, then nodded, apparently pleased. He gave a small wave off to the side, which must have been a greeting for Tulip.

"What happened to Yvette?" demanded Eliza before Silas could speak. She'd come up behind him again, quiet as a mouse.

Kerem's expression fell. He adjusted his spectacles. "There's no verdict yet. Afshin is understandably hesitant to lose another professor, so she's being held by the guard while the examination continues. He's asked me to fetch the Artifact we found with Havva's daughter."

"Where is Ceyda?" Silas asked.

The pause did not bode well.

"In the healing hall," Kerem said at last. "By the time I found her, the tissue damage was extensive, and it's a miracle she was still breathing, but she'll likely lose her leg. It may be the best-case scenario if that's all she loses. The Casters have her unconscious, and treatment is in their hands now."

A knot of guilt settled at the base of Silas's throat. He hadn't meant to encourage the cobra to aggressiveness—his only command had been to *appear* threatening—but his own stress must have bled into his magic.

As if sensing his guilt, Kerem rested a hand on his shoulder, waiting for Silas to look up before he said, "No Affiliate has perfect control every time. There are environmental factors we can't manipulate, and animals will always have their own disposition and instincts."

"But I put it there," Silas said quietly.

"And suffered consequences as well," Kerem said with a meaningful glance at his leg.

The guilt eased slightly, but it didn't disappear.

"What did Ceyda tell you?" Eliza asked.

Kerem lowered his hand. "Her father was part of Iyl Yvette's team for constructing the prison. He laid the tunnels beneath the kuveti stronghold, instructing his daughter to use the hidden room in an emergency. It's possible he did so without Yvette's knowledge. However . . ."

He trailed off uncomfortably, and Silas heard the unspoken.

Yvette was the strongest Stone Caster at the university, and her attention to detail was legendary. The idea that someone could lay a Cast directly under her nose was improbable at best.

"So she knew about the tunnels," Eliza murmured in Loegrian. "That doesn't prove she killed anyone in them."

Silas looked at Kerem. "There's more," he prodded, "isn't there?"

"It's best to leave the details to Afshin. He'll be thorough and fair in his inv—"

"Please," said Silas.

Grimacing, Kerem shifted his weight. Finally, he said, "I went back to the tunnels and prison house, searching for Mazhar. I found a paper trail of arrests. All magic users. For weeks, the kuveti have been discreetly capturing targets and disposing of bodies under the employment of Yvette Sahin." He held up a hand to forestall Eliza's protest. "The kuveti may be amoral, but they are not unorganized. They keep careful record of who pays them."

Just like that, Silas's hope evaporated, leaving behind an empty hollow.

He had his conclusion.

And it was his worst fear.

When Kerem asked for the Artifact, Silas surrendered it without a word, but before the professor could return upstairs, Silas stopped him one last time.

"Iyal Mazhar?" he asked, dreading the answer.

Kerem shook his head. "I was too late."

CHAPTER

38

The silence weighed against Eliza's heart, making each beat slow and painful. After Kerem's departure, Silas quietly went back to the table and packed his supplies into his bag, like everything happening was just as he'd expected.

Well, it wasn't what she'd expected. She hated it. All of it.

"Why would Yvette do this?" she demanded.

Henry and Gill looked lost, since the conversation with Kerem had been in Pravish, but they must have read the tension in the silence, because they didn't break it.

"Why?" Eliza demanded again, trying and failing to catch Silas's eye. "She's a good person!" Her voice cracked, and tears stung her eyes.

She thought of her first visit to Yvette's office, all the gentle compassion in the woman's stern face as she examined the bracelets and asked, *Dear Eliza, what have you done?* She thought of the birthday celebration for Silas, the warm office transformed into a home. Baris's booming laugh next to Yvette's sly smile.

Real love is difficult, Yvette had told her, *because it requires the most vulnerability two people can ever give, and the most forgiveness.*

How could she talk about vulnerability and forgiveness while knowing someone was dragging bodies through a tunnel on her orders?

Silas slung his bag over his shoulder. His face looked drawn and ill. Resigned. "People aren't good or bad, *apta*. They aren't simple. They're just people."

He stepped past her and gripped Gill's shoulder. "I need a favor. A big one."

"Anything," said Gill without hesitation. He rested one hand loosely on the sword at his side, as if ready to go into battle on his friend's behalf.

"There's a girl in the healing hall who needs cobra venom out of her blood right away. She might already be beyond saving, but it's my fault she's there."

"I'll see what I can do," Gill promised.

Inside Eliza, the storm clouds billowed, and her breath came faster in her chest. Hadn't she *just* escaped this? She cast around desperately for something to anchor herself, something to *do* to outrun the threatening thunder, but she'd lost the quest to prove Yvette's innocence. There was nothing for her to do except be swept up in the storm.

Henry was looking at her with hesitation, one arm lifted like he might reach for her.

He already had a scar on that arm, already had a struggle of his own with his new magic. She couldn't hurt him again.

So she directed the storm the only place she could—

At the one person who'd been able to withstand everything she'd ever thrown at him.

Silas looked at her with steady, dark eyes, and he didn't retreat even when she marched forward and shoved both hands into his chest as hard as she could. He caught her wrists, stumbling on his bad side with a grunt.

He spoke with an infuriating evenness. "Gill, Henry, can you give us a minute? Henry, if you remember your way to the healing hall, you can point out Ceyda. We'll catch up shortly."

Henry looked like he wanted to speak, like he wanted to stay, but in the end, he led Gill out the door, leaving Silas and Eliza alone in the entry hall of the Yamakaz—as alone as they could be with groups of students whispering over homework at the corner tables.

"I bet you're happy now," she spat, yanking her hands away. "This is what always happens, right? People always betray, and they always turn out to be the worst versions of themselves."

She was doing it, too, blasting him with lightning instead of offering comfort when he'd lost more than she had.

Not that he cared. He didn't care about anything besides facts and experiments. He didn't care about people.

Didn't care about Yvette.

Didn't care about *her*.

"What I am," he said softly, "is heartbroken."

She faltered, the next insult dying on her lips. The waves pressed in, threatening to drown her.

Silas gripped the strap of his bag as if to keep his hand from shaking. "I didn't want it to be Yvette, and I don't have a good answer for why she'd do it. Ambition? Arrogance? They've gotten the best of good academics before. Maybe it's an old-fashioned lust for power. Maybe her own magic wasn't enough, and she wanted more. I don't know, Eliza. I don't have all the answers. Right now, I feel like I don't have any at all."

That made two of them. And in a single moment of clarity, all the answers and questions and storm clouds dropped away into meaninglessness, leaving behind nothing except a connection to Silas that went far deeper than the bracelet on her wrist.

"Silas Bennett without answers," she whispered. "That just won't do."

His lips gave the smallest twitch. "It's unnatural, we agree."

"I'm sorry. For goading you, for Yvette, for everything." She drew in a single quick breath for courage. "Everything except this."

Eliza grabbed him by the collar and pulled his lips down to meet hers. She expected him to tense or pull away, but he melted, wrapping his arms around her as if he'd been waiting for this. *Hoping* for it, even. He met her hunger with his own in a way that shot electricity down every limb like lightning strikes.

But this was a storm she could navigate.

She slid one hand up the back of his neck, sinking her fingers into his soft hair. The fingertips of her other hand traced his collarbone.

Silas pulled back, and she panicked, thinking she'd driven him away. But all he did was slide the bag from his shoulder, dropping it with a thump, before he flashed a wicked grin and recaptured her lips. She gave a quick smile of her own before her lips were far too distracted for expressions.

Then she was moving. Startled, she flung her arms around Silas's neck as he steered her backward to the nearest table. He lifted her onto its surface—staggering on his injured leg—just as a student reached for one of the chairs. The student hurried away, grumbling.

"Sorry," Silas called after him, his tone completely unapologetic.

Eliza laughed. She tightened her arms behind his neck, drawing him back toward her, and his dark eyes held hers for a brief yet fathomless moment before he dipped his head to kiss her jawline, trailing up to her ear. Her eyelids drifted closed as she savored every sensation of his lips against her skin. He made her feel understood and cherished and *seen.*

He'd once told her that if real love existed, it would be a simple thing. *Someone saying, I like you as you are.*

From the start, he'd *seen* her. He'd never flinched from her darkest moods, and he'd never dampened her brightest ones. She was under no delusion that he'd liked her from the start, but he'd always known the real her.

And she dared to believe he liked her now.

Eliza turned her head, catching Silas's lips again, and with everything inside her, she tried to kiss him in a way that said she felt the same. *Just as you are.* From his academic obsessions to his dry humor, from his endearing fascination with language to his irritating opinions about romance. He was bold and honest and wary, and she loved every part.

Even his magic, which was both dangerous and wonderful, which she'd seen both hurt and help.

He wouldn't be Silas without it.

So she loved it.

Silas breathed in rhythm with her, as if their heartbeats had synchronized to that message—*just as you are, just as you are*—beating together in a way to never be undone. His kisses unraveled every understanding Eliza thought she'd had of the world.

Once, in a moment of annoyance, she'd thought him the antithesis of every romantic hero. While it was true that he would never go charging anywhere on a white stallion—indeed, it was unlikely a white stallion would even tolerate him as a rider—she hadn't given him nearly enough credit.

Because no romantic hero ever imagined could kiss in a more passionate or tender way than Silas Bennett.

A sudden *clang-clang-clang* startled them apart. Eliza looked down, watching a golden bracelet roll across the polished floor. Silas lifted his hand from the table, turning his bare wrist as if he didn't recognize it. When he straightened, Eliza's arms slid free of his shoulders, and her own bracelet followed, hitting the floor and ringing through the domed hall.

In the echo of it, she recalled Yvette's words about the Cast. *If you aren't both in love with each other, then the kiss won't strike the right chord for the Cast.*

Her heart stuttered and then surged. She looked up at Silas with a radiant smile.

Only to find him staring down at the pair of bracelets in clear horror.

"Mr. Bennett?" said an apologetic librarian, speaking from several feet away. She kept one foot in the stacks while her head was in the entry hall. She said something about noise and "displays of affection."

Eliza's face heated beyond any sunburn. Without the Cast, she could no longer understand every word, but the meaning was clear.

"Sorry," Silas said, his tone genuinely apologetic this time. "We were just leaving."

He snatched up his discarded bag while Eliza grabbed the two bracelets. She couldn't say why, since they were useless now, but it felt wrong to leave them on the library floor.

The outside air only added heat to her face, and the humidity stuck to her skin, making her as uncomfortable as possible. Silas walked with quick strides, and she realized he could actually leave her behind now, so she caught his arm, dragging him to a stop.

"Can we talk about what happened in there?"

He shrugged. "Getting thrown out of the library—that's a first for me."

She was too nervous to muster a smile. "No, I mean the kiss."

Kiss was hardly adequate. There had been many kisses, more than enough to leave her head still spinning.

He looked away, and the avoidance constricted her stomach. She clenched her fingers more tightly in the fabric of his sleeve, as if to prevent him from running away, and words spilled from her one after another.

"You kissed me back. Why? Were you declaring love? Asking me to stay? Taking *pity* on me? Use your words, Silas Bennett, in whatever language you want, and tell me what this *means*."

He raked his free hand through his hair, trying to pull away, but she held fast.

"Tell me!" she insisted, forcing him to look at her.

"It doesn't mean anything!" he burst out. "It just . . . happened. It doesn't mean anything."

She released him, her arm falling slack to her side. With her other hand, she clutched the twin bracelets to her chest, as if to shield them. Perhaps to shield herself. Tears welled in her eyes.

She *knew* what it meant—the Cast breaking had been evidence enough. But if he couldn't admit it, if he was determined to lie and to hide in his old avoidances that love didn't exist or that a kiss meant nothing at all, then it didn't matter.

It didn't matter if Silas loved her. He didn't want to.

"Thank you," she said softly, "for being clear. Because, for a moment there, I thought it meant I loved you. But I suppose it was just one of my romantic whims."

She dropped the bracelets on the path at his feet, and then she ran. It was cowardly, but it felt good, knowing he couldn't catch her if she didn't let him, knowing he wouldn't be dragged along on a tether. She was physically free of him.

If only the same could be said for her mind and heart.

Silas cursed himself in every language he knew. He kicked at one of the bracelets, wishing he could blame the Cast or the Caster behind it, wishing he could blame Yvette or Eliza. But his failings were all his own.

For a few precious minutes, he'd held the entire world in his arms, and at the first opportunity, he'd thrown it away. Eliza's voice haunted him from memory.

Be better than that, Silas. Be braver.

But he didn't know how.

The instant he'd seen the Cast broken, all his fears had come rushing in. So before Eliza could leave him, he'd left her. Before she could betray him, he'd betrayed her.

As a cornered snake, he'd spat venom.

And even if he wanted to transform back . . .

He didn't know how.

He rubbed at the scar on his throat. His first impulse was to go to Yvette for advice, and that made everything worse. Clearly, Silas's judgment when it came to people couldn't be trusted.

He tried to convince himself to head toward the healing hall, but the command swirled in his mind without ever reaching his feet. Standing rooted, he imagined what would happen if he went. Gill would see right through him.

What have you done? his best friend would ask, like Silas was one of his younger brothers, guilty of mischief.

I kissed Eliza.

Surely that would go over well.

You? A royal?

Yes, yes, lay it on. I remember everything I said when you told me you were in love with a Loegrian princess.

Are you in love with a Loegrian princess?

Even in his mind, Silas couldn't say a simple yes. The ground had vanished beneath him, and maybe he would never move forward again.

I don't even know what love is, Gill.

Eliza wanted him to be braver than he was, but even if he tried, what then? She could never stay away from Loegria indefinitely, and he could never go back. They were at an impasse. Any confession—any attempt on his part to make his feelings clear—would only end with a parting even more brutal than this one. A betrayal.

He remembered her devastation after her fight with Henry. Silas had been a hypocrite, wanting to comfort her after her unanswered confession, thinking Henry a fool for walking away.

At least Henry had only retreated.

Silas had offered her the world, then said it meant nothing.

She really was better off with the knight.

Eliza ran without caring where she was going. She left campus behind, taking the path out onto the Izili cliffs, but she didn't turn left into the city or right toward the Sarazan tabernacle. She raced out to the cliff edge, until she ran out of ground, until she slid to a halt, panting, her face streaked with sweat, seagulls crying above her and the ocean stretching out below.

It was beautiful. Blue and sparkling with a white haze of promise. Endless.

It was beautiful, and she hated it.

Dropping to the rocky ground, Eliza released a scream, pitiful and swallowed by the vast landscape before her. She bent forward. Inside, she clutched at driftwood and fought the currents, but the water was too strong this time. And she was *tired.*

It was time to surrender.

It was time to go home.

But for the moment, she sat back on her heels, and she let herself sob for every lost dream.

CHAPTER

39

Silas found there was only one person he could face, so he took an automatic, familiar path, returning through the Yamakaz and climbing the stairs to the third floor. He knocked woodenly at Kerem's office door, remembering too late that the professor would be with the dean, examining the Artifact.

But just as he started to leave, the door opened.

"Silas!" Kerem peered into the hallway, clearly looking for a girl-shaped shadow.

"Just me," Silas said quietly.

"You're always welcome."

The open door and greeting didn't heal anything, but it offered a comfort, one Silas didn't deserve but needed. His leg throbbed after all the stairs, so he lowered himself onto one of the stools beside the desk.

"You're not with Afshin?" he asked.

Kerem waved a hand. "It's not my place to overstep, and I don't envy the dean's job in circumstances like this."

"I thought you'd want to evaluate the Artifact at least. When I ran my own tests, I discovered it's composition warlockry." Usually, he could drown any emotion in research, and he turned to the tactic once again, opening his journal to his Artifact notes. "I need to turn these over to Afshin, but I was hoping to translate them to an actual essay first."

"May I?" Kerem extended his hand, and Silas surrendered his

journal. The professor pushed his spectacles into his black hair, peering closely at the detailed but chaotic notes. He flipped the pages slowly.

Silas found himself holding his breath, waiting for a grade. Though he was no longer a student, the old habits and mindset came easily. Would that change once he was a professor?

Then again, did he have any hope of becoming one? The discovery of composition warlockry between three magic types was certainly groundbreaking, but it wasn't as if he'd created the Artifact himself, and the person who *had* was also on trial for murder. Silas had become nothing but a fringe figure in a complicated situation.

Maybe if he could get Gill to work with him, he could present research on his venom interacting with Fluid Casting. But Gill had only come to convince him to return home—and to escort Eliza. He wouldn't want an extended stay away from his brothers and fiancée.

"Have you ever been in love?" Silas didn't mean to ask the question, and his neck heated. But it wasn't as if he could ask advice from his parents. Yvette and Kerem were the closest he had, and Yvette was . . .

"Hmm?" Kerem asked without looking up. He flipped a page. "You mean marriage? No, I never saw the benefit. I imagine my work habits would be a problem for a spouse, and I prefer the freedom to do as I please."

That answer should have placated Silas. It would have a few weeks ago.

Yet the itch remained.

"I always thought a relationship was just an opportunity for betrayal," he whispered.

"Considering I was sold into slavery by a friend," Kerem said bitterly, "I can't argue."

How could Silas feel *more* miserable to be agreed with?

He fell silent, trying and failing to direct his mind toward research while it wanted to chase a girl who was already gone.

"This is spectacular," said Kerem, resting his hand on the open journal. "Working from the outside, given the barest information, and you've still managed to deduce so much. I always said you were the brightest mind on campus." He met Silas's eyes, and he smiled, though it held a touch of regret, a contradiction to his words.

"Thank you." Silas's neck heated again, and he wasn't sure what else to say. He should have been thrilled at the praise, but his emotions felt dulled, slow to engage. He'd left at least half of himself behind in the library, kissing a princess.

"It's lucky for me," Kerem went on, "that you've been distracted of late. But I can't count on that forever. Eventually, your mind will catch up, so it's better that we navigate this crossroads now."

Silas frowned, sitting more stiffly on his stool. His skin prickled with awareness, and he tried to force himself to be fully present in the moment, ignoring the ache in his calf and the pull of a princess.

"What do you mean?" he asked.

Wrong question—her voice came back to him as an accusation. *Tell me what this means!*

He flinched.

"I would much rather have you on my side, Silas. It's one thing to work with your venom, but to work with your mind . . . I'm sure we could revolutionize everything. Not to mention I've always enjoyed working with you more than with either Havva or Mazhar."

Something's wrong, Silas thought, unable to form anything more coherent than that. He should have gone to the healing hall. Should have . . .

Kerem's voice remained even, as if this were any normal day, any one of the hundred times Silas had come to his office to work. "You would just have to convince me you can be objective about the sacrifices required for advancement. After all, the Artifact I created did not come at low cost."

Silas found his focus at last, and it sent his heart plummeting through the floor.

He really was the worst judge of people.

Eventually, Eliza dragged herself to the healing hall. Part of her wanted to slink away without telling anyone, to return home the same way she'd left it, but she'd done enough intentional hurting, and if Henry really wasn't returning home, she wanted a proper goodbye.

With Silas, she . . .

She didn't know. But she owed herself a chance to decide while calm.

Unlike the Sarazan tabernacle, the healing hall had permanent beds and rooms separated by doors rather than curtains. Mint permeated the air, perhaps used for calming patients or to cover any unpleasant smells.

After asking directions to Ceyda's room, she found Gill and Henry already there. No Silas.

But Ceyda was awake.

She looked dreadful, all the warmth leached from her dark skin, her dry lips pale and her face thin, but she still had both legs—judging by the shape of the blanket across them—and she didn't seem to be ringing the bell for death.

"You were unconscious!" Eliza blurted.

Ceyda watched her suspiciously with crystal-blue eyes before giving a shallow nod toward Gill. "I believe he fixed that."

"It's relieving to have a translator," Gill said mildly, pulling on a set of white gloves and adjusting them across his hands. He rubbed his head as if it ached. "I managed the magic but nothing since."

Eliza blinked, then realized she'd spoken Pravish to Ceyda. It had just . . . come naturally.

She rubbed her bare wrist.

"Where is Silas?"

The question could have come from anyone, but it came from

Ceyda, and since the answer could only be understood by her, Eliza indulged herself in a raw truth.

"*Bikmayak kalamak*," she said. *My sword breaks here.*

The severing of a relationship.

Ceyda sagged against the pillow, as if relieved. Eliza wished her own emotions could follow a similar track, but deep inside, she felt a gaping hollow. It was all that was left after she'd cried the rest out.

Henry caught her eyes, but neither of them spoke.

One of the female physicians entered, and Eliza did her best to translate for Gill. Apparently, the Casters at the healing hall had tried both drawing out the venom and spreading an antivenom to counter it but hadn't felt confident about either treatment since their lead healer was missing.

"I'm aware how difficult working with blood is," said Gill. "Luckily, I've had some recent practice. I drew out what remained of the venom, which stopped her fever, but I can't reverse any of the damage already done."

"I've never learned the word for 'fever,'" Eliza muttered. She squared her shoulders and tried her best, calling the fever "head hot" and touching her own forehead.

The physician smiled and seemed to understand well enough. Then she spoke to Ceyda briefly, the girl's face growing more frightened with every word. She couldn't have been older than Eliza.

"They're going to evaluate her leg again," Eliza translated. "See if . . . if they have to remove it."

As the physician left, Eliza seated herself firmly on the edge of Ceyda's bed. She took the other girl's hand, giving it a squeeze. Ceyda didn't pull away. When she muttered a curse about snakes, Eliza's sympathy reached all the way to her soul.

"It doesn't matter," Ceyda rasped, her thin voice high and frightened. She clenched her other hand in the blanket. "Even if they heal me, he'll just come after me again."

"Who?"

"*Shedskin*," Ceyda spat.

Eliza pursed her lips. Of all the terrible things Silas Bennett was, he wasn't a killer.

"He never meant to hurt you," she said. Pointing at Gill, she added, "He sent a Caster so you wouldn't die."

Ceyda shook her head, clearly swallowed in panic. "The cobra was too gentle for him. He'd rather kill me with his Sarazan."

"Sarazan?" Eliza frowned. "What do you mean?"

The girl glanced at Henry, who looked back with cluelessness.

"The Sarazan tabernacle?" Eliza asked. "Did something happen there?"

"I . . . made a wave." Ceyda swallowed, gripping Eliza's hand tightly enough to leave grooves from her fingernails. "The Artifact felt wrong to use, like—" She said something Eliza couldn't parse. Heart painting? Perhaps an idiom. "I made a wave to sink the ship."

She started speaking in longer, rushed sentences, and Eliza snatched translations from any of the words she could scrape together. "A monster from the ocean. Snake as big as Sarazan. Drowned the sailors."

Ceyda's eyes darted toward Henry again. "I used magic to get us to shore. No one else."

"She keeps looking at me," Henry said softly, the question clear.

Eliza offered him a quick summary. Then, to Ceyda, she said, "Silas didn't send Sarazan. It's just a monster in the ocean."

Ceyda yanked her hand back, shaking her head and then seeming to regret it. She pressed her palms to her temples, squeezing her eyes closed.

"It was after *me*," she insisted, her voice cracking. "Everywhere I go—snakes. Hunting me. I hid underground, and even then, he still found me."

Eliza frowned. Silas had sent out snakes, yes, but he'd said they could never find any trace of Ceyda. She made it sound like she'd been dodging them on every street corner, not to mention in the ocean itself.

"Are you certain . . ." Eliza's voice trailed into silence as she realized one awful possibility. *Silas isn't the only Snake Affiliate here.*

She stood, shying from the thought.

But once it presented itself, she couldn't shake it.

She remembered standing in the alley with Kerem and Silas, remembered the ease with which Kerem banished the cobra. His exasperated voice: *You should have let it bite her the second time.*

Silas had felt so guilty over Ceyda's condition.

But he'd never ordered the cobra to bite in the first place.

Henry moved to stand next to Eliza, his hand hovering above her shoulder. "What's wrong?" he asked.

"No," she murmured. "Why would he save her then?"

He could have told Silas he was too late. Clearly the threat of death had been real enough from her injury. Why bring her to the healers?

Unless he needed people to see he had a witness. A witness who, conveniently, fell unconscious before speaking to anyone else. Who would likely not last the night.

Eliza leaned over the bed again, speaking urgently. "The man who found you after the cobra. What did you tell him?"

Ceyda kept her eyes closed, hands pressed to her head.

"Please! Did you tell him about Yvette?"

"Who?" Ceyda looked up at last, her blue eyes cloudy.

"The Stone Caster your father built the prison with."

"I don't know anyone from his work except Silas Bennett."

Eliza stumbled back, feeling sick. She had focused on trying to prove Yvette innocent, but she'd never considered what it meant if she was. She'd never looked for who was actually guilty.

Silas worked with Kerem. Trusted him more than anyone else.

She had to warn him, before it was too late.

CHAPTER

40

Each passing second dragged through Eliza's heart like a needle, leaving behind stitches of dread. She told Gill and Henry her suspicions, and then they just *looked* at her, like they expected her to know how to solve everything.

They're looking to their princess, she realized. It was the same look people had always given Aria. Whether Eliza wanted to be or not, for two members of the Loegrian court, she was the authority figure in the room.

Silas had never looked at her like that. He might have called her "Highness," but he had no difficulty taking charge, no qualms about making his own intentions clear. When they'd infiltrated the kuveti prison, they'd made the plan together.

"I need some input here!" she burst out. "I don't know where Silas is. Do we search for him first, or will that waste too much time? Would it be better to go straight to the dean? Kerem may already be there. As soon as he knows we're suspicious, we'll be covered in cobras."

Gill took the invitation first, resting one hand on his sword. "We can split up. I'll search for Silas. You and Henry inform the university's dean."

As always, Eliza found herself a walking contradiction. She'd asked for opinions, yet upon receiving one, her instinct was to protest. The thought of running to the dean instead of to Silas felt like asking a famished woman to ignore a feast. Her willpower cracked.

But she was the only one who could speak Pravish, however roughly.

"Fine," she forced herself to say. "If you—"

"I can't protect her," Henry interjected, his voice pained. "I don't have a weapon, and even if I did, you're the far better swordsman. You go with Eliza, and I'll look for Silas."

"You have a weapon," Eliza said. "You have magic."

And Silas was right; it was nothing to be ashamed of.

"Baron," Henry said, ignoring Eliza.

But she refused to be ignored.

"You can both look for Silas, then! I'll protect myself!" She threw her hands up. "I don't know why all the men in my life are so eager to be rid of me, but I'm taking it personally. Good riddance to you all."

She stormed from the healing hall, passing physicians and Casters. The late afternoon sun slanted into her eyes, set against her just like everything else, and she raised a hand to block it.

After a few minutes, Gill caught up. Henry was nowhere to be seen. Eliza clenched her jaw but said nothing, practicing silently what she would say to the dean.

They climbed to the fourth floor of the Yamakaz, and although Eliza had never personally met Afshin during her time at the university, she pretended full confidence when knocking at his door.

A pair of guards answered, and Eliza gave her name and title, certain to say *crown princess* properly this time. They looked skeptical—she was just a frazzled girl in Pravish clothing—but, thankfully, Gill had the official paperwork and seal from Aria to legitimize an ambassador claim. After a brief conference between dean and guards, they were admitted.

The dean's office had a welcoming feel, with curved walls and a domed ceiling. Overhead windows beamed in sunlight. Afshin greeted them both with a warm smile, although he looked haggard around the edges. His collar sat askew, as if he'd been pulling at it, and stress shadowed his eyes.

"A Loegrian delegation!" Afshin said, ushering them to a cushioned seating area.

Eliza stifled a groan, realizing he spoke perfect Loegrian. So much for her practice.

"This is exceedingly rare," he went on. "It may be the first time while I've served over the university. But I had hoped, with the recent changes in your government, we might open a communication."

How would he feel if he knew she'd been sneaking around his campus for weeks, chasing her own problems without ever worrying about the bigger picture between countries?

"What brings you here, Your Royal Highness?" Afshin asked.

"Actually, I've been here for . . . a short while. Accompanying Silas Bennett. We happened to become entangled in recent events, and I've found information you need to know relating to the deaths of Iyal Havva and others."

Clearly, Afshin hadn't expected the conversation to turn this direction, so Eliza plowed on.

"Iyal Kerem is framing Yvette. Ceyda never offered a witness against her, and I'm certain he planted the research journal and forged the documents from the kuveti as well."

Afshin struggled for composure. "You have an extensive knowledge of what's happening at our university. These are . . . serious accusations."

Eliza frowned. "They've already been laid against Yvette. I'm only directing them at the right person."

"What proof do you have to offer?"

"You can speak to Ceyda, for a start. She can tell you about the giant snake Kerem sent after her."

Afshin tensed. His fingers tapped slowly against his knee, as if he were considering a variety of responses and trying to choose the right one.

"I *have* had reason to consider a Snake Affiliate's involvement in this matter," he finally admitted.

Eliza's flash of triumph died as quickly as it appeared. Because she heard his silent implication. *Snake Affiliate.* Not a name.

Sitting as tall as she could, she declared, "I can account for Silas Bennett's whereabouts and actions every minute of the last weeks. While we were linked by a Cast, I was unable to go more than a few feet from him, and I would stake my own crown and reputation on his innocence. Any involvement he may have suffered was a result of Kerem's manipulations. *Kerem* is the real snake."

She felt Gill's eyes on her, and she wondered what he was thinking about her involvement with Silas, but she kept her gaze facing resolutely forward.

Eventually, Afshin shook his head. The shadows beneath his eyes darkened, as if he was actively growing more tired.

"Ceyda Polat," he said. "You claim she's awake. I was told by our healers that she would not regain consciousness for days, that her odds of even surviving were quite low."

Unable to help a touch of smugness, Eliza gestured to her side. "Well, I brought my own Fluid Caster, and he's impressive enough to be a king."

Gill gave her a flat stare for that, but she didn't care.

"Come with us," she insisted. "Speak to her yourself."

Together with Afshin's four guards, they made their way toward the healing hall. As they passed the third-floor landing, Eliza looked down the row of faculty offices. Kerem's door was closed, with no sign of movement. She hesitated on the landing.

Was Silas there? Was Kerem?

Her feet took one step toward that office, longing to charge forward.

Afshin's gaze weighed heavily on her.

"I'm worried Silas is in danger," she said. "He's Kerem's research assistant, and he doesn't know what the professor's done."

"Allegedly," Afshin said with all that weight.

Somehow, Eliza stopped herself from running off in spite of him. She held her ground instead. "You arrested Yvette on allegations, but Kerem's allowed to remain a potential danger to students on your campus?"

As she'd hoped, protection of his students was the correct appeal. With a nod, Afshin sent the guards to Kerem's office.

It was empty.

Eliza's dread doubled. What were the odds Kerem and Silas could both be missing and not together?

Silas went back to his dorm, she told herself, trying to believe it. *Kerem is off doing evil snake things, and Silas is sulking in his dorm.*

She reached in her pocket, curling her fingers around the leather-bound snakeskin Silas had given her, tucked against her book of sonnets.

Silas is fine. He's fine. He's too stubborn to get hurt.

Yet she remembered wrapping his wounded leg in an alley. The last snake he'd come up against had won, and she had a feeling Kerem was far more ruthless than a cobra. For all Silas's bold opinions, he was softhearted. He comforted crying princesses. He tried to rescue strangers from prison.

He was going to get eaten alive.

Gill touched her shoulder, and for a moment, they shared a silent worry.

"Henry will find him," said the Caster.

She wondered if he was having as much difficulty talking himself out of the fear as she was.

Once at the healing hall, Afshin talked with Ceyda until he ran out of questions and she ran out of energy. Eliza caught highlights of the conversation but missed large chunks as well. For all her improvement, her Pravish still had a long way to go. As far as she could tell, Afshin's suspicion of Kerem grew during the conversation.

He ordered a search for the professor.

Unfortunately, Henry returned to the healing hall out of breath and empty-handed. He'd searched the dorm and campus buildings but hadn't found Silas anywhere.

Silas couldn't die. If he didn't want to love Eliza, fine. If he wanted to be a stubborn, ill-tempered snake hermit all his life, *fine*. But he couldn't die. She wouldn't allow it.

"Henry," she said softly, reaching for him.

He must have anticipated the request she was about to make because he shook his head, taking a step backward. She caught his hands anyway, drawing him back toward her.

"I've seen the way Silas can use snakes," she said. "It's how he found me. Please. Whatever animal link you have, you can find him."

"I can't," he said, voice cracking.

She wrapped her arms around him. After a hesitant moment, he pressed his hands to her back and rested his chin on her shoulder, breathing deeply. The irony struck her—how she'd once tried to convince Silas to help her find Henry, and now it was the other way around. She remembered throwing herself into Silas's arms in the library, partly as a ploy to get the bracelet on his wrist and partly out of genuine fear of the python at their feet.

Here she was again, just as fearful but of different things. Manipulating with another hug.

But she would do whatever it took to find him.

"How long have you been an Affiliate?" asked Gill with some wonder.

Henry tensed, pulling away from Eliza. Color stained his cheeks. "Just recently."

He seemed bolstered by the fact that Gill didn't run screaming in the other direction. Instead, the Caster gave a gentle smile and said, "You'll be pleased to know Her Majesty has repealed the laws against Animal Affiliates. You're safe to be yourself in Loegria now."

Eliza's heart swelled. She could always count on her sister's compassion.

"My family will still hate me," Henry whispered. "My father . . ." He trailed off, clearly thinking of how things had gone between Silas and Lord Bennett.

"Actually, as a member of the Upper Court, your father has spoken in defense of freedom for magic. Aria is relying on Lord Wycliff quite heavily to help champion all the changes she's making."

For a moment, Henry just stared, as if he had to repeat Gill's words in his mind before he could make sense of them. Then he gave a small smile, meeting Eliza's eyes once more.

As if steeling himself for a tournament, he said, "I'll try."

"Thank you." Eliza sagged in relief. "Now will you finally tell me what your animal link is?"

It likely wouldn't be as widespread as snakes, but she could still hope for a miracle.

"It's better if I just show you."

With that, the noble knight puffed into a tiny brown rat.

After learning Kerem was a murderer, the smartest action would have been to call for help and try to escape. Instead, Silas willingly followed him out of the Yamakaz and away from all its guards and fortifications. After everything that had gone wrong, he couldn't help clinging to a sliver of hope that Kerem had a good explanation for what he'd done, that if Silas just listened, he'd find the misunderstanding.

He finally understood why Eliza had been so stubborn after the shipwreck. Better to cling to a fragile hope than to embrace a nightmare.

And he'd already lost everything else.

His former professor led him into a series of tunnels beneath campus. They pointed toward the ocean, and soon enough, Silas heard the distant crash of waves, echoing dully against the rock walls. The narrow tunnels opened into wide caverns, some of which must have led to caves in the cliffside.

They stopped in a low-ceilinged but expansive cavern. Natural rock structures had clearly been used as tables, some still bearing abandoned cups or surrounded by chairs. Notes had been scrawled in chalk across the rock walls. As far as research rooms went, it was more atmospheric than anything on campus.

Kerem set his lantern on a table, correcting an overturned cup like a wayward student. Silas thought of corrected essays, of afternoons in lecture hall, of the surge of pride he felt whenever Kerem noted his contributions in class. Mentor and murderer—Silas could not reconcile the two identities in his mind.

It was like trying to understand his father all over again.

"It began with a dream," said Kerem, his voice echoing surreally in the cavern. Lantern light flickered across the rock walls. "First, a dream of achievement. My grandfather raised me, and he believed in experimentation and potential. Everything was an achievement waiting to happen. I was ten years old when my magic activated, and he encouraged me in every exploration of it. He paid for my education. I saw an open world, with nothing barred to me."

Silas's eyes roamed the white letters across the walls, but his mind focused on Kerem's voice.

"That dream dissolved, running like sand through the hands of Cronese slavers."

One by one, Kerem shuttered three sides of the lantern, throwing the cavern into deep shadows. The remaining light illuminated only one cavern wall, jagged rock cut deeply by trickling water over the course of time.

"Eight years I spent being sold from one wealthy family to another, a snake on display, transforming for their entertainment or suffering the consequences in blood. I had only one dream left to me. A dream of escape."

In the echoing shadows, Silas felt the walls pressing in.

"I thought once I achieved it," Kerem said quietly, "I could go back to where I was before. But the world never turns backward. When I finally came home, I'd grown from child to adult, and it was home no longer. My grandfather was gone. I had no family, no friendships, no path forward. Even my magic—forever damaged.

"Freedom, which should have been everything, was nothing."

Silas pressed one hand to a dark wall, leaning his weight off his throbbing leg. A deeper pain pulsed beneath.

He knew what it was like to lose a home.

"Another ten years of struggle," said Kerem, "advancements and accolades, a professorship and a name for myself. Yet I could never forget what had been taken. It was time for a new dream."

He turned the lantern, throwing its focused light onto a different wall, white with chalk. Even at a distance, Silas could distinguish three sets of handwriting woven together.

"A Stone Caster, Fluid Caster, and Affiliate, all coordinating magic. A project with almost zero chance of success, but I had nothing to lose."

Silas spoke at last, his voice hoarse. "Iyal Havva did."

The wire frame of Kerem's spectacles cut shadows like scars across his face. "I predicted the Artifact creation would draw out a single bone, that he would survive the process, however painfully. Havva thought so as well, and he agreed to that sacrifice. We planned for it. I never imagined the true result."

"Is that why you felt guilty and took his body home?" It would have been smarter to dump it in the ocean or pass it to the graveyard like the other magic users, though the thought made Silas ill.

A tic passed through Kerem's jaw. "That was Mazhar's sentimentality. Since Havva was our collaborator, Mazhar insisted his death be known and his sacrifice respected, even if no one knew the truth. I never should have agreed. It cost me the Artifact after I'd already begun experimenting with it. A monumental setback, especially when I failed to capture the thief."

It was a wonder Ceyda had survived. If she had. Silas prayed Gill had been able to find and help her in the healing hall, that her presence there wasn't simply one more lie.

"How did you recruit Havva and Mazhar? You just knocked on another professor's door and asked him to offer up one of his bones for your secret project?"

Kerem shook his head, as if disappointed in Silas's reasoning. "Initially, I carried a hatred of Cronith. Of the slavers who sold me, the people who purchased, the government that refused to outlaw a barbaric practice as long as it stayed limited to foreigners rather than its own citizens.

"But it was my own country that was most to blame. The shackles I wore that damaged my magic were not made in Cronith but in Pravusat. It was Pravusat's black market that allowed them to be created and smuggled into dangerous hands. It was Pravusat's lawlessness that allowed me to be captured and sold in the first place, and it was Pravusat's selfishness that turned a blind eye to the outcome."

Eliza's voice echoed in Silas's mind. *What is wrong with this place? No one cares.*

"I was not the only one enraged by Pravusat's deficiencies." Kerem stepped up to the wall, touching one set of handwriting, then another. "Mazhar was orphaned by senseless violence, the attacker released from justice on a bribe. Havva lost his wife when the Nephew King burned a city for a crown. We'd all suffered, and we all hungered."

"What was the dream?" Silas asked.

This time, he received a quick glance of approval, like he'd given the right answer in class. It made his heart ache more than his leg.

"A stable government." Kerem unshuttered one side of the lantern, spilling new light. "An end to corruption." He opened another side. "And the power to achieve it." The final side.

The lantern glowed like a beacon in the dreary cavern.

With a hollow smile, Silas said, "I should have known it was a revolution. It's Pravusat."

Kerem smiled to match, as if they were sharing a joke. "To survive a viper's den, you must be the bigger viper. There is no way to save this country from itself except by overwhelming power, and the greatest power resides in magic."

"So you made an impossible Artifact—one that could steal and hoard magic—to set yourself up as king."

"Dictator," Kerem corrected. "Despot, perhaps. Let's not be soft about the terms. I intend to pull this drunken country from the gutter, clean it by my own hands, and *force* it to remain upright."

"No regard to freedom."

"I know the price of freedom," he said sharply. "And I know when it's undeserved."

Silas shook his head. "Maybe so. But I've never believed anything good comes from unchecked power."

Loegria's monarchy had ruled without challenge for centuries, yet held an entire country in oppressive tradition.

Shifting, Kerem leaned against the table, his shadow long and dark beside him. "Imagine this, then. Imagine yourself back in the moment your father drew his sword."

Silas tensed.

"You're helpless. Death is approaching. Except—" Kerem lifted a finger. "When he swings, you catch the blade."

Silas swallowed. "I can't do that."

"A Stone Caster could. Bend the metal or blunt the edge, your choice. Imagine it, Silas. Imagine staring into your father's eyes and knowing he *can't* hurt you, because you hold a power he can't match."

Despite himself, the image hung in Silas's mind, rewriting the past. He felt the cold press of harmless metal against his hand, saw the shock in his father's dark eyes. His worst memory, transformed.

And the emotion seizing his chest was no longer terror. It was empowerment.

Before Silas could dispel the dream, Kerem pressed on.

"Now imagine how much more you could do. Fluid Casting, Stone Casting, a dozen Affiliate links—all at your fingertips. Imagine walking into the palace unhampered, knowing that whatever you said, they would have to listen. What message would you bring the monarchy?"

Silas gritted his teeth, reining in his mind even as it eagerly offered up a dozen lectures.

"You're simplifying," he ground out. Just because a problem could be solved by force didn't make it the right solution.

Hypocrite, said his own mind. The first thing he'd done when meeting Eliza was threaten her with snakes. He'd made a show of power, even thought of himself as royalty, and relished the feeling that she could do nothing to stop him.

Silas winced.

Dictator. Despot.

He could understand what Kerem wanted to do and why. But there was still a disconnect in the *how*.

"Explain the graveyard pattern to me," he said. "The bodies of magic users buried by the kuveti. Tell me honestly—when your Artifact harvests magic, it kills, doesn't it?"

Kerem grimaced. "Unfortunately, yes."

Silas remembered his first meeting with Ceyda, the way he'd felt his soul unstitched from his body. He'd been mere footsteps from death.

All thanks to his favorite professor.

"You blame Pravusat for letting slavers target the innocent," he said. "Meanwhile, you're dragging them off the street into open graves. How is it any different from what was done to you?"

He'd struck a nerve. Kerem straightened, shoulders tensing. He reached out to touch the lantern, like drawing renewed magic from a serpent.

"I wish the path were different," he said at last. "But the deaths happening now will end, and they'll accomplish an exponential saving."

The calm voice of reasoning was one Silas had heard so many times from a podium. His hand twitched, as if unnerved to not be taking notes.

He wanted so badly to justify Kerem. But he couldn't justify this.

"Pravusat is a disaster," Silas admitted quietly. "But to me, it's been a paradise. It's saved me from something worse. You let your bias control your perspective, Iyal. You fixated on the rot instead of seeing everything worth saving."

Had Silas done the same with Loegria?

"Without cutting out the rot," said Kerem, "there will be nothing left worth saving."

"And with the way you're cutting, there will be nothing left at all."

Kerem lowered his hand from the lantern, his expression mournful. "Advancement has never come without sacrifice; this is only more bitter than most. My best student is strong enough to see that. Tell me I haven't lost him to idealism."

Idealism. If so, it was Eliza's influence.

And Silas could never regret that.

"I can't be your research assistant on this," he said, and despite his best effort to be firm, his voice cracked. Not because he wasn't resolved, but because he hated everything about what was happening.

This was the worst day of his life.

"I'm truly sorry to hear it," Kerem whispered. He turned his back on Silas and stepped away from the table.

On the far side of the cavern, where it narrowed and led to other caves, a large shadow moved. For an instant, lantern light reflected off one massive, yellow eye.

Silas hadn't realized how distraught he was, how unstable in his magic, to not have sensed what was right in front of him.

A scaled nose as wide as his forearm poked into the cavern. Following it came a scaled, diamond-shaped head, which lifted to brush the ceiling. The serpent stared down at him through yellow eyes with black slit pupils. Its head alone was half his height.

Despite the horror of the situation, Silas couldn't help a little thrill of wonder at the creature before him.

"Sarazan, I presume." He licked his lips. "So I suppose there's no point in saying, 'Sarazan save me.'"

CHAPTER

41

Henry was doing his best, but magic was a skill he'd never practiced. Gill could only coach him on Affiliate abilities from secondhand experience, and Eliza didn't have any insights to add. Even if Henry had been an expert, trying to find one person in a sprawling city of thousands would take time, and time was a precious resource.

Rather than standing around uselessly, she had her own plan.

It was madness to think it would work, but she had to do *something.*

While Gill and Henry were distracted, she slipped from the healing hall and made her way back to the Yamakaz, winding through the stacks until she reached a wide planter with a tree sprouting right in the middle of the library. It took her a moment to spot Tulip among the branches, and she'd never been so grateful to see a twelve-foot snake.

"*Nirhaba,* Tulip." It was best to be as respectful as possible, since she was about to ask a python for favors. "I'm Eliza, if you remember."

The python cinched herself around the branch, stretching out her neck to look Eliza in the eye. Eliza swallowed, then took one step closer. Tulip's dark eyes appeared solid at first, but up close, she could distinguish the light-brown iris and the thin black pupil.

"We have the same eye color. Sort of." She swallowed again, her mouth suddenly dry. "Tulip, I need your help. Silas is in danger. You love Silas, right?"

Tulip flicked her tongue, which Eliza chose to take as confirmation and not as her simply thinking of a meal.

"I have to find him. Can you . . . sense him? The way he can sense you?"

Another tongue flick. The snake didn't move.

Eliza rubbed her arm, shifting. She was talking to a snake. What had she expected? With a sigh, she turned away. The library stood empty, haunting her with memories of sitting at a table beside Silas, throwing herself into his arms, peering over his shoulder at books, kissing him senseless.

She was not an Affiliate. She had no reason to believe she could communicate the way they could. But even with every evidence against her, she could believe in the impossible. That was her specialty.

Closing her eyes and drawing deep, even breaths, Eliza tried to remember exactly what Silas had said about talking to snakes.

It's magic and sensory input, not rational thought and language.

Eliza gathered all her feelings about Silas. She didn't worry about putting them to words the way she would have with a human—*I love him; I'm scared for him*—but instead tried to hold him in all her senses. The image of the last time she'd seen him, blurred through her tears. The scent of almond-spice on his skin as he carried her to a library table, and the taste of his lips against hers. The sound of his voice, not from memory but as she imagined it, broken after Kerem's betrayal.

Most of all, her empty arms, longing to hold him. He was out there, facing danger, and she would claw through any obstacle to reach him.

Turning back to Tulip, she stretched one hand out, slowly, slowly, until her fingertips brushed scales. The snake was softer than she'd imagined—not a sensation like touching fur, only the softness of a living thing, with muscles and skin that flexed beneath her touch. Eliza pressed her hand to the python, and she willed Tulip to feel what couldn't be said, the threat and the need and the urgency.

Then she opened her eyes and gave her command. "Find Silas."

The snake held perfectly still, as if frozen by the contact. Her brown eyes never twitched. She didn't appear to breathe.

"Find Silas." Eliza repeated, begging with all her stubborn willpower and every hope. "Find Silas. *Find. Silas.*"

All at once, the snake unfurled, causing Eliza to jump. Tulip's tail dangled from the branch, twisting over itself in the air, and she stretched out her neck until her head contacted Eliza's shoulder.

"What are you doing?" Eliza whispered, almost a squeak, but she managed to hold still.

With an awful sensation, Tulip's head slithered over her shoulder and down her back, then twisted around her torso, as if Eliza were a convenient tree. She was *heavy*. Enough to make the princess stagger. And as Tulip coiled, she constricted.

"Do *not* squeeze me to death, Tulip," Eliza gasped out, wishing she could expand her ribs. "We are better friends than that."

The snake continued her descent, and within moments, her tail dropped from Eliza's waist, landing with the rest of the serpent on the floor. Eliza gave in to an irrepressible shudder, flapping her hands and stomping her feet, though it did little to actually shake off the sensation of *snake* all over her body. She was going to have nightmares for certain.

If this worked, it would be worth it.

Tulip slithered off, headed for the library entrance, and Eliza stumbled to follow.

Like a polite guest, the snake waited at the door until the princess opened it for her, then continued on her way, twisting around the corner of the Yamakaz, heading for the edge of campus. Eliza glanced back at the healing hall, but Tulip was fast, and she refused to risk losing the snake's guidance.

So she followed, praying for the impossible.

Until Tulip led her to a concealed trapdoor in the cliffside.

Eliza heaved it open and stared down into the dark bowels of a stone tunnel like the one beneath the prison house.

Without any hesitation, the python plunged down, a lattice of browns quickly blending into shadows.

"Wait!" Eliza tried to catch the snake's tail and missed.

She couldn't hope to navigate without a lantern. Besides that, she needed to tell Henry and Gill about the tunnel. But with every second, she was losing her guide.

Spitting a Pravish curse worthy of Silas, Eliza unwound her scarf and tied one end to the handle of the open trapdoor, draping the rest out across the ground, bright pink against a sandy landscape. A flag visible at a distance. It was the best she could do.

Then she scrambled down the stairs into the tunnel.

Sarazan seemed to smirk. The snake held perfectly still, poised in the lantern light as if giving Silas the opportunity to appreciate its power. Behind its pale yellow eyes, the diamond-shaped head held two streaks of black, thinning into stripes down its sides. Between them, the snake had a dark back and lighter underbelly, both in rippling shades of blue-gray. It must have been completely invisible in the water: a sailor's worst nightmare.

The serpent hadn't yet opened its mouth, but based on head size alone, Silas expected its fangs to be more like curved swords than teeth. A bite would impale him clean through.

The wound on his leg seemed like a mosquito bite in comparison.

"I wish we'd met under different circumstances," Silas said, mind racing as he tried to decide the best approach.

Leaning into his emotions would give him the strongest magical commands, but they were a swirl of grief and regret and anger. That would agitate a snake, make it more aggressive, and he wasn't trying to get either himself or Kerem killed. Besides that, he didn't know how loyal the snake already was to Kerem. Revealing himself to be at odds with the professor might encourage the serpent to strike.

He tried to project calm. "I'm not a threat."

The serpent shifted its head, knocking free a stream of pebbles and dust from the cavern ceiling as its scales scraped the rock. With deliberate precision, it lowered its jaw, revealing pointed fangs like rapiers.

Clearly, the calm had not communicated.

Out of the corner of his eye, Silas had been watching Kerem. The professor had retrieved a bone-white Artifact from a chest, this one bearing no sign of damage. *Two Artifacts.* Silas remembered the Stone Caster from the market, buried without bones in the graveyard, like Iyal Havva.

With the first Artifact stolen by Ceyda, Kerem would have been forced to craft a replacement. Ceyda had created a tidal wave that overturned a full-size merchant galley. What would Kerem be capable of?

Run. The instinct rattled his bones.

Sarazan struck. Its head lurched forward on a stretching neck, jaws closing over the spot Silas had been only a moment before. Gray mist puffed in the air.

As an adder, Silas shot toward the edge of the room.

Artifact glowing, Kerem pressed one hand to the wall, spreading a jagged crack like a bolt of lightning. Chunks of stone tumbled free, threatening to crush Silas. He transformed back, hissing as a large rock rebounded off his shoulder.

Sarazan coiled for another strike.

Silas lunged forward as the massive serpent crashed into the fallen rocks behind him. Its furious hiss echoed across the cavern.

His eyes darted to the closest tunnel, trying to gauge the distance.

With a calm exactness, Kerem directed Stone Casting again, collapsing that exit. His low voice carried across the room. "There's no escape, Silas."

That was narrow-minded thinking. There were at least five escapes left.

Until another rumble of Stone Casting left four.

The sea serpent twisted farther into the cavern, brushing up against the table holding the lantern and throwing part of the room into darkness as it blocked the would-be sun. Half its body still filled the tunnel it had emerged from.

Silas fixed his gaze there. Kerem couldn't collapse that tunnel without risking damage to his pet.

Transforming again, Silas shot in that direction. Behind him, he heard Kerem curse.

Unlike its master, Sarazan gave a satisfied, echoing hiss, one that shivered against Silas's mind in a single, clear impression.

Hunt.

It would have been wise to figure out what she was going to *do* once she found Silas, especially if he was with Kerem, but Eliza had to focus on the present. The sunlight behind her faded quickly, the tunnel growing darker until it was pure night.

She kept one hand on the wall, orienting herself. It was a good thing the tunnel had been made with magic because, as she hurried forward, the unnaturally smooth ground remained clear of obstacles, though she still walked with every muscle tense, anticipating a sudden drop or fall.

Tulip slithered ahead, a hiss of scales against stone. At one point, she turned left, and Eliza almost missed the turn, then stumbled when she found it but lost the wall. She hit her knees, giving a soft cry of pain.

Then she dragged herself upright and kept going.

"Tulip," she panted, "slow down."

But the snake paid her no mind. Eliza had been lucky to communicate once—assuming that was what had happened and these awful tunnels weren't just the python's preferred hunting grounds when she grew tired of library rats.

Rats. Eliza winced, thinking of Henry. Even if he found her trail and tried to follow her, he'd become prey in a country of predators. No wonder he'd been frustrated by the form of his magic. A wolf would have been useful. Or perhaps a dragon. Were there Dragon Affiliates?

With a spike of panic, Eliza realized she couldn't hear the slithering.

"Tulip?"

Distantly, she heard a rumble, like one of the Stone Caster earthquakes at the dorm. Had something frightened the snake into changing directions?

Another rumble. Was she hearing earthquakes or ocean waves?

She increased her pace, then even more, until she was running in the dark. What if she stepped on Tulip? Better to be bitten by the python than to lose her completely. Her knees wobbled. Her hand on the wall grew clammy, sliding at a breakneck pace.

Then she saw the tunnel curving around her in the dimmest outline.

Eliza ran faster, and the glow increased until she could see faint rays of light streaming through a pile of fallen rock. Half of the mouth of the tunnel had collapsed. She strained her ears but could hear nothing beyond, so she clawed her way up the rocks, slipping and scraping her hands until she finally wriggled over the top, sending a few smaller rocks tumbling down ahead of her.

She'd reached a cavern, wide and recently vacated.

She based the "recently vacated" idea on the fact that the light was fading, bobbing through a tunnel on the other side of the cavern, like a lantern being carried away.

She almost shouted for Silas, then stopped herself. If it was him, she'd catch up in a moment. If it wasn't . . .

Eliza swallowed hard, then carefully picked her way to the cavern floor, trying to disturb as few rocks as possible.

She crept toward the light.

Silas was faster than a regular snake, but enhancing his speed drained his magic, and it didn't take long before he felt the strain. He tried to head toward the ocean, basing his direction on the scent of salt in the air. It wasn't ideal to seek Sarazan's hunting grounds, but if he could find the ocean, it meant an exit from the cave system.

The floor sloped down abruptly, dumping him into a new cavern. This one had a shallow pool of water filling its center, and his adder form glided across the water, but left a wet streak across the rock on the other side, easy to follow.

He transformed into a human, then immediately cursed at letting his panic take charge; human eyes were terrible in the dark. Not to mention he'd done a string of transformations in a short period of time after already being wounded both physically and emotionally. His magic felt like a cup with only a few swallows remaining.

Meanwhile, Kerem had an Artifact that offered him a deep well's supply.

Silas's only chance of survival was to stay ahead of pursuit.

He limped on in the dark.

CHAPTER

42

Silas knew he was dead when he sensed Sarazan ahead of him. Kerem must have directed the serpent through a side tunnel, a shorter path. There were no diverging paths for Silas to take. He was trapped between snake and master.

In that case, he'd take the snake.

He got as close as he dared, relying on his magic to locate a snake he couldn't see. He was panting, his forehead dotted with sweat, and the ache of his leg paled next to the ache of his regret.

The slice of scales against stone cut through the darkness, quiet in his ears beneath his rapid heartbeat.

He should have written a letter to Maggie.

He should have told Eliza the kiss meant *everything*.

Faint light grew behind him, like the beginning of dawn. Ahead of him, a blue-scaled head rose in the shadows.

Silas's pulse throbbed against the scar on his throat.

I want to live. He focused that single thought into a tether, connecting him to the serpent in front of him, and he poured his remaining magic into a one-word command: "*Leave.*"

Sarazan resisted, head pulling back under the physical force of the order. Its tail thrashed, knocking into the tunnel wall, vibrating the rock. The serpent unhinged its jaw, straining to strike the prey directly in its path, furious at being forbidden.

Silas stood his ground, bristling with fangs of his own.

And, finally, the serpent turned, slinking into the dark.

Before he had the chance to feel any victory, Kerem's voice came from behind.

"*Bikmayak kalamak.*"

Silas spun, taking a blind swing at the professor he expected to be directly behind him, but Kerem was out of reach, crouching with his hand on the ground. The rock directly beneath Silas melted into a liquid, muddy sand, sinking him up to his knees, then thighs. He grabbed for the wall but couldn't find purchase. With the movement, he sank up to his waist.

"At least fight with your own magic!" he spat.

"The magic you're so familiar with?" Kerem shook his head, the angles of his face dancing with shadows from the lantern on the ground beside him. He cradled the Artifact against his chest, like a child to protect. "Can you picture it now—the kind of power afforded to a person with magic of *any* type? I can even create compositions by myself. I've no need for research partners any longer, and perhaps that's for the best. Mazhar's betrayal caught me off guard even more than yours. He started with vision but lost it halfway."

Apparently Silas hadn't given the short-tempered Fluid Caster enough credit for his conscience. It may have kicked in late, but it was more than Kerem showed.

"Hypocritical of *you* to talk about betrayal," Silas said bitterly.

"In what way did I betray you?" Kerem's eyes flashed. "I believed in you, mentored you, made it possible for you to remain at the university. I wanted you involved in all my greatest achievements, because I've always seen you as . . ."

The unspoken hung between them, and Silas halted his struggle against the quicksand.

"You can still stop," he found himself saying. *Begging*. "You can stop this. Please."

Kerem looked away. Quietly, he asked, "What could I do instead? Stand aside and watch the corruption grow? I can't, Silas. I tried."

He stood, curling his fingers more tightly around the Artifact, any sign of compassion gone.

"I need your venom. At least I can promise I'll use it to save the country you love."

Scales flickered across Silas's skin, but he remained himself, too exhausted to complete a transformation. Pain lanced his skull at the attempt, and for a moment, he couldn't even open his eyes.

But in the dark, a faint impression came to his mind.

Find Silas.

Slowly, he blinked. Kerem had taken a few steps toward him, but the man faltered, looking down.

A familiar python slithered between the professor's legs. Tulip reached the edge of the quicksand and tested it with her tongue, then glided forward like the strangest sailboat. She curled protectively around Silas's waist, pulsing with a contentment he could feel, like she'd accomplished an important mission.

She distracted them both from the second familiar visitor.

With both hands, Eliza slammed a dagger into Kerem's back, dropping the professor to his knees with a scream of pain. He released the Artifact to clutch his shoulder, grasping for a hilt he couldn't reach, and Eliza rushed forward to grab Silas's wrists, trying to yank him free.

Realms, she was gorgeous. Haloed with frizzy hair and scowling with determination, a better saving angel than any portrayed in art or statue.

"Pull!" she shouted, shaking him from his stupor.

Silas did, almost pulling Eliza into the muddy pit along with him. But contact with Tulip had given him a new surge of magic, so he transformed into a snake and then back so quickly he left the princess blinking.

Frantically, he looked for the Artifact that had fallen close to Kerem.

The professor saw his attention and lunged at the same moment Silas did.

Kerem was closer, but Silas was faster. Desperation could do that to a person. His fingers closed around the box just as Kerem's hand clamped over his. They wrestled, but Kerem's injury weakened his grip, and Silas managed to wrench away.

Kerem rose to follow but collapsed again with an agonized grunt.

Silas hesitated, his eyes on the dagger hilt protruding from his mentor's back.

"*Gravmak*!" Eliza ordered. *Outrun the strike.*

She seized his hand, and he ran with her, just as they'd run from the kuveti.

An echoing hiss through the tunnels told him Kerem was calling Sarazan back.

Eliza had snatched the lantern, and the light wavered wildly as they ran, painting the world with dizzying shadows. A few rats scattered from their path.

They rounded a corner, splashing through the cavern with the shallow pool, and Silas's injured leg slipped on wet rock. He stumbled, catching himself on the wall.

Awareness prickled the back of his neck.

Eliza turned, darting back to his side before he could warn her.

A massive blue sea serpent filled the cave behind him, body sliding through the water, displacing it in tides over the rock.

Jaw unhinged for a fatal strike.

"*Not her!*" Silas bellowed, and the blast of magic he sent out froze the massive serpent in place, fangs still exposed.

Eliza didn't hesitate. With a battle cry, she threw the lantern directly into the snake's open mouth, spilling oil and fire across its forked tongue.

Rearing back, the serpent's shriek rattled Silas's mind. It thrashed in the cavern, slamming walls and loosing rocks from the ceiling, and Silas grabbed Eliza, pulling her to his chest and shielding her head. The closest rocks splashed into the pool, spraying them both.

With one last shriek, Sarazan whipped around and fled, almost tangling itself in its haste to retreat.

Silas managed to breathe again.

Without the lantern, the cavern was a dark pit, and even holding Eliza, Silas couldn't see her. He held tighter.

"What was *that*?" she whispered in the dark, fisting her hands in his shirt like she couldn't bear to be separated either. "Regular cobras aren't dangerous enough for you, so now you're picking fights with the snake gods?"

Despite the situation, he laughed. He smoothed her hair with both hands, then cradled her face, leaning his forehead down to touch hers.

"How are you here?" he whispered.

"I told Tulip to find you," she said, her breath warm against his face. "And I followed."

She was a wonder.

"Just how many languages did you learn from me, *apta*?"

Somehow, he could *feel* her smile. Even without sight, every other sense tingled with an awareness of her.

He wished to never move, to hold her forever, but they weren't safe yet.

"We have to find the Artifact," he murmured. He'd dropped it when shielding her.

Together, they searched along damp rocks until Silas located the box. Unlike the damaged version he'd previously examined, this one brimmed with power, humming against his skin. Tentatively, he focused on it, trying to access the magic.

It was like plunging his head into the ocean. The raw force inside the Artifact stole his breath, a vast collection of magic swirled together, the bottom distant and murky.

Coming up for air, he gasped.

The Artifact retained a hazy glow, gilding Eliza's face in the dark.

"Can you break it?" she asked.

He barely heard her, swept away by a wave of possibilities. Kerem's hypotheticals took on color, and Silas imagined himself as an unstoppable force, changing entire countries. What use was an army in the face of a flood pulled from the ground itself?

The power lust lasted only a moment, replaced by something far more enticing—the *research* opportunities. What could this well of magic do for the medical field, for communication, for transportation? It could revolutionize the world.

"Silas?"

Those who had died to create it were already dead; he couldn't change that. Should their power go to waste? Wouldn't it be more honorable to do something with it?

Kerem's voice echoed in his mind. *The deaths will accomplish an exponential saving.*

"Silas." Eliza's hand covered the box's glow, light leaking through her fingers. She rested her other hand along his jaw, her thumb stroking the edge of his mouth. Her brown eyes carried a clear worry as she whispered again, "Can you break it?"

"I can't," he rasped. Then, with as much willpower as he could muster, he lowered his hand, leaving the box in her grip. "I need my research assistant's help."

A resource-draining assistant, he'd once called her. *Resource-draining* was just what the situation called for.

Her eyes widened. "I don't know how to use magic!"

"You don't have to use it well. Just use it up."

Taking her other hand, he pressed it to the wall, then stepped back. She should feel the resonance in the Artifact, the Stone Casting begging to be used. The glow grew sharper, and Eliza's jaw fell slack with wonder.

"Be reckless with it, *apta*." Silas smirked.

Eliza met his gaze for a brief moment—accepting the challenge—then closed her eyes. Beneath her touch, the rock wall rippled. Shadows crawled outward, cast by rivers of golden light, leaping forward and twisting in on themselves like snakes.

Words, Silas realized. She was carving words.

An entire book of sonnets, to be precise.

The poetry flowed from her fingers, spilling onto the floor and ceiling, engraving the full cavern and beyond. Perhaps the entire system of tunnels. Flower silhouettes curled across the lines, creating leaves and vines and blossoms. Reflections of light swayed in the water.

Until, finally, the glow faded, lingering only in the copper sparks of Eliza's opened eyes and a misty haze around the Artifact.

Spots flickered in Silas's vision like persisting stars.

"I think that's all the Stone Casting," she said hesitantly. "Should I . . . try the water?"

Silas almost joked that liquid wouldn't hold words as well as stone, but as he turned to look at the pool, something launched out of it at him.

A horned viper.

Kerem aimed well. He struck Silas almost exactly where the cobra had, flaring the damaged muscles anew. Even without venom, the bite seared pain all the way to the bone, and Silas dropped to the floor with a cry.

"Silas!" Eliza fumbled the Artifact, and its glow vanished, plunging the cavern into solid black.

But Kerem was still in his snake form, able to navigate the dark.

Eliza screamed, piercing Silas more than any wound could.

With a snarl, he transformed, launching forward even before his senses adjusted, but his jaws closed over nothing but air. Kerem twisted sharply, making a strike of his own that Silas barely reared away from.

They circled as snakes at the edge of the pool, testing each other, fanged mouths snapping.

One bite. That was all Silas needed. One successful strike with venom could paralyze Kerem, and—

Kerem plunged in the other direction, toward Eliza's colorless, shadowy form.

No! Silas dove to intercept.

Which was exactly what Kerem wanted.

Twisting back, the horned viper sank its fangs into Silas's neck, just behind his head. No matter how he thrashed, he couldn't free himself or get off a bite of his own, and his magic drained like blood through a fresh wound.

With no other choice, he turned human, collapsing on the cave floor and gasping through a throat that still felt trapped between jaws. The world tilted, his vision spotted and dizzy.

Kerem turned human as well, his fingers clenched around the Artifact, lighting its glow.

And he rounded on Eliza.

Eliza's leg throbbed where she'd been bitten, but when Kerem turned toward her, visible at last, she didn't cower.

She launched herself at him.

She was smaller, but she hit his legs, bringing him to the ground. She tried to wrestle the Artifact from his hands, but he cursed at her and held fast.

The Artifact's glow flared.

"Eliza, get back!" Silas shouted.

It was too late. She made one last desperate grab.

Kerem shoved her backward, sending her tumbling into the pool of water. She sputtered, shaking water off her face. Before she could do more than that, ice crystals spread throughout the water, freezing over.

Eliza gasped as ice enclosed her hands and feet, trapping her in place. The cold sliced down to her bones.

Without hesitation, Kerem turned on Silas, kicking him before he could transform or retaliate. The professor's shirt carried a bloodstain on his back, but the dagger was gone. Even as she watched, the wound glowed briefly, halting the bleeding.

Kerem kicked again, knocking Silas against the wall. He fought with a chilling detachment, without words, focused only on the outcome.

She'd never seen someone accustomed to killing before.

He was going to kill Silas.

She struggled, yanking uselessly at her prison. Her skin burned against the ice. Her teeth chattered.

Silas pressed against the wall, trying to rise but only making it halfway.

Artifact glowing, Kerem grabbed him by the throat, and Silas screamed in clear agony.

"S-Stop it!" Eliza shrieked, barely able to manage the words.

She couldn't help.

She couldn't *move*.

Then, new light danced through the tunnel, the bob of an approaching lantern. An eerie chattering of squeaks heralded it, just before a horde of rats burst into view. They swarmed over Kerem, trying to scurry up his body. His hold on Silas slipped, allowing Silas to wrench away.

Gill charged down the tunnel, sword drawn. He swung at Kerem, and Kerem transformed—not into a snake, but into a large eagle Eliza had seen before. Stolen magic. He swooped at Gill, but he was limited by the narrow space, and Gill dodged with the reflexes of a swordsman, preventing the eagle from drawing any blood. Kerem transformed back to avoid running into the wall.

Behind them, Henry held a lantern in the tunnel. When his eyes met Eliza's, his face set in determined lines. He crouched, setting the lantern down and then vanishing in a burst of brown mist. She could barely track the little rat that scampered between the two figures fighting in the tunnel.

Until, a moment later, Henry reappeared at her side.

"You d-did it," she managed through chattering teeth, her breath puffing in the air. "Used y-your m-magic."

"Let's worry about you instead of me," he said, trying and failing to lift her from the ice. His expression grew worried, and he looked around as if searching for help.

The army of rats scurried over, surrounding Eliza, little pockets of heat against the cold. They gnawed at the ice, occasionally nipping her skin, which she could only tell from little pinpricks of blood. She'd already gone numb.

Henry grabbed her face between his hands, his touch scorching, his hazel eyes fervent. "Why did you run off like that? You could have been killed!"

Tears stung her eyes, because she couldn't bring herself to tell Henry the truth. *Because I love Silas.*

She couldn't see him past the knight. Had he collapsed? Was he helping Gill?

She heard a shout of pain and prayed it was Kerem's.

CHAPTER 43

The first time Silas almost lost his magic, the process had been subtle and slow. Perhaps that was Ceyda's inexperience with the Artifact, or perhaps it was a reflection of her personality. Maybe she was reluctant to kill even while longing to avenge her father.

When Kerem grabbed him by the throat, it was clear he intended to be efficient. Rather than feeling the threads of his magic quietly cut, Silas felt it ripped away all at once, like a sheet of parchment torn in two. Thanks to Gill's arrival, he was able to pull free, but the damage was done.

Unable to stand, Silas collapsed. His head swam, and while he was vaguely aware of Gill fighting, of Eliza trapped, he couldn't seem to grasp the details. It was as if everything had happened a long time ago, and he was trying to look back while something dragged him away.

I'm dying, he realized with an academic detachment. An experience he'd never be able to write about, never be able to share the results from. Useless.

He tried to fight the sensation, but it was like fighting an enemy without a form. There was nothing to kick, nothing to bite.

Only an inevitability slowly devouring.

By the time the rats chewed Eliza free, she'd lost sight of Gill and Kerem as their fight moved down the tunnel. But she'd seen a glimpse of Silas. A glimpse that chilled her more than any ice.

Henry had wrapped his arms around her to keep her warm. Her skin was reddened where it had been in contact with the ice, but the numbness had receded, replaced by a painful prickle in every limb.

As soon as she could finally pull her last foot free, she wriggled away from Henry, half stumbling and half crawling to where Silas had collapsed. She pulled his head into her lap, running her frozen fingers over his cheeks.

He gave no response to her cold touch. His eyes were closed, and for a terrifying moment, she thought he wasn't breathing, before she saw the shallowest dip of his chest.

"Is he—" Henry started.

"He's alive," Eliza said sharply, determined to keep him that way through sheer willpower.

A shadow moved nearby, and she curled protectively over Silas before realizing it was Tulip. The python moved in tight shapes, flicking her tail. She coiled her head and neck atop Silas's chest, tongue darting in and out rapidly, beady eyes fixed on Eliza as if demanding to know how she'd allowed this to happen.

Earlier, Tulip's contact had rejuvenated Silas, yet he didn't stir. Aside from the wound on his leg, he wasn't bleeding. Kerem had done something else to him. The problem was magical.

"We have to stop Kerem," said Eliza.

Henry nodded. "You stay here. I'll help Gill."

"No," she said fiercely. "*I'll* help Gill. You get in close enough to transform Kerem."

She remembered her brief moments as a snake—the disorientation, the lack of control. As long as Kerem held the Artifact, he was powerful, but he wasn't invincible.

Silently, she thanked Silas for all his lectures about magic. They resonated with her now, reaffirming her plan.

"He's already an Affiliate," Henry protested.

"But he's not *your link*. He could turn you into a snake and you'd be under his command, but you can do the same to him as a rat. You just have to bite him."

She very much wanted to see Kerem as a helpless, cornered rat. Then she could use the Artifact to fix whatever he'd done to Silas.

With reluctance, she shimmied away from Silas, resting his head on the ground. Leaving him to Tulip's care, she ran in the direction Gill and Kerem had disappeared, her legs needling painfully with each step.

"Eliza, wait!"

But she couldn't afford to. Every second mattered.

In the next cavern over, Gill and Kerem circled each other, dimly lit, neither one able to get the upper hand. Each time Kerem attempted Fluid Casting, Gill canceled it, and vice versa. Gill had the longer reach of a sword, but Kerem kept transforming into different animals to dodge the strikes, and if Gill got too close, he risked being turned into an animal himself. Then it would all be over.

Eliza was suddenly grateful she'd drained all the Stone Casting from the Artifact; otherwise Kerem could have brought down the cavern in a quake or trapped Gill in the floor as he'd done to Silas.

Instead of representing deadly potential, the rock surrounding her gave her courage, carved as it was with familiar words, the poetry grounding in a new, literal way. She strode across declarations of love and faith, and her heart beat to their rhythm. Without magic or dagger or defense, she would manage *something*—because even if Silas could not be hers, she would still save him. That was the very essence of love.

Love, my crown.
Love, my armor.
Love, my sword.

Without magic or blade, she still had words.

"He trusted you!" Eliza shouted in Pravish, stopping just out of reach of the circling combatants.

Kerem's dark eyes found hers with a special hatred, the kind reserved for a pest that had already been dealt with but came crawling back. His gaze darted to the ground, and she didn't understand why until a flurry of squeaks caught up to her, rats spilling past her legs to leap and gnaw at Kerem as he fought.

At first, she felt a surge of hope that Henry would be one of them, that the battle would already be finished.

But the Artifact in Kerem's hand maintained a steady glow, and each rat that touched his skin fell to the ground, twitching. Eliza's heart lurched until she realized Henry had to be safe, or else the remaining rats would flee. Instead, they circled, making lunges but held at bay by the threat of Fluid Casting stopping their hearts.

Eliza had to do something.

She jumped atop a jutting portion of rock, making herself as noticeable and distracting as possible. Then she laid into Kerem with all the fire she possessed, determined to keep his attention.

"I knew there was something wrong about you from the moment we met. I knew you were a predator, but Silas believed in you. He looked up to you. He *loved* you!"

Gill lunged, and Kerem dove aside. His face dripped sweat, and he'd lost his spectacles. He clutched the Artifact to his stomach, his fingers digging like claws into its bone surface.

A few daring rats nipped at his ankles, but though the bites landed, the rats still fell dead.

He was an Affiliate with decades of experience controlling his emotions. What could Eliza say to break his focus?

"How could you?" she demanded, raising her voice. "You called it a shock that his father tried to kill him. You said you'd *never* do the same!"

Kerem's eyes cut sharply to hers, and for a moment, the hatred was gone. The snarl on his face now held a mixture of frustration and pain.

Gill took his opening in a surging attack. Kerem dodged, but too slowly, and the sword point tore through his side, spilling blood. He cried out, but he managed to grab Gill by the throat, his other hand on the glowing Artifact.

Eliza remembered Silas being held in the same position. Remembered his scream. She leapt to the cavern floor, running forward but already knowing she was too late.

Gill clamped his hand down on Kerem's arm, and they both recoiled as if struck by lightning. While Gill spat blood, Kerem clutched his side.

Then he transformed into a familiar black-patterned adder, launching a strike.

Eliza halted, sick to her stomach at witnessing the stolen magic.

Could she still save Silas if his magic had already been taken?

Gill's sword swung a fraction too late, only skimming the gray scales. Either he was thrown off by Silas's magic in the wrong hands or he was hesitant to kill.

Regardless, Kerem's bite landed, and in a puff of mist, Gill transformed into a snake. As Kerem turned human once more, the new snake lay curled and cowering at his feet.

Eliza swallowed. She stood only a few feet from Kerem.

With a weary sigh, he touched his side, stopping the blood. Perhaps, in that moment of delay, she could have run if she tried.

Instead, she seized her final chance to distract him.

"You're using *his* magic?" Her heart cracked in her chest, pain in every beat. "Silas would have given the world for you, but to you, he's just a source of venom. Just another power in an Artifact."

Kerem's eyes flashed, and he took a menacing step forward, but Eliza beat him to it. The storm inside had never been stronger, and she steered full-speed ahead, crashing into him with all the rage she held. He stumbled with a grunt, but even so, he caught her by the throat. Quick as a snake.

His eyes narrowed in a smug victory.

Then they widened. "You're not an Affiliate? But the rats . . ."

"The only rat I see here is you," she snarled, clawing her nails into his arm. "How could you, Kerem? How could you be like a father to Silas and then kill your son?"

He flinched from her words, his fingers slackening.

After all she'd done to encourage Silas to trust Yvette, to trust *her*, to let go of the hurt caused by his father and not see betrayal around every corner . . . Kerem had ruined it all.

She hated him. For what he'd done to Silas, she hated him more than she'd ever hated anyone.

"How could you?" she whispered again, wishing she had stronger words, piercing words, words she could plunge like daggers through his chest and into his cold-blooded heart to make him realize exactly what he'd done.

But, sometimes, words fell short.

For a moment, Kerem's gaze held hers, his dark eyes unreadable.

Then he winced.

Looking down, he seemed to spot the little brown rat clamped around his ankle in the same moment Eliza did. The glow of the Artifact died, the box tumbling from his hand.

In a puff of brown mist, Kerem was a rat.

And Henry was a breathless, triumphant knight.

"Kneel," he ordered, cowing the rat at his feet. It trembled against the ground.

Gill transformed back, and Eliza crouched to stare down a black-eyed rat. "My first day in your office, you said, 'Magic is a powerful weapon, not a shield against all ills.' You forgot your own lesson, Iyal."

Snatching up the Artifact, she ran back to Silas.

Tulip hissed a warning at her approach, perking up to strike, but then the python settled.

Dropping to her knees, Eliza grabbed Silas's hand and pressed the box between his palm and chest, willing it to return his magic, to give him healing or strength or whatever he needed.

What little color had been in his face was gone, leaving him pallid as death.

Please, she willed, and then she was whispering it aloud, "Please. *Please*."

Please come back. I won't ask for anything else. Just come back.

Warmth pierced the darkness. Just a pinhole of it, hardly enough to discern.

He'd almost lost all sense of self, but he felt the warmth. And with it, he heard a whisper.

Please come back.

It wasn't clear how he heard it without ears. Even less clear how he grasped it without fingers, but he did, drawing in the warmth, holding to the whisper.

Until, slowly, Silas remembered himself, and his world faded back into focus.

A world that hung above him in the form of a familiar, reckless princess.

"*Apta*," he whispered, reaching for her face. Tears spilled down Eliza's cheeks even as she burst into a smile, clutching his hand with her own.

When he tried to lift himself, he realized there was a weight on his chest, holding him down. A disgruntled python hissed out her opinion of his death scare.

"It's not like I enjoyed it either," he griped, his voice barely a croak. He ached all the way down to his soul, but that soul seemed to be more or less intact again.

Tulip hunched herself into a tight S shape, and in so doing, she displaced something else from his chest.

The bone-box Artifact.

It fell to the ground with a clatter, displaying one side cracked all the way through, the edges blackened as if burned. Silas wasn't sure what to make of that. Prodding at the awareness of his magic felt different, like entering a familiar room where the furniture had been rearranged and new paintings hung.

But he was *alive.*

Full of the triumph of that, he shifted his hand from Eliza's cheek to the back of her neck, drawing her down. She didn't resist, kissing him with a tenderness that taught his heart to beat again. Her tears left his face damp.

"Thank you," he whispered. "I'm uncertain of a few details, but I know you saved me. Again."

Even after all he'd done to hurt her.

She answered with a prim little smile. "Well, I had to do something. You're an academic, not a fighter."

He tried to laugh, but between the python on his chest and the exhaustion sweeping in, it emerged as a strange cough. Hesitantly, he asked, "Kerem?"

"He's a rat."

"I wasn't asking for a personality assessment, *apta.* I meant—"

"Oh, no, he's currently a rat. Henry has him under control."

Silas's lips twitched. "Well done, Henry."

He was quickly losing his hold on consciousness, but before he could fully sink, he brushed his knuckles across Eliza's cheek, wiping the last of her tears. She caught his hand and kissed his palm, whispering something he didn't catch. He didn't like the cadence of it; it sounded too sad for the wake of a victory. Almost . . . resigned.

Before he could investigate, a nonthreatening darkness pressed in, closing his eyes.

CHAPTER

44

Silas spent three weeks in the healing hall, asleep. Apparently, after hearing about his injuries—specifically his magic being ripped out and replaced—the physicians decided the best treatment was to put him in a *tasumak* and hope that, without interruptions, his body could sew itself back together.

He woke rested and ravenous, with a greater appreciation for the disorientation Henry had experienced when coming out of his own Stone Caster's coma. The physicians brought him enough food to feed an entire class, but they brought something else, something that cracked his heart and made him wish he was still asleep.

A worn, red book, familiar in every threadbare edge.

When he asked about the girl behind it, the news was simple: Gone. She and Henry and Gill had taken a ship back to Loegria. Apparently, they'd tried to delay until he woke, but he'd needed more time to heal, and the ship's schedule only had so much to give.

Gill had also left him the pardon. Silas stared at the Loegrian royal seal and Eliza's sonnet book until his raging stomach finally forced him to set everything else aside and eat.

He was grateful when the physicians admitted his first visitor; he needed the distraction.

"Iyal Afshin!" Silas almost sprayed a mouthful of rice, catching himself with the back of his hand. He struggled to untangle from his food tray, but the dean waved for him to stay seated.

"I'm pleased to see you out of bed," Afshin said, smiling widely.

Silas had taken up residence on the floor, preferring a thin cushion to the blanket that had held him hostage for the last few weeks. He gestured to the other cushion beside him, and Afshin settled atop it.

"If it's up to me," Silas muttered, "I'll never sleep again."

"I'll leave it to Iyl Daria's team to warn you about over-taxation during recovery." Afshin looked him up and down, as if trying to perceive cracks in his skeleton. "You're feeling better?"

Silas managed a nod, stuffing his mouth with beans to avoid expounding on that. He *was* feeling better. Physically.

Even if his eyes kept darting to the red book on his bedside table.

"Good, then we have some things to discuss."

Understandably, the dean wanted his account of everything that had happened. Although Silas would have preferred to deliver it in written form, he muddled his way through a retelling of his discoveries and the events in the tunnels, filling in gaps as he realized them.

Afshin was clearly familiar with most of it already, but he filled in some gaps of his own.

Yvette had been cleared of suspicion. One of the kuveti captains had surrendered the details of his agreement with Kerem. In addition, Iyal Mazhar had left behind a more detailed research journal than Iyal Havva's, and in combination with all the witnesses, the condemnation was clear.

"What will happen to Kerem?" Silas asked. Even after everything, he dreaded the answer.

"The execution is already done," Afshin said gently. "Our guards turned him over to the palace, and, as you can imagine, the Nephew King did not look kindly on a would-be usurper."

Silas's stomach lurched, almost rejecting everything he'd eaten thus far. He set his tray aside, his shaking hands rattling the dishes.

"I'm sorry, Silas."

He couldn't respond. He was busy trying to remember the last words he and Kerem had said to each other, but he couldn't. Everything in the caverns had happened so quickly.

What he remembered with clarity was Kerem's voice saying, *Bikmayak kalamak.*

My sword breaks here.

Silas pressed his palm to the scar on his throat, feeling his pulse through it, slow and disbelieving.

In the heavy silence, Afshin sighed. He lifted a journal he'd been holding. "I brought this for you, though I'm not certain it will improve anything. Perhaps it might even make matters worse. It was Kerem's."

Silas lowered his hand, eyeing the worn brown leather. "I would have expected you to keep all his research."

"Anything pertaining to what we're calling the 'Bone-Box Incident,' yes, but this is the venom research you conducted together. He kept meticulous notes, and many of them include his thoughts on your specific contributions. He was quite proud of your work."

Though it went against his better instincts, Silas took the journal. When he opened it, the familiar handwriting nearly undid him, and his own voice haunted him, a warning he'd given to Eliza: *People aren't good or bad,* apta. *They aren't simple. They're just people.*

He closed the journal and set it as far from himself as possible. One more relic to taunt him with what could have been.

The dean watched him closely. "There's one more thing before I go."

"It can't be worse," Silas said quietly.

"No, I hope not. Thanks to the Bone-Box Incident, I've had three deaths on my faculty. Another professor, displeased with my handling of the situation, handed in her resignation yesterday. Our warlockry department is suffering. In light of the circumstances, and in consideration of your efforts to uncover and avert this disaster, I would be honored to have you join that department."

Silas blinked, trying to absorb that. The room felt too small, like the ceiling was lowering and the bed was growing. Perhaps he was shrinking.

After opening his mouth twice, he finally managed to speak. "I'd be replacing Kerem."

"Kerem Aytac is irreplaceable, I daresay. As are we all." Afshin's voice softened. "There are many people indebted to him for his creation of antivenom, for his clarity of teaching, for his relentless encouragement to discover the unknown. There are also many people dead at his hands. If you could somehow separate and build upon the good of his legacy, I'm sure there would be benefit.

"Regardless, I'm certain you will have your hands quite full building your *own* legacy, and I look forward to the results. Of course, if you need time to consider it . . ."

He left it hanging.

A real professorship. Mere weeks ago, Silas had begged for this opportunity. It was everything he'd wanted.

Yet the reality of the moment clashed with that vision of weeks ago, and, like a fool, he found himself saying, "This isn't . . . what I pictured."

"Nor I. Believe me, I wish the offer were under brighter circumstances." Afshin leaned forward, his expression candid. "But even in duress, I would *not* offer if I didn't think you worthy, Silas."

Silas latched onto that like steady ground beneath his feet. The university was where he belonged. This chance was what he'd been fighting for.

"Yes." He swallowed. "Yes, I'd be honored."

But although he said the words with conviction, they felt strangely hollow.

Eliza passed the ten-day journey home in a daze. She watched the rolling ocean waves, the tranquil blue reflected in sea and sky, and she tried not to think about anything beyond the present moment.

There were some things she couldn't avoid, however, trapped in the small space of a single ship.

"Captain says we'll dock this afternoon," Henry said, standing beside her at the railing. How he could look so relaxed at sea after experiencing a shipwreck was beyond her. Eliza's own hands white-knuckled the railing whenever she stood on the deck.

For the hundredth time, she told herself to speak to him about the important things, the things they hadn't addressed.

She was down to her final day to do it.

After a stretch of silence, Henry said, "We haven't actually been gone that long. A few months. Feels like an eternity."

Eliza swallowed. "We crossed into the new year."

That felt symbolic for how time had stretched into something bigger. How it could feel like she'd left half her life behind with Silas.

Had he read the note in her sonnet book? Or had he set the love poems aside without a second glance?

It didn't matter either way. She had to look forward. That was the decision she'd made by coming home.

"Henry, I—"

Her voice deserted her. The coward.

Henry watched her with gentle hazel eyes. "How do you say 'new year' in Pravish?"

"*Yeni basi.*"

She remembered toasting with Yvette and Baris, remembered the happy smile on Silas's face that he couldn't hold back. *New year, new skin.*

Eliza had shed her skin in Pravusat. When she'd first arrived, she'd been determined to pretend she was still the same girl as before her curse, to ignore the shift inside that changed how she navigated the world. She'd clung to the same beliefs, the same love—whatever could anchor her to the past. But whether she wanted it to or not, the past drifted away, and she couldn't hope to sail while fastened to an anchor. That would only tear her apart.

And maybe, if she kept looking, she'd come to appreciate the new girl in the mirror, through both the storms and the swells.

"I thought you might stay." Henry kept his eyes on the horizon as he spoke. He hesitated, then said, with obvious significance, "For Silas."

Eliza's restraint broke, her voice hitching as she turned. "Henry, I'm so sorry. I didn't mean to keep it secret. I just—"

A surge of the ship interrupted, making her stumble. She reached out with one hand, and Henry caught it, steadying her.

"You didn't." His voice remained gentle. A faint smile even crossed his face. "Anyone could see the way you look at him."

She struggled to catch her bearings again, torn between wanting to cling to his hand and feeling like she should let go. Inwardly, she screamed—because love shouldn't hurt so much. It should be joyous, like the sonnets promised. It should be simple and straightforward, with lonely princesses always swept up by gallant knights.

But life wasn't straightforward; it was messy. And on her way to a knight, she'd fallen for a snake.

At last, Eliza released Henry's hand, standing on her own.

"I didn't mean to be unfair to you," she choked out.

"Eliza, you *saved* me. Unfair isn't what I'd call it." But she could see the tight lines in his throat, the pain carefully held back while he maintained a reassuring expression.

She swiped at her eyes with the heel of her hand. "Then why does it hurt?"

"Sometimes life takes a different path than we wanted."

"Like when it turns us into rats?" She tried for a smile, then faltered, wondering if she'd caused him more pain. "You're still a knight. You're still just as wonderful as before."

"I felt like a knight again, using it to help people." He cleared his throat, folding his arms. "Anyway, I really thought . . . you would stay."

Eliza had considered it. Part of her had entertained a grand vision of loving Silas and living as a university student instead of a princess, playing the *kiyum* while he listened and then listening while he read, stealing kisses in the library—

But that was a fantasy.

There was duty to consider, but it was more than that. It was missing her sister so much she ached. It was knowing that if she stayed in the harsh climate and culture of Pravusat, she would wither up inside. She would shed another skin, but this one would put her too far from herself.

It was knowing that as much as Silas belonged in Pravusat, a place where he could be wholly himself, she belonged at home.

And it was knowing that she had no right to force Silas to choose love, to choose *her*. He had his own goals, his own fears, and if she tried to force him to be the romantic hero of her dreams, then he wouldn't be Silas anymore.

"You must hate me," Eliza whispered, "knowing I'm choosing not to be with you when I can't be with him either." She gripped the railing, eyes on the waves breaking against the ship.

Henry rested his hand gently over hers. "I'll always be grateful," he said, "to the girl who crossed an ocean to save me."

He squeezed her hand, and then he left the deck.

The carriage ride from the port to the castle felt more excruciatingly lengthy than the entire ocean voyage. Snow dusted the landscape, welcoming Eliza back with a glittering, sharp cold that pricked her lungs and made her feel alive.

But it wasn't until she saw her sister that she felt *home*.

Aria waited impatiently in the palace courtyard, braving the cold in a thick cloak rather than staying inside where it was warm, even though she'd surely been advised otherwise, even though she was now a *queen*. And before the carriage even rolled to a stop, she ran to the door, throwing it open and shouting Eliza's name.

Eliza threw herself into her tall sister's arms, relishing the warmth of her embrace and the familiar scent of her lilac perfume. As she listened to Aria's scolding and her worry and her relief, all of it echoed in Eliza's own heart.

And later that night, once they were finally alone in Aria's room, snuggled in quilts before a crackling fire, Eliza told her sister *everything*.

CHAPTER 45

As crown princess, Eliza was now a part of the Upper Court, and Aria held twice as many meetings as their father ever had, so most days, Eliza found herself slowly going mad on a cushioned chair in the throne room, listening to people argue about the best ways to handle changing the laws around magic.

She spoke out in defense of Affiliates whenever she could, but it always left her thinking how Silas would have said it so much better.

When she wasn't in meetings, she was planning the quickly approaching wedding for her sister. Just as Aria didn't care about the details of her birthday celebrations, she'd left her wedding in the hands of their mother, and Eliza stepped in to make sure the dowager queen didn't get too carried away in her own preferences.

It gave Eliza something to do other than play a harp to an empty room, pretending it was an echoing university music hall.

Family meals had been scarce before she left home, but they were nonexistent now. She saw her family members one at a time or not at all, as if they lived on separate islands instead of within the same castle. And with her father's reclusiveness, she'd begun to think his island had floated away, until, one day, she rounded a tall shelf in the library and ran directly into the former king.

"Father," Eliza squeaked out. "I didn't expect . . ."

He and Aria were so alike: tall and dark-haired, skin a half shade darker than Eliza and the queen's, and a presence that made it seem they could accomplish anything. But where Aria carried an abundance of compassion, their father had always been severe.

Eliza braced herself for a lecture or a silent, curt nod.

Instead, her father's voice emerged in a softer tone than she'd ever heard it. "What book are you looking for?"

At first, she sputtered. Then she managed, "Something on Loegria's founding. I'm trying—for Aria's wedding, you know. She . . . she likes history."

He scanned the shelves, and in the end, he took down a book she wouldn't have been able to reach without the footstool. He extended it like a peace offering.

All Eliza could do was stare.

"I heard the knight returned with you," Father said at last, his voice a little stronger, a little more like his old self. "If you'd like, I could make arrangements with Lord Wycliff."

Offering her a book was one thing, but a *wedding*? The old Eliza would have been thrilled, would have been so swept up in the joy of it as to swoon against the bookshelves.

Now, she swallowed.

"I brought Henry home," she whispered, "but I don't want to marry him."

Guilt flared within, and before he could criticize her, she rushed to say it first. "I'm a subject of *whims*, just as you said."

Her father looked away.

After a moment, he opened the book in his hands, searching the pages. His eyes remained down as he spoke. "I taught you that an unyielding path is the only strength. Your sister believes a greater strength is knowing when to change."

He handed her the book, opened to a chapter entitled "Arthur and Louise: The First Royal Wedding of Loegria."

"Follow Aria's example," he said gruffly. "Not mine."

The condemnation that had followed Eliza for months evaporated, and she wondered why she'd put so much weight on her father's words to begin with. If only she'd thought of her *whims* as paths to change. Paths that *she* could choose.

Suddenly, she realized where she'd gone wrong since being home.

Eliza wrapped her father in a hug, the poor book crushed between them. Silas would have suffered a rage transformation to see the literary mistreatment.

Her father patted her back and stepped away. He left the room immediately, without even a goodbye, but she saw tears in his eyes. Apparently she wasn't the only one who'd shed a skin in the past months.

Using meetings and frantic planning, Eliza had tried to distract herself from her time in Pravusat, tried to forget. She'd never considered what to *do* as a result of it.

She remembered Yvette's voice. *I'm asking you to sail with your eyes open.*

Her mistake was trying to fit back into her old life without any accommodations for who she'd become.

And, truthfully, there *was* something she wanted to do.

Clutching the book, she made her way to her mother in the music room. The dowager queen looked right at home surrounded by instruments, a tea tray, and servants taking her directions for wedding plans.

Which made it awkward for everyone when Eliza blurted out, "Mother, I want to attend university."

After a moment of clear alarm, her mother finished giving instructions on feast details and then dismissed the servants. Once they were alone, she spoke with obvious care. "Eliza, we were lucky the first time that no one took advantage of a princess far from home. If you tried to return—"

"Not in Izili." Eliza blushed. "We have our own university. I know you teach there sometimes."

"As an amusement, darling. A way to keep busy. If it's musical learning you'd like, I am willing to teach you anything I haven't already, and if it's anything else, we can bring the tutors here, just as we always do."

"That's all learning was for me before." Eliza huffed. "A way to *keep busy* while I waited for marriage. I don't want that anymore. I want *real* learning, and I want new experiences too. I want to interact not just with tutors but with other students."

"What happened to my romantic little girl who cared only that she'd come of courting age?" Her mother didn't sound chiding, only baffled.

Eliza gave a breathy laugh. "Ironically, she fell in love."

It was more complicated than she'd expected, more bittersweet, and she was going to *do* something with her life because of it.

"I'm going," she said stubbornly. "I've already decided."

Silas climbed the stairs in the Yamakaz, but he didn't make it to Afshin's office.

Instead, he froze on the third-floor landing, his eyes fixed down the walkway on Iyal Kerem's office. The door still carried his name.

When he finally tore his gaze away and resumed walking, it was not up the next flight of stairs. It was down the hallway in the opposite direction, to Yvette's office.

She was at her desk, bent over a piece of stonework, and she smiled when she saw him. "Iyal Silas, I presume. Congratulations on the teaching position."

"I was afraid you were the professor who'd resigned." It was a more abrupt greeting than he'd meant to give.

Yvette huffed as if offended by the thought. She tossed her hair over her shoulder, the beads clacking. "Why should I surrender doing what I love just because others tried to force me from it? I'll be at this university until I die. Even if it burns to the ground, I'll raise it back up."

With a wry smile, Silas thought Afshin had better watch his back. There was clearly someone else interested in the position of dean.

He meant to say academic things—specifically about how his magic had changed since his death scare, how, in reclaiming it from the Artifact, he'd somehow pulled other abilities with it. How he could Fluid Cast now, an ability he'd tested that morning by heating the water in his washbasin. He meant to ask Yvette's help with experiments.

Instead, he said, "Eliza's gone."

"I'm aware. Unlike you, she knows how to say goodbye to friends before leaving the country."

She'd said goodbye to Yvette but not to him. Even knowing he'd been asleep, his irritation refused to bow to logic.

"Are you going to hold that over my head indefinitely?" he grumbled.

"Depends if you're remedying the mistake now."

It took him a moment to understand, and then he tensed, gripping the strap of his bag more tightly. "This isn't a goodbye. I'm not going anywhere."

"Hmm," she said, with the air of someone deliberately *not* saying something.

He swallowed. "Can I read in here?"

He expected her to ask why he couldn't go to the library or his dorm—or even his own office, which he would have been given as soon as he spoke to Afshin. But all she did was wave him toward the cushions and resume her own work.

It was senseless not to read in the library, but the books weighing down his bag felt too private for that.

Silas sat cross-legged on a cushion, and he opened Kerem's research journal. The information was all familiar, presented with Kerem's subdued enthusiasm, sickening now to read.

On one page, he'd made a note about Silas's insight, then added, *He reminds me of myself—ambitious but realistic, wounded, and hungry for justice. There are countless achievements in his future, I'm certain.*

Silas wanted to tell himself he was nothing like Kerem, but that was a lie; Kerem had captured the truth exactly. Ambitious but realistic. Both unable to let go of wounds from the past. Silas may not have leapt into Kerem's plan, but he'd heard it out, been tempted by the Artifact and all its potential to fix things.

If he and Kerem were the same base form, the question was how to avoid evolving in the direction his professor had, how to avoid succumbing to bitterness and cynicism.

From the corner of his eye, he saw a worn red book peeking from his bag. He set Kerem's journal aside and replaced it with Eliza's.

And *journal* was an accurate descriptor, no matter how the book had started.

She'd written notes in the margins of more than a dozen sonnets. Her writing was as flowery as expected, both in word choice and in flourishes at the end of her lines. Most of the notes contained Pravish vocabulary, but while Silas would have written something like, *arakl: magic*, she refused to be simple.

Arakl means magic, or something like it. It seems to be multipurpose, used on both Affiliates and Casters, because Pravish refuses clarity whenever possible.

He snorted.

He read two dozen sassy dictionary entries before he reached her favorite sonnet, marked by a pressed flower.

Love, my sword.

She hadn't written any notes in the margins, but he was shocked to see his own name at the bottom of the page along with a painfully short message.

Silas, I hope you find love.

He snapped the book closed, almost catching his face in it, since he'd bent in ridiculously close. Without seeing them, he could still feel the words, carving an ache in his chest the way she'd carved poetry in a stone wall.

The irritation surged again. Of all the things she could say, of all the goodbyes she could leave him with, she'd chosen *this*. He clenched his jaw against the press of fangs.

I hope you find love.

As if he hadn't found it already.

As if he could just move on to some other girl.

As if she could be so easily replaced.

Finding wasn't the problem. The problem was that he didn't know what to *do* with it. The problem was that he was a complete wreck inside, and the one person he wanted to be with most was in the one place he couldn't go. Loegria was still a sword, eager and waiting to impale him again. Even if laws were changing, mindsets wouldn't. Even if Eliza accepted him, her family wouldn't. *His* family wouldn't.

Yvette stood from her desk, and for a disoriented moment, Silas thought he'd lost track of hours and lecture hall had started.

"Come with me," she said.

Welcoming the distraction, he grabbed his bag and followed, but she didn't lead him anywhere on campus. They crossed into Izili proper, and then out to the city wall. The marketplace buzzed with chatter, angry voices rising more often in the particularly humid heat, vendors shouting at each other across the way.

Baris grinned to see his wife, and he made space for both of them in his stall. Silas hesitated, but Yvette was insistent, so he finally sat.

"Baris," she said, whacking her husband lightly on the arm. "Silas needs to hear the story."

An ambush. Silas glared at her, but she remained unruffled.

Baris didn't hesitate. Allowing Yvette to take over the bartering, he scooted back on the blanket, angling to face Silas and cracking his knuckles like he was prepping for a fight rather than a story.

"This is the story," he said grandly, "of how I lost my two fingers!"

Silas blinked, unsure what he'd expected. He squinted at his professor, but her secret motives couldn't be discerned at a glance.

Baris snapped with his good hand. "Focus, now! Thrilling story! Perhaps as good as *The Advent Moon*. I was at a magnificent festival where everyone brought food to share, where we bellowed songs and made memories to last. My family brought papayas, and I was knife tossing. Like this, see." He flicked his wrist back and forth, spinning an invisible knife. "Toss and cut the papaya, very flashy, very fun. There was a beautiful girl, one I'd fancied for months, and she came to share our papayas. I thought, 'I will impress her.'"

The direction of the story wasn't hard to guess, and Silas winced. Baris laughed at his reaction. If anything, his voice boomed with more energy.

"One confident chop, one slip—that's all it takes! One plus one makes me short two fingers, and there's blood and bone in the papayas, and I have impressed a beautiful girl into throwing up over my brother's feet."

The image was almost vivid enough to gag. Silas grimaced instead. "I'm sorry."

"So was I! Very sorry. Here is the snake's tail." Baris leaned in. "I sacrificed two fingers for her, and it was not Yvette. That beautiful girl was never my wife."

He sat back, presenting his three-fingered hand as if displaying a trophy, and his proud grin was the most confusing part of the story. Yvette looked as satisfied as if she'd finished a lecture of her own. They certainly matched—both baffling.

Scale patterns rippled across Silas's hands. He tried to rub them out of existence but only sharpened the pattern.

Yvette had to have guessed his feelings for Eliza. She'd been the one to tease him about it from the start. She'd practically pushed him into this situation. Now she was telling him to forget about the princess before he lost fingers reaching for something he wasn't meant to have?

"Sometimes we sacrifice for nothing," he grumbled. "Very comforting. Thank you, Baris."

But Baris shook his head. "You miss the point entirely, Silas the student."

Silas frowned, leaning forward despite himself.

"I should make you buy ten papayas to hear it. No, it is too valuable. Ten *baskets*."

"You don't even have ten baskets here."

"Not anymore—I have been very successful in the heat. Fine, because of my success and good mood, and because of my love for my wife, I will give you this lesson for free." Baris grinned. "The point is, if I would give two fingers for the girl I did not marry, imagine what I would give for Yvette."

He captured Yvette in a long, drawn-out kiss.

Silas rubbed his hand over his face. Though the scales had faded from his skin, they threatened a return. He pulled the book of sonnets from his bag, tracing his thumb across the rippled pages, darkened and frayed by use.

Baris was right.

The lesson was worth at least ten baskets.

"I might give everything," Silas whispered, "and then I would have nothing left."

"Risk is inherent in every experiment," said Yvette, speaking at last. She leaned back on the rug, pressing her shoulders into her husband's chest, and he shifted to wrap one arm around her. She brushed her hand over his bearded cheek, looking up with pure adoration. "But imagine what you might discover."

"Easy for you to say, after your risk has paid off." But Silas's gripe didn't have any real heart.

His heart was already somewhere else.

And it was time to trust it.

CHAPTER 46

When Eliza finally visited Loegria's university, her mother required her to bring a carriage and a lady-in-waiting and a royal guard, so she felt like an overstuffed pillow arriving in the middle of a collection of practical paving stones, but she didn't let it stop her.

"It's bigger than I expected," Jenny whispered, peeking out the carriage window at the university campus.

Eliza smiled. At least Jenny had agreed to be her lady-in-waiting. Even as a maid, she'd always been more sister than servant.

"It's less than half the size of Izili's," Eliza said, enjoying the way Jenny's jaw dropped.

University de Loegria was near the border to Patriamere, surrounded on either side by two wide forks of a river, making it a stranded sailor, huddled on an island, just trying to survive. Unlike Izili's grand offering, the architecture was nothing to boast about, a collection of square edges in granite blocks, squat and perhaps even dreary. But the campus had wide-open lawns, beautiful gardens, and winding paths, a splash of hopeful paint on an otherwise disappointing canvas.

And the students traversing the paths—rosy-cheeked and puffing clouds of cold air as they laughed—reminded her of the ones in Izili.

She could make this work.

Ignoring the stares she received for her entourage, Eliza walked confidently to the dean's office, practicing what she would say. If he suggested private tutors, she would argue about the unique experience of a campus environment. If he claimed her status would be a distraction to other students, she would remind him of the benefits of a royal perspective. They'd never had a student like Eliza before, and that came with both good and bad; she had to convince him to focus on the good.

She entered the antechamber outside the dean's office, a collection of cushioned chairs and plush rugs. There was a refreshment tray set out for guests, a simple arrangement of cucumber sandwiches and mint tea, which permeated the room with a calming scent. Eliza wistfully recalled the healing hall where she'd left Silas.

Then, abruptly, she halted.

Another person had just exited the dean's office, his hand still on the door, his dark features familiar to her from her dreams, from her nightmares, from every recent memory she both treasured and struggled to forget.

Silas Bennett was standing in Loegria, looking right at her.

And saying, "*Disi dokmek*."

For a moment, she couldn't move. Couldn't believe the evidence of her eyes. He didn't look like himself—dressed as a Loegrian noble in a buttoned shirt and vest, dark trousers, dull colors. He could only be an imposter.

He couldn't be *here*.

"Eliza—" he started.

The sound of her name from his mouth stoked her fury. To the great concern of Jenny and her guards, Eliza grabbed a sandwich from the tray and hurled it at the imposter, who lifted his hand too late and instead got hit in the face by a wad of bread and cucumber.

"Your Highness?" said one of her startled guards, apparently unsure if she needed help or not.

She did not.

"You couldn't leave!" she shouted at Silas. "I *knew* you couldn't leave. That was why I cried while you were in the healing hall and why I left you my *book* and why I didn't let myself—"

"You're not supposed to be here!" he shot back.

"*I'm* not supposed to be here?"

He barely ducked the next sandwich.

It hit the dean, who had opened his office door to see what the commotion was.

Eliza spent the next twenty minutes apologizing to a man she'd meant to impress and trying to plead her case while her mind was still in the antechamber where her guards were preventing Silas from slithering away.

Fortunately, the dean was thrilled by the idea of a princess attending his university. He hoped it would set an example and encourage even more children of court to attend. Rather than arguing, he thanked her.

Good. She could save all her arguing for the imposter outside.

"I'll start on a schedule at once, Your Royal Highness," the dean promised. "Since it's variety you want, I'll make that my priority, and I'm sure you'll be pleased by the classes we have to offer."

"One last thing." Eliza glanced toward the door. "The boy who was in here before me—what did he want?"

"Silas Bennett!" The dean said it with as much pride as if introducing his own son. "The prodigy of Fairfax. I tried recruiting him years ago, but his father insisted he study abroad, something about gaining an appreciation for Loegria.

"Now he's bringing me a letter of recommendation from the dean of Izili University. Apparently, Izili wants to start an information exchange between our universities, and they want Bennett to run the program."

With each word, Eliza's heart sank. Silas had come on behalf of Iyal Afshin. He wasn't here to stay. Apparently, he'd meant to slip in and out without ever seeing her.

Woodenly, she thanked the dean, and then she returned to the antechamber.

Silas's eyes met hers at once, and he tensed, perhaps anticipating another edible projectile. She ordered her entourage to wait outside the room; she wanted as much privacy as possible.

Forcing composure, she said, "I'm sorry to have interrupted your diplomatic mission, and I'm sorry for the . . . sandwiches."

He stood from his chair, and he opened his mouth but closed it with a grimace.

"I'll leave you to it, then, Mr. Bennett."

As she stepped past him, his hand snaked out to catch hers. Not in any innocent way, but with fingers tangled, his grip desperate. He pulled her into his arms.

She shoved away. "You can't *do* that! You can't keep giving me hope only to—"

"It wasn't supposed to be this way," he interrupted. "I was supposed to get my professorship here settled first. I was supposed to get your sister to approve establishing a warlockry curriculum. I was supposed to face my family, and *then*—"

"What are you talking about?" she demanded.

"I had a plan! A well-thought-out and reasonable plan, and when I *did* face you, it was going to be after I'd written everything down, after I had the right words and knew where I stood at court and at the university and regarding a princess. After I knew what I had to offer."

Eliza's fury puffed out like an extinguished candle, leaving the slow smoke of hope wafting in its place.

"Silas," she whispered, "what are you saying?"

"Nothing well," he muttered. He rubbed his hands over his face, and she noticed the subtle pink shade to his ears that marked his blush.

Her lips twitched, but she didn't dare smile yet.

"Use your words, Silas Bennett, and tell me what this means."

The last time she'd insisted on that, he'd broken her heart. But broken things could mend. She believed in that as strongly as she believed in love.

And she would take the risk to hear that one impossible word from him.

He drew her into his arms again, and this time, she didn't resist. Gently, he brushed his knuckles across her cheek, as if memorizing her outline. And then his dark eyes met hers.

"In three languages"—his voice cracked—"I can't find the words for what I feel, because language can't describe the depth of it. Poetry has never penned, tongue has never tasted, magic has never matched the connection my soul feels to yours."

Eliza's eyes misted with tears, but she smiled through them, leaning into his hand. "Careful, I might think you believe in love after all."

"Someone did recently tell me I was wrong more often than I'd admit."

"She sounds wise. Maybe you should cross an ocean for her."

"Maybe I did."

Everything inside her swelled, pulled toward him as if gravity itself had reoriented. Her feet had surely left the floor.

"I'm in love with you," she said. "Some of it happened by accident, some by dare, and some, I insist, by fate. But from this moment on, it's a choice." She pressed her hand to his chest, feeling his heartbeat match the same erratic, joyous rhythm as hers. "I'll choose to be yours, Silas, if you'll only choose me too. If you tell me you want me, then I'll choose to love you *forever*, snakeskin and all."

He held her more tightly, and his response almost broke her heart again, but for a different reason.

"I'm afraid." He paused, drawing in a shuddering breath and blinking away a sheen of tears from his eyes. "I really do hate this country, Eliza. I hate what's happened to people like me here, and I'm afraid I'll wind up just as bitter as . . ."

Just as bitter as Kerem.

"But you still came back for me?" she whispered.

She'd been so certain he would never leave Pravusat, so certain he would never choose *her*.

But he had.

"You came back for me first," he said. "After the library, I was cruel. I pushed you away. And you still came to save me—even when it meant facing snakes and worse." Tilting his head slightly, bangs falling in his eyes, he added, "You chose a flawed donkey over a perfect ideal when I never thought anyone would."

Eliza started trembling, and Silas's brow furrowed. Before he could worry that he'd said something wrong—because he hadn't; she'd loved every single word—she rushed to confess.

"I'm afraid too!" she blurted. "I said I would never hurt you, but I'm not certain that's a promise I can keep. I might hurt you on *purpose*. You changed your entire life for me, but in a single bad day, I might get swept up in a storm and—"

He caught her chin, smirking in his roguish way. "I can forgive a few rage transformations," he said, and then his expression softened, his thumb tracing the edge of her lips. "Because there's a difference between a momentary hurt and a real betrayal. I realize that now. And because I love you, Eliza, just as you are."

All her life, she had obsessed over every romantic story she could find. She'd swooned over men fighting monsters, knights undertaking quests, heroes trekking across deserts, everything in the name of saving the women they loved.

Now she realized she could never be saved more than she was by Silas's promise of forgiveness for her mistakes.

"I'll be your sword," she vowed. "Any prejudiced law, any tradition, any sheep trying to spread hate—I will fight for you. I'll reshape the entire country until you don't have to hate it."

He drew her closer, one hand pressed against the small of her back, the other caressing her face.

"Good," he murmured. "I'm really better suited to a pen."

Then he kissed her in a way that put every romantic story to shame.

EPILOGUE

With the queen's approval and help—as well as with the assistance promised by Iyal Afshin—Silas established a warlockry department at Loegria's university. It started small, just one other teacher representing Casters while Silas represented Affiliates. He kept his residual Artifact abilities under wraps. He was still struggling to trust his home country with the knowledge of his animal link, and he wasn't about to invite more danger by coming out as some never-before-seen magical hybrid.

But he chose to trust Eliza with the truth.

"Don't turn *me* into a cup of tea," she said when witnessing his Fluid Casting, followed by a grin, and, "Show me again!"

With her help, he set up experiments to test how his Affiliate magic might have changed. The result was an office filled with small animals and a collection of avians knocking sharp beaks against his window. While Silas tried and failed to banish them all, Eliza sagged against his desk from laughter.

He could only transform into a snake, but now he could establish a communication link with basically any other animal. The resulting obedience, however, was . . . variable.

"This is not how Affiliate magic works," he grumbled, scratching frantic notes in his journal while someone's lost hunting dog chased a gopher out the door.

"You're discovering how *your* magic works," Eliza said, rescuing a rabbit from the chaos. "Good thing you have a research assistant to help."

Silas smiled down at the page. "Research partner. It's more accurate."

Even though they were no longer bound by magic, he preferred having her by his side. She made good things more enjoyable and difficult things easier to bear.

When he was finally ready to visit his family, he told her she didn't have to come, but she insisted. Truthfully, he was grateful. What he was about to do was hard enough—at least he could know there was one person on his side.

The Bennett estate remained as he remembered. Grim black gates and square hedges surrounded a manor house with dark trim. His father wanted to appear sophisticated, but the end result was simply oppressive.

Eliza pursed her lips. "We could splash some orange on the front, Izili style."

"I'm here to speak to my father, not stop his heart."

The family butler greeted Silas stiffly, like he was a stranger in his own home. Rather than introducing herself as the crown princess, Eliza had worn her Pravish clothing and called herself Yvette, a friend from university.

"So I can be dramatic, if needed," she whispered as they followed the butler to the sitting room. She touched the scarf over her hair. "I'm prepared to throw back my scarf and make royal decrees if he so much as touches you."

Silas slipped his fingers around hers and squeezed.

He'd gone over what he wanted to say repeatedly, but once he was actually in the same room as his family, his carefully chosen words fled. His mother took his hands and kissed his cheek, speaking as though he hadn't been gone more than a day. Maggie complained about the lack of any letters, and though she presented it as teasing, he saw the genuine pain in her eyes. He was about to cause worse.

Could he really go through with it?

His father remained on the other side of the study, regally composed, hands clasped behind his back.

It was only when his mother sent for a tray of refreshments that his father finally spoke.

"He won't be staying long," Lord Bennett said.

Eliza didn't bother to conceal her scowl at the man. Court manners would have required an impassive expression, like the one Silas's mother now wore, but Eliza preferred honesty.

As did Silas.

"No," he agreed. "Just long enough to say what's necessary."

His father's nod approved of the direction he thought this was going. "It's about time. Your attitude in recent years has grown increasingly dismal, and I'm pleased the banishment seems to have been sufficiently humbling. If you have aspirations about regaining your title and inheritance, you'll accept strict requirements, beginning with a prestigious marriage arrangement. Marquess Haskett's daughter is a fine target, or perhaps the spare princess, if you can be trusted not to squander a second opportunity at a royal connection."

Eliza nearly threw back her hood, but she restrained, folding her arms tightly across her chest.

Clearly trying to be delicate, his mother said, "Silas, dear, your friend is lovely. Is she here . . . visiting family?"

Silas ignored the question, addressing his father. "Keep the title, Lord Bennett. I know what it means to you. I came for only one reason. Since it's no longer a death sentence, I can be honest about who I am."

He transformed in a puff of mist.

In control as he was, he did it quickly, just long enough to make the point. The silence in the room was thick as ice, and he couldn't bring himself to meet Maggie's eyes.

Silas could have left it there.

He considered it.

But he thought about Kerem and the easy path to bitterness.

To his father, he said, "I forgive you for believing what you were always told about shapeshifters. Now you know it was all wrong. Moving forward, I hope you can see me as a son, but I'm not going to follow requirements or leap hurdles to *earn* your love. I'm either enough or I'm not, just as I am. You decide. I'll be myself either way."

Glancing at his mother and sister, he added, "If you have any interest in finding me, I'm a professor at the university here. I'd love to show you what I'm working to create."

He bowed, and then he turned away, taking Eliza's hand as he walked.

The new queen's wedding was the biggest celebration Silas had ever attended, and though he desperately wanted to slink off to some corner of the castle with a book, he stayed in a dressing room with his best friend, dodging servants and tailors. It should never require so many people to get dressed.

"I thought you'd have a quiet wedding, Gill. Something in your lemon orchard."

Gill held perfectly still for the tailors, but he smiled through the mirror. "Can I ask you something? Why do you insist on using 'Gill'?"

"You don't have more pressing questions on your wedding day?" Silas smirked, then looked away. "When we met, you told me everyone had called you 'Baron' since you were six. I asked what they called you before that."

"And then you took up 'Gill' without any further explanation."

"Because I wanted to pretend I'd known you all my life, and if I had, I would've been too stubborn to change your nickname when everyone else did."

The tailors finished their work, leaving Guillaume Reeves dressed in a white suit trimmed with red—the royal colors of Loegria. The dress sword at his hip had been handed down through the royal family for centuries and looked too delicate to actually swing.

"Since I've known you all my life," said Gill, "I can say with confidence that it will be you under the tailor's pins soon."

Silas felt ill at that. Marrying Eliza was one thing, but looking at Gill in that red-and-white costume, all he could think of was joining the royal family, a family that had persecuted magic users for centuries.

"They branded you," he said quietly. "Now you're joining them."

He meant it less as an accusation and more as a question for his best friend of what path he could possibly take.

"I would choose different in-laws if I could," Gill said frankly, "but not at the expense of Aria."

The sounds of a faint argument echoed in the hallway, and then Gill's thirteen-year-old brothers spilled into the room, Leon complaining about the frills on his shirt and Corvin telling him to stop whining on their brother's wedding day.

Since the ceremony was imminent, Silas decided to give them a few minutes of family time, but before he left, he gripped his friend's shoulder. "Thanks, Gilly," he said quietly. At Gill's confused frown, he added, "Don't make me list why. There's too much. Just marry your queen."

The castle chapel had been strung with yellow and green banners in defiance of the snow outside. Yellow flowers lined the aisle, and Silas smiled, remembering Eliza's complaints about flower availability in winter. Clearly, she'd prevailed against the challenge in her usual determined way.

Despite being overcrowded and formal, the ceremony was nice—or, at least, it was nice to see how happy it made his best friend. Eliza cried more than the two people actually getting married, and even when the celebration moved to the castle's expansive ballroom, she was still weepy. Before Silas could offer comfort, she folded herself into him first, clinging like she would never let go.

"It's a happy occasion," he drawled.

"I *am* happy," she griped back, rubbing at her freckles. "I'm also jealous and sad and confused and desperately in want of a lemon tart."

"One of those things I can remedy, but you'd have to let go."

"Then forget the tart. I'm more desperately in want of you."

The words sent a little thrill up his spine, and he rubbed his hand gently over her back, enjoying the way she relaxed in his arms. Any of the gossips at court who didn't already know the crown princess was courting a disinherited scholar would know by the end of the day, because Eliza was never shy about affection in public, and she made no effort to hide Silas or to present him in a more socially respectable light.

All at once, the answers to the questions he thought were terrifying became simple.

"What are you looking so smug about?" Eliza squinted up at him.

She wore a green silk gown tailored to her figure, her brown hair half-gathered in curls beneath a tiara. She looked like a princess.

Silas tapped her crown. "Dangerous weapon you're wearing."

Authority could be wielded in the same way as a sword. The same way as magic. And trusting her to wield her power well was no different than trusting her with a blade. His father and hers had both proven to be dangerous with a weapon, but Eliza and Silas could be different.

Just as he'd once handed her an Artifact in the dark, trusting her to help him, he trusted her now.

Maybe it *would* be him under the tailor's pins soon, and maybe he didn't mind the idea.

Maybe the best day of his life would be the day he chose to share it forever with Eliza.

Eliza's hand flew to her tiara, and she pulled back, eyes wide. "Weapon? Did it poke you?"

Silas snorted. As the orchestra transitioned from atmospheric music to sultry waltzes, he kissed her hand and led her onto the dance floor—not because he cared for dances, but because he knew she did. The sparkle of joy in her eyes was well worth it.

Between songs, a familiar, timid voice spoke from behind him.

"Silas?"

He turned to find Maggie, rumpling the front of her dress in nervous fingers.

"Excuse me, Y-Your Highness. I was hoping I could . . . dance with my brother."

Eliza beamed. "I'd planned on keeping him all evening, but I suppose I could make *one* exception." She leaned in to whisper loudly. "If he tries to make a run for the library, let me know."

Silas would have glared at her teasing, but he was busy watching his sister, his every muscle tensed.

"You aren't afraid of me?" he asked, hardly daring to believe it.

Tears shimmered in Maggie's eyes, but she shook her head. "Now I know why you never wanted to come home."

He couldn't manage a response to that, so he hesitantly offered his arm, but Maggie slipped beneath it and gave him a hug, sniffling against his vest.

Eliza started crying again, too, and the princess excused herself for lemon tarts.

"I love you," Maggie whispered. "Please don't leave again."

Swallowing hard, Silas wrapped his arms around his sister.

Not so long ago, he'd thought his only chance for happiness was in a different world. Now he'd have to write Yvette a letter and tell her she was right about risks and discoveries.

"I'm not going anywhere," he promised.

He danced with Maggie before leading her back to Eliza, where the two girls quickly fell into an enthusiastic conversation about their shared love of snow. At one point, he noticed Maggie's eyes straying to a boy across the ballroom—none other than the familiar knight, Henry Wycliff. Silas wasn't certain how to feel about that, so he excused himself from the entire situation.

Roughly an hour later, Eliza found him in the window seat of the library, and when she scrunched her nose at him, he gave a helpless shrug.

"It's dark already," she said, nodding toward the windows.

Silas glanced over his shoulder, where a chill seeped through the glass. "Winter nights."

"Do you miss the warmth?"

"A little," he admitted, "but weather never made it into my top reasons for loving Pravusat."

He scooted over on the cushion, making room for her, but she shook her head with a smile.

"The observatory tower is empty," she said, "and it's the best view in the castle. Come watch the stars beside me."

When she extended her hand, Silas set aside his book and entwined his fingers with hers, letting her lead him up to the stars.

ACKNOWLEDGMENTS

This book was a particular challenge for me, partly because it included things I've never attempted before and partly because of the season of life I was writing it in. I love the final result so much, and it wouldn't be here without all the people who supported me while I struggled to make it happen.

My beta readers: Brooke Adams, Brianne Bird, Rachel Bird, Roma Blackham, McKenna Gillette, Alyssa Green, Brady Lowham, Karen Lowham, Ashley Nicolaysen, Ashlie Olson, Moriah Pond, Jessica Shepherd, and Konstanz Silverbow. Thank you for being my extra eyes—for telling me all the things you loved and for helping me catch the flaws.

My critique group: Allison Mathews, Bri Stephens, and Katie Stone. You guys are the best for reading my choppy nonsense and somehow believing that nonsense could turn into a real book. Also, let it be known: If this book totally flops, it is all Katie's fault for not reading it on time. It has nothing to do with marketing, reviews, bad luck, or me as the author. It's all on Katie.

My snake expert: Cami Dalrymple. Thank you for fielding my relentless ophidian questions, for teaching me about snake musks and milking, powdered venom, shedding fangs, and everything else that inspired details of this story. Silas is indebted to you, and so am I.

My publishing and marketing team: Bre Anderl, Tasha Bradford,

Garth Bruner, Troy Butcher, Bri Cornell, Heidi Gordon, Callie Hansen, Amy Parker, and Chris Schoebinger. Thank you for believing in this book and working to make it available for readers.

An extra shout-out to my editor, Lisa Mangum, for putting in extra work on this one and giving me extra encouragement, and for working around my tight schedule while I tried to get everything done before my baby arrived.

Finally, and very importantly, a special thanks to Jami Diewald, who served as both beta reader and my consultation expert on bipolar disorder. Thank you for being vulnerable, for sharing your experiences with me, and for helping me bring Eliza to life in the way I wanted. Any justice done to her portrayal is thanks to your guidance, and any errors are a result of my own shortcomings in writing. I love you, friend.

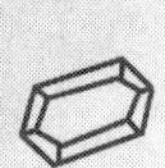

Olmak means have, but only sometimes. Other times, it's kendik. I cannot tell the difference of when.

While I Have Your Love

The flurry is frozen and carried in whorls,

While on each circling lake neck, frost glimmers like pearls.

Each breath in the air is the puff of a cloud,

While snow drapes the hills like a white, woolen shroud.

The world is adorned in its mourning attire,

Yet through crystal chill, I nurse embers of fire.

No winter's touch can freeze

Nor cold give unease

While I have your love to please.

Inci is pearl.
Or maybe it's gem.

The word for clothing changes if it's worn by men or by women.
Giyfa: women
Giyfal: men
By this logic, if I throw my scarf on Silas, it becomes giyfal.

Pravish has no word for winter, as far as I can tell, which is proof of its awfulness as a language.

At least Pravish still has the most important word.
Sevmek: love
There's also an idiom.
We would say "fall in love"
They say "bitten by love"
Sevda isirigi
Because of course they do.

Cont. Ahmet Khatib notes

Fluid Casting is transformative magic, rooted in transition. Change what is there. Stone Casting is enhancement magic, rooted in enrichment. Enhance what is there.
—The Essence of Casting, *chapters 7–12*

Building on his work, Usanee Ratan and Nasret Fenari attempted a composition experiment. Hypothesis: Fluid Casting draws out magic like blood. Stone Casting contains it in stasis like tasumak. Highly anticipated results, eventual failure. WHY?
—Fenari Research Journals, *compiled and abridged*

Mirim Mattei, positive effects of focusing magic through written language, research incomplete.
—Transformative Language, *chapter 21 plus author's concluding notes.*

Experiment: words painted on snakeskin
Hypothesis: native language strongest effect **NULL**

	Control (no word)	*Loegrian*	*Pravish*	*Cronese*
"hold"	*Expected capacity*	*Expected capacity*	*Expected capacity*	*Increased capacity*
"strength"	*Expected strength*	*Slight strength increase*	*Expected strength*	*Notable strength increase*
"last"	*Expected duration*	*Expected duration*	*Slight duration increase*	*Extended duration*

Results: Variable results, but Cronese strongest in each case.
Roughly 10% increase?
More experimentation needed.

GLOSSARY

MAGIC TYPES

Caster: Stone Casters can apply magic to bone and other hard substances, like rock and metal. Fluid Casters can apply magic to liquids, including blood. There is an extinct third type of Caster, of which little is known.

Animal Affiliate: Magic users who can transform into animals and imbue some of their animal link's attributes into Artifacts. Affiliate types are, from most to least common: small mammal, avian, large mammal, reptile. There is no documentation of aquatic or insect types, although there is speculation about mythical, such as mermaids and dragons. *Shapeshifter* is a derogatory term for Affiliates.

PLACES

Cronith (crow-nith)
Izili (ih-zee-lee)
Loegria (low-egg-ree-uh)
Patriamere (pah-tree-uh-mare)
Pravusat (prah-voo-saht)
Thesland (thez-land)
Yamakaz (yah-muh-kaz)

PRAVISH IDIOMS

Bikmayak kalamak ("My sword breaks here")—severing a relationship

Disi dokmek ("swallowed tooth")— expression of bad luck
Gravdan kazmak/gravmak ("Outrun the strike")—run for your life
Kemik kirmasi ("the flesh rip")—term for Affiliates transforming without control
Yeni basi, yeni cilt ("new year, new skin")—blessing for a birthday

PRAVISH PHRASES

Buraya ne ka ("Come to me")
Gik ne seyahat ("Go home")
Gunadin ("Good morning")
Nirhaba ("Hello"/"Welcome," most common greeting)
Sarazan kurta beni ("Sarazan save me")
Sen tatli al gozumek ("You look beautiful")
Seykeli atin al ("Buy what you please")
Tezekurler/teze ("Thank you"/"Thanks")

PRAVISH WORDS

Abajur (lantern)
Abakar (priest)
Abide (memorial)
Analamak (understand)
Apta/aptal (foolish girl/boy)
Arakl (magic)
Birahan (alehouse)
Enelemek (memorize)
Erkal (age-neutral man/male)
Erkek (affectionate term for a male)
Genca/gencal (young girl/young boy, used for children under ten years old)
Hana (wife)
Iyanal (snake-blessed)
Iyl/iyal (feminine/masculine form of an honored professor)
Kuveti (peacekeeping force in Pravusat)

Lirina et/lirinal (feminine/masculine address for an heir to the throne)
Muhetsem (beautiful object)
Palem (pen made by a Fluid Caster)
Sarazan (mythological sea serpent)
Senen (singular you)
Seravat (peace)
Sizen (plural you)
Tasumak (Stone Caster-induced sleep)
Tatli al (beautiful person)
Utamas (ashamed)
Utanmas (gentle)
Yalan (lie)

Fantasy and reality collide in this retelling of "Beauty and the Beast" about a young woman's heroic quest to save herself.

BEAUTY REBORN

ELIZABETH LOWHAM

"Beauty . . . is an intriguing, well-crafted original. . . . Readers who appreciate narrative risk-taking are well served."

—*KIRKUS REVIEWS*

"A sensitive and slow-burning retelling."

—*PUBLISHERS WEEKLY*

"A darker and bittersweet retelling of the familiar fairytale, laden with an equal dose of humor and tragedy."

—*COMPASS BOOK RATING*